THE CROSSING

**Center Point
Large Print**

**This Large Print Book carries the
Seal of Approval of N.A.V.H.**

THE CROSSING

WILL HENRY

CENTER POINT PUBLISHING
THORNDIKE, MAINE

Affectionately for
John Starr Niendorff

This Center Point Large Print edition
is published in the year 2008 by arrangement with
Golden West Literary Agency.

The text of this Large Print edition is unabridged. In other
aspects, this book may vary from the original edition.
Printed in the United States of America.
Set in 16-point Times New Roman type.

ISBN: 978-1-60285-286-0

Library of Congress Cataloging-in-Publication Data

Henry, Will, 1912-1991.
   The crossing / Will Henry.--Center Point large print ed.
      p. cm.
   Originally published in 1958 under the pseudonym Clay Fisher.
    ISBN: 978-1-60285-286-0 (lib. bdg. : alk. paper)
      1. United States--History--Civil War, 1861-1865--Fiction. 2. Large type books.
I. Fisher, Clay, 1912-1991. Crossing. II. Title.

PS3551.L393C76 2008
813'.54--dc22

2008018122

PART ONE
THE BOY FROM TOPAZ CREEK

1

IT WAS a high, a lonesome and a lovely country.

Perched above the Llano River on the sunrise slope of Packsaddle Mountain, it overlooked the plains two hundred miles east to the timbered bottoms of the Trinity and stared out across the tumbled hills a like distance to the buffalo pastures of the Pecos on the west. There was no place in the prairie world, Jud Reeves thought, to match it in June of a good rainfall year like this one. The unbelievable green of the new grass, the windswept blue of the Texas skies, the muting gray of the mesquite, the creamy bursts of the Spanish dagger and the golden blooms of the huisache all conspired to cloak the arid realities of the harsh land beneath the soft deceptions of early summer.

Jud was well aware of this transient illusion. He knew it like an old friend, and like an old friend he found it difficult to face for the last time. Yet he had made his choice.

Below him in its warm shawl of hills nestled the pole corrals, weathered sheds and the low-walled adobe home of the beloved horse ranch he might never see again.

Beyond its snug buildings and small pens, up on the

crest of the cottonwood rise from which issued the creek to wander past the Reeves homeplace, his widowed mother slept her last sleep, that same day laid to rest by his own hand.

Away and afar beyond the hills and the cottonwood rise, the ramparts of Wild Rose Pass reared beckoningly against the western sky, calling his imagination toward distant Fort Davis and the great valley of the Rio Grande. But it was not to the west he must now turn his face. Nor was it homeward that he now must look, nor yet toward the silent grave beneath the cottonwoods. His destiny, delayed until this late day by his mother's lingering illness, lay to the east, and now at last he could ride to meet it.

Checking his restive mount, he took a final, searching look down at the tiny house, his intent blue eyes seeing through its mud-chinked earthen walls.

There was the French walnut grand piano freighted all the way from Loudon County, Virginia, to this remote nowhere in the Texas wilderness by his soldier father. There were, too, the old Victorian oak secretary, the circassian Louis Quatorze dining cabinet, the Salem maple Wakefield chairs, the Haviland china, the Sheffield plate and all the dozen and one other pitiful small reminders of a better past which had sustained his genteel mother here in this merciless land so foreign to her First Family breeding and Old Dominion upbringing.

And then the mantel over the old adobe fireplace.

Could a boy ever forget those stern pictures which

had watched him all these years from its smoke-stained ledge of mountain cedar? The one so huge and oval-framed of his grandfather, the original General Judah Beaumont Reeves? The other, smaller and even more severe, of his father, the second General Judah Beaumont Reeves? Ah, no, Jud Reeves would remember those portraits with pride and deep feeling all the days of his life.

He would remember, as well, the bookcase which stood at attention across the room from those pictures. The one whose ornate doors of settlement glass protected the complete works of von Clausewitz, Blücher and Thielmann. And the one which held, too, that thin calfbound volume which had been his own military Bible and bedside primer. The holy book his mother had pressed upon him with the ceaseless understanding that he, Judah Beaumont Reeves III, must also one day be a cadet at the United States Military Academy at West Point; and must after that, in his own inevitable time, become the family's third general officer in direct male line.

Jud knew he must not fail this proud heritage.

To make certain that he would not, he had brought away with him the calfskin manuscript which contained its commandments; that slim, terse monograph from the bookcase whose title was *The Professional Soldier in Command; His Obligations as a Leader of Men,* and whose distinguished author was his own dead father.

His mother had been a childlike and a fragile

woman. Her mind had never left Virginia, her heart had been buried with her general. Somehow, no matter the many years since gone, she had never replaced his loss with the homely, sunburned boy who was her own and his only son. That Jud should be the image of his father and his father's father was her passion; she never really knew the boy himself. So words of tenderness and compassion would not come now to Jud Reeves and in the end he turned the roan pony away from the hills of his surrendered boyhood with only the sober crowsfooted squint of his blue eyes and the determined set of his long jaw to show that he meant to bear himself like a Reeves in the dangerous way ahead.

Likely it would be a dangerous way, too.

The date was June 1, 1861, a month and more gone since the firing of the first Confederate rocket over Fort Sumter in Charleston Harbor.

The Civil War was six weeks old and Judah Beaumont Reeves III was on his way to the state capital at Austin City to join the Texas Army and drive the cursed Union troops forever from southern soil.

Jud reached the stageline settlement of Llano Springs at dusk of June 3, his plan to stay the night, continue on down next day to Austin City where he was to follow his mother's parting injunction about seeing the Governor for a commission in one of the Texas regiments forming up to go fight for the Confederacy.

He well knew his family name and connections

made this course a virtual certainty. He would have preferred to enlist as just plain Jud Reeves, then see what he could do on his own and from there. But his mother had written him that personal letter to the Governor, and he had promised to deliver it. He had naturally, now, to keep that promise.

Llano Springs, however, provided a quick and sudden turning to this path of easy influence.

Jud had been forced to travel a long, careful way to avoid the Comanches who were gathering like blowflies to a bad bait in all that far western land where the U.S. troops had withdrawn to go home and fight for the Union. As a result, he had used up his little roan gelding in a three-day, hundred mile detour to this halfway point in his journey to the state capital.

Since there was little to do with a lame horse save to shoot or sell him, he determined to get what cash he could from his outfit and go the remaining way to Austin City in style on the stage.

He got $40 for his horse, $60 for his saddle, very creditable prices indeed.

Now, though, with more hard money in his pocket than he had seen in the previous nineteen years of his life, the prospect altered.

It took Llano Springs about two hours to separate Jud Reeves from his $100.

The boy didn't really remember the details.

There was that first little drink which burned like a branding-fire coal in the pit of his stomach. Then the second one to put it out, and the third to rekindle it, and from there things got hazy and rough.

He did recall sketchily making a political address in the Cavalryman's Canteen in which he outlined the facts that he was a Southerner and a soldier born, the only son of a famous fighting father, Texas' own General Judah Beaumont Reeves, the "bright-haired hero of Vera Cruz," and the grandson in straight male line of the original Judah Beaumont Reeves, the old "Eagle of New Orleans," dependable right arm and best drinking companion of irascible old sot and soldier, Andrew Jackson; and that, moreover, he was right then on his way down to Austin City to get his commission as a major in the first Texas contingent to leave for the East, and that anyone who felt like drinking to that should step up to the bar and name his brand—the treat was on Judah Beaumont Reeves III!

His only other dim picture was of finding himself several treats later in the smoky cardroom of a second mud-walled saloon with a faded blonde on one arm and a fish-eyed faro dealer on the other. It was when the latter tried to take his last $5 without working for it by palming a needed ace out of his sleeve rather than slipping it from the casebox on the table that Jud rose up and bent a chair over his head and staggered back to his hotel to sober up.

It was there the town marshal found him an hour later with some news that did the job.

The faro dealer was in very serious condition, might not live out the night. Pending the outcome, Jud was under arrest on a charge of assault which could turn to one of second-degree murder any minute.

Shaky and sick, he was led away to the settlement's verminous two-room jail.

"You got a visitor, kid."

The marshal said it soft and quick behind Jud's back, startling him. He came around from the cell window all tied up inside and ready to fight.

"Simmer down," the marshal said. "You're in more luck than you know, boy. Right this way, Mr. Hampton."

"Thank you, Mr. Dowd," Jud heard the newcomer murmur. "Might I see the prisoner alone?"

"Five minutes," nodded the other. "I got his breakfast gettin' cold out here in the office."

The marshal stood aside for Jud's visitor, repeated, "Five minutes," and went out of the cell room leaving Jud to study his uninvited guest by the flabby pink light of the sun now staining the dank walls of the jail.

The latter got immediately to the point.

His name was Mr. Wesley Parnell Hampton and he was, among other duties for the Cause, a recruiter for Captain John Robert Baylor. His young friend had heard of Captain Baylor?

"Certainly," scowled Jud Reeves. "He's the one recruiting state militia down on the Salado. Been advertising for 'hide hunters' to go chasing meat and robes out along the Pecos, or some such nonsense." His scowl deepened with the belligerent nod which

11

backed it. "Listen, mister, I'm no buffalo hunter. Furthermore, I'm not interested in any volunteer militia units. I've got a commission in the regulars waiting for me down to Austin City."

"So I heard," said Mr. Hampton quietly. "It's what brought me here."

Jud flushed guiltily.

"I'm right sorry about that whiskey talk," he said.

"No need to be, boy. It might have saved you a jail term."

"How's that?" asked Jud uneasily.

"Your man's going to die. Marshal Dowd tells me he won't live to see sundown. I heard about your speech in the saloon and I'm here to get you out on my terms. You can take them or leave them. Sign up with Baylor, or stay here and take your chances on that man dying. What's it to be, boy? The Austin City stage rolls in an hour. You want to hear more about Captain Baylor's Brigade, or shall I send the marshal in with your breakfast?"

"Well sir, Mr. Hampton," grinned Jud palely, "I'm sure not hungry," and with that wan inducement Mr. Wesley Hampton began his brief résumé of the military opportunities for serving the South right there at home in Texas.

Baylor's regiments were very nearly ready to move, awaiting only informal approval from the Confederate Government at Richmond to start them on their way. That approval reposed presently in Wesley Hampton's letter pouch. Yes, it was true. He had with him the

12

South's official, if *sub rosa* blessing for Captain Baylor's Texas privateers to march into the military and territorial vacuum created by the recent withdrawals of United States troops from the various Texas, New Mexico and Arizona posts. This was nothing less than a politically phrased order to strike and seize the entire Southwest for the Confederacy.

Considering the family background of his young listener, there could be no doubt of his being given a preferential place on the captain's staff. Nor could there be any question of Wesley Hampton's ability to deliver him from the Llano Springs jail to start him on his way toward that place. Both Marshal Gil Dowd and Judge Mirabeau Potter Simms, who would try his case should it come to court, were personal supporters of Baylor's adventure.

Actually, however, let them be honest with one another.

No boy of Jud Reeves' good name was going to do more than token time in any Texas jail over assaulting that conniving faro dealer. Still, even a token sentence was no joke. It might run anywhere from six months to a year, and providing a part of it was suspended it still wasn't funny. Now that was all Wesley Hampton had to say on the subject of serving the South at home. The remaining chance was Jud's. Would he take it on the certain promise of a commission with Baylor's Buffalo Hunters, or on the doubtful extent and leniency of Judge Mirabeau Potter Simms' untried patriotism?

Confused and still a little whiskey-sick, Jud faltered. The halt was decisive.

Before he realized fully what he was doing, he was shaking hands with Baylor's courier-recruiter and their Southern gentleman's agreement was set on the basis of Jud's being a special scout for the entire Baylor Brigade (owing to his Llano County upbringing) and very likely head scout, at that, with no less than a first lieutenant's commission to start, and the positive guarantee of a chance to command and lead troops in battle once things were well organized and the column under way.

Thirty minutes later standing outside the stageline office down the street from the jail taking his last instructions from Wesley Hampton, Jud's head was still whirling.

His stage ticket was in his pocket and paid for.

It took him through Austin City, San Marcos and New Braunfels, clear into San Antonio, and Jud still couldn't believe he was sober.

The prospects for adventure and rapid advancement in the service of the dashing John Robert Baylor had, in fact, now begun to grow so impressively upon him that Hampton had to ask him three times if he had his ticket pinned in a good safe place and his father's valuable campaign watch put where it wouldn't draw any undue notice from possible toughs along the road, before Jud finally heard him and answered that he had. By then it was time to go. The stage was rolling up to the ticket office from the company corrals, the other passengers were pushing to get past Jud, and the slouch-hatted old driver up on the seatbox was bawling down his standard warning and welcome.

"Everybody in! Ladies to the back, gents to the front. A girl's got a right to see where she's goin' and a man to watch his backtrail away from where he's bin! Hee-yahh!"

"Well," smiled Baylor's courier, offering Jud his hand, "I guess this is goodbye, Reeves. I will be delayed here and again in Austin City. In all likelihood we shall not meet again. Good luck to you, young man."

Jud took his hand and said, "Thank you, sir," and Hampton waved the acknowledgment aside, continuing.

"Remember me to the Captain. Should you come to him ahead of my dispatches, which I doubt, tell him that Richmond considers the War all but won on the Potomac and that our glorious independence is assured by no later than September. Also remember, sir, to give him that letter of introduction I gave you. Do you hear?"

"Yes sir, I will surely do that, sir, and thank you again," agreed Jud. "But, ah well, there was just one other thing, sir—"

"Yes, yes boy? What is it? Be quick, we're being run over here by these confounded ticketholders. Damn you, sir! Will you please watch that umbrella. You nearly put out my eye. Oh, excuse me, madam, I didn't see you—"

"Well, yes sir," spoke up Jud stoutly. "It's that I haven't got a thin dime of my own to eat on, or anything like that. I don't reckon I can make out on my good looks, do you, sir?"

"No," winced Hampton, eying his sunburned, blue-eyed homeliness, "I surely don't. Here. I'm glad you reminded me, boy."

Out of his riding coat pocket, he took a large leather moneybag of the kind carried by traders and freighters through the backcountry. Digging down into its sagging load of U.S. gold eagles, he fished out two dollars in small silver coin and handed it to Jud.

"Sorry, Reeves," he nodded hurriedly. "I almost forgot."

Jud glanced dubiously down at the worn coins.

"You still almost did, Mr. Hampton," he said.

The latter patted him on the shoulder, turned him brusquely around, pointed him for the stage door, gave him an ungentle shove.

"Yes, well good luck again, boy. Don't forget to tell the Captain what I told you about the War. Up you go now—!"

Jud grinned and climbed aboard, feeling better than he had at any time since leaving home.

Hampton, relieved to see one more cocky young recruit safely on his way to fight for Texas in Texas, latched the door from the outside, waved up to the driver and stepped quickly back out of the way.

The driver let go a catamount squall, the four-mule hitch hit its breastbands together, the coach lurched, settled back on its thoroughbraces, rebounded and shot forward with a lunge that knocked Jud off his seat sprawling down onto his knees on the floor. He got up, still grinning, leaned out the window, gestured back at his benefactor with the closed hand which clutched the limited gift of silver. "Thanks for everything, Mr. Hampton!" he yelled happily. "I'm sure beholden to you and the Treasury of Texas!"

Mr. Wesley Hampton stared off after him a truculent moment, then shook his head.

"Impudent young scoundrel," he announced to the stageline agent standing on the board walk nearby, and turned and started back up the street toward the Cavalryman's Canteen, well satisfied that $2 was an entirely adequate amount to feed one Topaz Creek ranch boy from Llano Springs to San Antonio, Texas, in early June of 1861.

2

THE TRIP to San Antonio took three days. It was June 6 when Jud arrived in the sprawling camp on the banks of the Salado River.

The stage dropped him at the depot in town and he made the remaining five miles out to camp the best way he could. He had been better ways. But he thanked the obliging driver of the wagonload of shelled corn for Baylor's horses, who had given him the ride out, and got down off the seatbox with a great deal of unspoken gratitude.

There was much to see.

And to hear and smell.

First there were men and horses and wagons and buggies and buckboards beyond any number a boy might previously have conceived. Then, continuing out of eyesight around both elbows of the bend, there were still more men and horses and carts of every description to a total at which Jud could only gape and guess.

This amazing first sight taken, second impressions began to flood in.

These supporting details were without end or order.

A myriad wandering gaunt and hungry dogs, staring, blank-eyed tame Indians, scratching, roistering fighting cocks staked out on strutting ropes, crates of molty-looking eating chickens, tents, tarps, brush wickiups, clotheslines hung till they dragged in the dirt with dingy gray wet wash, cooking fires smoldering in every direction, a hundred nameless hills of boxes and bales and packs which might hold anything of great or no value, from a dozen modern Union arsenal Springfield rifles to a moth-eaten buffalo robe rolled around some oldtimer's muzzle loader saved up against just this very day from the issues made fifteen years before in the grand fever preceding Matamoros, Palo Alto, Resaca de la Palma and the other flourishes attendant upon Zach Taylor's Mexican advance. Then, dumped hither and yon and helterskelter to salt and season the endless picketlines were the sacks of feedgrain and makeshift ricks of loose hay for the work and saddlestock. And over all and everywhere roundabout the limits of an excited recruit's gaze stretched still more men and more horses and more hungry dogs and arms-folded Indians and dirty clothes and drifting campsmoke and libelous language, mule brays, rooster crows, mustering shouts, marching orders and nervous mustang whistles until hell wouldn't hold half the man stink and animal noise being put up by Baylor's teeming cantonment along the Salado.

Jud blew out through his nose and said, "Phew!" without realizing he had been holding his breath the whole time of his unbelieving look.

He scratched his head, pulled at his jaw, took the notion that he might as well plunge right into the middle of things. It was either that, or stand there and suffocate from the dust and smell of the outskirts.

Shouldering his old Ethan Allen shotgun, he started directly toward the nearest cookfire. At the edge of its circle of bearded loungers, he waited politely for someone to notice him and ask him in.

No one did either thing.

All of the men, after the alert way of the country, had given him a careful looking at before he drew up to them. But now that he was there, not a one of them would so much as glance in his direction.

Jud grinned wryly, grounded his riflebutt.

He knew these old boys.

Best idea for getting on with their kind was to pull up a chair and sit tight until they decided to discover you were there. Meanwhile, you could watch and listen and maybe learn a little something, so long as you kept your mouth shut.

One of the fireside squatters, an old gaffer as gaunt as a set of desert-dried steerhorns, was holding forth on the past glories of the Texas Rangers. From his age Jud figured he must have been there when Cap Tumlinson's original company had drawn first blood in the Indian scrape at Hornsby's Station in January of '36. The old galoot was sixty, or Jud wasn't sixteen.

Still, to hear him tell it, his fires were a long ways from final banking. Or from even the need of fresh fuel, or a little friendly fanning.

"Why for the luvva Christ," he was declaiming, "in them days there wasn't a house nor a hogpen between here and Austin City. It was so lonely you couldn't even strike up a conversation with the wind, and you know how the wind blows in Texas."

"Well I don't know," put in Jud out loud and out of place. "I thought I did, sure enough. But I'll swear I never heard it blow out in my part of the country the way it does down here."

He should never have opened his mouth. He meant it well and he backed it with a crinkly, sunburned grin to prove he did, but he simply never should have opened his mouth.

The old fellow got up off his hams. He shaded his eyes and looked all around on the prairie over the tops of his listeners' heads. He scanned right past and through Jud as though he were made of glass.

"That's funny," he said, squatting back down again. "I'd of swore I heard somebody say something."

"It was me, oldtimer," acknowledged Jud contritely. "And I'm right sorry."

He stepped in toward the fire, facing the storyteller.

"Didn't mean to cut in on your yarn." He smiled. "Honest to Pete, I didn't. Just new to camp and needing to know in a fair hurry where is Captain Baylor's tent."

"Captain Baylor, is it?" he heard one of the men say softly aloud.

"Yes sir," he replied. "You see I am to ride scout for him—head scout, I believe—and since I've been on the road all the way from Topaz Creek up yonder in Llano County, I reckon he'll be wanting to see me soon as he can."

He finished the statement with an unconsciously important chin lift and the same soft-voiced man said to the white-haired oldster, "You hear that, Elk? He's going to be head scout for the Captain. My, ain't that a grand thing? I surely do feel better for it already."

"Me too," said another. "By Jings, I will sleep a mort sounder tonight knowing that the new head scout is here."

Several others joined in, all good-natured and nothing unfair or nasty in their comments, but just the same planting them where Jud could feel their points.

"Well," the old man took out a pocket-linted plug of chewing tobacco, bit off a corner, cheeked it, spat toward the newcomer with the nod, "if you're a scout, I allow you won't have no insurmountable difficulties scouting out the Captain." He shifted the softening cud of his chaw, got richer color into his second shot of its juice toward Jud. "And if you're a smart scout, you'll squander no more of our time getting started doing just that." The third stream of amber lanced the ground between Jud's feet, making him jump to avoid getting his boots splashed. He wound up looking pretty awkward, and the men laughed quick and rough at his discomfiture.

For his part, young Jud Reeves did not admire being spit at.

"Don't do that again, oldtimer," he said quietly. "I told you I was sorry."

The old man looked at him. He looked at him a long thoughtful spell. At last he nodded and said just as quietly, "So you did, young un. Get down and come in."

Jud grinned all over and relaxed.

He moved on in and squatted down to the fire, reaching his hands out over the coals in that unconscious gesture of warming that a man will use on the hottest day in July.

One of the men shoved a bent tin cup into his right hand and another poked a grimy slab of smoked wild turkey into his left. A third poured the cup full of steaming *garbanza* bean coffee and a fourth grinned, "Fall to, son. She ain't much and them *garbanzas* cain't shine with real coffee nor even chicory, but she's hot and the pot's full and you're welcome to all you can hold."

Jud thanked the entire circle with an embarrassed wave, then said to the old man through the first mouthful of turkey, "Go on with your yarn, why don't you? It sounded mighty good to me. The Captain can wait."

"Well now thank you, son. I reckon he can. Let's see, where was I?"

"At the Battle of Salado," prompted Jud, wiping the turkey grease on his thigh and reaching for more coffee.

The old man hesitated, squinting suspiciously at him.

"How come you to know that?" he demanded. "I hadn't even got started yet."

"I've heard it fought a hundred times," said Jud. "I had kin there on my daddy's side."

"Oh," said the old man, relieved, and launched into his version of the Captain Jack Hays fight with the Mexican mercenary, Adrian Wall, on the Salado River.

"So there was young Jack Hays," he led off, shaggy brows contracted intensely, pale eyes alight with the rekindled flame of battle, "a-laid up in the brush on the north bank with less than two hundred men—"

"He had two hundred and twenty-five," said Jud.

"—So there he was," the old man set out again, not even looking at Jud, "a-laid up in the brush of the north bank with two hundred and twenty-five men and him but a week past twenty-five years old at the time. Then

23

yonder, there, a-marching up from San Antone with two hundred cavalry and six hundred infantry—"

"He must have been more than a week over twenty-five," said Jud. "He was twenty-five when he got sent to San Antone in August. The fight wasn't until September 10, so I figure he was—"

It was his turn to lay back on the reins, and sharply.

He looked up to see the enraged old man towering red-faced above him, his Sharps bullgun clubbed and backswung menacingly.

"So!" he roared down at him, "I figure you'd better shut your infernal big mouth! You say one more word, you little Llano brush-thicket son of a bitch, I'll lay your head open like a busted mushmelon!"

When Jud had turned pale and promised there would be no more interruptions, his threatener turned and handed the Sharps to a wizened little Lipan Apache tracker sitting back of the circle under a stovepipe sombrero and a bright red Caddo blanket. The giant old frontiersman next picked the tiny Indian up bodily and sat him down in the circle next to Jud.

"Junior," he said to him, "you *sabe* hold gun on boy with big mouth? You *sabe* pull trigger first noise he makes?"

"Sure, me *sabe*," grunted Junior, who might have been ten years older or twenty years younger than his white instructor. "Boy open mouth, me shoot."

"Right square in the threadholes of the third shirt button!" huffed the bony oldster, and got on with his story.

"So, by God, there comes the damned Dutchman, Woll, with his two thousand barefoot infantry and his ten pieces of eight-pound horse artillery, the Aztec Snake flag a'flying and the Mexican musketbarrels so thick you couldn't—"

"Shoot, Junior, shoot!" implored Jud, throwing wide his arms and baring his soiled shirtfront.

"Wagh? what matter now?" inquired the little Lipan curiously, lowering the Sharps and leaning forward with rapt attention to catch Jud's answer.

"Woll wasn't a Dutchman," recited the latter. "He had eight hundred troops. Those guns were four-pounders. There were only two of them, and they were both old high-wheel, flash-hole howitzers, handdrawn and wouldn't break the skin on a ripe persimmon at anything over six hundred yards." He motioned dramatically to the Sharps in the Indian's hands, concluded piously, "Go ahead and shoot, Junior. I would rather be dead than to sit here and bear false witness to such shameless distortions of true Texas history."

"Well, by Christ!" howled the old ranger, seizing his buffalo gun back from the Apache, "if Junior ain't of a mind to do so, we'll see if maybe I can't accommodate your desires to die honest!"

He laid the gun's sights on the young historian as though he intended to channel him then and there, but Jud had won a surprise ally.

He wasn't big enough to balance an elk's tooth on a vest pocket watch chain, and he was so dried up the burly old man could have blown him out of camp with one snort, yet the way he equalized the disparity was crushing.

"You no shoot boy," Junior told the white-haired plainsman. He laid hold of the Sharps barrel, pushed it disdainfully aside, stalked over and stood beside Jud. "Him tell better story than you. You all through."

"Why you mealymouthed Apache packrat!" bellowed the deposed minstrel, "I'll flay your dirty Injun hide right off 'n your back. I'll run you so far out—"

Junior held up a small red hand, haughtily abrogating the threat in mid-insult.

"Him no use to cry like old squaw. You all done. Me got new friend now. Boy tell truth, old man lie."

Far from resenting the little Indian's defiance of their white fellow, the other firesiders took huge delight from it. At once and without mercy they began rawhiding the old ranger. Shortly, they were giving him a very hard way to go indeed.

They berated him about being such a bad liar he couldn't even "wool-over the eyes of a dumbbrain Apache mule tracker," and such similar rough comments to the point where Jud could see someone was going to get hurt.

Naturally, that wouldn't do.

To let what started out as a goodtime tall-talk fest turn into a Bowie-knife brawl which could put them all in the guardhouse for the rest of the summer was no way for a new recruit to launch his career in a tough camp. But while he was standing there trying to think how he might throw a little water on the fire he had got going, help arrived in the form of Baylor's orderly.

The trooper surveyed the raucous scene a moment, then yelled, "Hey! quiet down. I got questions." Then, as the men held up a moment to his order, "Any of you seen a strange kid around here? Captain's expecting a boy in from Llano Springs. Must be kin to Sam Houston from all the fuss he's putting on. You all seen this rooster?"

Eyebrows went acock around the fire. Ears perked. Glances walled Jud's way.

"Well, no," answered one of the men thoughtfully. "We got a boy here sure enough. But he's from Topaz Creek. Besides, he wouldn't need to go pulling any kinfolk rank to get in good with the Captain. He's already our new head scout. Said so his ownself. Ask him. Yonder he stands."

"Him?" said the orderly, staring at Jud.

"As ever was," responded the other. "Ain't he a dandy?"

The orderly ignored him, stepped over to Jud.

"You Reeves?" he asked quietly.

Jud looked around, was relieved to see the men at the fire had not made anything of the name. He nodded to the orderly that he was his man.

"All right," replied the latter, "come on along. Captain Baylor wants to see you right off."

Crowsfooted glances once more ran around the chastened circle. By damn, the kid hadn't been horsing them after all. Baylor *had* wanted to see him.

Jud sensed the moment's surprise and straightened to stand a little taller because of it. He hunted up his rifle and fell in beside the orderly. They started off.

"Hold on a minute!" sang out the old ranger with belated urgency. He came trotting up, motioning Jud to step to one side with him. The latter did so.

The old man sidled around for a foot-shuffling spell, then brought up his craggy head and came right out with it.

"Say, kid," he asked, brow knit, "if Woll wasn't a Dutchman, what the hell was he?"

"A Frenchman," said Jud soberly, and followed the orderly on off.

At Baylor's tent the atmosphere changed abruptly.

John Robert Baylor was not a career army man but he was clearly intending to overcome that handicap at the earliest possible moment.

In and immediately about his headquarters the bearing, talk and actions of his aides were entirely military. There was patently no nonsense about Captain J. R. Baylor. No man could reasonably hope to make those tough old Texans look or act like regular soldiers, nor was Baylor quite innocent enough to try. But within the limits of his ability to control his long-haired volunteers, the Captain obviously aimed to run a tight camp. Jud sensed this at once and had presence of mind enough to salute properly when the orderly brought him before Baylor's desk—a packingbox lid balanced over a stump—and to stand stiffly at attention until relieved.

Baylor was pleased with the reaction.

He returned the salute and said, "At ease, Reeves," and motioned him to sit down. Jud planted himself nervously on the edge of the indicated campchair and waited, his carefully rehearsed greeting and his letter of aid from Hampton alike forgotten.

Baylor studied him for a kindly moment.

"I knew your father quite well, boy," he told him. "Both out here and back in Virginia."

Hearing his identity was known, Jud realized Baylor's recruiter or his intelligences had beaten him to the Salado. He thought then about the letter but only answered politely, "Is that so, sir? You don't hardly look old enough."

"I'll be forty soon, young man. That will about double your span I should imagine."

"Yes sir. I'm not twenty yet."

Baylor nodded, the kindliness back in his dry tones.

"I knew your mother, too, lad. Back in Virginia that was. Knew her before your father did as a matter of fact. Lovely, lovely woman. How has she been, boy?"

He put the question as people will when they are asking about someone they know to be in poor health; someone who never had any real chance to get well.

"She's gone on, sir," Jud said. "Passed away last week."

"Oh, I'm sorry to hear that, son. God rest her poor dear soul. She was a grand, gracious Virginia lady."

"Yes sir," said Jud.

His mother had been a practicing invalid and insistent Southern belle all her grown-up life, he clearly suspected.

In her pale philosophy men were born for two things alone—to wage wars and to wait on women. Lucretia Reeves had made the most of her opportunities in both directions by marrying a gallant young West Point cadet from her own home county of Loudon.

"Well, well—?" said Baylor.

Jud had wandered away in his thoughts, forcing the officer to clear his throat and break the growing pause.

"I understand you want to follow in the family tradition, young man. Is that correct?"

"Oh yes sir, that's right sir, I surely do sir," he stammered belatedly.

Baylor nodded, satisfied, and pulled a weather-stained document out of the dispatch pouch whose contents he had been studying at Jud's approach.

"From Mr. Hampton's report, here," he said, "it would appear you had some hopes of a place on my staff, perhaps even of a commission. Is that right?"

His listener shook his tousled blond head.

"No sir," he said. "That was Mr. Hampton's idea."

"And what was yours, sir?" crisped Baylor.

"To scout for you, sir!" broke out Jud. "I know that country out there like it was my Bible psalms, or my own backyard, Captain. Rode over every foot of it, one direction of another, ever since I was big enough to see over a saddlehorn. I've even been across the Pecos and up the Rio Grande a ways. Went with a bunch of hide hunters the spring of '58. They took me along because I could talk Comanche."

"So I see," said Baylor, looking up from Hampton's report. "A scout, eh?"

"Yes sir. Head scout, Mr. Hampton said. With likely a first lieutenant's commission."

Baylor's eyes narrowed, lost their paternal tolerance. "What's your full name, Reeves?"

"Judah Beaumont, sir. Like my father's and grandfather's. Everybody calls me Jud, though."

"All right, Jud, now let's you and me get off to a perfectly clear understanding. Do you expect any special treatment here because of your family's influence or its military reputation? Any favors at all, sir?"

Jud thought again of Hampton's letter of promise in his pocket, thought as quickly that he had better not introduce it as evidence at this late date.

"No sir," he said emphatically. "Not any at all, sir."

"I see," guessed Baylor shrewdly. "Were you led to expect any such favors or preferential treatment by Mr. Hampton's representations?"

"Well, uh—no sir."

"Of course you were," contradicted Baylor abruptly. Then after a moment's stern regard.

"Reeves, you're no different here from any other lad who comes into this camp from the Trinity bottoms, the brakes of the Brazos, or the big bend of the Rio Grande. Hampton was wrong to mislead you; he was carried away by nonmilitary enthusiasm. But I shall not deny his error any more than I shall compound it.

If you stay here you will start from ragged scratch, sir. Is that entirely apparent to you?"

"Yes sir, it certainly is."

"Well then, what do you say?"

Jud snapped out of his chair into a saluting brace.

"Private Reeves reporting, sir," he answered, backing it with his homely, crinkling grin.

Baylor laughed and got up. He clapped him on the shoulder and said that was the spirit he liked to see, and that now all they had to do was figure out what assignment to give a stripeless private whose father and grandfather between them had rated six stars.

"I'll tell you what we'll do, Jud," he declared. "We'll go as far as we can to honor Hampton's offer. We'll make you assistant to the head scout. That is to say a sort of journeyman apprentice to my chief of scouts. How does that sound to you for a starter?"

"Just wonderful," agreed Jud, forgetting to "sir" the smiling officer. "Who do I report to, Captain?"

"Captain *sir,*" Baylor chided him genially. "And you report to a chap named Cavanaugh. 'Comanche' Cavanaugh. You will find him around one of the fires. That is, providing he hasn't run off across the river to see his squaw again. Just ask anyone you see. They all know him."

"Yes sir, Captain *sir,*" Jud saluted, and got out of there as quickly as he could.

As he went Baylor, plainly pleased, called up one of his young aides and asked, "What do you think of him, Hugh? That's General Reeves' boy."

"The devil you say, sir! General Judah Reeves? And you sent him along to that crazy Cavanaugh? As a ragged-tail recruit, sir? Why that boy's family—"

"I know all about that boy's family," laughed Baylor. "Don't worry about that, Hugh. And I don't intend leaving him long with Cavanaugh. Just long enough for a bit of quick seasoning. I'll have him back up with us before we've marched far."

Then, adding it with an admiring headshake, "You just don't get in that kind of material to work with every day in the week, Hugh. He's Reeves right to his fingertips, that young gamebird. We'll have to see he's given a little something to try his spurs on directly."

He turned, nodding happily, and went into his tent and Second Lieutenant Hugh Preston looked over at his fellow staffer Second Lieutenant Darrel Royce, who had been standing by with him during Baylor's talk with Jud.

"You hear that?" he sidemouthed to the other officer."

"I heard it," vouchsafed Royce, shrugging. "What of it?"

"You watch," said Hugh Preston, jerking his head angrily toward the command tent. "He'll have that ignorant little son of a bitch a first lieutenant inside of sixty days!"

Jud walked back to his group's fire, thinking hard.

Something about Baylor bothered him.

Also vaguely disturbing was something he felt he

should remember about that name "Comanche Cavanaugh." But that could wait a bit. It was the dashing leader of the 2nd Texas Mounted Rifles who had him worrying right now.

First off, the Captain had a way of looking over a person's head while he was talking to him, giving the impression he was thinking much farther ahead than this disorganized camp and its makeshift corps of Texas Militia. Next, there was something intangible about Baylor, or about his snapping-eyed ambition, which simply did not go with these long-haired frontier adventurers which he had gathered together here on the Salado. Lastly, there was definitely an awkwardness existing between the Captain and his unruly troops, a lack of proper discipline and military respect very apparent to a boy of Jud's training and education.

However, this peculiarity of the kindly Captain's would have to wait for later observation.

Ahead lay Jud's fire.

He waved back to one of the men who saw him coming and greeted him with a friendly lift of the hand. A couple of the others called out to ask him if head scout work paid well and if it did what were the chances of his getting them on his staff. Another assured him he ought to give no least heed to the braying of jackasses, as the camp was full of them and it was just something a new man had to get used to. Still another said, "Here, have a fresh cup, she's red hot," as he came up, and reached to pour him the offered tin of coffee.

"No thanks," grinned Jud, feeling the glow of the rough welcome grow inside him. "I got a job to do."

It was plain they had accepted him. From then on, every man around that fire was his friend. It was wonderful to walk into a camp of a thousand strangers and be made at home inside half an hour. Still, that was the Texas way. What a grand state! And what grand people in it! Hampton had been absolutely right. Texas was worth fighting for every bit as much as Virginia, and a Texas boy's first duty lay in defending her and in helping her brave volunteers carry the flag of the Confederacy high and proud in the Southwest.

"Well?" inquired the bony oldster who had been intrigued to learn that General Adrian Woll was of Gallic rather than Prussian breeding. "What's your first assignment, boy? You got a job to do, leave us in on it. Which you going after first, the Comanches or the Apaches?"

"The Comanches, I reckon," answered Jud. "Leastways, I've been told to find a fellow called 'Comanche.'"

"Comanche Cavanaugh?" asked the old man dubiously.

"That's the one. Captain Baylor said any of you would be able to tell me where I could find him."

"Why for you want him?" It was still the old man asking.

"Captain told me to report to him."

"Report what?"

"Just report, that's all. I'm to be his new assistant, sort of apprentice the Captain said."

The old man looked sick. He went as white as though someone had struck him across the small of the back with a riflebarrel.

"Oh my God don't tell me!" he begged, and sagged weakly down on a convenient stump muttering and cursing in such a fluent string of Kiowa-Comanche that Jud had to guess at once who it was he had just injured.

"By golly, I'm sorry, Mr. Cavanaugh," he stammered. "I surely didn't know it was you I was looking for."

"You're sorry!" exploded Baylor's Chief of Scouts. "Oh by God I just won't put up with it! I'll resign. I'll run off and join up with the Federals. I simply son-of-a-bitching won't have it, you hear! *Sein-p'a'go dei-zounda, houdldh gyht-zounda! Tsou ei-tseidle tou-dougyh, gyh-zounda!—"*

He rumbled off into an unbroken addle of Kiowa and Comanche oaths out of which Jud picked, among the least foul of the references of himself, that because of Baylor's unforgivable act in assigning the boy to him, the old man was going to pull every hair out of his stubby white beard and that Jud was a stone in his moccasin which he was going to snatch out and throw so far over the side of the mountain it would never stop bouncing, and on and on in such similar rageful directions that at last Jud was forced to step in and call a halt to it.

"Old man," he said quietly, "stop babbling."

Startled, the other hesitated.

"I read that Wasp talk as clear as you spout it," Jud told him flatly. "And I don't care to hear any more of those mean things said in it of me or my folks. Now you slow down, you hear?"

Cavanaugh slowed down.

He shut his mouth and stopped altogether.

Cocking a bright, inquisitive eye at Jud, he squinted interestedly. "Well, now, that's right educational. So you know a Wasp from a Wanderer, eh?"

"And from a Yap-eater, or an Antelope, or a Liver-eater," nodded Jud, naming off some of the other better-known Comanche bands.

"And maybe even from a Burnt Meat or a Wormy?"

"Even from a Water Horse," said Jud, mentioning perhaps the most famous among the Indians but the least known to the average white man of all the Comanche families.

"Well, that does it!" declared the old scout.

He got up and came over to Baylor's newly appointed assistant to the Chief of Scouts and gave him a good, close looking over.

"By God," he said at last, "it ain't entirely impossible, at that. We might figure out how to do it somehow. Give me a little time, by Christ, give me a little time."

"For what?" asked Jud bluntly.

The old man stared at him witheringly.

"For figuring if you're fit to ride flank for the likes

of Elkanah Cavanaugh," he answered him with quiet, searing pride, and turned and stalked off into the gathering dusk still muttering and talking to himself.

Jud had it then; what had bothered him right from Baylor's first mention of the name Comanche Cavanaugh. The "Comanche" part of it had not rung familiar for that was not the way he had seen it written down in his father's military memoirs of the Mexican Campaign.

But *Elkanah* Cavanaugh!

Ah, that meant something else again.

Elkanah Cavanaugh was a name you wrote down right on the same line with the likes of Deaf Smith, Ben McCulloch, Captain Jack Hays, Old Cap Tumlinson or Bigfoot Wallace.

They just didn't come any taller in the border fighting business than that old man yonder.

Jud Reeves had struck it rich.

3

"WHERE'S the old man, Reeves?"

Jud looked up, surprised. Baylor's orderly was standing just beyond the fire, plainly impatient to have his answer and be off.

"Why, I surely don't know, Corporal," he replied. "He wandered off into the dark over an hour ago and hasn't come back."

Jud squinted across the flames at the young soldier, palming his hands to show that not only was he ignorant of Cavanaugh's whereabouts but innocent of any intent to inquire into same.

Not so Baylor's orderly.

"Well, wander off after him!" he snapped. "Tell him the Captain wants to see him. Tell yourself, too, while you're about it."

"I beg your pardon?" said Jud.

"Captain wants to see the both of you; on the double.

Corporal Bodie had served a hitch in the Regular U.S. Army, ran out his missions in a prompt and military manner. He was gone now before his listener could query him further, leaving the latter to figure out the details of the assignment for himself.

Shortly, Jud departed into the darkness in the direction taken by the old scout.

He found him sitting on a driftlog down by the river, smoking his pipe and tossing pebbles into the passing current.

"Why, hello boy," he said. "Come set down here and help me stone this stream. You won't learn much but it's fine for the nerves."

He was very subdued about it and Jud had to peer twice to make sure he had the right man. He had, all right, and couldn't resist asking about the change in weather.

"What's the matter, Mr. Cavanaugh?" he said. "Aren't you feeling well?"

"No, I ain't," sighed the old man. "You don't go forty years in this business without you develop some symptoms."

"You been scouting forty years?" exclaimed Jud incredulously. "I thought you were only about sixty."

"You'd ought to know, boy, that this country ages a man fast. I started scouting when I was twelve. I'm fifty-two years old this spring."

"By damn, that's something," said Jud, amazed. "What's your symptoms, Mr. Cavanaugh?"

"Lumped together, I call them my Comanche Twitch. It's something gets to bothering me like the damp and cold does some folks with the rheumatics."

"Well now that's right interesting; how does it work?" inquired Jud politely.

"It comes on of a sudden just before I'm due to get sent out on a scout, or any other time when there's a handclose likelihood of running into heavy Injun sign. Starts out with a crampy pain in the shankbones, pretty quick eases up into the tailbone. From there it runs square up my back into my head and I wind up with a miserable skullache."

"Where does the twitch come in?" asked Jud, puzzled.

"With the headache. When it starts to hurt, my eyes go to squinching up with the pain of it."

"Maybe you need spectacles," said Jud. "I knew an old man out on Topaz Creek used to get an eye twitch and he went to Dallas and—"

"Boy," Cavanaugh wanted to know softly, "did you come down here to fit me with eyeglasses?"

"No sir," answered Jud, remembering his mission but still worrying about the old man's twitch. "Captain

Baylor's orderly says you and me are to go see the Captain right away."

"I knew it," said the grizzled scout. "You might as well go roll your blankets, boy. We'll be gone by daybreak."

"Gone?" queried Jud. "Gone where?"

"To conquer the world," said the old man cynically. "Ain't you talked to Baylor yet?"

"What you mean?"

"You'll see," said Elkanah Cavanaugh. "You ain't no dummy. Come along and keep your mouth shut."

Jud wanted to explore the cryptic remark about Baylor, but had to settle for a swinging dogtrot to keep up with his companion's loping walk. He didn't get in another word short of the command tent and once there things went so fast he found himself hard put to keep up with the conversation, let alone take a part in it. Which in any case he was not invited to do.

Baylor talked.

Elkanah Cavanaugh argued back.

Jud Reeves listened.

The end point remained the same, and it was an eye-twicher, all right.

Baylor was going to break camp at daylight. He was losing ten men a day by desertion. As of May 1 he had had over 1000 troops on the rolls, as of June 6, the present date, scarcely 700 remained. The Texans were not disloyal, just restless. Action was imperative to hold the command together. It would be forthcoming at once in the form of a 500-mile surfaceline march from San Antonio to Fort Bliss at El Paso. Cavanaugh and Jud were to scout ahead of the column, watching out for Indians and reporting back as to the best grass and water for each night's camp.

They were to go in secret and immediately.

There must, moreover, be no general knowledge of the enforced move; Baylor fearing wholesale desertions to the point where he had not even briefed his own staff officers on the El Paso destination.

Cavanaugh tried to tell him that the type of troops he had were not the kind to care for surprises of this nature. But Baylor reminded him that he had been in Texas for quite some time himself, and might be presumed to know a little something of Texas and Texans in his own right.

The old scout granted that this was so, next asking for and being refused permission to go across the river and visit his wife and family before leaving. Baylor explained the refusal in terms of the pressing need for secrecy and dispatch, and Cavanaugh said not another word on the subject. He did, however, have a departing query as to the destination and aims of the 2nd Texas Mounted Rifles.

"Captain," he demanded, "where the hell we going and what the hell we going to do when we get there?"

"Mr. Cavanaugh," replied his commander, "surely you are familiar with the stated purpose of our undertaking. I've had the particulars printed and published, you know."

"Captain," the old man answered him bluntly, "I

42

ain't interested in what you're telling the newspapers. What I want to know is what you're telling yourself."

Baylor caught the challenge in his chief scout's scarcely delicate comparison. He returned the stare and the checkmate response with equal bluntness.

"I have just told you we are going to El Paso. Isn't that far enough for you, Mr. Cavanaugh?"

"Is it for *you?*" said the old man quietly.

Again Baylor understood him, but again refused to be drawn out.

"You'll know when we get there." He nodded curtly.

Cavanaugh looked at him an uncomfortably long time then wagged his shaggy head.

"No, Captain," he told him, striking Jud as more regretful than disrespectful about it. "I reckon I know already. Was there anything else, sir?"

"No sir," said Baylor stiffly. "You have your orders, please be about them as quickly as possible."

"Yes sir," acknowledged Elkanah Cavanaugh, and started off without another word.

"Just a moment, Mr. Cavanaugh," Baylor called after him. "How is young Reeves working out?"

"Young who?" said the old man, coming about.

"Reeves. Your new right-hand bower," smiled the officer.

"Oh the boy. Yeah. Well, he's working out just fine. What did you say his name was?"

"Reeves. His father was General Judah Reeves."

"My God! you don't mean it!"

"Aha! I thought that would cheer you up. Now go

43

along with you and no more second guessing my campaign objectives, you hear?"

"Yes sir," said Elkanah Cavanaugh, pushing Jud ahead of him to get the exodus under way and the more quickly clear of Baylor's tent. "Cuss you, boy," he growled under his breath. "Why didn't you say you was General Reeves' son? Ain't you got good sense? Your daddy's name—"

"Mr. Cavanaugh," interrupted Jud firmly, "it's not my daddy's name I enlisted under."

The old man looked at him, nodding his appreciation of the reprimand.

"Hell's fire, I know that, boy. You don't need to tell me you aim to stand on your own two feet. You're a Reeves. How else would you stand?"

There it was again, the honor of the name.

Jud winced and didn't like it, but said nothing to show that he did not.

"You and my father were pretty close, I guess," he offered to bridge the silence. "I read about you in his Mexican diary."

"I was his first sergeant in his first troop," said the old man. "We went all the way together."

"I hardly knew him," said Jud. "I was twelve the last time I saw him."

"A kid twelve don't know nothing. No, nor an old fool fifty-two, neither."

Jud didn't see the connection between the ages and admitted it. Cavanaugh just shook his head and told him to hush up and follow along to where their horses were picketed. Since he hadn't even known that he had a horse, Jud did as he was ordered with some interest.

Arrived at the picketline, he was astonished to find his bedroll already in place behind the cantel of a fine new saddle laced onto a good little flax-maned chestnut with a star and a snip and two white socks.

"Now who in the world—" he began to inquire into the identity of the horse's donor, but Cavanaugh cut him off.

"It was Junior," he said. "Them Lipans don't need to be told. They read minds. You'll catch on."

It was true. As the old scout spoke, the tiny Apache loomed up through the dark, white teeth gleaming. He put a hand on the chestnut's withers and grinned at Jud.

"Him good pony. Best can find in dark. We go quick now. Man maybe come looking."

"You mean you stole this little horse!" cried Jud. "Right off of somebody's rope in our own camp?"

"Other side camp," said Junior. "No take rope, just pony. Boy talk too much. Time we go."

"He's right," broke in Elkanah Cavanaugh. "We'd best mosey along."

"Well, good Lord!" objected Jud. "I'm not going to start off by stealing a man's horse!"

"That's his problem, not yours," grunted Cavanaugh, swinging up on his bony white gelding. "First rule in any man's army is to take care of yourself. Walk your horses," he ordered, dropping his voice and touching up the white. "We want to slip out quiet. We'll go up this near side of the river, right off. Easy now."

As Jud still hesitated, Junior touched him on the arm.

"You no worry about horse, boy. Me fix in morning." He patted the little chestnut, flashing his seamy grin again. "Cut mane. Bob tail. Color white foot brown. Make him look like Injun pony heap quick. You *sabe?*"

Jud grimaced unhappily, surrendered to the hard facts.

There wasn't any point in falling out with your own thieves, not in arguing with a patent expert. He got a leg up on the chestnut, followed Cavanaugh off through the cottonwoods. Behind him came the wizened Apache, humming some kind of a Lipan Brave Song weirdly offkey and perched on the saddleless back of a black Navajo mare which looked as though a strong gust of wind would blow her clear back to Arizona or wherever Junior had stolen her.

Catching up to Cavanaugh with the last of the camp safely behind them, Jud asked about the route they would take west.

The old man told him they would follow the abandoned San Antonio & San Diego Mail-line stage road through Fort Clark and up the Pecos to the old crossing at Fort Lancaster, below Horsehead Crossing, rather than take the better watered Butterfield stage route coming down from the north through Fort Chadbourne to the Pecos at Horsehead.

"But," he added, "I aim to make a little personal detour on the way and right shortly too."

"How's that?" asked Jud unsuspectingly.

"Like this," grunted the old man, and kicked his mount sharply to the left.

Jud was uneasy but said no more. They were riding due south where they should have been going straight west by a shade north. But the old man was a legend. If he thought it wise to ride south for a spell before turning west, Jud was not the one to argue his reasons.

Presently, they came to a small river and it was not the Salado. Jud frowned and said, "What stream is this?" and the old man said. "This here's the Medina and it's where you either set and wait overnight by your lonesome, or else come along with Cavanaugh to meet the wife and kids."

"Now hold on, Mr. Cavanaugh!" Jud remonstrated, reining in his pony. "The Captain said you weren't to do that. I heard him with my own ears."

"Well, you're hearing *me* with your own ears, too," nodded his senior. "And I'm a'going to do it."

"I won't go with you," maintained Jud stoutly. "Not against orders, I won't."

"Who's to know, boy?" asked Cavanaugh, eying him.

"Old woman she cook heap good," announced Junior, making his first speech since leaving the camp on the other stream. "Me go you, Tall Horse. We leave boy here."

Tall Horse was Cavanaugh's Indian name, Jud gathered. He judged it was taken from the old man's great height and from his loping speed afoot. In any event, he answered to it now, in no uncertain terms and in Junior's direction.

"You go to hell," he told the little Indian. "You like the boy's stories so damned well, you just stay here and feed yourself some more of them. See how they fill up your shifty red gut. I'll be cut and gelded if you ain't et your last of my old woman's *enchiladas*, you mealymouthed Siwash."

He turned briefly back to Jud.

"You coming, boy? I'd truly like to have you along."

"And I'd truly like to come along, too," Jud assured him earnestly. "I really would, Mr. Cavanaugh."

"Well then," said the old man, "you just do it and Baylor be damned. But there's one thing more I got to ask you, first."

"Yes sir?"

"What do you think of Mexicans?"

Jud was not a devious thinker. His mind, while sensitive, was not suspicious. He had learned early in life that a straight answer will turn away more trouble in ten minutes than a roundabout one in ten years. Accordingly, he simply said to his bearded questioner that he liked Mexicans fine, especially the girls. Who he thought had it all over American girls for good manners and proper, ladylike behavior. Taken by and large, he allowed, you would have to say he favored Mexicans a good deal, but what kind of a question was

48

that to put to a man when they had been talking about Captain Baylor and obedience to official orders?

"My woman's a Mexican," said Elkanah Cavanaugh meaningfully, and started his horse across the ford to the south bank.

Cavanaugh's place, a few miles down into Atascosa County, looked peaceful and pretty to Jud as they rode up on it in the early evening moonlight.

It lay in a nice kind of country, open and level prairie, with some big mesquite and medium-sized live oak trees scattered around just right to give good stock shade. A grove of very old, very big Spanish-planted cottonwoods towered over the house and barn, with some smaller stragglers growing in the pasture lot where Cavanaugh said his woman kept a milk cow and some angora goats.

The old man swore the goats gave more milk than the cow and the cow grew a better pelt of hair than the goats and none of them were worth the price of a rifle shell to shoot. But, he added, his wife was a sensible woman who made out with what she had, after the admirable manner of Mexicans, and so she and Cavanaugh had known a mighty good and satisfying life together regardless of the cow and the goats.

There were seven children, ranging from a boy barely walking to a girl seventeen years old.

As they stopped talking, now, and turned their ponies in toward the silent house, Cavanaugh's old white gelding shot his ears forward and whinnied hoarsely.

Almost at once a light bloomed inside the adobe and from around behind it rushed five or six rangy curs to start challenging the three horsemen to get down off their mounts if they dared.

Cavanaugh dared, and instantly the brutes had his scent and were changing their angry snarls to bawling yelps and boundings of unrestrained welcome. Before the old man could shout them down, the house was breaking out in a rash of other quickly made lights and its awakened walls were reverberating with a babble of eager cries and high laughter from the smaller Cavanaughs whose hearing, quite evidently, was as acutely tuned to the sound of the returned hero's voice as were the noses of the ranch dogs to his body scent.

It was clear to Jud that here was an old house with a lifetime supply of love and affection stored up in it. He sensed that before ever the front door swung open. And he had the feeling that something important and exciting was going to happen when that door did come open and the old scout's dusky brood spilled out of it.

There was that last brief pause of anticipation, then the rough planks were flung whoopingly wide to flood the yard with the expected wave of yellow lamplight and blackhaired halfbreed youngsters. But even as the latter stormed the night with their glad yells and delighted squealings, all sight and sound of them fell off and faded away for Jud Reeves.

There behind them, framed full in the open doorway

50

by the gleaming lamplight from within, stood the most startlingly blond halfbreed girl any Texas white boy had ever sat in his saddle and gaped at.

There could be no more doubt of her golden complexion than there could be of her obvious mixed-blood heredity.

In every sensuous line of the way she stood there this had to be Elkanah Cavanaugh's daughter.

4

HER NAME was Estrellita, the Little Star, but Cavanaugh called her simply Star and it was clear from the tender manner in which he held her when she ran to meet him in the threshold lamplight, and from the little-girl way he kissed her on the forehead and patted her gleaming hair while she laughed softly against his smoky buckskin shirt, that she was the old man's dearest favorite as well as fiercest pride.

The truly great thing which struck Jud about the girl and all the other children was the fact that from beginning to end there was no mention of his being any different than they were. They simply accepted him as one of the family with no awkwardness at all over the fact he was pure white *Tejano* while they were half Mexican.

Jud could not help wondering how his own father and mother, or any similar set of quality white folks, would have returned the favor, would have welcomed a halfbreed guest in their homes. He dropped the thought quickly and turned his attention to Cavanaugh's happy household.

Before long, the five younger children were sent back up into the sleeping loft with a bearhug and a whiskery kiss from the father they saw only between Indian wars. Left below in the ranchhouse kitchen, drinking real coffee and finishing up the last of a big iron pot of *arroz con pollo,* were Cavanaugh and the girl, her sixteen-year-old brother, Sam Houston Cavanaugh, called "Chulo," the mother, Maria Teresa Hidalgo y Samozo Cavanaugh, Junior, the Lipan Apache tracker, and the entirely absorbed, immediately adopted Judah Beaumont Reeves III.

Jud had never known a true family life or normal home atmosphere. Even guests were rare at the Topaz Creek ranch and of course he remembered nothing of the various military post residences which had preceded it, or of the Loudon County, Virginia, plantation of his mother's kinfolk. As for close or even distant relatives from "back east," these came not at all to the arid Texas plains whereon his father had willfully settled his ailing mother in the doubly mistaken idea that it would benefit her health while at the same time providing him with a fabulous future profit in land speculation.

Now, being so naturally and without question taken into old Elkanah Cavanaugh's voluminous clan, he was understandably touched.

And intrigued, too, at the manner in which so much of good feeling and family fun could show itself where there was plainly so little of actual value to be seen about the Cavanaugh place.

Poor they had to be; poor as Job's turkey.

A scout's pay, even a chief of scout's pay, would not run much over a dollar or two per day, and a good part of that would go at once for tobacco, powder, lead, percussion caps and, of course, drinking whiskey.

But deer and wild pigs were in the riverbrush and dove and prairie chicken and bright-eyed quail out upon the open prairie. Free land was everywhere, and it was rich land. If you were even half Mexican, like the Cavanaughs, you would understand how to engineer and dig the slender *acequias,* or irrigation ditches, with which the mission *padres* had long ago taught your forebears to bring fruit from the desert where a white farmer would sit and slowly starve while praying for the rains which never came, or against the duststorms which always did.

Jud understood these things about these people and this land; that they somehow got along with the country and climate in a superior way to their American betters. But he had never seen the spirit of "God will provide," their dominant philosophy, so happily demonstrated as in the destitute-of-worldly-goods household of Elkanah Cavanaugh.

It was long past midnight when the old scout at last began to weary of recounting his adventures since the previous homecoming and of being brought up to date on those of the family in the same time. Presently, he stood up to announce abruptly that, "She's deep enough for me, and I'm a-going to hit the hay.

"Jud," he went on, "you and Junior bed down in the barn loft with Chulo. Star, you show Jud around out in back while Chulo's making down his bed in the loft. Point out the pump and the trough to him so's he can find them in the dark. We're going to be cutting out before daybreak."

He turned to Maria and said, "Come on, old woman. You and me have got something better than talk to attend to," and fetched her a slap on her rounded backside that Jud thought would have staggered a steer.

Maria struck back at the grizzled scout, laying the back of her forearm across his broad chest with a whacking "thunk!" which sounded as though it had been administered with a stovelength of suncured mesquite. Then, even as he gasped with the force of the blow, she turned into him with her hips and slid the same arm around his neck and pulled his head down and laughed something into his ear in throaty Spanish.

Then, with a pair of quickly nodded, *"Adios, muchachos,"* the two of them were gone through the darkened front room into the cowhide-curtained alcove beyond it, which was their own cozy little *cuarto de dormir.*

Junior, plainly an old and familiar visitor here, grinned at Chulo and said, "Me you go now, *niño.* Girl she show new boy where pump is. *Me entiende usted, amigo?"* The little Apache shook his head sadly as he got up, adding with mock soberness to himself, "Poor boy. Him pretty old for not know where pump is," and went on out the back door with Chulo, still wagging his head in broad sympathy for Jud's ignorance.

The latter, left alone with the girl and the crude import of Junior's parting remark, was extremely grateful to Cavanaugh's slim daughter when she passed off the possible embarrassment with an easy smile and a matter-of-factly shrugged, "Come on, it's pretty late," and led the way out onto the shed-roofed back porch.

Past the black shadows of the porch the moon was shining brightly enough to read a cattle buyer's contract by. As Jud squinted to its brilliant whiteness, the girl blew out the coal-oil lamp he had carried from the kitchen. For a moment he could see nothing. Nor, actually, did he need to. The girl's satiny hand stole into his and she said again, "Come on," and moved out into the open moonlight.

Talking soft and low in the same throaty way he had noted in her mother, she showed him the dug well in the cottonwoods past the corral, and explained how it was piped from the pump to the stock trough by a square, box flume. She told him which end of the trough was free of moss for washing-up purposes, and said that there would be fresh coffee in the kitchen at 4 A.M. She did not actually say as much, but it was plain to Jud that she meant him to understand she would be there with the coffee, which pleased him out of all size to what it properly should have.

The girl was so inescapably pretty viewed out here

in the Atascosa County moonlight that he had to keep reminding himself over and over again as to who she was and who he was.

That Texas moon was doing things to her yellow hair and Aztec-green eyes which made a man mighty prone to forgive and forget her dark side. Still, to realize this was to be on guard against it. And so, if he kept a sharp watch of the girl and of himself, there ought to be no trouble.

Across the rear yard, now, she stopped with him in front of the barn and said softly, "The loft ladder is yonder in the feedroom corner." Then, after a hesitant moment. "You go along. I'm pretty well awake now and believe I will go down and sit by the spring a bit before I go in. Goodnight—"

She teased off the word as though she did not want to let go of it and reached out and put her hand in his once more.

"Come on," she murmured for the third, husky-voiced time and Jud went with her down through the cottonwoods and past the well into the little tall-grassed meadow of the pasture lot.

Star Cavanaugh had been to convent school in San Antonio for the better part of one winter term, and that was all.

She could barely read and scarcely write her own name.

Her father was an illiterate if locally famous "squawman." Her mother was a Chihuahua woman whose mother, before her, had been a pureblood

Sonora Apache. Her brothers and her sisters and herself might call themselves Cavanaughs until they were old and bent and ready for the burial plot. They would be deluding only themselves. To any of their Texas neighbors, and in cold fact to any standard of judgment in the Southwestern white world, they were "ignorant breeds." And they would never, ever, be anything else.

Hence, this *Tejano* boy sitting now so edgily beside her upon the log by the pasture spring, was a man from another planet.

Star had learned that fact in the past busy hours since Cavanaugh's homecoming. The old scout had troweled it on with a heavy hand, as to Jud's high birth and rare background. This, perhaps, was no more than natural in a simple-minded man, or rather in a man of uncomplicated mind, like Elkanah Cavanaugh. No normal person is apt to forget or to underplay his brief brushes with the lives of the famous, and Cavanaugh had not forgotten his service under the second General Judah Beaumont Reeves. But where he had dramatized Jud's bloodlines to make his little halfbreed family feel the same kinship with the white boy which he himself felt, the effort had backfired with his daughter Star.

The girl had been out in the world, even though but passingly, in that one winter away at school. She knew the bitterness of the halfbreed brand far better than the other children. She realized with equal sensitivity the tremendous advantages of birth and breeding in the white Southern man's way of life. Her time in San Antonio had taught her that much more certainly than it had any of her book lessons.

Accordingly, she hesitated with Jud Reeves, her original rash impulse to offer herself, really to demand that he take her, slowed and put in halting question by the nameless conflicts of instinct and reason momentarily whipping and sawing at her nerves.

And as she hesitated, Jud began to talk in his arid, easy-going Topaz Creek drawl.

The first flurry of excitement put up in him by the feel of the girl's hand, and by his guess as to its evident invitation in leading him toward the moonlit spring, had now calmed and disappeared.

It was clear that he had misjudged her intentions and of a sudden she looked very small and helpless and in need of real friendship.

She was, after all, Cavanaugh's daughter, he told himself. She could not be all bad or, in fact, bad at all.

He had just imagined he saw that open challenge in her first look at him there in the lamplight of the front door. In hard fact, if a person wanted to be entirely honest, it was not her fault he was sitting there in the prairie moonlight brief hours from starting west on the greatest adventure of his life. He had come along out here to the spring of his own free will, and indecently eager about doing so, too. No, she hadn't asked him along, as much, or any more, than he had asked himself along. So there was no blame on her for that.

Moreover, he was beginning to like her.

She had a sweet smile, a low, infectious laugh, a quick, frank way of talking and an easy, pleasant way of being with a man that set her apart from most girls.

True, he wasn't going to forget her background. But out here under the light of the 1 A.M. stars and the feathery touch of the early morning prairie breeze, even that charge did not seem any real province of his. It was not, certainly, Jud Reeves' job to try her case, nor to hand down any unasked decisions on it. Judge not lest you be judged, he reminded himself sternly, and so relaxed and began to talk in his easy, friendly way to Star Cavanaugh.

"It surely is a lovely night," he led off soberly. "And I'm mightily beholden to you, Miss Star, for the fact I'm out here to enjoy it with you."

He thought of her and called her by her first name and she smiled and said she was glad he had. In fact, she added, she was just as glad as he was that they were sitting there together on the log by the spring. Furthermore, she assured him with a touch of halting shyness, he owed her absolutely nothing while she, indeed, owed him everything.

"I don't understand that," he said simply. "I surely haven't done anything for you that I know of."

"You've done more for me than you will *ever* know of," she told him huskily, and he felt a meaning far beyond the few words in the lonely, humble way she said them.

He was suddenly quite ill at ease again.

"Now how is that so, Miss Star?" he asked. "You

came out here only because your father told you to take me around and show me the lay of the land. I had nothing to do with that."

"You had everything to do with it," said the girl, bringing her slant green eyes to bear on him. "I came out here for one reason—to be alone with you."

"You what?" sparred Jud desperately.

She looked away from him, out into the open moonlight.

"I wanted to get out here alone with you. I wanted to do that so I could talk to you. But it took your help to give me the nerve to do it."

She looked back at him and he felt the impact of her smoky glance as though it were a solid, moving force.

"I'm glad to have such a fine home," she concluded low voiced, "and no girl in the world has more reason to love and respect and be grateful for her folks and family. But I'll never lie to you. When you looked back at me the way you did out there in front tonight, I knew then I would have to leave them if you said so."

"If *I* said so!" burst out Jud, beginning to feel a great and spreading alarm. "Whatever in the world are you talking about?"

"About you and me going away from here," said the girl. She dropped her eyes, knotting her fingers and keeping her head down. "I didn't come out here to show you around. I came out here to make sure you felt the same thing I did from that look we had at each other out front. If you did, I want to go away with you and be your woman, that's all. I'll follow you forever and from here to as far as the road will wind or the trail bend, if you will have me. That's the truth and will stay the truth whether you will have me or you won't—"

She trailed off with a small choking sound and Jud, already startled and badly shaken, was terrified to see the quick glint of the tears streaking down her cheek.

"Miss Star!" he blurted in incipient panic, "it's plumb wrong for you to think and talk like that!"

He pulled away from her in fearful, awkward haste and she, misinterpreting the move as a rejection of her offered faith, sprang angrily away from him. Sensing that she had taken his meaning wrongly, and being reassured by her seemingly petulant action that her talk had been not so much serious as schoolgirlish, he lost his own fears.

Reaching an apologetic hand toward her, he murmured, "Now, please, Miss Star. I didn't mean anything disrespectful."

"Don't touch me!" she rasped, recoiling from the tentative gesture. "I knew I wasn't good enough for you. I knew it right along. I'll not bother you again, you needn't fear for that, Mr. Reeves."

"I don't fear for that, or for anything else about you," Jud told her gently. "I can't help who I was born any more than you can. And I don't want it to stand between us that we weren't bred and brought up the same identical way. Nobody is. But you're Cavanaugh's daughter, you hear? That's pedigree enough for me, or any man. Now you understand that, Miss Star, and you believe it. I wouldn't say it if I didn't mean it."

He saw the stiffness go out of her shoulders and was glad. There was no use deceiving himself. No matter the color of her skin, this green-eyed breed girl had taken a tremendous hold on him. He seemed to sense and to feel in her something of value and dearness which could not possibly be defined against the harsh realities of her mixed blood and illiterate upbringing. Not being able to put a name to it, however, did not help a man defend himself against its primitive disturbances. And so Jud admitted that blind fact to himself and got on with his peacemaking.

In the process he made an innocent but cruel blunder.

He led the passionate breed girl right back to the same dangerous point from which he had just so carefully and honestly guided her away. He did it by allowing the resumed talk to wander in the direction of his impression with the warm life and good times of the Cavanaugh family and to the contrasting barrenness of his own boyhood. From there, he and the girl got to talking as though they had known each other all their lives, for surely there is no key to tongues locked by past lonelinesses, like a trusting, mutual admission of that common background; and particularly so where the two locksmiths are not yet twenty and the medium in which they are working is June moonlight.

For the first time in his young memory Jud Reeves was thinking (and talking!) of a man's true place in the grown-up scheme of things, as husband and father, defender and provider, conceiver and creator of the family.

Under the influence of his educated if colloquially tainted language, Star Cavanaugh, too, was brought for the first time to see these inviting prospects of a home and children of her own. And to see them, unfortunately, through the natural error wrought by Jud's growing enthusiasm as a distinct possibility for herself and the tall blond boy by her side.

Carried away by the addition of this excitement to her previously existing fancy for Jud and knowing, within the simple limits of her out-settlement experience, but one way in which a woman might adequately express herself to a man, the halfbreed girl fell into the trap her companion had so unconsciously set for her.

In the highly charged moment of emotional silence following their brief exploration into the world of adult life together, she turned her soft body against his and sought his lips with a hunger as savage as it was honest and unashamed.

The heat of her parted mouth spread through Jud in a way that robbed him of both breath and sight.

He sensed, rather than felt, the swift twisting of their young bodies down off the log and into the dry prairie grass. But the feel of the ground under his shoulders and the panting weight of the girl's body pressing

fiercely atop his set off a wild panic of sudden conscience. He rolled away from her with a suppressed
oath and leaped to his feet to stare down at her with
the white-faced look of a man who has just jumped
back from stepping on an unseen snake.

It was not the way he meant to look. There was no
intent of disgust or anger in it. It was just the way that
his pure fright of her, and of his first feeling of any
woman's body against his own, made him look. It was
an expression of first experience shock, and nothing
else.

But the halfbreed girl was not experienced either,
and she read it only for what it appeared to be—a look
of loathing and revulsion for her, and of outraged
rejection of her impulsive embrace.

Star lay where he had thrown her, half against the
old log, her narrowed green eyes flaming up at him.

She had carried out with her on the moonlight walk
her shot-loaded Mexican quirt, as natural an instrument for pointing out things afoot as it was for encouraging a reluctant pony when mounted. The quirt had
fallen free when she kissed Jud, and she saw it lying
near to her now.

Her hand went out for it as quick and unthinking as
the act of a cat in unsheathing its claw.

As swift, too, as a cat she sprang to her feet and laid
the oiled rawhide thongs across the bridge of Jud's
nose and searing into the angular jut of his cheek-
bones.

He stood there in the moonlight, the black blood

starting to creep downward from the cutline below his eyes.

He did not move a hand to brush the blood away. Or to take the whip from the wild-eyed girl.

He just stood there.

At last he nodded and said without hate or hardness in his voice, "You shouldn't have done that, Miss Star. Not to a man who wanted to be your friend. Or to a boy who was beginning to believe in you."

And when he had said it, he turned away and went back up through the cottonwood grove toward the hayloft and the three hours' sleep which lay between him and Elkanah Cavanaugh's 4 A.M. start to scout the way westward for Baylor and his seven hundred buffalo hunters.

Jud was still staring at the hand-hewn stringers of the barn roof, squinting at the waning moon through the wide cracks between the sheathing boards, when Junior spoke. "Him time you me get up, boy. Tall Horse, him already got clothes on."

"How the hell you know that?" grunted Jud irritably.

"Me hear," shrugged Junior.

Jud cocked his head and listened hard. All he heard was the rustle of the dawnwind stirring the loose shingles on the roof above them.

"You're crazy," he told the Indian.

"No," denied his companion proudly, "me Apache," and of course that ended that, too.

They slid down the ladder without disturbing the

boy, Chulo, and went to the stock trough to freshen up. For one, Jud could use the cold water, and splashed it on generously. With an Apache's respect for such a scarce item, Junior stood well back so that none of the sinful waste should fall on him. *Wagh!* Water was for drinking. Only white men and muskrats used it for anything else.

Presently Jud was ready. There was a light in the kitchen by that time, and the sound of movement and the muted banging of pots and pans coming beckoningly from within. Jud's immediate thought was for Star but when he stooped to pass his six feet three inches under the low jamb of the rear door, he found only Maria and Cavanaugh there to greet him.

"Where's the girl?" he asked without any hesitation, or any attempt to disguise his direct interest.

Maria shot him a peering glance but Cavanaugh merely said, "Set down and dig in, we're late," as though he had not heard the mention of his daughter.

Jud did not question them again, obeying the order to sit down and eat. As soon as he had done so, Cavanaugh nodded and arched a furry eyebrow in his direction.

"Star's still asleep upstairs," he said accusingly. "I heard her sneak in pretty damned late. Guess she's plumb tuckered out."

Jud kept his head down.

"I guess so," he muttered, and went right on with his *enchiladas* and *frijoles refrescas*.

Ten minutes later he and Cavanaugh were standing

66

in the lamplight from the kitchen door and Junior was leading their horses up out of the corral darkness and saying, "Rain crow him talking down by spring. Going be hell of big rain I think. We go quick maybe. Get back across river before him rise."

Cavanaugh took the reins to his old white.

"I'd like to talk to that crow down by the spring," he said. "I'll bet he knows more than whether it's going to rain or not."

Jud flushed but said nothing. Quickly, he mounted up.

The three horses lined out, the white first, then the little chestnut, lastly the Navajo black.

Cavanaugh did not make any scene of saying good-bye to Maria other than to call back a grinning *"Adios, anciana,"* as he led the way around the corner of the house. Junior, whose good friend Chulo had just trotted up from the barn in time to miss his father, waved to the lad and bid him a cheerful *"Hasta luego, muchacho,"* before following Jud off into the thinning dawn.

Jud rode along for a moment feeling the tug of leaving the place pull at his heartstrings. Then he knew it was not the tug of the place at all, but something entirely different that was holding him back from departing without a farewell. As quickly as he admitted that, he turned around in his saddle, proud and tall about it as though it were broad day with everybody watching him do it, and stood in his stirrups and touched his wide hatbrim and called up

67

to the sleeping-loft window above the ranchhouse kitchen just loud enough for him and the passing wind to hear.

"Adios, Estrellita—!"

PART TWO
THE RED
BROTHER

5

Jud was riding with Cavanaugh. Junior was still trailing them, another of his endless repertoire of Apache songs desecrating the sunrise stillness. They had been in the saddle about two hours. The Medina and the Salado lay behind, the Cavanaugh homeplace rested, rose-flushed with the growing eastern light, twenty-six miles to the south and east. Ahead stretched the twin ruts of the San Antonio & San Diego Mail-line's old road, leading due away from the rising sun and toward the Fort Lancaster crossing.

They came in off the open prairie, put their horses onto the tracks of the stage road, pointing them west and giving them their heads.

The scout was officially on.

Its leader settled himself in his stirrups, shifted his breakfast chaw, spat to windward, checked his mount which was stepping out too fast, tilted his white beard Jud's way and said, "Well, what do you think of Mexicans now?"

It was the first sound he had uttered since leaving Maria and the ranch, and it took Jud a minute to get over the start it gave him.

"Nothing different than I did before," he answered

presently. "They're grand folks and your family's one any man would be proud to call his own. I know I sure would."

"Would you, boy?" said the old man, watching him closely.

"I sure would," repeated Jud. "How come you to ask like that?"

His companion shifted the point of his beard back to where it was aimed at the space between his horse's ears, thought over the youngster's question at considerable length. Finally, he nodded and began to talk.

He discoursed on love and life and growing old and how he came to meet up with Maria and get her into a family way and settled down with a brood of breed kids, and on and on with such personal things until Jud was embarrassed into saying, "Whoa up, oldtimer. Why all the lecture my way? I haven't asked you for the story of your past mistakes."

The old man looked at him and said bluntly, "I seen the whip cut on your face."

"Well, what of it?" snapped Jud. "It isn't smarting you any, is it?"

"Memories, boy, memories—" was all Cavanaugh said, forcing Jud to keep after him.

"What the hell you meaning to say? Quit mumbling into your chin stubble, will you. You sound like dry-spell steer gumming a mouthful of prickly-pear pulp. I'm not meaning to be flip with you, now, Mr. Cavanaugh, but, by God, I just can't get clear what it is you're trying to put across."

He was for a fact being flip with the old man, whether he meant to be or not. His nerves were raggy from no sleep and his temper was showing through from knowing, despite what he said, exactly what Elkanah Cavanaugh was talking about. He was talking about the girl.

And what he was trying to do was to say as much without actually naming names and thus making Jud feel any more awkward than he needed to.

But the boy's flare-up forced him to lay his hand down, rough side up.

"Well," he said, "I just hope you wasn't nice to her or didn't let her think you looked on her as a decent woman or the equal of a white man, for if you did you had better look behind you for she will be there following you to hell."

Jud laughed, a little too quick and loud, and said, "Precious small chance of that!" and they quit talking and rode on at a shade sharper pace.

The old man was way off the track, Jud told himself. He'd never see that girl again, unless he went back to Atascosa County to do it. Which he might, one day, when the War was over and the Yankees whipped. Just maybe he might, that was. It surely was no certain thing that he would.

Meanwhile Old Comanche was still squirrely as a peach orchard boar, and there was not one real chance in a million that his wild-hearted daughter would do any such crazy thing as to follow along after a homely no-rank assistant scout of Texas volunteers like Jud Reeves.

71

But "Old Comanche" was neither off the track nor out of his mind.

Thirty miles back, at the Atascosa homeplace, Star Cavanaugh was lying awake.

The loftroom was still cool and pink with the day's earliness, her little brothers and sisters yet dreaming peacefully away, when the restless girl arose silently from her pallet and crossed over and went down the loft ladder to the deserted kitchen below.

She listened for, and heard, her mother's deep breathing in the alcove bedroom, and that was good.

Maria, worn out with Cavanaugh's homecoming, had gone back to bed.

The way was clear, her course already chosen.

Quickly, the girl dressed herself in some of Chulo's old clothes, took a bag of tortilla flour and one of coffee beans. These she put into a larger wheat-flour sack, together with a frying pan and an old fruit tin and a half dozen cold *enchiladas* rolled up in a month-old San Antonio newspaper.

With that, and with the family plow mule sneaked out of his stall in the barn and hand-led around to the front of the house, she was ready.

She swung up on the bony brute's back, dug her bare heels into his scarred flanks, turned him out and away from her father's house.

Behind her, on the kitchen table, was a note to her mother saying she was gone for the day to see her father and the *Tejano* troops off from their big camp on the banks of the Rio Salado. But she was not gone

72

for the day, or to watch her father start westward.

She was gone for good and to follow Jud Reeves *"forever and as far as the road might wind or the trail bend,"* exactly as she had promised him in the moonlight of the pasture spring the night before.

The beginning lessons in military scout work proved nowhere near so difficult as they did monotonous.

It was all a deadly dull matter of memorizing the locations of every brackish waterhole and minuscule cluster of mud huts in West Texas, together with their names and the exact number of miles between them.

For example: the primary route march distances from San Antonio to El Paso were 100 miles due west to Fort Clark, 120 north by east up the Pecos River to Fort Lancaster, 120 by a north-circling westward bend to Fort Davis, 160 up the Rio Grande by way of Fort Quitman to Fort Bliss.

And again: the key place names reading west from San Antonio were Castroville, Delanis, Sabinal (Salt Springs), Uvalde, Fort Clark, Fort Hudson, Pecan Springs, Howard's Springs, Fort Lancaster, Escondido Springs, Fort Stockton (at Comanche Springs), Leon Hole, Hackberry Hole, Barilla Springs, Limpia, Fort Davis, Barrel Spring, Dead Man's Hole, Van Horn's Wells, Eagle Spring, Fort Quitman, Birchville, San Elizario, Socorro, Ysleta, El Paso and Fort Bliss.

Thus it went and thus it continued to go.

Over and over and over again Cavanaugh drilled the

distances and their place names into Jud Reeves' perspiring memory. The weather was fiercely hot for early June but the old man was as merciless as the copper sun overhead.

It was just as important, he said, for a scout to understand the locations of grass and water and fortifications as it was for him to learn to read animal and Indian sign, translate signal smoke, speak Kiowa-Comanche, savvy some Apache, and to ride, shoot, tell direction by sun and stars, recognize mirages or to judge true distances down to half a mile with the naked eye.

He hammered this contention home to Jud until he had it running out of his sunburned ears, and by the time they reached Sabinal the second morning out, the latter could have drawn a scale map, accurate to one-hundred yards, of every mile of ground between the Alamo in San Antonio and Jim Magoffin's general store in El Paso.

This labor was, in fact, precisely what the senior scout had his protégé engaged upon while he stirred the morning-halt coffee and Junior watered the horses at the spring.

Jud's map was done with a charcoaled stick in the springbank sand, the waterholes marked with circles, the trading posts or settlements with squares, the military establishments with crosses. It was the fifth one he had attempted—one for every coffee-brewing or horse-watering halt since the start—and the first one upon which he had gotten every circle, square and cross where it should be in relation to every other circle, square and cross in the five hundred miles over which they must guarantee the safe passage of Baylor's troops.

Peering critically at the frowning boy's masterpiece, the old frontiersman bobbed his white beard and drawled, "Well, anyways, by God, you will be able to find your way home happen you get lost," and by that Jud knew he had graduated from the first grade and might yet make a scout providing some Comanche didn't scalp him before Cavanaugh finished his schooling.

He said, "Well, thank you, Mr. Cavanaugh. I reckon it is about time I had it straight, don't you?"

Despite the fact he backed it with his best and biggest grin, the old man scowled and answered testily. "Yes, by God, and I reckon it's about time you got something else straight too."

He bobbed his beard again, spat acridly downwind.

"We're far enough away from Baylor and his soldier boys, now, for you to drop off that 'mister' any time you're a mind to do so. Like, for instance, right now."

"What you want to be called?" asked Jud, surprised.

"Cavanaugh, what the hell else? That's my name, ain't it?"

"It sure is if you say so." Jud paused, eying him a moment. "I got a name, too, you know," he advised him.

"Do tell," said the old man. "What is it, boy?"

"It's not 'boy,'" nodded the other.

Cavanaugh cocked his head and squinted his left

75

eye, in a habit he had when he was looking someone over while he got his answer together.

Finally, he nodded and spat into the fire. He reached out his big-boned hand and said with a rare warm smile, "All right, Jud, it's a deal," and so it was. From that day they were Cavanaugh and Jud to one another. Their callused palms came together there over the ashes of their coffee fire at Salt Springs, and that was all the contract they ever signed.

"We'd better catch-up and get along," said the old scout, standing up of a sudden and kicking out his leg as though to get a kink out of the calf muscle. "We can't squat here all day. Baylor'll be along before we get his next water spotted."

"What's the rush?" said Jud. "I thought you said we were going to lay up here and rest a day. Didn't you say Baylor could get here by himself and that the real work for us started from here on?"

"It's what I said," nodded Cavanaugh, "but my shankbones just give me a twinge."

"Him bones right," announced Junior, kicking dust on the ashes and looking around in a quick, wide-swinging way that brought Jud up off his hams without further argument.

"*Indians?*" he asked, in a voice much too small to go with his hard-muscled height.

"*Wagh!*" growled Junior. "Him damn Kwahadi!"

"The Comanches!" said Jud excitedly.

"As ever was," agreed Elkanah Cavanaugh laconically. "Let's ride."

Twenty seconds later, save for the wisp of blue smoke curling up through the dirt Junior had kicked on the fire, Salt Springs was as deserted and still of movement as the outer desert.

Twenty minutes later the red company arrived.

There were twelve of them, an advance patrol of a family band of fifteen lodges.

Their chief sat his potbellied bay paint on a rise of ground forty yards north of the abandoned coffee fire. Behind him, his braves crowded their ponies forward, flanking him right and left. None of them were looking at the white man's fire. All of them were staring off to the east, where more interesting sign by far was being put up.

"What do you think it is, Coyote?" asked the chief of the lean brave to his right. "It puts up dust like a mule, I think."

"That's right," answered the brave in thick-tongued Kwahadi. "It's a mule. A very big one and a very small rider. Either a boy or a girl."

"Well, which?" demanded the chief.

"I can't see," said Coyote petulantly. "Who else could even tell you it was a small rider from such a distance?"

It was true. None of them had eyes like Coyote.

"All right," said the chief, "then tell me this. Is it a good mule? One worth waiting for?"

"No, it's a skinny mule. Nothing but bones and harness blisters. I can see something else though, now. There were some sun wrinkles running in the air a moment ago, and they are gone now,"

77

explained Coyote. "I can tell you about the rider."

"Well, do it!" snapped his leader. "If it's not worthwhile, we may just as well trail those other three who left here as we came up. They may have a good gun or a fair horse among them."

"It's worthwhile," said Coyote, breaking off his slit-eyed peering to let his lips lift briefly above his filed canine teeth. "It's a girl."

6

THEY MADE their ride-up on Fort Clark late in the afternoon of the third day. There had been no pursuit from Sabinal and Cavanaugh was worried.

The post at Clark had been abandoned by the Union troops long enough for the lizards and the local Indians to move in and take over its rough buildings and small stockade. In the present case the human users proved to be not true redmen but a band of Comancheros, friendly half Mexican, half Comanche nomads who market-hunted buffalo as a way of life or, as Cavanaugh grumped it to Jud, "to avoid getting an honest job and going to work."

Also in the present case Junior proved to be an old and trusted *compañero* of Gomez, the breed band's leader and within ten minutes the two white scouts were squatting with their darkskinned hosts about a buffalo-chip and mesquite fire waiting for the fresh humpribs to broil and the *garbanza*-bean coffee to come to a drinking simmer.

Gomez, a walking barrel of a man with bowed toothpicks for legs and an inside as sunny as his exterior was ugly, asked for and was given the latest news from San Antonio.

He was glad to learn of Baylor's approach, as it would scare off the buffalo, he said, and thanked his white guests for the timely warning which would permit him to move his operations to the north before the soldier column got well into the country.

For his part, he went on to apologize, he had little to offer of news that was fresh or interesting. There was, of course, that Comanche lie being passed along about some yellow-haired breed girl at Salt Springs. But then, naturally, having come that way only the day previous, his good friends would know as much about that as did he, and perhaps more. Had they heard that story? Had they seen any Comanches at Sabinal? *Por supuesto, no. Quita!* The bragging red rascals! Gomez hadn't believed them for a minute. For himself and finally he would say that among the Comanches liars were quite plentiful, always, whereas blond halfbreed girls were very scarce indeed. Especially beautiful long-legged young ones with their hair falling down their backs to their buttocks, such as the Kwahadis claimed this one's did.

Jud and Cavanaugh just sat there.

They were so stunned that for a long breath they could neither answer Gomez, nor say a word to one another.

Then the old scout began barking at the halfbreed

chief in straight Comanche. Gomez gave him back his answers in the same harsh tongue. They talked too fast for Jud to catch it all, but there could be no doubt of what had happened.

The Kwahadis were not lying.

Star Cavanaugh had set out to trail her father and him westward and, at Sabinal, had ridden squarely into the same Comanche band from which he and the old man and Junior had barely escaped the day before.

Their coffee fire at Salt Springs had set a deadly trap for Cavanaugh's daughter.

Jud knew a thing or three about the Comanches. They had a long bad record for carrying off female captives. They made work-slaves, and far worse, of them and did not waste them like some of the other plains tribes, by burning their feet or pulling off their fingernails and suchlike ordinary refinements of red treatment. They had no hesitation to marry or take to mate any white, or half-white woman who met their fancy. The less fortunate who did not come up to this standard of comeliness were used as pack animals and camp drudges, the servants and whipping-girls of every old squaw or toothless harridan of a mother-in-law who might demand a helping hand, or carry an implacable grudge against the whole white race. The Comanches were, moreover, inveterate traders. They took captives with the idea, the sole idea, of selling them as slaves, and more than one poor girl from the Texas settlements had gone through their crafty hands to end up far down in Old Sonora as the concubine of some Mexican *jefe de bandidos,* or way out in Arizona cleaning up the wickiup of a Mimbreño or Mescalero Apache chief who fancied a pale-skin adorning his rancheria.

But instead of springing at once to horse, as Jud would have imagined he would, Cavanaugh only thanked Gomez for his information and went off to go sit outside the stockade and watch the sun go down.

Jud found him perched on a point of high ground half a mile from the post, chucking pebbles into a dry-wash which ran below his vantage. The action and its attendant attitude of distraction were the same as he had noted on the occasion of following him out of the Salado camp to fetch him up to Baylor's tent, and so he knew that the old man was thinking, not just sitting. He squatted down by him, stood the silence and the interrupting plink and bounce of the pebbles as long as he could, finally said, "Well, what the hell you going to do? Set there all night pegging rocks? Seems to me we'd ought to saddle up and get going."

"Seems to me," said the old man, "you'd ought to shut up and start thinking."

"What you mean?"

"Where you meaning to get going?" asked Cavanaugh.

"After those murdering Kwahadis, where else?"

"Suppose you got unlucky and caught up with them? Then what?"

"Well—" Jud started off, jawthrust, then just sat there. Pretty quick, he nodded and finished off lamely, "I'll be damned if I know. What would we do?"

"We wouldn't do anything," the old man nodded back, "because we'd never put ourselves into the position of needing to." He eyed Jud a minute, concluded quietly, "The first thing you got to learn about Indians is that you never pull out your pistol unless you mean to put a bullet into them."

"Yeah, guess I'd ought to know that," admitted Jud. And "Yeah, I guess you'd ought," the old man agreed with him.

"Now then, Jud," he went on, after a spell, "here is what we *are* going to do."

Baylor had given them orders to wait up for the column at Fort Clark. In view of that fact, the old man explained, they would wait. Orders were orders. When Baylor came up, the plan called for Cavanaugh to go ahead from Clark on long-range scout, with Jud riding day-by-day point for the troops, as a sort of link between them and Cavanaugh. This arrangement would obtain as far as Fort Stockton and, if it worked well that far, would be used the rest of the way across. Meanwhile they would sit right where they were until Captain Baylor came up, and no arguments out of Jud while they were sitting.

"Don't you mean to go after the girl at all?" asked the latter, unable to contain his indignation.

"I never said that," denied Cavanaugh.

"Well, you said the same thing. You said you were

going to wait right here for Baylor. I don't call that going after the girl."

"You let me handle it," said the old man. "She's my girl." He was short with it, but Jud was too worked up to catch the hurt it showed to be seesawing inside him, and so he bowed his neck and blurted out, "The hell! She's mine, too!" and then sat there wondering why in the world he'd said a thing like that when he had absolutely no call to do so, and no real want to, either.

But the irritated light died out of old Cavanaugh's pale eyes, and in its place a warm and almost hopeful glow began to shine.

"What'd you say, boy?" he asked softly.

"Nothing!" defended the latter, too quickly. "Not a damned thing. You must be hearing noises that aren't there."

"Reckon I must," said his bearded companion. "And you know something, boy?"

"No," said Jud obstinately. "What?"

"They don't make halfways bad listening," nodded the old scout, and went back to his sunset staring and his pebble chucking.

"Don't get any funny ideas about Star and me," Jud said sullenly, failing to find what he really wanted to say. "I didn't touch her, you hear?"

"Didn't say you did, boy. But you must have *said* something to her."

"What you getting at?" scowled Jud.

Cavanaugh looked at him and shrugged.

"She didn't get caught following *me,* boy."

"Damn it, you trying to blame me for her getting grabbed by the Comanches?" exploded Jud unbelievingly.

"Hell no," snapped the old man. "And shut up for Christ's sake. I'm trying to think."

"About time, by God!" sulked Jud, and got up and stalked away stiff-backed as a young dog scratching dirt.

The old fool was either crazy, as he had thought from the first, or he had lost his nerve and just didn't dare go out on the chase after those Comanches without waiting for Baylor to come up and furnish him a soldier escort for the job.

Well, either way it was not any of Jud's grief. Orders were orders as far as he was concerned. And Baylor's orders were for them to stay at Fort Clark until he got there.

At this righteous point in his thinking, the indignant boy took a slight chill of uneasiness.

Wasn't that what the old man had just said? Orders were orders?

Was he, Jud, using the same excuse? And using it for the identical reason—to keep from going out alone after the Indians?

No, that just could not be so.

He did have a proper regard for orders.

He was a Reeves, not a ragged-tail Texas recruit or an illiterate old dinosaur of a Sam Houston Ranger like Elkanah Cavanaugh. He did not take only the orders he wanted, leaving the others for someone else. No sir, not Jud Reeves.

He came to a halt, scowling.

What about the other night? Where was this huge respect of his for military authority when he had followed the old man across the Medina and down into Atascosa County, and the hell with Baylor's orders until Cavanaugh had said goodbye to his wife and Jud had sampled her *enchiladas* and her *arroz con pollo?* Not to mention the hungry and thirsting lips of her passionate daughter down by the pasture spring?

The thought of the inconsistency, together with the renewed memory of the girl's swift and startling emotions, upset him badly. He deepened his scowl, kicked at the dirt, started for the stockade again.

Damn it all! why wasn't Baylor here now? Every hour he and Cavanaugh had to sit here waiting for him was going to make it just that much harder for them to catch up to the murdering Comanche devils who had captured and carried off the old man's no-good daughter!

But Baylor's arrival brought no action.

The dashing adventurer was in very high temper and fine physical fettle. The march from the Salado had gone well, desertions had been very light along the route, the spirits of the men were right up on a level with those of their mettlesome commander.

After a consultation with his staff, the Captain of the 2nd Texas Mounted Rifles decided to drop off a garrison for Fort Clark, and continue immediately his march toward El Paso and the gateway to what Jud, standing restlessly in the background with Cavanaugh, was surprised to hear him call "Southwestern Empire!" And the exclamation point was Baylor's, not Jud's.

When the handsome officer made the reference to empire, Cavanaugh looked over at Jud and said out of the side of his mouth, "What did I tell you about watching this lad's ambition?"

Before Jud could even nod, Baylor looked over the heads of his officers and called, "I beg your pardon, Mr. Cavanaugh. I didn't catch what you said."

He must have cars like a kit fox, Jud decided. Or maybe the intuitive powers of a buffalo wolf. Either way, you would have to watch him.

"Me and the boy wants to see you soon as you're done, that's all," Cavanaugh called back without a bobble. "Guess I was mumbling a little too loud at the delay, Captain."

"Yes," said Baylor evenly, "I would say you were."

Despite the reprimand, however, Jud noticed that he was subsequently quick enough to accede to the old plainsman's "mumble," dismissing his staff and turning to his scouts almost at once.

"Well," he demanded of Cavanaugh, "what is it that you mean to try to blackmail me about this time?"

Jud could not decide whether he was good-humored and sarcastic or thin-tempered and caustic. So far he had a person fooled. One minute you felt he was a warm and human man driven only by fierce patriotism, the next, you were not so sure but what personal ambition and blind pride weren't doing more than their share of the shoving. He made Jud think a little bit of his father and grandfather. He was a grand figure of a man, and yet—

His analysis of Baylor was interrupted by Cavanaugh's answer, and he was glad enough that it was.

"It's family trouble again, Captain. I hate to bother you with it."

"Nonsense, man. If there's anything I can do, I'll do it."

Cavanaugh told him that indeed there was something he could do and that what it was would be to let Jud and the Lipan tracker take over the scouting for the column for a few days. This to allow him, Cavanaugh, to go out and get a trackline on a band of Comanche raiders who had reportedly captured a daughter of his back at Salt Springs.

"That," said Baylor abruptly, not even letting him finish, "is one thing I cannot do. You have a contract to scout for this regiment and I shall hold you to it. I do not trust the Indian, and the boy doesn't know enough. Was there anything else, now, Cavanaugh?"

Jud observed that when he was peeved, the C.O. didn't "mister" the old scout, and that when he was pleased, he did. He put the note mentally in his pocket for possible future use in his own case, and got back out of the way to watch the sparks fly when

Cavanaugh lit into his employer for the curt refusal.

Again the old man disappointed him.

He merely nodded, "Whatever you say, Captain," and turned around and walked off.

Jud started to follow him but Baylor waved his hand. "Hold up a moment, Reeves," he said. "How is everything going?"

"Fine, sir, just fine. I thought I knew a few things about this country and the Indians in it, but Mr. Cavanaugh is knocking that idea out of my head pretty quick."

"That's the spirit, sir!" enthused Baylor. "You'll make a soldier soon enough." He paused, a shade of annoyance tightening his tone.

"Speaking of that old hardnose," he nodded off in the direction taken by Cavanaugh, "I didn't get to tell him why I don't want him chasing off after those Indians."

"Yes sir," said Jud, and waited.

"I have every sympathy for his feelings about the girl, but higher stakes are involved here. We are most hopeful of winning over the Indians where the Union Government made enemies of them, and this particular Comanche band, I am informed, is desirous of coming in to talk peace and has asked for a meeting at Fort Davis. Their chief is a Kwahadi called Red Dog, a very influential man with the other tribes, I understand. My information is that he means to bring in all his white captives when he comes to Fort Davis, surrendering them as tokens of his desire to make peace with the new government. Now, surely, Cavanaugh can understand that there is no great concern over the safety of his daughter, while there is every need to be careful in every way we can not to alarm the Comanches or to frighten them away from that Fort Davis meeting."

"Yes sir," said Jud. "I should think Mr. Cavanaugh would understand that."

"Well," nodded Baylor, "it's your job to see that he does."

"Yes sir," said Jud, saluting smartly. "Anything else I should tell him, Captain?"

"Yes. Be sure and make it clear to him that I shall include safe deliverance of his daughter as an integral part of any agreement reached with Red Dog. Tell him he's to stay well out ahead of the column, with you for liaison in between. We'll start with daylight tomorrow, and I will not expect to see him again until we arrive at Fort Davis."

Jud gave him another salute and got away as quickly as he could.

There was still something about Baylor which made him ill at ease. He definitely did not enjoy being with him. He was one of those men who listened but did not hear. You got the feeling that your words got only as far as his ears, never into his head. He was a strange one, all right, but there was one thing about him that no boy of Jud's background and breeding could ever miss: whether you liked him or not, *John Robert Baylor was a leader of men.*

Determining to remember that, and to learn from it all he could of the art, he hurried off after Elkanah Cavanaugh to deliver the column commander's message.

7

EACH DAY from Fort Clark, Elkanah Cavanaugh ranged far out in advance of the Confederate column, looking for and never seeing trail sign of Red Dog's Kwahadi Comanche band.

Behind him, Jud Reeves rode closer point for the troops, maintaining contact with both Baylor and the old man by way of Junior, the omnipresent Lipan.

Progress of the column was routine, although the weather was beginning to turn very hot and desertions were increasing as the grass and water grew scarcer. Baylor's morale continued high. He either refused to see the holes in the daily muster rolls, or was rationalizing the desertions in some way not known to or shared by his worried staff. His lieutenants fretted and their sergeants fumed, but Captain J. R. Baylor rode confidently ahead.

Then, at sunset of the last day out of Fort Stockton, came good news.

Cavanaugh's Lipan Apache partner, riding with General Reeves' boy in advance of the column ("to hold the little man's hand so's he wouldn't get scared and wet his pants," according to Lieutenant Hugh

Preston) cut the pony tracks of Red Dog's band going west ahead of them toward Fort Davis.

His judgment vindicated by this show of good faith on the part of the Comanche chief, Baylor cheerfully granted Jud permission to go on to Stockton that night so that he might personally convey the discovery to Cavanaugh, who would be waiting at the fort for the troops to come up.

But when Jud reached Comanche Springs, whose clear cold waters were the reason for Fort Stockton's existence, he found that his news had run ahead of him.

Elkanah Cavanaugh already knew all about the Kwahadis going toward Fort Davis.

Gomez and his Comancheros had been at the springs when the old scout came into them yesterday afternoon. The halfbreed leader had caught him up on all the Comanche talk going along the prairie grapevine.

Red Dog was headed for Fort Davis, all right, and he still meant to make a peace talk when he got there. But he wouldn't be able to use that yellow-haired breed girl to show the new Pony Soldiers that his heart was good toward them. He wouldn't be able to do that because two suns past he had sold her to Sobre, the one-eyed New Mexican Mescalero Apache chief who had been warring on the western settlers since the day the old Pony Soldiers began to get out and go home to fight their own war.

Giving Jud this hard news, Cavanaugh's big hands went up in helplessness.

91

The Comanches were one thing, he said, the Apaches entirely another. They would neither of them ever see his girl Star again.

Or if they did, he added darkly, they would wish they never had.

Jud did not agree with him. He had heard of white people getting away from the Apaches. It was even on record that the army troops had taken a few captives from them unharmed. Why, he wanted to know of Cavanaugh, was it so impossible they couldn't hope to get Star away from them, or maybe talk them into giving her up?

The old man shook his head, hurting Jud with his sad, gray-faced look.

"It's this one-eyed son of a bitch, this Sobre," he said. "Gomez tells me he's never given up a prisoner and that he's particular hell on young white girls. Now, Star's near as light of skin and hair and eyes as most of your purebloods, boy, and I reckon she'll pass for white with Sobre."

Jud made an angry gesture with his big fist, balling it and drawing it back as though he could smash his way through a thousand Sobres just by the force of his hate for them. "Why, the dirty damned red devil!" he snarled. "The filthy, lecherous, murderous old Apache bastard! How can you stand there and throw in to him like that?" he demanded of Cavanaugh. "How can you set still a minute with the thought of some wrinkled old—"

"Jud," broke in Elkanah Cavanaugh, "he ain't old

92

and he ain't wrinkled. He's scarce twenty and he hates the white man worse than Mangas Coloradas does. And worse than the white man, he hates the white man's woman. Gomez says it's because some miserable, stupid Yank cavalryman shot down Sobre's Apache girl after the soldier had fooled around with her and she'd threatened she was going to tell her people what he'd done."

Cavanaugh paused, shifted his chaw, found it tasteless, didn't even have the spirit to spit.

"God damn these army bastards," he said deliberately. "A body sometimes wonders if he's fighting on the right side."

"Seems like a poor time," said Jud, "to be goddamning troops, Union or Confederate."

"They've stirred up more hell than they'll ever put down!" snapped the old man. "I tell you, boy, some of the things I've seen these uniformed sons of bitches get away with would break your heart. That's officers and men alike, by God!"

"You sound like Sobre," said Jud uneasily, not liking the wild look he saw growing in his friend's pale eyes, and thinking to jar him back to straight thinking by the comparison.

But the old man didn't blink.

"Maybe," he said softly, "I *am* like him."

He trailed off the strange admission, and Jud said impulsively, "My God, how can you take the Indian side against the soldiers'?"

"I don't," said Cavanaugh. "But when I say I'm *like*

Sobre, I don't mean I'll *do* like him, I mean I can think like him and understand what's going on in his head and heart."

"Such as what?" challenged Jud.

"Such as if I was an Apache I'd know what I'd do to any girl I caught of the breed that had raped and killed my own sweetheart of my own blood and color."

"Oh," said Jud, and let the silence grow, knowing now why the bearded scout looked so sad and hurt and grayfaced, and why he had said they would neither of them ever see Star Cavanaugh again. As soon as he could do so, he slipped quietly away and left the old man there to share his grief with the waning moon.

The next day and the arrival of the troops did nothing to improve the situation.

Baylor, alarmed over this new complication of his chief scout's daughter having been sold into certain death, or worse, by the Indians with whom he hoped to treat, refused to allow Cavanaugh out of his sight. His reasoning appeared to be that the girl was gone and that this fact, while regrettable, must not be allowed to interfere with the Fort Davis proceedings. The old man, left to his own discretion, was clearly of a mind to go out and start making treaties of his own with the Indians. This chance could not be risked and for the remainder of the long way to Fort Davis, via Wild Rose Pass and the Apache Mountains, Elkanah Cavanaugh and his apprentice rode within easy eye's and raised-voice's reach of the commander of the 2nd Texas Mounted Rifles.

But Baylor had been careless somewhere before putting his scouts under surveillance and after promising Cavanaugh to insist with Red Dog that Star's safe release be a condition of the peace talk. By what visiting friendly Indian or passing *Comanchero* or camp-sharing Mexican mule-train *arriero* the warning reached the Kwahadi chief would never be known. But the fact that it did reach him was certain.

When the troops threw down their bedrolls and turned their ponies loose outside the stockade at Fort Davis, there was not a Comanche within a long day's sight of the near mile-high mountain post.

There was only faithful Gomez, the *Comanchero* go-between.

And what he had to say was as brief as it was alarming. And lying.

Red Dog had heard that the new Pony Soldier chief was going to hold him to account for the safety of Tall Horse Cavanaugh's daughter. *Wagh!* Had he known who she was, he would have returned her with a glad heart and a proud hand. But the girl had said nothing to him of her identity ("trying to hold the ransom down, by God!" declared Cavanaugh) and he had been forced to surrender her to Sobre, the Mescalero, when the latter caught him, Red Dog, on the trail with only twelve braves and in a bad kind of country in which to start any arguments with New Mexico Apaches.

There was more, but it was only window dressing for the half-truths already told.

Baylor, outwardly calm, thanked Gomez and gave him an old silver bugle for his good part in reporting the matter. The latter, an intelligent man, was neither offended nor impressed with the gift. He knew the white officer regarded him as an ignorant savage, but he knew, as well, the social value of any such official presentation by a big soldier chief, and so he accepted the bugle with a proper show of appreciation.

When he had done so, Baylor wheeled away from him and would have forgotten him in the following five seconds had not Elkanah Cavanaugh stepped forward with a quick and quiet, "Hold on a minute, Captain. I've got a piece of an idea here." He turned and sang out to the departing halfbreed leader in the same breath, "Wait up, Gomez! Likely you ain't begun to earn that bugle, yet."

It developed swiftly that he was right.

Gomez agreed when he heard the size of the assignment.

Cavanaugh proposed that, having lost a minnow, Baylor go fishing for some real red trout. The specimen he had in mind was Sobre. Two things, he said, were in consideration. The Apaches, from the Rio Grande west and from El Paso north, were far more powerful and important than the Comanches. Sobre was, among the former, a much more influential and well-known chief than was Red Dog among the latter. It followed that if Baylor wanted to make a peace with

96

the redmen which might really bear upon the future of Confederate troops in their country, he had to begin and end with the Apaches. The first big tribe of them he would hit going west or north would be the Mescaleros. Get them quieted down and the rest of the bands, Mimbreños, Gilas, Tontos, Chiricahuas, the lot of them, might go along out of Indian curiosity.

Sobre, in any event, represented a rare chance to find out.

Why not send Gomez out to find him and tell him to come into the Fort Davis talks in Red Dog's place? The thing to do was to flatter the hell out of him, saying the new Pony Soldier chief had decided that Red Dog was not powerful enough to speak for his people, and that he had heard the great Sobre was in the vicinity and that, at once, all his desires had turned in the direction of talking with this famous Apache leader.

Jud stood by while Cavanaugh made this intense salestalk, and could not for the life of him understand the old man's change of heart.

Peace to the Apache?

To the very Mescalero who held his beloved "little girl"?

Offered by Elkanah Cavanaugh, the tough old "Tall Horse" of the Texas Comanches?

It did not make sense and he was sharp enough to see that Baylor's Chief of Scouts was running some other track than trying to help his commanding officer make a peace with the New Mexico Apaches. As he reached this conclusion, Cavanaugh wound up his suggestion with a deliberately underplayed shrug.

"Of course, Captain, it all depends on how far north or west you're aiming to go. If it's only to El Paso, we've no great need to worry about the Apaches."

Baylor grimaced and said, "Gomez, please be good enough to wait a few moments," then dismissed his staff with a wave of the hand and turned back to Cavanaugh, voice lowered.

"Now, sir," he nodded, "what the devil are you getting at?"

Jud, embarrassed, started to leave. Baylor waved him to stay. "You might as well hear this, Reeves," he said. "You'll be in on it."

"Now, sir," Cavanaugh smiled in smooth imitation of the officer's address, "you know pretty well what I'm getting at. If you've got any eyes for going past Fort Bliss and the Big Bend country, say like up Mesilla way, or maybe, happen the wind is from the right direction, on up to Santa Fe, why then you'd best make some kind of passport arrangement with at least the Mescaleros and Mimbreños."

"I see," said Baylor crisply. "And you're of the opinion that I *do* mean to push on up the Rio Grande?"

"Only as far as you can," answered Elkanah Cavanaugh steadily.

Baylor laughed, quick and a little harsh, Jud thought.

"Cavanaugh," he said, "educated guessing is a dangerous pastime on a military campaign. I'll not deny that you're quite sharp at the game, but I would like to ask you to keep your opinions to yourself. We've still a few miles to go and it's been a hard march. I don't want any trouble with the men. They've been told they're going to El Paso and I don't want any other ideas being put into their heads short of that destination. Is that clear, sir?"

"As mountain troutwater, Captain."

"All right. Now, sir, I think you have an excellent thought in regard to this Sobre. I mean to act upon it."

"Good," said Cavanaugh. "You want me to tell Gomez?"

"No, I'll tell him. Corporal Bodie—" He lifted a glove and his orderly came up on the trot. "Go bring that halfbreed up here." He was back to Cavanaugh and Jud without a break in stride. "Now, gentlemen, if you will excuse me, I have a great deal of staffwork to attend to. Preston! Royce! where the devil did you get to? Bodie, where's that halfbreed—?"

The old man said to Jud, "Come on, let's get shut of this," and slid around the command tent while Baylor's back was turned. Jud was a bit slow, and the officer caught him in the open.

"Reeves!" he called. "Tell Mr. Cavanaugh that we will bring Sobre into Fort Bliss, not Davis. I can't wait here all summer for the red rascal!"

"Yes sir," saluted Jud, and fell over a tent stake in his hurry to disappear before other ideas and orders might occur to the aroused officer.

He found Cavanaugh waiting for him at their cookfire. He told him about the change of location for the peacetalk, expecting it would upset him.

"That's fine," said the old man, and Jud noticed he was picking and chucking little clumps of buffalo grass into the fire as he talked. "I don't care where he comes into, just so long as he comes."

"What you mean?" asked Jud.

"Well," said Cavanaugh, "if he *arrives* at a certain place, sooner or later he's got to *leave* it. That's certain."

"So?" said Jud.

"So," answered the other, "when he comes into the meeting he'll find Baylor waiting for him, and when he goes out of it he'll run into somebody else that wants to see him powerful bad."

"You?" guessed Jud, low-voiced.

"As ever was," said the old man, and the look in his eyes when he said it put a chill up the ladder of Jud's backbone that he could feel clear up between his shoulder blades.

But things did not go right for old Elkanah Cavanaugh. His plan to ambush the Apache chief, Sobre, as he rode away from Fort Bliss after his conference with John Robert Baylor and the new "gray coat" Pony Soldiers, did not work out at all.

In the first place the crafty Mescalero would not come near Fort Bliss. His haughty refusal to come into the El Paso post reached Baylor at Fort Quitman on the Rio Grande, halfway between Davis and Bliss. Sobre and his subchiefs, the Apache sent word, were waiting to talk to the new Pony Soldier chief back at Fort Davis. Either the latter could come back there to smoke the pipe, or the pipe would not get smoked. Sobre was interested in peace, but it would have to be on his terms.

Baylor was nonplussed.

The Apache's word was not the only one which reached him from Davis. He had left a small garrison there, as he had at Clark, to guard and hold open his supply line from San Antonio. The green lieutenant in command of the Davis detail was getting the wind up. A rider had come through from him advising Baylor that there was no less than one hundred well-armed braves camped with Sobre just outside the Davis stockade and that he, the lieutenant, was very concerned over the extent of the coming and going in the Apache camp, and the plainly belligerent attitude of its members in seeking entry to the stockade and first-hand fraternization with their "new white brothers in the gray coats." The lieutenant did not like it and requested either relief from his unwelcome guests or reinforcements so that he might be better prepared to entertain them in case of necessity.

Baylor at once went into session with his staff, got nowhere at all, forthwith and wisely sent for his expert *sans portfolio* on Indian Affairs.

Cavanaugh chewed the matter over, gave it as his considered opinion that they had better be damned careful: Sobre was not bluffing, and yet they could not afford, either, to accede to his arrogant suggestion that they turn around and come back to pass the pipe in *his* wickiup.

The thing to do, the old scout decided, was to appeal to the Apache's pride. "They got more of that," he told Baylor, "than a four-year-old stud horse." Then, quickly, "Put it to him this way, Captain. Tell him it doesn't seem possible, but that it looks as though he was *afraid* to come to Fort Bliss. If that's the case, tell him, why then you'll be glad to come back and meet him at Fort Davis or any other place where he'll be more at ease. Get across the idea that you're surprised as hell that Sobre would show fear, but that you've got sympathy for the red brother's lack of courage running out your ears. You say it right, Captain, I'll guarantee you he'll kill his horse getting to Fort Bliss."

Baylor, like Jud, was beginning to learn that Elkanah Cavanaugh had not wasted his forty years of frontier schooling.

He sent Sobre the message.

The Apache chief received it and rode a staggering pony into El Paso only thirty-six hours after Baylor himself had reached the Big Bend settlement.

The peacetalk got under way at once.

Its atmosphere was good—Baylor treated Sobre with all the pomp and circumstance due a bona fide foreign potentate—and the results promised to be important and far reaching.

For Jud Reeves, the meeting and its haughty, dark-skinned principal subject formed a lasting memory.

The Topaz Creek boy had never seen any of the Arizona or New Mexico Apaches, the "wild" or "bronco" kind as opposed to the "saddlebroke" or "tame" Texas Lipans, and the prospect of meeting the fierce Ruidoso Mescalero in person stirred him mightily.

Sobre was a man to see once and never forget.

When he came into that low-beamed mud and brick barracks building at Fort Bliss, Texas, that July 2nd morning of 1861, you could have heard an eagle feather floating down through the hot and humid air, or the toenail scrapes of a frightened lizard scuttling across the rammed earth floor.

The tribute of silence was absolute.

Yonder was Baylor, back of a big oak desk trying in vain to look as massive and immovable as the piece of furniture behind which he waited. Flanking him in six canvas chairs, three to his right, three to his left, sat the members of his immediate staff, Second Lieutenants Hugh Preston and Darrel Royce uncomfortable among them.

Bulwarking Baylor's side of the room was a formal guard of forty troopers rigged out in the most complete Confederate uniforms to be had by a campwide levy among all the 350 privates of the line which had survived the three-week march from San Antonio, plus a representative gathering of the more hotly secessionist among El Paso's permanent citizens.

As for Sobre's side of the council chamber, it was singularly empty. *Sobre was, in fact, alone.* Stung by the calculated deceit of Cavanaugh's message, the Apache chief had come into Fort Bliss without his warriors. In doing so, he had come squarely to the old scout's bait, but the latter had not like the way he had done so.

When he saw him ride up by himself and heard Jud comment on his courage in coming without his braves, he had said tersely, "Yes, but that's not all he's come without, by God, and I don't cotton to it."

"What you talking about?" Jud had said, and the old man had answered, "The pipe, damn it! He ain't brought the pipe! The red bastard don't mean to talk straight and that's a fact."

"Well," Jud had felt forced to remind him, "neither do you, and that's a fact, too, ain't it?"

"It is," Cavanaugh had admitted through his teeth, and that had been the extent of that.

Now, however, with Sobre standing not ten feet from him surveying the assembled white citizens and their uniformed soldiers before continuing his proud approach to Baylor's desk, Jud did not feel the same sense of being sorry for the fearless Indian leader.

Quite to the contrary, he felt sorry for his nervous white confronters.

Sobre was six feet and one inch tall, a good head and shoulders above the average for his swarthy race.

He held himself with military erectness, yet walked with the ease and grace of a young mountain lion. He was dressed in the soft leather rider pants of his people, wore a scarlet head cloth knotted above his fierce, bobbed-off Apache bangs and black eye patch. Naked to the waist, he carried upon his person no arms nor ornaments of any description. In color he was exceedingly dark, in face and features bore a striking resemblance to Cochise, the fabled Chiricahua. He was, as Cavanaugh had promised, no more than twenty years old and yet when he glanced Jud's way in his sweeping view of the suddenly stilled gathering, the calm, deep piercing appraisal made the latter feel like a child by contrast.

But Jud did not mind.

It unsettled a person to be made to feel inferior in such a manner, of course. But the upset of that was more than matched by the *good* feeling this magnificent Indian gave you when you saw his grand pride, and also by the knowledge that you were seeing in him what you, yourself, one day hoped to become.

The Apache had what Jud remembered described in his father's military handbook as "the look of eagles."

He was, past all doubt and Jud knew it from the moment of that first fateful meeting of their glances there in Baylor's council chamber, a born warlord.

Jud did not yet understand enough Apache to make clear sense and so did not comprehend the details of Sobre's speech. He was, however, so overcome by his guttural voice and obviously straightforward manner that he knew the tall Mescalero was telling the whole truth and, moreover, was making out a very good case for himself and his people.

Nor was he the only one taken captive by the Apache's charm.

Baylor believed his story, whole skein, accepting

everything he said without serious question and waving aside all of Elkanah Cavanaugh's objections as they came along, which was frequently.

In the end the meeting broke up in complete accord or, as Cavanaugh growled to Jud as he went past him on his way out, "in a total massacree for the red son of a bitch!"

The grizzled scout's troubles were only beginning.

At the moment he could take what cheer he might from the fact that Sobre had been fool enough to come to Fort Bliss alone and that hence he would be leaving the post the same way, making the job of dry-gulching him all the simpler. But even that pleasure of antici-pated revenge was shortly denied him.

He was at the picketline with Jud, getting his can-tankerous old white gelding saddled and urging his young companion to do the same with his chestnut, when Corporal Bodie trotted up with the bad news.

"Captain Baylor wants to see you, Reeves. On the double."

"What's up?" said Jud.

"You're going on a little trip."

"Do tell?"

"Yep. All the way back to Fort Davis."

"The hell you say!"

"The hell I don't. Captain's sending that damned Indian back in style, and you're a'going to go along and see he gets there safe and sound. Ain't that one to peel your hair, Elk?" he finished up, grinning at Cavanaugh.

The old man did not like Corporal Bodie and he did not like being called "Elk." He made two long steps and one short grab, and Bodie was dangling in the air with his feet treading nothing.

"What did you say about that Indian?" he demanded angrily, setting Bodie back down with a jar that snapped his teeth together.

"Captain's sending him back to Davis in a stagecoach and Reeves has got the guard detail that's going with him."

"By God, you been chewing *peyote!*" snapped the old man. "This boy ain't got no business taking out a corporal's guard. He ain't even got his first stripe yet!"

"He has now," grinned Bodie. "And one more to go with it for good measure."

"Jesus, kid," husked the old man, suddenly seeing the trap Baylor had set for him, "you can't mean it." He stepped into Bodie, no longer threatening. "You dead certain you got it right?"

"I only know what I hear outside the tentflaps, Elk. And that's what I heard."

The old man turned away muttering and talking to himself and Bodie facetiously saluted Jud.

"Anytime you're ready we'd best be off to the Captain's tent, *Corporal Reeves,* sir!"

Jud looked at him and shook his curly blond head.

"If you're funning me, you're going to wind up getting a dislocated jaw out of it," he told the other youth.

"Not me," snickered Bodie nervously. "I never pick

on kids your size. Let's go, Reeves, I ain't the one that's sewing on your stripes. Tell it to the Captain."

Jud nodded and they started off. Cavanaugh called after them, and Jud held up.

"Boy," said the old scout, coming up to him, "what you aim to do, happen this is true?"

"If it is," answered Jud quietly, "I aim to do my duty."

"By me?" said Cavanaugh, "or by Baylor?"

"By my orders," said Jud, and swung away smartly behind Baylor's orderly.

Corporal J. B. Reeves rode alongside the jingling coach, his mind as busy as his ever watchful eyes. Fort Quitman was forty miles behind, Fort Davis yet a long day ahead. The rise and fall of the arid *llano* away from the old south-route stage road spread empty and still on all sides. There had been no trouble on the trip, and none had been expected.

Baylor had made a very sharp move sending Jud out in charge of Sobre's "honor guard." It was an important detail, a good chance to break in a promising recruit for whom rapid advancement in rank and command was a 2nd Texas certainty. Beyond that, it guaranteed against old "Comanche" Cavanaugh making any serious play to come at the Mescalero chief because of the Kwahadi claim that the latter was holding his daughter. The C.O. of the Mounted Rifles had assured his new corporal that full inquiry had been made of Sobre on the subject of Star Cavanaugh.

The Apache had labeled the story ridiculous, refusing even to discuss it. Baylor was satisfied he did not have the girl and the matter was dropped. Jud himself was of a mind to agree even if Cavanaugh had threatened to kill him for his "willful-blind stupidity."

The old man had gotten him aside before leaving Fort Bliss and told him for God's sake to watch himself and his Apache charge. The latter was dangerous as they came, he swore, and was certainly lying about not having the girl. "See what you can learn," he had instructed Jud, "and whatever you do, don't let the red scut out of your sight."

Since he could neither speak nor understand Apache, and Sobre either could not or would not speak English, he had had no luck carrying out the first part of the assignment. As for the second, Sobre was the very model of perfect behavior, making no effort to leave the vicinity of the coach at stops, nor to avoid the company of Jud or his six troopers at any time.

But the old scout's warnings were not entirely without weight.

Jud knew that.

For instance, he had admonished him to fight off any idea, such as Baylor was clearly getting, that the Indians would automatically be the friends of the Confederates because they had been the enemies of the Union forces. The Southerners, Cavanaugh had growled, had not yet learned the bloody fact that to an Apache a Pony Soldier was a Pony Soldier and a white skin a white skin, color of a man's uniform meaning not one damned thing.

Jud went with him on that, for he had known too many Comanches not to realize that you didn't make a wild Indian love a white man just by changing the cut and color of the latter's clothes.

But he did not go with him on his suspicions of Sobre in this case.

Cavanaugh had claimed that he had gotten to the Mescalero chief before he boarded the coach, and grilled him good about having the girl. Sobre had told him, *Wagh!* that now he had learned the girl was the daughter of Tall Horse Cavanaugh, he was sorry he did *not* have her. Tall Horse was *mucho hombre* and even Sobre would be proud to have a daughter of his in his rancheria!

This sidelong exchange had convinced the old man that Sobre was lying, and Jud that he was not. And so they had left it, Jud riding away from Fort Bliss with Cavanaugh staring a hole in his back and calling out bitterly, "If you *won't* believe me, boy, for God's sake *don't* believe that Indian—!"

Now, with four days to think it over, and not a word out of the Apache to help him do so, Jud was beginning to worry just a bit.

He had two of his six troopers out in front, the other four out on flank.

And still the miles and the silence crawled by without incident.

If the Apache meant to make trouble, this was his

last chance. Sundown would see them at Fort Davis and inside the safety of the post stockade.

But Sobre's word was good. The last mile was jingled under, the six-man squad safely brought into the stockade, and the Apache "guest" delivered to the gate of Fort Davis with the westering sun still an hour high and not a solitary Mescalero buck having been seen the livelong hundred and sixty miles of the way from Fort Bliss.

Corporal J. B. Reeves' first duty assignment was satisfactorily completed, his first command opportunity properly discharged.

He happily turned Sobre over to the Officer of the Day, and his chestnut gelding over to the first trooper who walked by with a stablebroom in his hand. He was very tired and very well pleased with himself. In that day and time and point in the history of the Confederacy in the far West, any command, well handled, could lead to a brevet for a brave noncom of good birth. Jud had done well in this first test, and he knew it. He did not expect to be made a brigadier general tomorrow morning, but this four-day escort duty was a start. It was his first *real* command, and he liked the feel of it far better than he had ever dreamed would be the case.

His last thought on rolling up his blanket in B Barracks an hour later was for his next chance in command: *when would it come? what would it lead to?*

He got the answers to both questions ten hours after he closed his eyes.

He and his squad were two hours out on the return ride to Fort Bliss the following morning when Private Arlie Kennedy, a sharp-eyed boy from the canebrakes of the Sabine, kneed his horse up alongside Jud's chestnut and said, "Hey, lookit yonder. What do you make of it?"

Yonder was due back along their trackline toward Fort Davis. And what Jud made of it was that somebody had fired the post.

The column of black and roiling smoke was already a hundred yards wide and twice that high. Even as they sat watching it, it billowed and ballooned to more than half again its present size and one of the young troopers said very quietly behind Jud, "My Gawd, boys, it must be the Injuns," and Jud grimaced and nodded back to him, "Well, I know one sure way to find out who it is—let's go."

They were back in sight of the post in but little over an hour. Surprised to hear no shooting, they rode on in to learn that a small band of Comanches had made a 4 A.M. rush on the post cattle pens and then, when Lieutenant May and eight men had gone out in the early dark after them, the main Comanche bunch had fallen on the whole post, firing everything in and around it that would fire and running off every head of beef and saddlestock belonging to the recently arrived Confederate troops at Fort Davis, Texas. The only horses left to Baylor's burned out garrison were the ones Lieutenant May's command had ridden out in pursuit of the first Comanche fein-ters. The only clue left behind by the red raiders was the black and towering column of smoke which had brought Jud and his little squad back to the stricken post.

To this last statement winding up the white-faced report of the dismounted troopers guarding the charred ruins Jud shook his head and shrugged, "Well, I wouldn't say it was the only clue but it will do for a starter. How come you are so sure the Indians were Comanches?" he added, asking it of the soldier who had been doing most of the talking.

"Lieutenant May, he's got a tame breed tracker he hired on after Captain Baylor left us off here. The breed he seen two, three of the first bunch before they got away from the cattle pens. He was the one said they was Comanches. Said you could tell it from their outfits."

"Yeah," broke in a second trooper, high-voiced, "and from the fact they attacked in the dark. He said the Comanches was the only ones that worked at night like that."

"Could be," Jud agreed, tight-lipped, "but I wish that breed tracker was here right now, all the same. Maybe he could tell us something else, happen he was."

"Huh?" said the first trooper.

Jud stood in his stirrups, shading his eyes into the climbing sun, eastward, toward the site of Sobre's big Mescalero camp on the high ground half a mile beyond the smoldering stockade.

He nodded once, eloquently, eased back down into the saddle.

"If all those Indians who hit you this morning were Comanches," he asked quietly, "what's become of our Apache friends, yonder?"

While the shocked troopers were still staring off at the deserted Mescalero camp, a nine-horse dustcloud moved out of an arroyo to the northeast and young Lieutenant May and his "Comanche" chasers rode up to report a loss of contact with the enemy in the field.

Jud promptly identified himself, gave May his theory of the Apache treachery, added that in his respectful opinion the Lieutenant was lucky he had not caught up with his Indian quarry.

The youthful officer was not interested in his military opinions, only in his claimed profession.

"Well, Corporal," May said abruptly, "if you're a scout this is your chance to prove it. My breed tracker disappeared an hour ago. Tell your men to fall in. Column twos. Be quick about it. The rascals already have a five-hour start."

Jud did his best to dissuade him, but it was not to be. May had been made to look bad and he was going to have somebody's blood for it.

He did.

At four o'clock that afternoon, with the sun a ball of smoky, sickening heat, and the fifteen men and horses of his little, command exhausted by eleven hours of continuous marching, Lieutenant May fell into a broad daylight ambush by five times his own number of New Mexico Apaches masquerading as Texas Comanches.

The result was as certain and no less brutal than as if his brave troopers had been steers and he the bell ox who led them up the slaughterhouse ramp to the killing hammer.

Inside of ten minutes the last of them was dead and Jud Reeves was sitting, a dazed and bloodyheaded captive, under the echoingly silent stare of seventy-five Apache riflebores.

PART THREE

A SERGEANT'S STRIPES

8

JUD KNEW he must stand up. He could not continue to sit there on the haunch of the dead chestnut gelding and let them shoot him like that.

He pushed with his hands against the still jerking muscles of the horse's sweated quarter. He got himself almost raised up, then his bracing hands slipped in the acrid lather covering the chestnut's twitching skin and he went down into the dust, caroming off the gelding's croup and landing heavily with his face buried in the bloodied dirt of the battleground. A dozen Apache rifles leaped at once to follow his fall, but the tall darkskinned young chief said two words and made a small motion with his left hand and his nervous tribesmen let their guns come back to their hips and sat once more waiting.

Jud did not know where he was hurt, nor how.

He only knew that a great roaring filled his ears and that a blinding pain coursed from the base of his skull to the small of his back. When he raised his head to look for his enemies, he could not find them. At first he thought it was impossible that they should all have vanished so quickly. Then he realized what had happened. The Apaches had not moved, but he was blind.

It came to him, then, that he was dying, and it somehow seemed more important than ever that he should not do so in this way. *He must stand up.*

With the strength gathered by the bulldog determination to be on his feet at the end, he surged, twisted, fought his way upward. This time he managed it. But by the time he had, the sound in his ears had increased to an enormous booming pulse and he was not only blind but he could not hear.

"We ought to shoot him," said Grito, Sobre's fierce-eyed first lieutenant. "He is helpless."

"That is why we cannot shoot him," answered Sobre. "Tie him across one of those horses and we will go."

He gestured toward the half dozen mustangs still unwounded and standing among Lieutenant May's fallen men, waiting for the riders who would never gather their reins again.

"All right," said Grito, "but we ought to shoot him. You'll see. There will be trouble because we didn't do it."

"There will be trouble enough because of what we have already done," suggested Chavez, an older member of Sobre's advisory group and a man whose word carried weight. "I don't care what you do with this tall young *guero,* but we've killed sixteen Pony Soldiers and we had better get out of here as Sobre said."

"All right," repeated Grito scowlingly. "But you will see. Chebo, Askanay—" he barked at two of his comrades "—put him on that big gray pony, the one the soldier chief was riding. Tie him on tenderly. Sobre is afraid he will fall off and hurt himself."

"Sobre is afraid of many things," admitted the young Mescalero chief quietly.

"Aye," added Chavez, the elder statesman. "Only fools are not."

"Are you calling me a fool?" challenged Grito, swinging angrily about.

"Have I ever hesitated to do so?" Chavez asked him evenly. "You *are* Grito, aren't you?"

"Bah!" snarled the younger warrior, and wheeled back to the work of getting Jud laced aboard Lieutenant May's rangy gray.

Jud opened his eyes to a vault of blackness illuminated by a million blazing white diamonds. It took him ten seconds to realize that he was alive and looking up at the midnight sky and myriad glittering stars of West Texas. Another half minute was consumed in remembering the details of his Apache capture and the brutal May massacre which had preceded it. Before the first full minute of returned consciousness had passed, he had added the facts that he was presently in the middle of an Indian nightcamp, that his head hurt with an impossible pounding wickedness, that it had been cleaned off of caked blood and carefully bandaged, and that he was being nursed by a sleepy Mescalero squaw who, heavily blanketed against the desert cold, was hunched a few feet away nodding in her unwanted vigil over the gringo prisoner.

He lay for a minute or two longer, thinking, as clearly as his throbbing head would let him of what he should do about speaking to his drowsing guard.

Judging from the reputation of Apache women—Cavanaugh had said they made the men look gentle as monks in a charity mission—an innocent question of this napping squaw might fetch him anything from a kick in the head to a riflebutt in the ribs. Yet, in the end, he could not resist the risk.

"Señora?" he queried her softly in Spanish. *"A thousand pardons, señora, but—"*

She was instantly at his side, her slim hand covering his mouth.

"Not Señora," she whispered in English. "Señorita!" Then, her throaty voice dropping lower still, "For God's sake, Jud," she ordered, "be quiet!"

Ahead, blurred and black in the starlight, lay Fort Quitman. The Apaches sent their ponies past it and on toward the river beyond it. They were not so many now, for a scout had come in with news that the old man whom the Comanches called Tall Horse and the white men called "Comanche," was heading south out of Fort Bliss with thirty Pony Soldiers. He was coming along the river toward Fort Quitman and he was looking for the Apaches who had attacked Fort Davis. He had found out which Apaches they were and he knew they had with them his yellow-haired daughter and also the *Tejano* boy Sobre had insisted on sparing back at the ambush these three days gone. Under such a set of circumstances no Mescalero in his right mind would waste any time getting across the Rio Grande and into Mexico.

Nevertheless, Sobre already had wasted precious time.

He had camped two whole days at an Apache watering place only forty miles from Fort Davis, and would still have been there had not the scout come in with the disturbing news that troops were on their way to intercept them before they reached the river. He had stayed at the hidden spring because the *Tejano* boy had started to vomit and get fainting spells from riding in the hot sun with his cracked head, and Sobre had said he would die quickly if they did not stop and let him revive himself. None of the one-eyed chief's followers had liked that idea. It was no time to lie up in the shade when you were only a four-hour lope from those sixteen bodies you had left bloating in the sun back there below Fort Davis. *Wagh!* Sobre was getting soft.

This latter possibility held fascinations not alone for the Apaches. Jud Reeves, too, was thinking of it.

Riding in front of Chebo and Askanay at the rear of the Mescalero column as Sobre led it silently toward the river crossing below Fort Quitman, he was reviewing his position with desperate urgency. He had the feeling that for him the stream ahead marked more than the boundary between Texas and Mexico. Once across it, his premonition warned him, the odds against his getting away from the Apaches would become insurmountable. That wasn't the Rio Grande ahead, he told himself grimly, it was the Rubicon.

The strange relationship with Sobre had begun at the moment of his regaining consciousness in the first nightcamp when Star Cavanaugh had put her hand over his mouth and begged him to be quiet.

The halfbreed girl had no more than gotten the warning out than the one-eyed Mescalero had loomed up out of the darkness and added to Jud in perfectly good English, "Yes, my brother, do as the girl says or I will kill you."

Perforce, he had kept quiet, but his obedience had cost him the chance to talk to Star.

The following day the long march back to the Mescalero homeland in New Mexico had begun, with Star being held by Sobre at the head of the column, Jud, under guard of Chebo and Askanay, at the rear. Thus there had been no further chance to talk to one another and whatever Star may have wanted to tell him about her capture and treatment, or whatever he could have gotten out of her about these things, had to remain unsaid.

That first afternoon was when the sun had gotten to him and then Sobre had called the rest halt at the Apache oasis forty miles west of Fort Davis.

Sick as he was, that halt had amazed Jud. It was more than the chief would have done for one of his own warriors. Why was he doing it for Jud Reeves? It did not make sense. Not Indian sense, anyway. Indians just didn't care that much about life and death. Not their own, nor anyone else's.

As he gained strength the second day of the halt, another question had arisen to plague him. Star was not being held the same way he was. She did not have her hands bound, nor was any noticeable guard assigned her. She didn't even act like a prisoner, laughing and talking with Sobre and Chavez as though they had all three been raised on the same rancheria. Not once did she more than glance Jud's way and by nightfall of that second day he had begun to wonder if she were a captive or a companion of the Apaches.

Then, an hour after dusk, had come that scout from the north.

His news, pieced out by Jud from the half Spanish, half Apache conversation of Chebo and Askanay, was as exciting to him as it was to the Mescaleros.

The scout had eaten that noon with Gomez's Comancheros. Gomez himself had not been there. He had gone into Fort Bliss the day before with a half-breed who said he had been a scout for the Pony Soldiers back at Fort Davis and who wanted to talk to the new soldier chief at Fort Bliss. What the halfbreed had wanted to tell the latter was that he had followed the lieutenant who had gotten killed and had seen which Indians it was who had killed him.

Gomez could not risk keeping such news from Baylor any more than he could tempt sudden death by informing on Sobre without warning the Apache chief that he had done so. So what he *had* done was to take the halfbreed to Fort Bliss, while leaving behind a message for the Mescaleros that he was doing so and that they had better get out of Texas at once. In fact, a messenger from Gomez had come into the Comanchero camp while Sobre's scout was still there, reporting the departure down the Rio Grande of Cavanaugh and the thirty troopers. There was one other member of that soldier party who made it more dangerous yet. It was that shriveled-up little Lipan devil who was not right in the head but who could track a weanling mouse across bare rock in a sandstorm.

Jud, already feeling much better, had perked up even more at his news of Junior being with the Fort Bliss patrol. If anyone could find and follow the Mescalero trail, it would be Cavanaugh's small red shadow. But the white boy had been given no time to enjoy his freshened spirits.

At once, Sobre had run in his grazing ponies and split his band into two sections, the smaller group of two dozen braves going with him, Grito taking the main band of fifty or so. Sobre had accepted the riskier Fort Quitman direction in order to determine the truth of his scout's report about Pony Soldiers coming down the river to look for him. Grito, not at all happy about it, had been ordered to swing far south, through Old Mexico, and to keep traveling until he got his braves back up north to the remote Tres Cerros hiding place in Sobre's "Three Hills" rancheria above Ruidoso in *Nueva Méjico*.

There was supposed to have been a second scout waiting at the crossing with immediate news of the approaching Pony Soldiers, when Sobre's band reached there at midnight. It was this knowledge which now tightened Jud's healing scalp as the Mescalero ponies slid down the low bank into the Rio's bottomlands and strung out on the lope, directly toward the starlit shallows of the ford ahead.

Sobre was on time. It could not have been more than minutes off of midnight, one side or the other. Question remaining: was the expected scout also running on Apache schedule?

Three minutes later the Indian mounts were drawn up in a soundless circle, flanking their leader, on the graveled sand of the east bank just clear of the heavy willow scrub which choked the approaches to the river. Between them and the water's edge the open sand of the streambed stood empty. Sobre's scout was not there.

They waited five, ten, fifteen minutes.

No scout appeared.

Chavez, who could do such things better than the imitated creatures themselves, barked once like a lonesome dog fox, scolded two or three times in the manner of a mallard hen disturbed at night nest, threw back his head and howled dolefully in such a precise matching of a buffalo wolf's howl that the small hairs at the nape of Jud's neck stood on end.

Between each signal there was a long, disciplined

wait so that no chance listener would wonder at such a sequence of sounds.

But there were no listeners, chance or deliberate.

Something had happened to Sobre's scout.

The Apaches closed up their circle, began to talk in their guttural, harsh-syllabled tongue. Chebo and Askanay, Jud's guards, moved their ponies a little forward to hear what was being said. All that had been going on in the Texas boy's mind came together as they did.

This was the time.

For himself he did not care. But the only chance Star Cavanaugh had of eventual rescue lay in his getting away. He had to escape, finding Cavanaugh quickly enough to put Junior on the Mescalero trail no later than daylight. The Apache ponies were worn down. If the troopers rode hard there was a possibility of bringing Sobre to bay by sunset of the coming day. There was no place for him to hide in that merciless Mexican desert ahead, and the Apaches could not turn back from it. The odds against all this working out were slim. The odds against Jud ever seeing Star again if they did not work out were nonexistent.

It was a bobtailed flush against no bet at all.

Jud set his teeth and laid down his hand.

Lieutenant May's tall gray grunted with pain and surprise as its rider's spurs went into its rough-haired ribs. In the same second and shattering the stillness at the ford with the piercing screech, Jud raised the Rebel yell at the top of his lungs. As the yell broke, he sent the gray bombarding through the exact middle of the Mescalero meeting and on across the shallow waters of the crossing toward the west bank.

The Apaches' nerves jumped as far in that first second as did the dead lieutenant's startled horse. By the time they had wheeled their ponies to take out after the fleeing gray in obedience to Sobre's belated shout to "Shoot him! This time put a bullet in him!" it was already too late. The white boy had won his desperate last-chance gamble. And he had won it in a way that was as much of a shock to him as it was to the pursuing Mescaleros.

Jud Reeves had raised the Southern war cry only as an instrument of diversion, to startle and to rattle the Apache raiders for the life-and-death instant he needed to get the jump and the start on them.

But the last echoes of his own yell were still bouncing around between the river's low banks when its shrill cry was picked up and flung back from the far side of the stream by no less than two dozen sympathetic Confederate voices, and riflefire began to bloom among the willows of the west bank like fireflies in a piney woods pasture lot.

Seconds later Jud was across the river safely into the bottom scrub, getting the wild-eyed gray caught and held by Baylor's dismounted troopers and receiving his hero's welcome from the bony giant of an old man who reached up and literally dragged him down off Lieutenant May's gelding.

"You miserable crazy son of a bitch!" snarled

Elkanah Cavanaugh. "Thirty seconds more and we'd have had the lot of them riding right into our goddam laps! But you! you yellow-bellied young bastard—!"

He stepped away from the white-faced boy, taking his hands off him and dropping his voice with the defeated sag of his bowed shoulders.

"Thirty seconds more and I'd of had my little girl back," he said brokenly. And then, even more bitterly soft, *"I've a mind to kill you, Jud Reeves."*

The Apaches, of course, disappeared into the east-bank darkness like raindrops into deep and thirsty dust. The troopers cut their fire after the first token volley, and not a man moved for his horse to pursue the vanished redmen. They were *Tejanos muy versados,* these ragged volunteers of the 2nd Texas Mounted Rifles, and knew all the percentages of chasing after shot-at Indians by starlight.

They might as well, said Cavanaugh dispiritedly, forget the whole thing and head back for Fort Bliss. Their only chance had been to ambush the Mescaleros and Jud had taken care of that with his brave dash to save his own hide.

The latter was mightily humbled by the whole turn of events but had certainly not been trying to save himself, and at once proceeded to set the old man straight on that score. It developed that Cavanaugh and the troopers had thought he had somehow spotted their ambush while the Indians held up to talk about their missing scout, and had made a reckless run to get inside their lines.

As soon as the angry boy swore that he'd had no more idea they were there waiting for the Apaches than Sobre and his bunch did, things took a more friendly turn. Cavanaugh, after cooling out a spell, could see that such a thing could be just the plain atrocious bad luck that the boy claimed it was, and began to let down and to question Jud closely about his capture, the strength of the Mescaleros, his daughter's condition and frame of mind, the destination of the Indian band and the like. He even went so far as to sandwich in a gruff apology for doubting his spunk (seeing he was a Reeves) and making a show of him in front of the men.

For his part Jud told his listeners only what he knew, saying nothing of what he suspected, this to spare the old man any hurt over the apparent possibility that his daughter had "gone" Apache.

This entire brief discussion took place in the presence of Second Lieutenants Hugh Preston and Darrel Royce, both young staffers sent along by Baylor for a little "seasoning in the field," and to keep a hard eye on old man Cavanaugh in case they caught up to the Indians rumored to have his daughter and young Jud Reeves captive.

Jud concluded his report by saying that for future reference they could all remember that Sobre spoke better English than most white men and that while he appeared absolutely implacable in his hatred for the gringo there was something about him that was different than the run-of-the-wolfpack Apache like Grito.

This difference, whatever it was, Jud averred, was responsible for his being alive. He had heard his Mescalero guards discussing his captivity and had learned that Sobre had ordered him taken alive *before* the May ambush. It was Sobre himself who had knocked him off his horse with a blow of his riflebutt that had nearly killed him, but he had understood his guards to say that he had done so only to keep Grito or one of the others from shooting him *accidentally* in the excitement of the fight. Later, when the dissidents had challenged the idea of leaving the white boy alive, Sobre was supposed to have answered them that "the young two-stripe soldier treated me like a chief when he could have laughed at me," and to have added, "His life belongs to Sobre, remember that."

Preston and Royce were not impressed with Jud's report.

Neither did they believe his story that his breakaway at the Fort Quitman crossing had been a heart-twisting coincidence.

Preston, in command, ordered the immediate return of the troop to Fort Bliss. Baylor's orders had been explicit: *Go down only so far as Quitman and if you cannot intercept the Fort Davis Indians by or at that point, do not go beyond it in pursuit of them, no matter the circumstance.*

Jud had sense enough not to make anything of Preston's unfriendly attitude and, in fact, could not honestly blame him a great deal for his opinion.

He felt quite lucky that Cavanaugh, Junior, and the

greater part of the men seemed to believe him and to be glad to see him back alive and with nothing worse than a cracked head to show for his three days with the Apache war party.

The march back up the river was made in two days, the troop coming into Bliss at sundown of July 12.

Baylor had them all in at once.

He heard Preston and Royce and Cavanaugh through, then asked for Jud's story.

The latter gave it to him without sparing himself for the fact he had been unable to keep Lieutenant May out of the Apache trap, that he had lost six of his own men in the same shambles, that his rash action at Quitman Crossing had ruined the return ambush set up so skillfully by Cavanaugh and the two lieutenants.

Jud had in truth nothing to be proud of in his dispatch of the assignment which had led to his corporal's stripes. He realized it, he admitted it, he fully expected to be broken back to private if not given more severe disciplinary treatment.

His astonishment, then, was certainly as great as that of any of the others present when Baylor, upon hearing him out, stood up and said quietly, "Well, I think under the circumstances that you have handled yourself quite properly and have in fact carried out your orders, in every way, to warrant and repay my confidence in you." He smiled happily, put out his hand.

"Congratulations, *Sergeant* Reeves," he said.

9

LIEUTENANT HUGH PRESTON, stalking out of Baylor's office with his friend Royce, was so angry he couldn't talk for ten steps. Then he clenched his jaw and said, *"Jesus!"* Royce, a youth of less temper, grinned an Amen and they walked another ten steps before Preston could go on.

"What did I tell you!" he snapped. "Sixty days and he'd have a commission? Well, here it is July 12 and I'm a liar by three weeks so far."

"Nothing to be ashamed of," shrugged his companion. "Give yourself another two weeks and you'll still win your bet. Sergeant in thirty-six days isn't bad. Wonder why Baylor kept him up there?"

They both glanced back at the C.O.'s office.

"Maybe he didn't have the guts to promote him again in front of us. Likely he's pinning his bars on him right now."

"Not quite," guessed Royce. "But something's up. You notice he even ran old man Cavanaugh out."

"I didn't notice anything except that he didn't pay a damned bit of attention to what we said about Reeves."

"What do you mean? Reeves was just as hard on himself as we were."

"Well, then, he didn't pay any attention to what *he* said, either."

"What's your point, Hugh?"

"My point is that it doesn't make any difference what Reeves does or says. He's going to get that commission regardless. Oh to be a general's son!"

"Oh, hell," said Darrel Royce. "Why not be fair about it? We weren't exactly commissioned for our outstanding ability either."

"Well," defended the other, "at least I had two years at the Point and you a year at V.M.I. We were being trained as officers anyway."

"Yes," countered his friend, "and why? Because our fathers wanted it that way, had the money to pay for it, and because military service was a tradition in both families. We're no different from Reeves, Hugh. Just a year or two ahead of him, that's all."

"I'm not going to argue with you about it," said Hugh Preston, with the lofty tolerance of the already beaten. "If you haven't got sense enough to see the difference, I can't help you."

"Forget it," shrugged the other. "I'm not in love with this job as you are. You and Reeves fight it out. Personally, I think I'll go over the hill the first dark night."

"Don't talk like a damned fool!" warned Preston.

"I mean it," said his companion. "We were told we were coming out here to occupy the abandoned Union posts. It sounded like a nice clean excuse to sit the war out in safety. Now that Baylor's got us here the truth comes out."

"Shut up, Darry. Those orders were secret."

"Sure they were. If they got out, half the hairy-eared Texicans in this outfit would saddle up their damned cowponies and skeedaddle. Hell, you know that."

"I won't discuss it," said the other tight-lipped. "And you'd better not either."

Royce stopped walking and looked at him.

"Listen, Hugh," he said, "I'm not forgetting we were brought up together. You're the best friend I ever had. But we don't see eye to eye on this war business and I doubt we ever will. I wasn't happy in military school and I'm not happy here now that I know there's going to be a fight. There are men cut out to be soldiers and men cut out to be cowards. You're one, I'm the other. I haven't got guts enough to touch a horned toad. What's more I never did have and you know it. So let's not play soldier with one another, Hugh, please."

"You're tired," said his companion. "That was a hell of a ride."

"You're right it was a hell of a ride," agreed Royce disgustedly. "Goodnight."

Baylor had some orders to sign and other papers to initial directly after he had asked Jud to stay. It was perhaps half an hour before he got back to him. Jud had used the dragging minutes to think, and the net result of his thoughts was that his new rating had a very bad odor to it somewhere.

He couldn't quite smell out just where, but he was satisfied the situation merited the scowls of Lieutenant

Preston, the shrugs of Lieutenant Royce, the shaggy eyebrow-raisings of Elkanah Cavanaugh.

The least thing he could figure out was that Baylor was promoting him simply because he was General Judah Beaumont Reeves' son. The worst was that, through rewarding him, the ambitious officer was trying to cover up his own grievous blunder in being so completely taken in by Sobre. And the case for the latter charge looked very strong.

Cavanaugh had argued strenuously for an immediate big push to go after the Fort Davis murderers and wipe them out as a warning to all tribes that the Confederates were not going to tolerate the same sort of Indian nonsense the Union Government had. But Baylor had refused flatly. He had not qualified the refusal, either, making it all the more suspicious to Jud. It simply looked as though he would pay any price to stay out of a war with the Indians, nor was Cavanaugh able to persuade him that a punitive force sent after Sobre was the very best way to guarantee staying out of such a war.

Now, Corporal Bodie was lighting the coal-oil office lamps and Baylor was at last turning back to Jud, his smile as bright as ever.

Before he could say whatever it was he had in mind using for a starter, his new sergeant saluted him and asked, "Beg pardon, Captain, but could I say something, sir?"

"Certainly, certainly. Go right ahead, Jud. That's why we're here, to get things said."

"Well, sir," replied the latter bluntly, "I don't want these stripes. I haven't done anything to earn them, and I don't deserve them."

Baylor lost his smile.

"How is that, sir?" he asked quietly.

Jud gulped, started to back down, decided, instead, to go all the way.

"Well, sir, I said I wanted to earn all my advances, and I truly meant it."

"Well, sir," said Baylor, even more quietly, "you will earn this one, I promise you."

"Beg pardon, Captain?"

"I'm giving you this promotion beforehand, just in case you don't get back from the assignment that will earn it for you."

"How's that?" said Jud again, forgetting the "sir" this time.

"You told me you knew all this country out here as you knew your own backyard. In fact I recall you claimed to have ridden over every foot of it, one time or another. Is that right?"

"Yes sir."

"Would you ever have gotten as far as Mesilla on any of those rides?"

"Not quite. I was at Fort Fillmore once."

"Well, that's only four or five miles from the town."

"Six, if I remember rightly, sir."

Baylor glanced down quickly at a field map spread on his desk. He nodded, getting a little of his smile back. "Six, it is," he said. "That's pretty good remembering, Jud."

"Yes sir. What was it you wanted to know about Mesilla, sir?"

Baylor lost the smile again, not liking to be brought back to business by a thirty-minute-old sergeant. *"Everything!"* he snapped. "The men from Fillmore go up there to do their drinking. That's officers and enlistments alike. I want you to take ten men and go to Mesilla and bring me back all the information you can about the fortifications at Fillmore. I want to know the quality of the troops stationed there, the identity of their outfits, the morale of the garrison as a whole, everything about that post. Do you understand me, sir?"

"*Ten* men?" asked Jud, shaking his head. "I heard Major Lynde has got seven hundred up there. Isn't ten kind of scant for going up against seven hundred, sir?"

"Don't worry, Sergeant. You're not going as soldiers."

"Not soldiers?" said Jud uncertainly.

"No sir—spies," said Baylor.

"That means we get shot if we get caught."

"It does."

Jud was not going to let him see that he was scared. At the same time he *was* going to let him know what he thought of such an assignment for a youth who had seen only thirty-six days service.

"That's just great, sir," he said level-voiced. "Anything you'd care to add to your instructions?"

"Yes," said Baylor. "Don't get caught."

• • •

It was 10 P.M., July 13th, 1861.

Jud had his patrol halted six miles out of El Paso, with forty miles yet to go, due north up the Rio Grande, to Mesilla. He had just come out of the pass over the Franklin Mountains through which the big stream flowed at this point; and was now back on the river-level grade of the Butterfield mail road. The route had been through rough and broken foothills and down a tremendously steep and tortuous arroyo, tiring the horses badly.

Ahead in the darkness, now, lay the tiny way station of Frontera, where the old crossing to Mexico went over the Rio Grande. The place was utterly dark. Jud wanted to stop and find out what he could of the situation at Mesilla, but did not dare. The old mossybacks out in this Big Bend country ought to be Southern sympathizers, but you could never tell.

"We'll go along directly, boys," he told his waiting troopers. "Get down and give your horses a blow. Smoke if you like."

"Well, thanks," said one burly soldier. "It surely does help to have a kind and considerate commander. Ain't we lucky, boys?"

Jud got down off his gray and walked over to the man. "What's your name?" he said.

"Lipscomb. Buddy Jack Lipscomb. They call me Big Boy," leered the huge trooper. "What do you think of that?"

"Well, Buddy Jack," nodded Jud quietly, "*I* call you Big Mouth. What do *you* think of that?"

The big man growled like a kicked dog.

He had been grumbling ever since the patrol set out. At this stage of the war the Southern troops were still electing most of their own officers and all of their non-coms, and Jud had not been chosen by the men but appointed by Baylor to lead them. It wasn't right and fair. This curlyheaded little snob had been getting petted and pampered from the start, just because his old man had been a big general, or something. Buddy Jack didn't like generals' sons worth a tinker's dam, and this homely blond boy had been a special peeve with him from the minute he'd first heard tell who he was. If the stuck-up son of a bitch was looking for trouble he had walked up to the right man when he'd walked up to Buddy Jack Lipscomb.

For his part Jud knew what he had to do.

He had kept his ear tuned on the ride through the pass and had pretty well pinned down the hulking private as the potential company malcontent.

There was one in every detail, apparently.

And on a detail like this one it could mean somebody getting killed to have a hardnose sounding off and stirring things up at the wrong time.

"Well?" he now said, breaking the foot-shuffling stillness. "I'm waiting."

"For what?" rasped Lipscomb. "You think I'm stupid enough to swing on you with them stripes on?"

"All right," said Jud, "so you're a smart soldier. See that you're smart enough to get one other thing straight about me and this patrol. You don't have to like it, or me. All you have to do is obey orders."

Lipscomb couldn't stand the challenge.

"And who says we have to do that?" he demanded, loud-voiced and feeling the bully's need to blow strong where the situation looked safe.

"You might try me," said Jud quietly.

"Sure! Look at the hero now he's got three stripes," jeered the other. "And me with eight years in the state militia and a lousy damned private's rank to show for it!"

Jud stepped back carefully and said, "Lipscomb, you're forgetting something. I'm not wearing any stripes now. We're spies, remember?"

"By God, that's so—!" breathed the beefy giant. "I plumb forgot." Then, shucking grinningly out of his fringed buffalo hunter's coat, "Watch yourself, sonny boy. I'm going to show you how much help it is being a general's son six miles from the fort!"

Jud said nothing.

He slid in and smashed a left hand to Lipscomb's belly and a following right to his slackened jaw as he doubled forward. The other soldier was in the dirt almost before he got the words about Jud's being a general's son out of his mouth. He came up to his knees shaking his head and spitting twigs and blood and river gravel. Jud stood back, waiting for him. He came up on to his feet, squinted, found Jud in the darkness, said, "All right, you son of a bitch I'm gonna kill you for that," and lunged at him like a wounded bear.

Jud weighed one hundred and ninety pounds. Every pound of it was where it ought to be. He had an eye like a lynx, the reflexes of a fighting cock. He hit naturally, he hit hard, he hit often. And he had a fist the size and consistency of a rail-splitter's maul.

Buddy Jack Lipscomb outweighed him forty pounds. He had a big paunch, small hips, tremendous shoulders, arms the length and toughness of shagbark hickory fenceposts. There was no softness in him or about him and he hated young Jud Reeves.

It was a fight—a beautiful, terrible, classic frontier brawl which ended, as must all such savageries, with one man down senseless in the dirt, the other standing over him little the better off for his bloody victory, except in the eyes of those lesser men always on hand to disown the loser and embrace the conquering, if barely conscious, survivor.

Buddy Jack tried every gouge, hairpull, dust-in-the-eye, bite, kick, scratch, knee-in-the-groin tactic known to the inherently dirty fighter. Jud took what he had to offer, above and below the belt, and never once hit him when he was down or laid a boot into him when he was getting up. The exchange was so unequal that before it had gone a full minute the soldiers were pleading with Jud to "for God's sake go on and kill the bastard" every time he had a chance to take unfair advantage of Buddy Jack's being down or off balance. But he did not do so, going on to the end fighting clean.

Thus it was that when he saw Lipscomb was not

going to get up again and said to the gaping soldiers, "You'd best take him down to the water and clean him off, boys, we got a far piece to go yet tonight," he had done more than win a bare-knuckle, broken-nose brannigan. He had shown nine ordinary privates that there *was* something special about being a general's son, even if he'd had to nearly kill the tenth one of them to do it. From now on, he thought grimly to himself, he doubted if he was going to hear much more about his name being Reeves.

He was right.

One of the soldiers, a cocky little towhead from Uvalde, stepped in and picked up Lipscomb's feet.

"You sure you don't want us to put his head under and hold it there, Sarge?" he grinned. "It'd be a mortal pleasure."

Two other troopers moved in, each taking a huge, slack arm. One of them said, "Yeah, Sarge. Say the word and we'll sink him with a sack full of rocks."

"Just rinse him off," nodded Jud. "He won't be any more trouble."

"He's plumb crazy if he is," muttered the third soldier admiringly. "By God, Sarge, you got a poke like a packmule's hindleg. I sure thought you'd kilt the son of a bitch."

The three went off dragging Lipscomb across the rocky ground to the river, still happily evaluating Jud's victory. But for the latter they were only adding details that did not count. They had paid him his main compliment without knowing they had done it when three of them had called him "Sarge" in six seconds where the whole ten of them hadn't said it once in the six miles ahead of that.

Maybe Baylor had been right about those stripes after all!

Jud held up his hand.

The men behind him slowed their horses. Chigger Denton, the grinning towhead, who was up for his corporal's stripes and whom Jud had named his second-in-command after the understanding with Lipscomb, moved on up to Jud's side.

"We'll pull off the road here and lay up," Jud said. "First, though, we'll boil up a can of coffee and go over the plans once more."

The other boy nodded, turned and called back to the two troopers who had helped him drag Lipscomb to the river.

"Sherm, you and Little Jo rustle up some dry wood. We're going to pull off here and make a fire. Sarge wants to talk to the boys again. Rest of you," he waved to the others, "get off the road and put your horses under cover."

The patrol turned aside quickly, heading for the nearby riverbank cottonwoods. The two foragers, Sherman Gates and Little Jo Shelby, whose uncle was the famed "Missouri Raider," spread out to scout for firewood and also anything else the river brush might hold which would be of interest to eleven Confederate troopers masquerading as Texas buffalo hunters only

143

four miles from the Union town of Mesilla, New Mexico, and but two miles past the hundreds of Yankee troops at Fort Fillmore.

It was broad daylight of the 14th; a fine bright morning with little wind, no clouds, and the prospect of heating up considerably by noon.

Jud checked this matter of the weather, swung his own mount after those of his men.

It was a sobering moment.

Directly ahead lay the riskiest piece of work he had ever been a party to. The important thing he had to do now was explain it to the patrol one more careful time and then start praying that the Yankees were just half as far offguard as that hothead Magoffin and the other rabid secessionists in El Paso had talked Baylor into believing they were.

As soon as the coffee fire was lit and the water on, he had Chigger run up the boys.

"Now hold your questions till I'm through," he told them. "This is the last go-round on our orders and I don't want to be interrupted."

He waited a minute to give any company lawyers their opportunity to cross-examine the command, but none did and he went on with the details of Baylor's brash reconnaissance.

"First thing to get straight, once for all," he led off grimly, "is who we are and what we're doing here. Back at Fort Bliss we were soldiers sent out to reconnoiter the enemy. Up here we're spies and what we're doing is spying. If we get caught at it they'll shoot us."

He waited five seconds, letting that sink in.

"All right, now. We rest here through the heat of the day, and come dark tonight break up in twos and threes and drift into town from different directions. We go to wherever we see any Yank soldiers, or can expect some to be. That'll mostly be the cantinas, naturally. There's four main ones, and the biggest is La Golondrina. We'll all gather together there at ten o'clock. That's so we can see that everybody's present and accounted for."

Again, the watchful pause. Then, "After that we'll scatter and meet back here. If we're lucky we'll have all the information we need and can keep right on going. One more reminder. Forget it and you're apt to get left in Mesilla. No, not apt, certain to. Here it is: no matter if you've had any luck or not, you be in that main saloon by ten o'clock. Any man not there could mean big danger to the rest of us. He could have been captured and made to talk, or got drunk and done his own talking. We can't chance it either way. Are there any questions?"

There were none. The men had been thoroughly briefed before this, both by Baylor and his lieutenants at Fort Bliss and by Jud on the long ride from Frontera to Fort Fillmore.

Now they only shook their heads, and Jud was satisfied they were as ready as they ever would be, or any men would be, for a job as chancy as this bold stroke of Baylor's to get the "feel" of the enemy "beyond Texas."

Jud knew the odds against his venture better than most, because he knew the country around Mesilla better than most.

The Mesilla Valley, and the town itself, were heavily Spanish-American. What white men there were, of pre-war settlers, were anti-Texas in their feelings. Texas had long had hungry eyes for New Mexico and Texans were about as popular there as they were in Old Mexico. However, Texans went where they pleased, popular or not, and so Mesilla was used to seeing them and might not make any trouble over a ragged-tail bunch of stray buffalo hunters moving up toward Santa Fe looking for the herds which had been reported by the Comancheros to have gone north.

The danger was that somebody might get to adding up all the stray buffalo hunters suddenly in town and get the idea they were after something more than hides and humpribs. But that was a part of the gamble. If they went in with fewer men, and did run into any kind of difficulty, they wouldn't have a fighting chance to get out. This way, there was enough of them to bluff anything but a full company of cavalry. Providing, of course, that they hung together and didn't panic and split up at the first challenge.

Jud shook his head and set his jaw.

There were just too many "providings" and "of courses" inherent in Baylor's idea. A man might just as well forget them and concentrate on carrying out his orders, win or lose. *That* was the soldier's job.

The day passed swiftly enough. The men were tired

and so were the horses. They cooked food at noon but made no fire that evening, eating what had been prepared, extra, at noontime. The horses were put on picket at sundown so that they would not take on any more water and could "run" if they had to when they got to town.

At eight o'clock the first groups began to leave.

At the last minute Chigger Denton, who had been fretting about him all afternoon, asked Jud once more about trusting Buddy Jack Lipscomb.

"We got to trust him," said Jud. "What we going to do with him, shoot him?"

"Might be the best idea," replied the Uvalde towhead.

"Best thing to do with a bad actor is give him a job of work," disagreed Jud. "I'm going to put him in charge of his group, which will be him, Gates and Shelby. That'll give him a good feeling of being trusted and at the same time give us somebody we can trust to keep an eye on him."

"Well, they'll love that," predicted Chigger, "but it ain't a bad idea. Next to shooting the son of a bitch, that is."

By eight-thirty the last of the men were gone and only Jud and Chigger Denton were left.

They legged up on their restless horses, headed them out of the cottonwoods. They followed the Butterfield mail road on up the east bank for a mile of so, halting where it forked just before the crossing. Straight ahead, stretching up toward Doña Ana, the main branch continued two hundred and eleven miles north-ward to Santa Fe. Westward, the "Tucson Fork" continued across the Rio Grande one and one half miles to their objective, Mesilla.

Jud looked at his companion, gave him a tight grin and said, "Well, here goes nothing," and reined his gray hard left. "Nothing plus a hundred and twenty-nine pounds of Confederate sweat!" said Chigger Denton, and sent his own mustang splashing after Jud's across the shallows of the stage-road ford.

In Mesilla everything went off, in the worried Chigger's words, "slick as steer guts through a slaughter-house floor chute."

He and Jud Reeves hit the big strike in La Golondrina itself. There, about nine-thirty, they managed to get a table behind a heavy-drinking party of Fillmore officers. By the time their own company started drifting in about a quarter of ten, they had learned that the Union morale at the big fort down the river was practically nonexistent. His officers regarded Major Lynde, the C.O., as a rank incompetent, a "barracks-room brigadier," and lacking in every attribute of a suitable field commander, including courage. Further information, in detail, came right along with the main course. Lynde indeed had a large body of troops under him but they were a pickup outfit of regulars, mili-tamen, overdue transfers and raw recruits. Nevertheless and including the unpopular C.O. and the poor morale, Fort Fillmore's garrison was well aware of Baylor's thinly disguised intentions toward New

Mexico, was correctly informed as to his strength both in numbers and quality of troops, and did not doubt for a moment its ability to repel any Confederate advance which might be mounted by "350 self-armed Texas ruffians," under an "out-and-out adventurer like that damned Baylor."

Excited by his and Chigger's own luck, Jud could scarcely wait for ten o'clock.

The minutes sat back on their haunches and dug in with their forelegs. The big wallclock behind the bar seemed to have locked its hands together at ten of ten. Jud nodded to Chigger at 9:55 and the two of them got up and drifted toward the bar. They paid no heed to their men already there, until they had ordered and been served their whiskey. Then Jud made a quick count. Everybody was present except Sherm Gates, Little Jo Shelby and Buddy Jack Lipscomb.

Chigger made the same count at the same time and looked at Jud.

"They'll show," murmured the latter. "They still got two minutes."

Chigger shook his head, and he was right.

At ten, straight up, Gates and Shelby came in alone.

They picked out Jud at the bar. Sherm Gates waved at him and called across the crowd, "Say, by God, look who's here! Old Tex and Shorty, sure enough!" And Little Jo Shelby added, "By Cripes, it's good to see you all! You boys by any chance going up north? We hear the herd's headed up thataway."

With the loud bluffs they moved through the crowd,

149

forced grins working full blast. Gates got to Jud first, slapped him on the back, dropped his voice and said, "We're surrounded, Sarge. That son of a bitch Lipscomb got away from us and went to talking. We caught up with him and beat it out of him, but there's a Yankee captain and upwards of thirty men gathering up outside."

Jud shot a look at the door.

Outside he could see the splash of the lamplight on Union uniforms moving to scuttle across the cantina's open doorway and get to their positions.

His glance swung to the rear of the big room.

There was an adobe archway there, leading out to an alley no doubt. But Gates had said "surrounded." That meant troops front and rear of the place.

He thought of the motto engraved beneath his grandfather's picture hanging over the mantel of the Topaz Creek homeplace, "When the Issue Is in Question—Charge!" and he gritted to Sherm Gates, "Pass the word to the boys. Chigger and me will bust the lights in thirty seconds. Everybody out the front way."

In the next half minute, in the mysterious way that danger will broadcast its alerting seed through an alien, unwarned crowd, the big room of La Golondrina grew as still as the street outside.

As it did, Jud kept up his silent count. When he reached twenty-nine he nodded to Chigger and went for his Colt.

There were three overhead oil lamps.

Chigger was carrying a sawed-off double-barreled

150

shotgun and got the first two in the same deafening blast of sound in which the blending shots from Jud's Colt broke the third. Flaming oil and shattered chimney glass showered down for half a flaring, wild minute. Then the place was plunged into smoking darkness and the ten trapped Confederates were pouring through the street door, guns bucking and jumping in their hands.

But the Union troops had gotten under good cover on both sides of the exit and they had good shooting light from the lamps of the two smaller cantinas which flanked La Golondrina.

Three Southern boys went down and did not get up.

A fourth was added to the toll when Jud, racing for his rearing gray at the hitch rail, found his way blocked by a brutish giant in fringed buckskin. The man was drunk and he had a shotgun aimed waveringly at Jud's head and his name was Buddy Jack Lipscomb.

Jud ducked twistingly down, wrenched the shotgun out of his hands and shot him in the belly with both barrels so close the burning powder set his fringed hunting shirt to smoking.

After that it was just lie flat on your pony and pray to God neither you nor he got hit. For Jud Reeves and six of his original command it worked. A half hour later they were at the rendezvous and an hour after that they were fifteen miles out of Mesilla and still not looking back. For the other four of his command, including the brave Sherman Gates, it was already too late for prayers before ever Jud got to his pony.

Back in Mesilla they lay quietly in the dust of the main *calle,* waiting for the burial detail from Fort Fillmore. Over them a Yankee sentry grinned at the crowd of Spanish-American curious who stood back to mutter and stare at the dead *Tejanos* and to cross themselves uneasily as they did so.

"Step up and have a good look, you Mexican bastards," the Union trooper invited them. "They ain't going to bite you."

But the dark-eyed villagers only looked at the Yankee sentry and crossed themselves again and murmured "God forgive him," in Spanish, and went away quickly from that place where the Texas Devils lay dead in the streets of Mesilla, New Mexico.

10

JUD and his badly bruised command reached Fort Bliss at high noon of the 15th. Baylor already knew there had been trouble when Jud reported in to him only minutes later.

"Well?" said the handsome officer. "What happened? I mean," he qualified warningly, "*precisely* what happened?"

Jud told him.

When he had done so, Baylor deliberately let the silence run on. Finally he inclined his head toward the open door, outside which Jud's remaining six men waited to be dismissed.

"Four men lost," he said. "Forty per cent casualties. Do you think you made the right decision, Sergeant Reeves?"

"I don't know, sir."

"Don't you think you ought to know?"

"Yes sir."

"Your information is all we could have hoped for, I must say that."

"Thank you, sir."

Baylor shook off the acknowledgment.

"But I must also say that the price you paid for it is exorbitant. A commander's first responsibility is toward his men, Sergeant. That goes for a corporal on patrol with a squad or a colonel advancing on the field with a regiment. Your men come first, sir. Always remember that."

Jud knew from the way he said it that he was going to dismiss him in the next breath, and no more made of the whole unfortunate affair than that.

But he was not ready to be dismissed.

"Sir," he said, "may I say something?"

"Certainly."

"Thank you, sir. Now, what you just said about a commander's first responsibility being to his men?"

"Yes?"

"That's not what my father said, sir."

Baylor's fine features sharpened, along with his voice.

"And what," he asked, "did your father say?"

"That there's only one way and reason to fight."

"How's that?" said Baylor.

153

"To win," said Jud, and saluted and stood back.

The older man got up out of his chair. This boy he had chosen to sponsor might not prove to be all he had assumed he would be from his background. He could not put his finger on the trouble with him, but it seemed as though, despite his family heritage, he might not be quite the superior officer material a man had hoped. He would, in any event, bear careful watching from now on.

"Thank you, Sergeant," he nodded in belated receipt of Jud's oblique rebuke. "And now may I say something to you? *You talk too much.* Goodnight sir!"

Jud saluted and went out. Baylor watched him through the window as he dismissed his men and led his horse across the parade ground toward the stable-area lean-to he shared with Elkanah Cavanaugh. While he was thus still engaged Second Lieutenants Preston and Royce entered his office from the adjoining staffroom. Without turning, Baylor said to them, "Did either of you happen to hear what young Reeves said to me just now?"

"No," answered Darrel Royce, for a notable brusque change not waiting for his friend Preston to take precedence. "But we heard what you said to him."

"How do you mean that, sir?" Baylor came around with the sharp question, eyes narrowing.

"You said he talked too much," replied Royce, unabashed. "That's not his main trouble, sir; not viewed as potential material for a combat command, it isn't."

"I see," said Baylor, frown darkening. "And exactly what *is* his main trouble, viewed as a potential leader of troops in the field, Royce?"

"He *thinks* too much," said Second Lieutenant Darrel Eugene Royce, and meant it precisely the insulting way it sounded.

Very clearly, something big was in the wind.

For the following eight days Jud and every other volunteer in the 2nd Texas Mounted Rifles trained from reveille to taps. Jud, who could recite backward the basic cavalry drill procedures when he was five, was given forty men to whip into combat marching condition. It was merciless work. By the night of the 22nd, he was so tired he could not take his clothes off. He went to bed at sundown, not even bothering to eat. Four hours later he came cursingly awake. Cavanaugh's foot was in his ribs, the rising moon in his eyes.

Cavanaugh gave him twenty seconds to get himself together. Then he dropped it on him like a bucket of cold water. "On your feet," he said. "I just been with Baylor. The column's moving out in the morning. We're going tonight."

"You got a mouse in your pocket?" asked Jud, eying him rebelliously. "What you mean 'we'?"

"Don't get flip with me, boy. I mean you and me. Colonel's orders. Let's go."

"*Whose* orders?" said Jud, holding back.

"Colonel's," said the old man, staring him back.

"What the hell's a few grades of rank between old family friends? Come on." He started off, stomping toward the stables.

"Whoa up!" challenged Jud, getting in stride with him. "You mean the Captain's been promoted since I went to sleep? All the way to colonel?"

"Sure," barked Cavanaugh. "Why not? Who's to care in Richmond?"

The old man had been born in Tennessee and was as independent as Davy Crockett. He had gone to work scouting for Baylor as a matter of needing the money, not from political conviction. As an old Ranger and early settler, he was violently for Texas. But like many a hardheaded border-state Southerner before and after him, he did not consider that love necessarily synonymous with being a red-hot Secessionist. Jud knew this about him but called him on it just the same.

"What's the matter with Richmond?" he growled.

"Oh, hell!" snapped Cavanaugh, lengthening his steps, "you know them jackasses back there are ladling out the chicken guts like there was enough to loop around the sleeves of every right-born son of a bitch in the South. It makes my butt ache!"

"Say," said Jud, "whose side you on?"

"I ain't made up my mind!" snorted the old man, and Jud didn't know whether he meant it or not.

They got their horses, setting out north, toward El Paso, neither saying anything more.

Going up El Paso Street, they struck San Francisco

Street and turned left, heading west. They went right on through town, still not talking. Presently the road bent sharply northwest, up over the low terraced foothills bordering the east bank of the Rio Grande. Jud knew the way well enough, having taken it only two nights before, and now he scowled quickly.

"What the hell's the idea? This here's the Butterfield Road."

"Do tell. Butterfield, you say? Now it does seem like I've heard that name somewheres."

Jud hauled in the gray, not amused.

"Where we going?" he demanded flatly. "Back up to Fillmore?"

"I am," said the old man over his shoulder, not even slowing his own mount. "Don't know about you."

Jud touched up the gray, came alongside him again. "Why?" he said.

"Baylor don't believe you," Cavanaugh told him straight out. "He wants me to check on your information while he's bringing the troops up behind us."

"And did he want me to go along for the ride?"

"No, that was my idea."

"Thanks. How come, for God's sake?"

Cavanaugh looked at him. "An old man gets lonesome, boy," he said. "Don't you know that?"

He said it softly and with no sarcasm and Jud said back to him, "I'm right sorry. I didn't mean to sass you. It's just that I'm sort of shook up, I reckon."

Again the old man searched him with his pale eyes. "Over what?" he asked. "Seems to me you're doing pretty good, boy; private to sergeant in less'n six weeks."

"It's not me," said Jud.

"I know it ain't," nodded Cavanaugh. "You want to talk about it?" He reached out a long bony arm, put a hand the size and weight of a cantaloupe on his young companion's shoulder. "You know, Jud," he said, "nineteen ain't so old but what a boy still needs somebody to listen. I'm listening."

The simple gesture broke loose the floodgates of Jud's thoughts, pouring his worries through them.

"It's those poor boys, Cavanaugh!" he blurted out. "They didn't have to die! I know they didn't!"

"They did," said the old man quietly. "*I* know they did."

"How do you know that?" asked Jud, half hopefully, half honestly puzzled by the old scout's flat certainty.

"I know," said Elkanah Cavanaugh, "that when a man will lead other men he's got to be ready to accept casualties. Some will come unavoidable as catching cold on damp ground. Others will be from getting careless. Some he can help and others he can't. But they'll come sure as sin, both kinds, and they're only a part of the price he pays for being a captain or a corporal or whatever."

"By God," said Jud a little touchily, "you sound just like Baylor. He read me the same rules when he was dressing me down yesterday. That throws me. You and him quoting out of the same book."

158

"Well, boy, you got some things to learn about both of us. Especially Baylor."

"Yes, what about him?" countered Jud. "I got the idea you figured him for a damn fool."

Cavanaugh shot him a look that would have poisoned a waterhole and said, "Jud, let me tell you a little something about John Robert Baylor."

Having asked the permission, he did not wait to receive it but launched straightaway into a one-breath biography of the head of the Bexar County Buffalo Hunters.

"Baylor," said the old man, "was born in Kentucky, but raised out here on the *llano*. His daddy was J. W. Baylor, the best damned doctor the army ever had in Texas or the Indian Territory. He was the post surgeon with the Seventh Infantry up at Fort Gibson for a long time. He was a family man and Little John, that's the Colonel, now, was brung up eating out of a messkit and nursing a canteen. He's regular army clear through to his tailbone.

"He's got more education than most schoolteachers, more manners than a Mexican ambassador being interviewed on the Alamo, more unadulterated brass than a Spanish-cast cannonbarrel, more grit than a gravel pit and more ambition than a mustang stud in early spring. He'll charm you or kick you to death either way he has to, to get where he's going. And where he's going as of this here minute is Mesilla, New Mexico, or Arizona Territory, or whichever the hell you want to call it. He's aiming to go there with

300-and-some untrained Texas volunteers and I will not bet you ten cents against the Confederate Treasury that he don't arrive on schedule. Here's a boy, barely forty, got his toe stuck in the crack of the door to the whole southwestern quarter of the U.S.A., with a good idea he can kick it on open and grab California for the South before the North knows there's a war on west of the Mississippi! And you've got the gall to sit there on that wall-eyed gray wolfbait and tell me I been putting it out that I got him figured for a damn fool. Jud," concluded the bearded scout witheringly, "I don't know about you. Sometimes you don't strike me as being more than about one quarter bright."

Jud laughed and felt better.

He accepted the lecture on Baylor as he had the preceding assurance that those boys' being killed in Mesilla was not his fault. He wanted to think the older man was right, and right because he *was* older.

But the idea would not hold.

What he had accomplished in Mesilla could have been achieved without the loss of a single life, or without so much as one shot having been fired.

What had he done wrong?

Where had he failed in his leadership of those men?

Why had they had to die?

Seeing the shadow of the question still on his young companion's face, Cavanaugh began to talk again. His theme was the same blunt one as before: in a war men had to die, and someone had to lead them to their deaths. War was a cruel struggle, which he likened to that in nature, where the strong survive not by right but by might. Wars were never started, he said, except to promote the advantage of the aggressor, to add, principally, to his personal glory in connection with the cause. He cited, bitterly, the Mexican War. Who but its leaders had profited from it? he wanted to know. And was there any doubt but what they were after a personal profit to begin with? No, he said, a man had to face it: if he wanted to be one of the leaders, he had better realize *why* he wanted to be one, and *what* it was going to cost him to get his commission. The price, said Elkanah Cavanaugh, was always the same—death for his followers.

The old man's words cut Jud inside and deep.

He didn't like them and he didn't want to believe them.

And he fought back against them.

War was still what his father and grandfather had seen it for, as taught to him by his mother—a pure crusade in the name of continuing freedom, the only true way in which a man might serve his country unselfishly. To die in such a cause was the greatest honor which could come to a man, the greatest service he could render to his native land.

Cavanaugh literally snorted at this high-minded diatribe.

Dead men, he growled, did nothing for any country. It was the live ones who made the speeches over their graves and then went home to marry their widows and inherit their personal fortunes. The only service a man performed by dying for his side, was to shorten the war by just so much. The more killed, the sooner over. Jud would see. This little fracas just getting under way between the States was going to prove Cavanaugh's theory. It wouldn't end until enough men had been killed on both sides to sicken everybody concerned with it. And that would be the whole and the total and the entire result of the damned thing, and the ones who could be blamed for starting it and keeping it going, and hence for the death of every single poor son of a bitch who went under in it, would be the leaders.

It still went, what he had said in the beginning.

If a man wanted to be a leader, fine. If he simply had it in him to be driven by ambition, like Baylor and that sneery-faced Lieutenant Preston, and if he couldn't control his itch to wave a sword and holler Charge! why then, good enough. Let him admit it, and admit he didn't care how many other men got killed so long as *he* got where *he was* going, and then let him get on with the job. Just don't let him try to tell Elkanah Cavanaugh how noble it was to get somebody else's guts blown out in the process, nor even how exalted it might be to take a cannonball or a charge of grape through his own belly.

Cavanaugh had brought the argument full circle: *Was it, or was it not, Jud's personal fault that Sherm Gates and those other brave boys had died in Mesilla?* It was an argument without an answer. Wisely, Jud let the subject rest.

All other talk shortly dwindled away. They rode on through the night.

It was only minutes before sunup, the morning of July 23, when they came in view of Fort Millard Fillmore. What they saw left them staring and shaking their heads. Baylor had been right. Jud's Mesilla report had needed some checking.

Fillmore was an obvious fortress.

It was teeming with men, bulging with supplies, crammed with arms and ammunition.

Freight wagons stood hub to hub outside the Q.M. sheds south of the parade ground quadrangle. The enlisted men's barracks flanking the quadrangle north and south were overflowing with troops. Row after row of auxiliary tents stretched behind the permanent buildings. Sentries walked their beats with alert briskness. The barking cries of the drill sergeants were already stabbing the early morning quiet. The snap and roll of their "hup, two, three, four!" together with the sharp responses of their wheeling squads to the manual orders gave clear evidence that these troops were anything but the "pickup" companies Jud had reported back from his Mesilla scout.

"I don't understand it!" exclaimed the latter, unslinging his fieldglasses and fastening them on the drilling companies. "To hear those officers carrying on in that cantina the other night, you'd have thought they didn't have a soldier on the post with sense enough to spit downwind. No, nor with spirit enough to go to the latrine by himself in the dark. I just don't understand it!" he repeated obstinately.

"I do," said Cavanaugh, lowering his own glasses after one quick look. "The liquor goes in, the truth comes out. There never was a West Point man didn't sneer at his troops and snarl at his C.O. They all think God, not Congress, gave 'em their commissions. You didn't listen in on nothing but a bottle of whiskey talking, boy. This post is no more ripe for picking than a green persimmon. If Baylor tries it, he's going to wind up with an awful pucker in his mouth. Them's regulars down there, Jud. There ain't a militiaman among 'em."

"I don't believe it, by God!" gritted his companion. "I heard what I heard up in Mesilla. There's no officers going to talk like that for nothing."

"Well," grimaced Cavanaugh acridly, "you can't see morale through a damned spyglass, I'll grant you that. But you can see soldiers. And them down yonder are the real issue article. If they're a fair sample of the rest, our boys are going to get their butts put in a sling."

"What are we going to do?" asked Jud, tight-lipped. He still believed he had heard the truth about the bad morale of the Fillmore garrison. But what he had heard and reported to Baylor along that line did not match up with what he and old Elkanah Cavanaugh were looking at right now. He had to admit that.

"Do?" said Cavanaugh. "What the hell can we do but go tell Baylor you made a little mistake?"

"What you going to say?" Jud frowned defiantly.

"Just what I think," said the old man, and turned his rawboned gelding away and sent him on down off the ridge just as short and straight as that.

PART FOUR

THE COWARD
IN COMMAND

11

MAJOR ISAAC LYNDE appeared to have an overwhelmingly powerful force situated in a virtually impregnable position.

In his command at Fort Fillmore, at the time Baylor's scouts rode back to warn their commander of the Union strength, were seven companies of crack frontier foot troops, A, B, D, E, G, I and K of the 2nd and 7th Infantry. Further, he had four companies of cavalry and mounted infantry, plus an artillery detachment with a battery of excellent medium-range eight-pound howitzers, bringing his total force to in excess of seven hundred combat effectives. His officers as well as his men were experienced both in terms of general service and local duty. Lastly, Lynde himself, as were nearly all of the field-grade officers in New Mexico at war's outbreak, was a West Point man. He was, as well, an experienced commander entirely familiar with the surrounding terrain and having at his disposition the largest, best-armed garrison of veteran troops in the Southwest.

There existed, then, at Fort Fillmore that July morning of 1861, every obvious military element needed to explain the continuing confidence of Union

Colonel Edward Richard Sprigg Canby in the ability of his subordinate to defend successfully the Federal Government's southernmost salient in the Department of New Mexico.

Indeed, not only was Colonel E. R. S. Canby seemingly certain of Lynde's ability to defeat Baylor's three hundred San Antonio irregulars at or before Mesilla, but announced himself satisfied that the Fillmore forces would subsequently "drive him back" and very quickly retake Fort Bliss for the Union.

Canby's optimism, in view of Lynde's own directly opposite opinions of the same situation, was, if nothing worse, singularly ill-considered.

In response to repeated frantic appeals from Lynde dating from the day of his June 16th assignment to the Fillmore command, Canby had been forced to send down to the lower fort three hundred stands of spare small-arms, 12,000 rounds of ammunition for same, plus 20,000 extra rations of subsistence from the main departmental depots at Albuquerque. In addition, he had before him by mid-July, instant, Lynde's pleading letters of the 7th and 9th, practically crawling for permission, despite his apparent great advantages of troops and equipment, to immediately abandon post. In these completely unwarranted communications Lynde represented Fort Fillmore, one of the strongest redoubts in the Southwest, as totally indefensible on the grounds that it was located in a depression commanded on three sides by hills within six pounder range, and water for men and animals had to be brought from the Rio Grande a mile and a half away.

That a man of Canby's high professional reputation could feel any confidence whatever in a commander who would not only write, but repeat, such baseless—and base—appeals, was the ultimate in tributes of blind faith to the value of a United States Military Academy education.

It was, additionally, a disastrous error in personal judgment.

There can be little doubt that Colonel Edward Richard Sprigg Canby was a brave and competent commander.

There can be none at all that Major Isaac Lynde was a cowardly and incompetent one.

Baylor was advancing with caution up the west bank of the river. He had Junior, the Lipan Apache, out looking for Cavanaugh and Jud Reeves on the east side, while his some dozen or so enlisted scouts (with whom Cavanaugh would have nothing to do) probed ahead of the column up the far side. These troopers were under fiery Hugh Preston, who burned to get a field command, and timid Darrel Royce, who did not. Each of the young lieutenants had a sergeant and six men. The idea of their being out on a scout at all was simply another of Baylor's imaginative conceptions of an improved military operation: a logical projection as it were of his previous theory that staff officers should be given field experience—absolute heresy in the regular army.

Just before sunset Royce's outfit, returning to head-quarters, was spotted by Cavanaugh and Jud. They hailed the patrol and joined it. By dark they were with Baylor in his command tent fifteen miles south of Santo Tomas on the old westbank Indian Road.

Cavanaugh spoke first and as promised earlier to Jud, said what he thought. This turned out to be the opinion that Fort Fillmore was swarming with crack troops, was obviously informed of Baylor's approach, and was impossible to take without staggering losses. He recommended it be let strictly alone; bypassed, in other words, and left to sit on the riverbank while the "buffalo hunters" went on up the stream after the main herd under Colonel Canby at Fort Craig.

When he had heard the old scout through, Baylor merely nodded and asked Jud what his previous, con-flicting report now looked like to him.

The latter hung tough.

He said he still thought his original intelligence was basically correct: the garrison was shot through with bad morale because of its widespread distrust and dis-like of its commanding officer. He remained con-vinced the fort could be and ought to be taken.

Baylor beamed approvingly.

The boy's position was patently the sounder from the military viewpoint. Cavanaugh must be getting old. To leave a powerful force in one's rear to get at a second powerful force on one's front, while greatly lengthening one's supply lines in the process, could be a deliberate act of suicide. Young Reeves had expressed this thinking logically and well. It became Baylor's pleasure to reward him for it by saying that he agreed with him completely. As soon as Preston's patrol came in, he decided, they would move up.

The order was passed through the camp, the men told to "sleep on your rifles within reach of your reins."

Preston returned shortly after midnight, having gone all the way up to the Santo Tomas crossing below Fillmore. His report only added fuel to Baylor's fire of restlessness. The crossing was wide and shallow and hard-bottomed. All the wheeled vehicles could be driven across. Hence, with no need for time-consuming lashing of log floats to the wagon sides, swimming of the teams, hooking on of additional "pull-out" teams, etc., the entire column could be gotten back across the river to the Fort Fillmore side, in position for a dawn attack, well before the break of day.

When he heard Preston's detailed description of the Santo Tomas crossing, Cavanaugh said disgustedly to Baylor, "Hell we could have told you that!" and Baylor snapped back at him, "Well, then, sir, why didn't you?"

The old scout looked at him and growled, "Because I didn't figure you'd ought to go across there, that's why. And what's more, you still oughtn't to do it."

"I pay you for information, Mr. Cavanaugh, not advice!" Baylor was incensed, and showed it.

"Speaking of pay, Colonel," said the latter, uninterested in demonstrations of highbred temperament, "I ain't seen any since signing on. When *is* the eagle going to scream?"

This was a question which could not be ducked, nor thrown aside. Cavanaugh was not the only one of the buffalo hunters beginning to wonder about Confederate financing. Baylor sensed the need for candor when he saw his two most trusted aides, Major Waller and Colonel Herbert, join the general push of his assembled staff forward to catch his reply to the grizzled civilian scout's blunt query about his backpay.

John R. Baylor, sometimes rash, sometimes impudent as well as imprudent, sometimes impetuous, short and dictatorial with those around him, was at the same time a man of fundamental good humor and warm friendliness. Both a fair soldier and a fearless leader, he was to the end a hopeless victim of the impossible Southern Dream. This early in the Confederate adventure his belief in Richmond's political promises and the private words-of-honor of his Texas backers was as yet unshaken.

His answer to old Elkanah Cavanaugh, therefore, was as honest as it was naïve and instant.

"Things have indeed been a bit uncertain, Mr. Cavanaugh." He smiled. "But I am happy to tell you that I have received assurances of forty thousand dollars being advanced to our account by Colonel Magoffin and his associates in El Paso. As soon as this Mesilla campaign is concluded we shall bring our books up to date, I assure you. By that time, our lines to Richmond will be straightened out and the regular arrangements made. If it's any comfort to you," he added with a wry shrug, "we hear that Colonel Canby up at Fort Craig has had to guarantee payment of forage levies with his own signature against his personal property. His troops have not been paid, in the case of some of his regulars, for as long as twelve months. I believe we should be able to accept twelve weeks, Cavanaugh, don't you?"

By the dropping of the "mister" he let the old man know they were friends again, and the latter threw in with an embarrassed grin and a gruff, "Hell yes, if you say so, Colonel."

The staff meeting broke up in very high spirits. The troops were roused out of their four-hour sleep and the march taken up toward Santo Tomas. The crossing was reached at 3 A.M.; the entire force of two hundred and fifty men and their field equipment, gotten over to the east bank and into position only six hundred yards south of the Fort Fillmore stockade by ten minutes after four. The Confederate command's presumption at that time was that the complete operation had been carried forward without the knowledge of the Union garrison. An hour later it was light enough to see that Elkanah Cavanaugh knew what he was talking about, that Sergeant Jud Reeves and Second Lieutenant Hugh Preston did not, and that the presumption of enemy surprise needed drastic revision.

Fort Millard Fillmore was wide awake. Her catwalks were bristling like the guardhairs of an angry dog-wolf's neckmane with the outthrust barrels of four hundred silently aimed and waiting rifles.

"Son of a bitch!" snarled Lieutenant Hugh Preston. "They're onto us!"

"You didn't say your prayers," laughed his friend Darrel Royce. *"I did—!"*

"What does that mean?" glared Preston, wheeling on him, white-lipped with anger.

"It means we won't attack the fort," shrugged the gentle, dark-haired boy. "And that I can live another day without being found out."

Baylor fretted in his lines all that day, the 24th.

The following morning, without a shot having been fired on either side, he fell back. Going over the Santo Tomas crossing once more, he marched on up the west bank of the Rio Grande and occupied Mesilla without enemy resistance.

Meanwhile, the timorous Major Lynde was emboldened by the enemy withdrawal. About 4 P.M. that afternoon of July 25, he came out of Fort Fillmore and marched up to Mesilla with six companies of infantry and one of his eight-pound artillery pieces.

Jud sat with Elkanah Cavanaugh on the roof of the adobe house in which Baylor had set up his field command post, and watched the blazing Battle of Mesilla which now ensued with bewildering suddenness.

Coming along the road to within sign of the beginning dwellings of the town, including the one which housed Baylor and his staff, Lynde halted his troops and lobbed two tentative rounds from the eight-pounders toward the plaza at the city's center. He then sent forward his aides, Post Adjutant Edward J. Brooks and Post Surgeon James Cooper McKee, with his formal demands for unconditional and immediate surrender of the town and of the Confederate forces within it.

Baylor's scarcely worried aides, Major Waller and Colonel Herbert, set out at once to intercept the bearers of the Union truce flag.

Waller and Herbert, carrying double barreled shotguns on the front of their saddles, accomplished this mission without trouble and demanded to know of the Yankee gentlemen what it was that they might do for them.

Upon being informed of Lynde's weird demand, Waller smiled and said, "Well, sirs, Colonel Baylor has anticipated Major Lynde's natural confidence in the superiority of numbers, and has instructed us to tell you that if he wants Mesilla and our men with it, he has only to come along and take them."

After half an hour of apparent indecision on the part of the Union command, the Federal forces began to advance along the road, laboriously hauling the howitzer by hand through the deep and treacherous sands, the troopers cautious but entirely confident.

When the first of them drew near Baylor's headquarters, a scattered Rebel fire from the Southern pickets falling unhurriedly back upon the command post killed three and wounded six of the Yankee skirmishers, including two officers. Jud, watching from the roof, was amazed. The rifle fire sounded like popgun "pips" and the falling men appeared no more real than tin soldiers being knocked over on a child's playboard. But his astonishment at the unreal effect of the "toy soldier" tableau spread before him down the dusty road was nothing compared to the surprise wrought by the Union commander's reaction to these trifling casualties.

Lynde ordered an immediate full retreat. The move was so completely unexpected that it had the effect of a well-conceived tactic. Caught with no plans at all for an advance (who could have anticipated the need for one that afternoon?), the Confederates could not pursue, but had to content themselves with making camp where they were and staying the night in Mesilla.

Squatting with Cavanaugh in the cottonwood-shaded yard of the command adobe, where they waited Baylor's next need for them, Jud still could not believe what he had seen.

The Battle of Mesilla was over. It had consisted of two long-range howitzer shots, both of which had fallen in Guadalupe Fernandez's cornpatch five hundred yards short of Mesilla proper, and some hundred rounds of small-arms fire resulting in nine casualties of which only three—one less than Jud's Mesilla Scout had taken in front of La Golondrina on July 14—had been deaths!

Three men the price of a formal clash between 380 Union regulars and 250 Confederate volunteers?

Three men the cost of a Federal commander's courage?

Of a Confederate leader's failure to seize and follow up an advantage of such easy opportunity?

It simply passed belief.

There had to be something wrong here somewhere.

It developed shortly that Baylor agreed.

"On your feet!" barked Corporal Bodie, trotting up to them about seven o'clock. "Colonel wants to see you both. On the double. Hup—!"

"'Hup' your chili-picking butt!" rasped Cavanaugh, glaring him down. "Next time you come up to me, you come up with a 'Excuse me, Mr. Cavanaugh,' you understand?"

"Yes sir," grinned Bodie. "Excuse me, Mr. Cavanaugh, but the Colonel would admire to have you join him. On the double—huppp!"

He ducked the shard of brick the white-haired scout hurled at him, laughed and loped off chuckling at his own dubious humor. .

The old man calmly picked up his Sharps bullgun, levered in a cartridge, laid his sights and squeezed off. Corporal Bodie's battered slouch hat spun around one complete revolution, but stayed on his head, and Cavanaugh put down the gun and said, "Son of a bitch, I drilled it half a inch off center. I got to get me some eyeglasses."

"Eyeglasses my back!" yelled Bodie, yanking off the wounded article. "You got to get me a new hat, you crazy old bastard!"

"You're going to need a new head to go under it," allowed Cavanaugh, picking up the Sharps again, "less'n there's a powerful improvement in your memory. Not to mention your manners. And somewhat suddenlike in both directions, I'd recommend—"

He was actually lining up the white-faced corporal again when Baylor appeared in the low doorway of the adobe and called out sharply, "*Mr. Cavanaugh,* might *I* bother you for a few moments?"

"No bother at all, Colonel," drawled the impervious one. "The light's getting bad for close holding anyhow." He knuckled his shaggy right eyebrow in what he imagined was a salute, or, rather, what he imagined Baylor thought was one, and asked blandly, "What can we-all do for you, Colonel?"

" 'You-all,' " Baylor mimicked him good-humoredly, "can get yourselves down the river and see what that rascal Lynde is up to. I can't understand the sense of his actions this afternoon, and I definitely believe he is trying to draw us in."

Jud stood silently to one side, waiting. He could see that Baylor was at once highly pleased with his blood-less occupation of Mesilla and concerned over Lynde's peculiar counter action.

"Appears to me, Colonel," replied Cavanaugh, "that he's got a whiff of the same skunk. Way he backed off just now you'd have thought he smelled a whole litter hid out under the kitchen stoop."

"I think he was trying to make me believe just that," nodded Baylor. "That he sensed my trap and was just too timid to put his foot in it. He hoped to get me to come after him, don't you see?"

"No sir," said Cavanaugh honestly. "But me and Jud will run along down there and find out what we can. Was there anything else, Colonel?"

"Just be careful," smiled the latter. "I can't afford to lose my 'eyes' at this stage of the game."

Cavanaugh held up, letting Jud move on out of earshot. "You can't afford to go on ignoring what your eyes see, either, Colonel, and that's a fact, all due respects considered."

"I don't follow you, Cavanaugh."

"All right, then, was I right about that fort being loaded for wounded bear? I was," he answered his own question, "and if you hadn't of slowed up and backed off they'd have slaughtered you down there yesterday morning. That was just pure luck, Colonel. Next time you might not make out so well."

"And—?" said the officer quietly.

"Next time," vouchsafed Cavanaugh, bobbing his beard decisively, "you'd better listen to me."

He had expected another flare-up about advice not being what he was paid for, but Baylor fooled him.

He put his hand on his bowed shoulder and gave him a quick grip, strong as a closed bench vice, and laughed unaffectedly. "You know, Cavanaugh, I believe I'll just do that! Now run along and tell me what we ought to do about our Yankee major, down yonder."

Jud was waiting at the horses, and they mounted up

without talking, Cavanaugh moving out in the lead. They went across the river at the Mesilla ford, figuring Lynde would have the Santo Tomas crossing picketed. A half mile from the north stockade they nose-wrapped their horses and tied them well off the road in some river willows, going the rest of the way in on foot.

At the fort all was quiet. They lay in watch for an hour, then made a circle of the entire stockade from the Butterfield stage road on the north, back to the same road on the south. The unnatural lack of ordinary garrison noise continued to intrigue them.

"By God," muttered Cavanaugh, "for once Baylor was right. The Yankee sons are up to something."

"Sounds to me," shrugged Jud, "like they're up to no more than getting a good night's sleep."

"No," said Cavanaugh abruptly. "Now you listen. Listen real hard. What do you hear?"

Jud started to say he didn't hear anything, then he suddenly *did* hear something. "My God," he whispered, "it sounds like a beehive getting set to swarm!"

"You named it!" snapped Cavanaugh. "Let's get out of here!"

"Hold on. Why for? We don't know anything for certain yet."

"Add it up, Jud," said the old man tersely. "It's moondark and they know we can't spy on them from the hills by night. Not unless they show some lights. But there ain't any lights. Not one. Nor do we see a damned sentry on the skyline of the catwalks, nor do

180

we trip over a solitary picket out in the brush past the stockade. Now what does that give you so far?"

"Nothing," said Jud just as tersely. "Keep going."

"All right, then. No sentries, no pickets, no lights. And at first, no noise. That is, we don't pick it up right off. But this is a big post, boy. Six, seven hundred men and the families of quite a few of them. Women and kids and dogs and the whole kaboodle. Plus freighters and packers and the crew that works for the post sutler—why, my God, boy, there must be enough people inside them walls to start a new territory! And what do we hear? Nothing but a low hum, and that only after an hour of cocking our ears. Now what you got?"

"I can't believe it!" exclaimed Jud. "It's plumb crazy!"

"It is," said the old man. "Likewise it's true."

He waited a long minute while both of them again listened to sustained, sibilant, rustling and humming sound of several hundred people moving with secret, almost distracted purpose behind the darkened stone and adobe walls of Fort Millard Fillmore.

Then he spoke again, and sharply.

"Let's go, Jud. That Yankee major's up to something, all right. Happen Baylor don't stop him, there won't be a bluebelly trooper south of Doña Ana come sundown tomorrow night."

Jud didn't argue it. The eerie sound of the preparing departure, once translated, was unmistakable. There was no question but what Cavanaugh was right and

181

that Union Major Isaac Lynde was getting ready to abandon Fort Fillmore.

They recircled the lightless post, found their horses, mounted up and galloped north.

At his Mesilla headquarters, Baylor stunned them by refusing to take seriously their report.

"I *can't* believe it," he insisted candidly. "Where would he go? And for what possible reason?"

"He'd go north, and to save his shrinking hide!" said Cavanaugh. "Listen, Colonel, that garrison's pulling out. They couldn't be doing nothing else. Thet Yankee commander is scared, just plain scared. He ain't setting no trap for you no more'n you're setting one for him."

Baylor looked at him, pulling at his chin in the way he did when he was really thinking. Finally he said, "All right, Cavanaugh. I'll go down there with you in the morning and take a look. Meanwhile, we can all do with a good night's rest. What time do you want to start?"

"Four o'clock. That'll give you time to get back up here and get your column on the road. That is, providing there's any Union troops left to chase by then."

"I'll see you at five," said Baylor. "I'll not get up at four o'clock in the morning for any reason short of a barracks fire. Goodnight, gentlemen."

As good as his word, the C.O. of the 2nd Texas Mounted Rifles went down the river at five the following morning. With him went Waller, Herbert,

Preston, Royce and three other officers of his staff, in addition to Jud Reeves and Elkanah Cavanaugh.

The latter found them a fine spot on a sheltered ridge eight hundred yards northeast of the stockade, and the watch began.

The foul luck which had stuck with the old man's scouting since Jud had spoiled his Apache ambush at the Fort Quitman crossing was not due to improve.

The appearance and activity of Fort Fillmore, by day, was completely normal. The sentries walked their posts, the companies drilled on the parade ground, the work details tended the horses and cattle in and beyond the north-side stock corrals. Two small signs, alone, gave evidence of any undue intentions. The post ferrier was shoeing more horses and at a greater rate than would appear to be normal, and the beef herd was being held closer to the fort and more tightly bunched than it had been on the 24th and 25th.

Cavanaugh argued these exceptions for all they were worth, but Baylor was not impressed. By 9 A.M. he had seen all he cared to see. By ten, he and his staff had finished an excellent breakfast back in Mesilla and were enjoying a box of fine Havana panatellas that same morning come in by courier from Fort Bliss, sent on from that encampment by the just-arrived new bride of Colonel Bertrand Foote Horton, a veteran of the Mexican War and one of Baylor's few regular army officers.

All that day of the 26th Jud and Cavanaugh watched

from the north ridge. Nothing had happened by sundown. They rode back up to Mesilla very much puzzled, still suspicious, entirely worn out from their three-day unrewarded surveillance.

They reported in to Baylor, who told them to take the night off and get some sleep. Regardless of the instruction, they left their horses saddled. After they had eaten and gotten forty winks, they would ride back down and see if the fort were still "buzzing," as it had been the night before. But full stomachs and deep fatigue betrayed them both. It was a quarter after three in the morning when Jud awoke with a start to find himself still sitting with his back to the adobe wall of the headquarters house. Propped up beside him, mouth open, beard sagging chestward, Cavanaugh was still snoring a gale. Their forty-wink nap had stretched into a seven-hour full sleep. Neither of them had moved a foot since easing down against the wall at 8 P.M. to "rest up" for the ride back down the river.

Jud roused the old man at once. They were mounted up and riding within five minutes, but the enemy had not waited even so long as that. By the time they got over the Rio Grande at Mesilla Crossing, the leap and lick of the supply-dump fires lit by Lynde's demolition squads were staining the southern blackness blood-red, and they were already too late.

Major Isaac Lynde and his huge garrison with him, to the last man, woman, child, family pet and head of livestock in Fort Millard Fillmore, were gone.

• • •

On the afternoon of July 25, within one hour of his return to Fort Fillmore from the fifteen-minute clash with Baylor's pickets outside Mesilla, and without consulting a single member of his staff, Lynde issued his infamous order to abandon post.

He gave as his only reasons his concern that the fort could not be defended against Baylor's light artillery and his conviction that the Confederate commander meant to set up a blockade beyond Mesilla so that he, Lynde, could not reach the safety of Fort Craig, one hundred miles north.

His peculiar alternative was to try to reach Fort Stanton, a blistering hundred and fifty-four miles northeast across a country as rough and arid as the Libyan Desert. It was a tragic, a fantastic decision.

For several hours immediately before the abandon-ment on the second night, the garrison slept uneasily, rifles to hand. The wagons had been crammed with all manner of supplies, the field ambulances readied for the women and children. All the team-stock had been watered and fed during the day. Everything had been done, which could be, to tighten up the traces for the dash (twenty-two miles by a bad road) from the fort to San Augustine Springs, which had been designated the first objective.

In that last hour it became apparent that some of the supplies would need to be left behind. Word spread quickly that unbroken cases of hospital brandy and full kegs of medicinal whiskey were to be in this category.

The first signs of resentment now appeared in the ranks.

Abandonment, shameful or otherwise, of a military post under orders was perfectly acceptable, but the orphaning of "officer quality" drinking whiskey was unthinkable.

Shortly, every other soldier was emulating the example of one tough old sergeant of Company A, who promptly pulled the cork on his canteen and replaced its "sweet wine of the Rio Grande" with the odorous "sourmash of old Kentucky."

The officers either did not, or dared not see, and the travesty was repeated until the last bottle and barrel had been violated. This substitution got the march off to a roaring start, and it is doubtful if any command ever began a disgraceful rout in better or more ebullient spirits.

But the wagon road to San Augustine Springs was sheer rock and shifting sand, and the day turned off insufferably hot by 9 A.M. Without cooling water in their canteens and with the burning whiskey in their tortured stomachs, Lynde's men collapsed in dozens and scores along every mile of the way. By noon the column was strung out for five miles and the tragedy was apparent.

WITNESS: Col. John Robert Baylor, C.S.A.

On July 27th, a little after daylight, my spies reported a column of dust seen in the direction of the Organ Mountain distant 15 miles on the Fort Stanton Road. I could from the top of a house with a glass see the movements of the enemy. I immediately ordered the command to saddle and mount for the purpose of intercepting them at San Augustine Pass.

Upon gaining the summit of the pass, a plain view of the road was presented. For 5 miles it was lined with fainting, famished Union soldiers, who threw down their arms as we passed and begged for water. I was in a few moments sent for by Major Lynde, who asked upon what terms I would allow him to surrender. I replied that the surrender must be unconditional. To this, Major Lynde assented, asking that private property should be respected.

The articles of capitulation were signed, and the order given for the enemy to stack arms.

WITNESS: Union Post Surgeon James Cooper McKee

Everything was in unutterable and indescribable confusion. Ruin was on every side of us. The enemy was steadily advancing.

On or about noon I drove my two horse buggy into camp at San Augustine Springs, found the companies in camp and Lynde comfortably enjoying a lunch as if nothing were going on and his command safe, instead of a wreck and scattered along the road for miles. It was the sublimity of indifference.

In a short time the Texans were seen advancing in a line of battle to the number of some 300. Our men, numbering at least 500 infantry and cavalry, trained, disciplined, and well drilled soldiers, were drawn up in an opposite line forming a striking contrast to the badly armed and irregular command of the Texans.

The enemy advanced to within 300 yards of us, when Lynde raised and sent out a flag of truce, which was met and negotiations commenced with a view to surrender.

They demanded an unconditional surrender, the same that Lynde had demanded of them at Mesilla. Lynde sought to modify this, but his request was refused, and to do the Texans full credit for humane conduct, they stated that two hours would be granted to remove the women and children to a place of safety, a most marked contrast to the cowardly conduct of Lynde at Mesilla, when he ordered the artillery to open fire on the town full of them.

At this time all the officers assembled, and proposed waiting on Lynde and protesting against the surrender on any terms. One by one, from the senior down to the junior, we gave in our protests. It was farcical and ludicrous in the extreme. And it was too late. Even had any of the senior line officers been bold enough to seize the command by displacing Lynde, and putting him in arrest, the issue was already lost. Blind, unreasonable obedience to orders was the ruin of our command.

There were other witnesses to the Union shame who did not consign their sentiments to paper.

Jud Reeves was one.

Broiling with his two hundred fellow troopers of the 2nd Texas Mounted Rifles on the rocky slope above the springs at San Augustine that July afternoon, Jud was not alone heat-, but heart-sick. To Elkanah Cavanaugh, sitting with him on the slope just beyond the springside shade and within embarrassingly easy earshot of the pitiful surrender parley now going forward immediately below their vantage, he grated harshly, "God help me, I can't go on with it. I'm going to quit the minute we get back to Mesilla."

The old man only shook his head, not even looking at him.

"You won't quit," he said with acid softness. "You'll go on. You're a Reeves, ain't you?"

Yet despite his Tennessee hillman's unshakably dim opinion of high Southern traditions, Cavanaugh concurred in his protégé's angry disillusionment.

"Don't mistake me, boy," he appended in gruff apology. "You and me ain't got no arguments about this here spectacle. The whole thing stinks worse than a week-old gangrened leg."

It remained, however, for a simpler, less cynical mind to conceive and deliver the last, best summation of the San Augustine surrender. Junior, the Lipan Apache, lately kept apart from his two friends by having been made a special courier for Baylor (the Indian situation had worsened to the point where a white rider could seldom get through), was now with them again.

When Cavanaugh made his rough comment on the bad odor blowing up from the springs below, the wizened little Texas Apache grimaced, made an eloquent hand-sign gesture, added expressionlessly, *"Wagh,* him like buzzard break wind. Even noise smell sick."

PART FIVE
STAR LIGHT, STAR BRIGHT

12

BAYLOR designated the Federal disgrace "the Battle of San Augustine Pass," and so entered it, without apology, into the Confederate record. It was held to be a military engagement with the same peculiar logic which had described the preceding timid skirmish outside Mesilla as a "great victory"; and Jud Reeves was learning more things about the anatomy of war and leadership than he cared to.

First was the ugly rumor that, shameful as the Fillmore affair had been on the surface, there was even less honor in it than met the eye. One of Lynde's highest officers bitterly and publicly charged immediately upon the surrender that Lynde's trusted adjutant, Lieutenant Brooks, was "a Secessionist, a traitor, and a paid spy," and had used his position to subvert and assist "the old imbecile Lynde" to the point of the collapse and panic which had resulted in his "infamous and cowardly scheme" for abandoning the fort.

Baylor did not dignify this accusation by denying it, leaving Jud to decide for himself whether or not his side had officially struck below the belt in seducing Major Lynde. Loyalty forbade him accepting the

191

story, but logic would not let him entirely reject it. It had that "certain smell" of rotten truth about it which the nose of conscience would not expel.

Next, there was the August 2nd abandonment and burning of Fort Stanton by Union Colonel B. S. Roberts, for no more reason than Baylor rattling the saber on the Rio Grande 154 miles southwest. This obvious act of panic was different from Lynde's only in two regards; it was carried out successfully, and it had 148 miles less reason for ever being carried out at all. Yet the Stanton commander was not even censored for his lack of courage, whereas his Fillmore counterpart was crucified for his.

Jud worried a lot about that and finally had to accept old Elkanah Cavanaugh's cynical opinion as the military truth. Said Baylor's Chief of Scouts, when asked: "Oh, it ain't being a coward that counts, boy; it's getting caught at it."

Then he had overheard Second Lieutenant Hugh Preston and Second Lieutenant Darrel Royce talking in Baylor's office about Lynde's having been given the Union command in the first place. "Where's the mystery?" Royce had asked. "He had the rank, he got the job. Since when has the army done business on the basis of ability?"

That was the same day of the Stanton abandonment and the issuance of Baylor's unauthorized proclamation declaring all that part of New Mexico lying south of the 34th parallel to be the Confederate Territory of Arizona, with Mesilla as the capital and himself the military governor thereof. Here was the naked hand of that ambition of which Cavanaugh had warned so long ago, revealed bold and clear. And it did not go unchallenged this time. Jud now saw added to the other unpleasant aspects of leadership never touched upon in the flowing prose of his father's and his grandfather's *Memoirs* the nasty facts of political maneuver and the counterattacking of hidden influences above the level of field command.

Somebody back in Richmond was already at work making sure that the career of Lieutenant Colonel John Robert Baylor stopped right where it was. The San Antonio adventurer had assuredly "kicked the door to the whole Southwest wide open," just as Cavanaugh had predicted he meant to do. But it rapidly became as apparent that he was not to be allowed to "walk right on through it," as the old man had said he planned to.

Baylor, of course, understood this situation and was proportionately discouraged by it. His resultant gloom, and Jud Reeves' growing depression over the seaminess of the maneuvers going on behind the lines of the "intrigue brigadiers" in the Capitol at Richmond, was further compounded the second week following the San Augustine surrender by the arrival of news from the north that Canby's command had been reinforced to 2,500 troops and that the Union commander had suspended the writ of *habeas corpus* in New Mexico.

This was on August 8.

Jud's rebellion against himself at once reached a point of absolute frustration.

Ten or twelve days ago, when Cavanaugh had talked him out of it by reminding him his name was Reeves, he could easily have gotten his discharge from the Mounted Rifles in the flush of victory. Now, with everything piling up against Baylor, there was no honorable way out. He had to stay with the Confederate commander, win or lose. All thought of going on back east to get in on the real war, as he had started to do in the beginning, and as he had been recently thinking he might still do, had now to be put unhappily out of mind.

It was in this uncertain mood that Cavanaugh found his young assistant the early evening of August 9.

The day had been another bad one. The Indian trouble had overnight turned deadly serious. A Confederate scout patrol up near Santa Rita had been ambushed and four men killed. A Southern cavalry troop had trailed the raiding party away from the Mexican settlement of Lagunas and shot down five of the red marauders in retaliation. Baylor, no longer ignoring the Apache threat, had been closeted with Cavanaugh and his staff since 4 P.M. trying to decide what to do about it. Now, having just left the meeting, the old scout came to a stand over the despondent Jud and queried softly, "What you thinking about, boy?"

"Lots of things," grunted Jud.

"Like maybe there's more to running a war than wearing a soldier suit?"

"Maybe."

"And like you wish you could chuck the whole thing along about now? Maybe head on back east and get in on the big fight? Or just forget you ever wanted to be a soldier in the first place and go set on a high lonely rock somewheres?"

"Could be."

"Boy?"

"Yeah."

"I just been three hours with Baylor."

"Hurrah for you."

"He give me a thirty-day leave to go hunting. I told him I thought you ought to go along."

"Why don't you mind your own damned business? Furthermore, what the hell you think you're going to hunt this time of year?"

"Indians. Baylor wants we should bring in the Apache who bosses this country from Santa Fe, south. The one who's been raising all the hell. He says to tell him to come on in and talk peace with the new Pony Soldiers, and all that usual line of rot. You know the stuff. Now what you say, boy? You want to go along?"

"I say you're crazy," shrugged Jud. "There's only one Indian I'd be interested in hunting up and his name isn't Red Sleeves."

"Red Sleeves?" queried the old man. "What the hell has he got to do with it?"

"He's the boss Apache in these parts, isn't he?" demanded Jud, referring to Mangas Coloradas, the implacable "Red Sleeves" who, next only to Cochise, was the most powerful of the Apache chiefs.

"Sure he is, but he's a Mimbreño. Ranges mostly west of the river. These birds we're after are Mescaleros. They're the big ones in the Mesilla Valley."

"I don't give a damn if they're the White Mountain Chiricahuas out under Cochise himself. There's still only one Apache I'd be interested in tracking down and I would think you would be too!"

"I am," said Elkanah Cavanaugh quietly. "And this is the one."

The truth broke over Jud Reeves like an upturned *olla* of ice water.

"Sobre—!" he gasped.

Cavanaugh's grin widened mirthlessly.

"You know any other Mescalero needs a dose of peacetalk any worse?" he asked.

"Whoa, boy!" shouted Jud, leaping to his feet, the tensions and disenchantments of soldiering with the 2nd Texas Mounted Rifles disappearing like desert rain before the sunshine of this new exitement. "Let's be on our way!"

They went immediately to the picketline and got their horses.

Jud's beautiful dapple gray had been eating oats out of a nosebag for better than ten days. He was as full of scat as a catnipped kitten. Even "old Whitey," Cavanaugh's shambling bone pile, was laying back his ears and showing a little ginger. Then, as they mounted up and swung away from the picketline, a third familiar horse loomed out of the gathering dusk to side their two with whickers of recognition and welcome all around: Junior's miserable black Navajo plug.

"Me decide go long by you," announced the Lipan tracker to Cavanaugh. "You get too damn old. You no smell him Indian like used to."

"You go to hell!" growled the white-haired army scout, but Jud could sense that what he meant was more like, "Glad to see you, you little redtailed bastard. Come right on along, you're welcome as the flowers in May."

They went up, that night, only as far as Dripping Springs, a rock-seep waterhole on the Apache trail to San Augustine Pass. Junior herded them into some rocks above the water and said, "Keep him pony quiet. We wait now. Him be here pretty quick you see." Before Jud could so much as ask who "him" was, a little cactus owl hooted three times out on the desert to the east and, when Junior had hooted back at him, floated on in to join them at the Springs. It proved to be a very paunchy owl with a Spanish accent and an Indian profile.

"*Buenas noches, amigos,*" said Gomez, the *Comanchero.* "We are all in good time. Let us make the best of it."

"*Despues de usted,*" nodded Cavanaugh, waving him to lead the way. "We are right behind you, my friend."

They rode at a brisk but not pushing gait until shortly before dawn when Gomez brought them to a well hidden *tinaja,* or pothole watertank, on the far side of the Organ and San Andreas Mountains. They made a fireless camp and lay up all the next day.

That night, and the nights thereafter, they rode steadily northeast up and across the great dry Tularosa Sink, past the weird and lifeless gypsum drifts of the White Sands to Alamogordo at the foot of the Sacramento Range. Here, Gomez left them. And here they turned due north toward Tularosa Town, then hard east to Bent's Mill and again northeast past Ruidoso and on into the brooding, timber-dark jumble of the Tres Cerros, Jicarilla and Capitan Mountains; so coming at last to the cedar and granite-guarded homeland of the Mescalero Apache.

It was four o'clock in the morning of August 13 when Elkanah Cavanaugh pulled up his old white gelding and grunted, "She's deep enough. We'll hole in right where we are, till there's light to see by."

"Me no like," complained Junior. "Too close. See too much." But he got down off his gaunt black mare despite his guttural grumbling, quickly taking both his white companions' mounts, along with his own, to "hide him damn horses so even sun no see."

Jud gave up his gray without any argument.

It was, for sure, high time to be holing in.

As of the old man's halting wave, they were one hundred crowflight miles out of Mesilla, standing 8,000 feet up on the north flank of 12,500-foot Sierra

Blanca Peak. And they would be, come daylight and according to the precise trail instructions furnished them by the hastily departed Gomez, staring straight down into the secret mountain valley rancheria of the one-eyed Mescalero war chief, Sobre.

In the blackness before dawn, Jud's weary mind marched clear back to the Topaz Creek homeplace, then on to Cavanaugh's ranch in Atascosa County, and from there to Fort Davis, El Paso, Mesilla and, finally, back to the darkened flank of Sierra Blanca Peak above Sobre's rancheria in the Tres Cerros Range of central New Mexico.

It was a long, long journey—a thousand miles and more by the turn of the trail and the bend of the river—but all that remained of it, that burned most brightly in the memory of Jud Reeves, was the luminous, faintly smiling face of Star Cavanaugh. All the rest of it was as though it had never happened. Or, happening, still did not matter in the least. To the lonely boy it was suddenly very clear that the sole thing which really did matter, then or later, was the tawny-skinned breed girl.

He had thought of nothing else in the four days and nights of their wary advance from Baylor's encampment outside Mesilla to this high mountain hiding place. Now, with daylight but minutes away, the feeling of her nearness seemed almost more than he could bear. Sleep, he would have thought, would be as far away from him as the coldest star. Yet drowse he did, and Cavanaugh's low-voiced words nearly jumped him out of his skin.

"She's out there, boy—out there somewheres—"

"Don't you ever come up on me like that!" gritted Jud. "Jesus. You like to scared me to death."

"Shouldn't have," said the old man bluntly. "We're in Apache country, Jud. You got to stay awake forty-eight hours a day. You were dreaming with your eyes wide open."

The silence set in, ran unbroken for several seconds. "Yeah, I know," admitted the younger scout at last. "I was thinking about her."

"Sure," said Cavanaugh, putting his long arm around his companion's shoulders. "So was I."

Again the silence set in.

Down below them on the mountainside, the first blue quail were beginning to argue about getting up. Over east, away over east, the rim of the prairie world was turning pale.

"Cavanaugh—"

"Yeah, Jud."

"You think we will find her?"

"I dunno, boy, I dunno."

"You think she will be all right, providing we do?"

"It ain't hardly likely. We got to admit that, no matter our praying it won't be so. They've had her long enough."

This time when the silence settled back in, it stayed a long, lonesome time. Finally, there was only the morning star left way over on the horizon. Jud shivered and said, "Cavanaugh, how's your Comanche Twitch?"

The bearded scout shook his head.

"I got the ache in my shankbones right after Gomez left us. The pain has been working up my backbone a joint a mile ever since. My head just now started to ache."

"Damn. That means they're powerful close."

"We *know* that, boy."

"Your eye twitch hasn't set in yet, though, has it?" asked Jud anxiously naming the last in the sequence of symptoms in his friend's legendary ability to "feel" the nearness of the red enemy.

"Funny thing," said the old man, "it just did."

Jud felt his stomach grow small.

"Where's Junior?" he whispered, glancing around in sudden alarm. "He's not come back from seeing to the horses. I *must have* dozed off!"

"He ain't," muttered Cavanaugh, "and you did. The red scout just took them crowbaits of ours and kept traveling."

"That's near an hour gone!"

"It is, boy. We might as well face it. *We're afoot.*"

The eerie stillness of the mountain daybreak seemed all at once magnified. Even the quail had quit calling on the slope below. Eastward, the rose flush of the coming sun was tipping the Capitans. Jud's voice sounded unnaturally loud to him in the echoing quiet.

"Maybe he was right about us having got too close

to Sobre's village," he croaked, hoarse with nerve strain. "What you think?"

"I think he was right," said a deep voice from the hillside behind them. "What do you think?"

The two white men froze, looking straight ahead.

"Don't move," rasped Cavanaugh. "Answer the bastard, but don't move!"

Jud swallowed noisily. His jaw muscles were so tightly strung it was an effort to get his lips parted far enough to form the words. But when he had done so, his reply did credit to the Topaz Creek strain of toughness which was his lean heritage.

"I think," said Jud Reeves, "that we have made a little mistake."

"Turn around," ordered Sobre, the darkskinned chieftain of the Three Hills Mescalero, "and see *how* little."

The white scouts came around very slowly. They left their guns where they lay in the rocks, their muzzles gaping down toward the Apache rancheria below.

"Jud," announced Elkanah Cavanaugh succinctly, "we're gone up."

"Cavanaugh," the tight-lipped boy nodded back as briefly, "that's so."

And with that they stood and waited.

The rocky flank .of the mountain immediately behind their boulder lookout was literally acrawl with swart, slant-eyed riflemen. In the complete stillness of the discovery moment, the musical clinking of triggers being put on cock throughout the scowling

Mescalero ranks seemed deafening. To Jud it sounded as loud as the clean ring of drill-steel under a six-pound jackhammer in pure quartz. He straightened with instinctive pride, wanting to stand tall before the smash of the Indian bullets cut him down. As he did, Sobre raised his hand.

"Welcome, *schichobe,*" he said gravely to the white youth. "Where have you been? We expected you much sooner than this."

"Watch it!" hissed Cavanaugh, pale blue eyes narrowing at the sound of the Apache word. "Either he's being funny, which an Apache never ain't, or he's actually tooken a shine to you. Treat him gentle, whichever. He just called you *old friend.*"

13

THEY WENT down the mountainside to the rancheria, which lay at about seven thousand feet. The valley which held the Apache "town" was an exquisite miniature of all high mountain valleys, the West and Southwest over. Although the growing season was short, the sunshine at that altitude was intense and what was put into the virgin soil would bear fruit. There was a plenitude of water from two forks of the crystal stream which spilled down off Sierra Blanca, to run lazily and loopingly across the little valley's floor, before plunging once more into its steep millrace of descent on the far side of Sobre's hidden paradise. With this water, the Tres Cerros Mescaleros, with an industry not common to the Apache, had irrigated a few fields of the vari-hued Indian corn and some patches of the hardy Rocky Mountain melons native to the regions farther north. The jacals, or beehive-shaped mud and cedar dwellings of the Mescaleros, were especially well built and maintained in this Three Hills rancheria of the proud young chief who now led the way down off the mountain. The women, old ones and button-eyed smaller children who stared from jacal or field as the white captives approached, were well dressed and well fed. Out beyond the irrigation ditches bordering the stream, the several pony bands grazing the fat mountain grass under guard of the older boys were in superb condition and showed a surprising amount of breediness and good conformation for an Indian *manada*. Jud had never seen an Apache rancheria and could not get over his astonishment at the evident high order and prosperity of this one. But his interest in Sobre's people was subdued by his awe at the spectacular place in which they dwelled.

"My God!" he said, *"it's beautiful!"*

He had spoken to himself and only half aloud, but Cavanaugh, marching a step behind him, had heard him.

The old man looked past the tall youth's squared shoulders, letting his eyes run the rearing granite walls of the hidden valley which was to be their prison or their tomb. He nodded as he did. It was in truth a place of unreal beauty. A wild and a brooding and a lonely place, too. Full of solitude, and splendor, and frightening silence. It was an unbelievable green jewel of lush grass, aspen, birch, poplar, pine, cedar, bending willow and seedling wild grape, all set in a fantastic mounting of platinum water, harsh red rock and raw blue sky. The pagan impact of it struck a man simultaneously dumb, humble, sad and afraid. It left him shaking his head and thinking inside himself, My God, my God, it *is* beautiful! And it left him, too, with a deep and poignant ache of wanting to tell, so powerfully bad that it hurt like a heart pain, just how truly wonderful and mind-staggering was this great work of the Lord's. Yet, finally, he could think of nothing more expressive to say than had Jud Reeves, and so had helplessly to leave it in the end as he had found it in the beginning—undescribed because undescribable.

Cavanaugh had seen many places like this. The haunting lure of them was what had driven him on these forty years of nomad wandering. Each time a man thought "next time" I will be able to understand. "Next time" I will feel the gladness without the lonesome fear. "Next time" I will stay and seek no more, for I will have found my trail's end and will know it and so will wander no farther. The inside hurting and the outside awesomeness will be gone and, "next time," I will have come home. I will have found my *querencia*.

Querencia was a Spanish word meaning an animal's loveplace, his natural home, his place of retreat and safety above all others. It told, better than any English word, what restless men who are born without the capacity of tolerance for the close company of their fellows are looking for when they roam the outtrails of the wilderness.

Yet in forty years Cavanaugh had not found his *querencia*. Now the bitter swiftness of time's flight was telling him more strongly with each passing day that he never would.

It was a strange moment for such thoughts—being marched under guard into a life or death of Apache cruelty—but he saw, in the way Jud Reeves looked at that valley of impossible beauty which walled them in, the same yearning and hunger he had felt himself those useless, squandered years ago; and he was determined that, live or die, the boy should not suffer the hurt and the heartache of that phantom, hopeless dream which had destroyed his own small chances of a home and happiness. Come what may, Jud Reeves had to be gotten out of that valley before its wild call lured him away from his own color and kind, as another valley beneath another mountain in another time had lured Elkanah Cavanaugh.

The days became weeks and their endless, sunny chain extended into September. The Mescalero Autumn Songs and the Apache Corn Prayers were danced away. The days, still golden with warmth, became shorter. The nights grew cold. The high air became thin and sharp with the hoar-frost warning of coming winter. And still the white scouts languished in their granite-barred prison, listening to the drums and the dance chants and wondering when the savage rhythms would change into the chilling, minor key cries of *Dah-eh-sah,* the Dance of the Dead.

But the drums did not summon them with the dread cadence, and their strange imprisonment went on.

By night they slept in the big jacal of Chavez, Sobre's iron-gray second in command. By day they were sent to shuck or grind corn—women's work—or taken to the pastures to help in horse-breaking or branding—the labor of men—or put to digging new *acequias* for the irrigated fields—a menial indignity fit only for slaves. And always and wherever they went, they went in company with Chebo and Askanay. They were not chained or physically restricted in any way during the daytime. But they understood the typically Apache terms of their parole. If they broke for freedom Chebo and Askanay would shoot them. If Chebo and Askanay did *not* shoot them, then Chebo and Askanay would be shot. It made for a very clear understanding all around, assuring the docility of the prisoners in the same arrangement which guaranteed the alertness of their guards. At night the problem was simpler. Chavez padlocked them by ancient stake chains and iron collars (the relics of some Conquistador's slave column) to logs in the wall of the jacal. Each time the bachelor subchief would turn the great key in the rusted locks and replace its leather thong around his bronzed neck he would nod, not unpleasantly, "If I hear the slightest sound of a chain being worked with, I will kill you both."

Beyond these fundamental restraints there was one other which puzzled them. They were not allowed at any time to talk to, or to be with, any of the Apache women. Jud thought this might be because their captors feared they might "work on" the softer sex, possibly soliciting them successfully for aid in escaping. Cavanaugh scowled and said it was a sight more likely it was being done to keep the women from working on them, and Chebo, who overheard the remark and was as good-natured as Apaches came, had grinned and said that Tall Horse was right as rain in the sprouting month and that the big young *guero* would do well to remember as much.

The final peculiarity of their imprisonment concerned Star Cavanaugh.

They had neither one of them so much as seen the girl since their arrival at the rancheria, and their repeated attempts to question their guards about her whereabouts and well being drew only blank stares or grunting shrugs. Finally, two days ago, Askanay had struck Jud across the mouth with the flat of his rifle-butt and said in Spanish, the common language, "I am tired of hearing about the cursed girl. Ask me once more and I will kill you." He had added, *"Sabe usted, 'zas-tee?"* emphasizing the Apache expletive for "kill!" and Jud had nodded that his growing Mescalero vocabulary did indeed include the definition of *zas-tee,* and that he was grateful to Askanay for the reminder in the mouth, just now, and would remember him for it.

"De nada, it is nothing," Askanay had answered him straightfaced.

There, was one thing, and one alone, which the white scouts *did* understand about their situation. The indecision and delay in their case, the half friendly Chebo let slip the following day, was due to an argument of fundamental politics going forward between Grito and Sobre since the day of the taking of Tall Horse and *El Guero* on the mountainside above. Sobre was holding that Tall Horse would not lie; that he was telling the truth when he told them he was coming to ask them in for another peacetalk; and that if the Apaches had not taken him and *El Guero* prisoner, they would have come into the rancheria of their own accord and without fear. Grito would have none of such nonsense. The two gringos would never have come down off that mountain except as captives, and the only reason they had been up there was to spy on the rancheria so that they could lead the *soldados* back down upon it and destroy it. As for Grito, he would never believe a white man and had but one ambition for all of them.

Dah-eh-sah. Death.

The entire matter, Chebo now informed Jud and Cavanaugh on the morning of the third day following Askanay's attack on the former, was presently coming very close to a vote. In fact, Chebo believed, the short sticks and the long ones were being counted up at the medicine man's *kinh* right then, while they stood there talking outside the jacal of old Chavez. In further fact, the roundfaced brave added thoughtfully, he was as glad that this was so. It was not that he had anything against Tall Horse or Guero (Jud was identified as *El Guero,* The Blond, and this shortened to "Guero" in the familiar) but they must realize that guarding them was tedious work. *Anh!* yes, and dangerous, too. Chebo grew mightily weary of it. He would frankly be very happy to be rid of them.

Cavanaugh eyed Jud when he heard that term "rid of." He did not care for the particular way in which the squat warrior had used it, and asked him for a clarification.

"Oh, well," the affable savage did not hesitate to shrug, "that is a very simple matter. You see, if the vote goes in your favor you will be set free, and if it does not, you will be shot. *Sabes ustedes?*"

"*Completamente,*" the white-haired scout nodded politely. "*Un millón de gracias. Es usted muy amable.*"

It was nearing 8 P.M. that same night, September 16, 1861, that Sobre sent for Jud to be brought up to his jacal.

In the guttering light of the lamb's-fat lamp set upon the earthen floor, the darkskinned Apache seemed more fiercely handsome than ever. Jud's gesture of respect toward him upon entering the windowless structure—a quick touch of the left fingertips to the

210

forehead—was spontaneous. Sobre recognized this. He returned the sign with graceful dignity and said in Spanish, *"Sientase, señor, por favor."*

It was a peculiar admixture of the imperative command and the polite personal, Jud noted, and he wondered what that meant, if anything.

But he only answered, *"Gracias,"* and sat down as directed, leaving the lead where it belonged, with the Indian youth.

Sobre studied him for some minutes, his look of grave dignity growing more and more tinged with doubt and distaste of what he had, shortly, to tell the white boy. Presently, to put off the time of the telling, he held out a doeskin pouch and asked, in Apache, *"Na-to?"*

Jud, who did not smoke, shook his head.

"Dah, na-to. No, no tobacco," he replied haltingly in the same tongue. Then in explanatory Spanish. "Thank you, but I do not use it."

"Nor do I," nodded Sobre. "We are much alike, my brother." He paused, thoughtfully studying his guest. Presently he nodded and went on, his rich voice deep with emotion. Jud listened, spellbound.

Sobre was a troubled redman.

The son and grandson of chiefs, he said, he had come into his position by heredity among a people who did not believe in, nor practice, the policy of tribal power being passed down by blood. Among the Apaches, any man could be a chief. And the Apaches preferred that any man should be chief. So jealous and savage was their love of their wild freedom that any hint of authority was resented and in the case of Sobre, where that authority was now in its third generation, the resentment became first a nameless restlessness, then an outright fear, eventually an active anger.

The basic truth was that the Apaches were, as all horseback Indians of the far West, fanatics about personal freedom. To them, democracy was not a political label, it was a pure religion.

With every brave in the tribe thus doing exactly as he pleased, when he pleased and in the manner which most appealed to him at the moment, concerted effort of any kind was impossible. The result was more frequently anarchy than democracy. And the whole ugly weakness of the redman's war against the white lay precisely in this area of stubborn refusal of the warriors to follow orders, or even to listen to them. Young Sobre's cross was that it had been given to him by his father to understand this weakness of the Apache people, and charged to him by the same proud source to see that he used his life to protect his people from this disease of individual liberties. The way, and the only way to do this, was to give them leadership. And to give it to them whether they wanted it or not.

"Remember always," the old man had said, "that to buy a little freedom, much freedom must be spent."

Teach that to the people, Sobre had been told, and if they would not accept the lesson in good part, then beat it into them with a lancehaft. If stronger instruction were needed, there was always *besh,* the knife, or *besh-e-gar,* the rifle.

So far Sobre had not used either club, dagger or gun. But in this second year of his leadership big trouble had come upon the Desert People. Despite all that Cochise, the great Chiricahua, had been able to do, hot-heads and cultists of the old Apache *Hesh-Ke* Sect—a secret lodge brotherhood whose name was taken from the Apache word for "a rage to kill"—had begun to raid the white settlements. Grito and a band of Tres Cerros Mescalero had been among these renegades.

Now, Sobre himself was no friend of the white man's. He had never been of such a mind. His father's advice had not included any instruction that he should be. "Only avoid them," the old chief had said. "As the wolf avoids the poisoned bait. Circle wide around them when you see them. If you do not see them and are forced into a fight, then kill all that you can. And, if you can, kill *all.* For if there is one left to bear the tale, a hundred will return in his place and the Desert People will die again."

This was the way that Lieutenant May and his fifteen Pony Soldiers had died at Fort Davis. They had followed too close and made the Apache fight. And again it had been Grito and his fanatics who had started it all by raiding the stockpens and setting fire to the fort.

Sobre did not claim innocence of blame for that massacre. The responsibility was his and he accepted it.

But he was not the hater and the killer of white men that the latter said he was.

He did not blame the white men for thinking so; he only denied to his friend, Guero, that it was true.

He had killed, yes. And he would kill again. The white men would not have it any other way. They hated the Apache and the Apache did not love them. It had been so from the first, save for the little time of Cochise. Now that was over and Mangas Coloradas was the leader. The Mimbreños were in power and Mangas Coloradas, their chief, was a *Hesh-Ke*.

Now there would be war.

No white man could stop it, no Indian would want to. War was in the autumn air. The excitement of it was too strong in the Apache nostrils to be expelled now. The new Pony Soldiers had made a great mistake in trying to talk peace and to be brothers to the Apaches. Sobre's people had taken this as a sign of weakness in the *Tejas soldados*. Sobre himself knew better. He, for one, was sorry about the Fort Davis treachery. It was the whole trouble with the Indian way. While one chief made peace, his brother chief was making war. While Sobre shook hands with the enemy at Fort Bliss, Grito was killing him at Fort Davis. This was not the white man's fault. It was the Indian's. But until the white man could be made to understand that this was the Indian's way, there could never be any peace or any sensible talk of peace. The Pony Soldiers could not go on killing one Apache's people for what some other Apache's people had done. When a white man murdered a white man, did the *soldados* go out and hang six other white men who never even heard of the murder?

"*Dah, schichobe,* no, old friend," he concluded, reaching to place a slim red hand on Jud's shoulder, "until your people stop killing mine simply because they are Apaches, there can be no peace between us. I tell you all this, Guero, so that you will understand what I must next say."

He fell silent, then, dropping his glance from Jud's face and plainly not wanting to go on.

After a moment, Jud hesitantly returned the shoulder touch, and Sobre at once brought his face up from its brooding study of the jacal floor.

"Will you tell me one other thing," said Jud, "before you say why it is you have sent for me?"

"Ask it," nodded his companion.

"Why do you call me 'old friend'? We are enemies, you and I. And for more reasons than the colors of our skins. Do you know what I mean?"

Sobre knew well what he meant. It was the yellow-haired girl.

"*Anh,*" he said, "I know."

"Well, then?"

Sobre looked at him for the better part of a full minute. It was the Apache way. Unlike the white brother, the Indian had a habit of thinking before he talked. That was because what he said was important to him, and would have to be stood by. It was not just words. Not just pebbles in the mouth to be spat out so that the tongue might be more comfortable, or given more room to wag.

"In our lives," he replied at last and slowly, "we meet many men. Their numbers are as the leaves of the aspen. And as the leaves of the aspen they talk too much and say too little. You and I have not said three score words before tonight. But in the first instant we met, our eyes talked and your eyes said to me, 'I am your friend. My heart is good for you. I am glad to see you.' Do you remember that time, Guero?"

"Yes," said Jud. "It was when you came into the room at Fort Bliss. The first time you talked to Baylor."

"And did I read your eyes wrong?"

"No. I was thrilled to see you. I felt a great pride in the way you stood so tall and unafraid."

"Did you feel only pride? Nothing else?"

"Yes, there was something else," Jud admitted. "I felt sorry for you. I wanted to put my arm around your shoulders and tell you that you had a friend there. I wanted you to understand that, but of course we couldn't talk."

"We *did* talk," said Sobre softly. "I understood you. I knew I had a friend there, and that it was you. That is why I call you *schichobe;* that was a long time ago, but an Apache does not forget. Among all those we meet upon the long trail, only a few, no more in one life than the fingers of a man's right hand, do we remember as our true friends."

The Apache youth paused, holding up his hand.

216

"Here is my right hand, Guero. I count you first among its fingers."

Then, before Jud could think to answer this simple testament of instinctive trust, the Indian boy reached out and offered the upheld member to his white companion.

"From this night when our hands touch," he said, "we are brothers."

Jud took Sobre's grip, returning it with impulsive feeling. Then belated embarrassment overcame them both, and they pulled their hands apart with awkward haste.

"Now," said the Apache youth, after a moment of emotional recovery, "I must tell you what it is that brings you here."

"Gracias," nodded Jud. He was confident now, feeling far better than he had when brought up to the young chief's jacal only minutes before by the scowling Askanay and his talkative mate, Chebo. Whatever it was Sobre had to tell him, it could not be as bad as he had feared. Probably he and Cavanaugh were going to be banished, taken down the mountain and turned free, their peace mission a complete failure. Since such a failure involved a man's pride, Jud could see where an Apache would think it was a pretty bad thing. This would account for Sobre's unhappy earlier looks, as well as his present worried frown. To the Indian youth he said graciously, "Do not be concerned. Whatever it is, I will understand that you had no choice but to do it. *No es verdad?"*

"Yes," said Sobre, "it is true; I had no choice. Among my people, where such matters of the entire band's good are involved, the vote of the headman is final. In this case, where the security of the rancheria was at stake, you could not win."

"De nada, my brother," shrugged Jud, still magnanimous with the relief of a simple expulsion from the Apache camp. "How did the vote go?"

Sobre looked at him, his single fierce eye afire in the shadowed light of the lampwick.

"It went bad," he said, low-voiced. "You will be shot in the morning, when the sun strikes the peaks of the Capitans."

Askanay pushed Jud with his moccasin sending him sprawling through the low-beamed door of Chavez's jacal. "Lock him up!" he snapped at the old man. "Sobre is going to shoot him in the morning. Yes," he sneered at Cavanaugh, "and this bony old horse with him." He eyed Chavez a moment, then added, "You'd better not sleep tonight. If anything happens to these two, Grito will cut your liver out."

"Grito will do well to worry about his own liver," replied the gray-haired Apache quietly.

"When he is chief, I will remind him you said so," growled Askanay.

"Do that," nodded Chavez. "But now do something else. Get out of my doorway. The wind is from your direction and the stink is like a sick dog."

"I will remember that, too!" snarled the ill-tempered

brave. "All things will be remembered when Grito is chief!"

"I fear your bark like the yapping of *Enh,* the fierce prairie dog," Chavez advised him. "You are a fit companion for Grito. Both of you are great fighters with your mouth." The grizzled subchief picked up his rifle. "I am cocking *besh-e-gar,"* he explained. "That is because I am going to fire a shot through my doorway."

Askanay cursed and leaped aside as the belch of smoke and flame from the old man's rifle burst in Jud's and Cavanaugh's ears. The big .50-caliber slug from the Pony Soldier carbine splintered the door-beam, whined wickedly off into the night. There was a raving string of Apache profanity from outside, then dead silence as Chavez fired a second shot right through the jacal wall in the direction of Askanay's curses, *"Besh-e-gar,"* said the old man, putting down the gun, "speaks a language they all understand."

"That is a true thing," answered Cavanaugh in Apache. Then, quickly, "What do you think, Old One? Will the young chief truly shoot us?"

Chavez lifted his shoulders.

"We are both *ancianos,"* he said. "Why should we lie to one another? If the headmen voted with Grito, you will be shot. Sobre has no choice."

"That's what he said," put in Jud aimlessly.

"He said a true thing," grunted Chavez. "Now be quiet. It is late. I want to sleep."

"One favor," requested Cavanaugh. "Let me ask

about my daughter of Guero, here. You must know how a father feels."

"I am not a father," said Chavez. "But I have seen your daughter. I would want to know about her if she were mine. Go ahead, but be quick."

"Gracias," Cavanaugh thanked him, and turned on Jud. "Well, what did he say? Is she all right? Where is she? What have the bastards done with her?"

"By God!" blurted Jud, "I don't know!"

"You what!!" cried Cavanaugh.

"I honest-to-God don't know!" pleaded the guilty youth. "I was so bowled over by him telling me we were going to get shot, I plumb forgot to ask him. Before I remembered, Askanay was booting me through the doorway yonder."

The old Indian fighter sagged down in his iron dog collar, his back against the jacal wall.

"Cavanaugh," muttered Jud, "I'm just as sorry as I can be. And as ashamed. I guess I just stampeded when Sobre hit me with that bad vote. I thought they were going to turn us loose. It looked to me like everything was going to wind up friendly, and that we'd no great need to worry about Star, right off. I mean, providing she was all right and just being hid out while they powwowed what to do with us."

Swiftly, then, he told the old man about his meeting with the young chief, up to its abrupt ending. But Cavanaugh wasn't buying any extenuating circumstances.

"Jud," he said, "you'd ought to have knowed better.

I went all over it with you a dozen times. Maybe your friend Sobre is different, like you say, and maybe he ain't. But this here Grito is pure Apache. He'd argue that once we had seen the rancheria we couldn't be let go free, no matter why we had come in the first place. I told you that would be his line and I told you he'd make it stick." He shook his shaggy head and looked at Jud in a way that went into him like a knife. "The least thing you could have did, boy, was to find out what you might about my girl. It would have helped me a mortal lot to stand up to the red devils in the morning to know that she was all right."

While Jud struggled for an answer to his companion's rightful reproach, a tall shadow fell across the packed earth floor between them and the vibrant voice of Sobre startled them both.

"I will tell you about the girl," he said to Cavanaugh. "You are her father. I understand."

"Thank you," said the old man.

"*De nada, anciano.* I meant to tell Guero, and forgot. So I came now." He paused and both his white listeners could see that it was not easy for him to talk about Star. Shortly, they knew why.

"I love this *nah-lin* with the yellow hair," he murmured. "From the moment I saw her with Red Dog, I knew my heart was hers."

He paused again, the effort to continue such a confession to white men clearly a great one.

"But," he went on at last, "a proud man will not take by force what he cannot gain by willing surrender.

221

This *nah-lin* loves another: She told me this and I believed her, for I had seen the other one. I have not touched her, my friends, and she is well. Let me tell you, *anciano,* that I shall never take her unless she comes to me, and I shall protect her against all others while I wait and pray for her to do so. And let me tell you, Guero, something that turns in me like a rusted lanceblade: *you are the other one that she loves!"*

As silently and swiftly as he had come, the Apache chief was gone.

Jud and Cavanaugh sat looking at one another, searching for something to break the heavy silence Sobre had left behind him.

Presently the old scout muttered, "You're dead right about that Indian, boy. He's a stray, for sure."

"Shut up!" grated Chavez, from his blankets across the room. "Women. Love. Pride. Bah! Shut up." He turned his face to the wall, sighed wearily and began to snore. He was deep in sleep before the light of the new moon had crept an inch across the packed earth floor of his stale-aired jacal.

Jud came awake, startled that he had dozed.

He listened, as a man will, when everything is dead quiet in the night.

He heard nothing. The Apache village was asleep.

Three or four ridges back from the valley, a lonesome coyote barked without answer from the rancheria dogs. Striking full into the doorway now, the moon threw its light across the floor of the jacal like a lantern. Over against his wall Chavez was snoring fit-fully.

He lay on his back gasping and hawking in the top of his throat for air the way an old person does. It seemed nothing short of the earth opening would awaken him, yet Jud knew the least chain rattle or whisper of guarded talk would bring the wrinkled sub-chief out of his blankets with *besh-e-gar* cocked and aimed.

He glanced at Cavanaugh.

The white-haired scout sat on his hams as he had since moon-up, staring out the jacal door, wide awake yet far away in his thoughts. For some reason Jud glanced back at the doorway himself, perhaps just to make sure the old man was not seeing some-thing out there which he was not. As he did, his spine stiffened.

There was a shadow in that moonlight, one which had not been there fifteen seconds before.

Instantly, he flicked his eyes toward Cavanaugh and saw that the latter had lost his staring look and was leaning forward, head cocked, watching the shadow on the floor as an old hound watches a bug crawling across the boards of the back stoop.

Their eyes met. Cavanaugh nodded. Jud nodded back. They waited.

The shadow moved. Stopped. Moved again. Froze.

Seconds slipped by. A full minute passed.

Suddenly, a naked human figure stood in the doorway. Next instant it had slid inside the jacal, was invisible against the front wall. They waited, listening. There was nothing.

Then there was something. In the moonlight over by old Chavez. The naked figure again. Crouched and leaning over the sleeping Apache, an iron-hard burl of mesquite root in its hand. The hand moved. There was a grunt from Chavez as the heavy wood struck him behind the ear. Then the dry rattle of his bear-claw necklace being disturbed by probing fingers was heard. With that, the sinister figure had stepped back into the doorway moonlight. There it stood, grinning at Jud and Cavanaugh, the ancient Spanish padlock key from Chavez's neck dangling in its small dark hand.

Could it be? Was it possible? Junior, the thieving Lipan tracker? The traitorous red scoundrel who had stolen their horses and fled with them to save his own cowardly skin? Yet, indeed, it *was* he. There could be no mistaking that puckish grin, those quick, monkey-like movements, nor, God bless him, that wonderful gift for reducing a complex situation into simple English.

Said the little Texas Apache unhurriedly, "Me unlock collars. Goddam. We all run like hell."

With this sentiment, he put the rusted key into the socket of Jud's verdigrised dog collar and gave it a grating turn. When the latter was free, Junior handed him the key and scuttled back toward Chavez, who was beginning to sit up and groan. By the time Jud had uncollared Cavanaugh, the Lipan was back dragging Chavez by the heels.

"What in the world you got in his mouth?" whispered the white boy, noting the crude gag jammed between Chavez's straining jaws.

"Him 'Comanche bridle,'" shrugged Junior. "Him open mouth to yell, him strangle. Him got to hold bit in teeth so can breathe. One way or other, him keep quiet."

Jud hunted up Chavez's Springfield carbine while his companions locked the subchief into one of the dog collars. They knew the inside of the jacal by heart after their many weeks in it. Everything they needed was there, and they took it. Minutes later, laden with a sack of corn grist, three belts of Pony Soldier ammunition for the carbine, an army canteen of water and a new pair each of soft-tanned *n'deh b'keh,* the blunt-toed, calf-high Apache moccasins, the three friends stole out of the jacal.

In the sharp clean bath of the outer moonlight they waited a moment, letting their cramped limbs get the blood into them for the life's run which lay ahead.

There was still no sound in the village.

The black beehives of the Mescalero jacals stood dark and silent, dotted at rest upon the valley floor like sleeping buffalo. No smoke showed from any of their central smokeholes, indicating the lateness of the hour, all cookfires having died to cold ash hours gone.

"What time you reckon it is?" muttered Jud, shivering to the dawnchill of seven thousand feet in September.

"Late," said Cavanaugh, eying the eastern grayness over behind the Capitans: "Damn late."

Junior, as usual, narrowed down the observation.

"Sonbitch," grunted the laconic Lipan. "Him time we go."

14

ONCE PAST the last jacal and out beyond the final field, they swung into a dogtrot across the valley, away from the stream. Cavanaugh followed Junior. Jud brought up the rear. None of them spoke. Without horses and with daylight and discovery of their escape only an hour away, there was no breath to spare for speeches. Nor time to waste on argument. Junior's course, furthermore, was clear.

The Lipan tracker was heading due southwest, to get into the gorge of Tres Cerros Creek, one of the two forks which formed the little Sierra Blanca River which flowed down the center of Sobre's beautiful valley.

The rough floor of the tumbling creeklet led upward so precipitously and so badly broken by ledges, slips and dykes in the naked baserock that initial pursuit by horseback was impossible. With typical Indian cunning, Junior had planned an escape route which would guarantee them a minimum two-hour start. And more. Once they hit the canyon of the Tres Cerros, they would leave no trail. The going was granite heart-rock all the way. The suede leather soles of their stolen *n'deh b'keh* would leave no more print upon it than the passage of a falling leaf through the autumn wind.

They climbed in continuing silence, taking cruel punishment from the sharp rocks and slashing creek-brush, yet as daylight tipped the Capitans they stood two thousand feet above the floor of Sobre's valley and had won their race against the sun.

Below them, even as they watched panting and gasping from their lung-bursting ascent, the Mescalero rancheria came suddenly, swarmingly awake.

"*Wagh,*" grinned Junior. "Good thing we got him horse."

"What!" cried Cavanaugh and Jud together. "You've got the horses?"

"Sure. Me got more than horse, too. You come see. Just over hill on other side. What you think me do all time you sit on bottom?"

"By God!" said Cavanaugh, "you tell me! I thought you was still running for home."

"You damn old fool. Me say you that back him soldier camp Mesilla." He jerked his birdlike head toward Jud. "Boy, him remember me say you need mother on trail now. *No es verdad, niño?*"

"*Verdad* as all hell!" laughed Jud. "Let's get on over the mountain. Our friends down yonder aren't waiting for breakfast."

Junior glanced down toward the Apache rancheria.

The Mescaleros were mounting up and streaming

off *down* the valley, almost directly away from the line of flight taken by their released prisoners.

The Lipan's deep-seamed face darkened.

"Me no like," he said abruptly. "Sonbitch."

"What the hell you mean?" challenged Cavanaugh, still smarting over being accused of senility by an Indian he personally knew to be older than Yosen, the Apache God. "We'd ought to give 'em three cheers. They're going the wrong way."

Junior looked at him, really worried about his old friend now. Tall Horse should know better than what he had just said. It was true he was getting too many years for this work, but still—

The wizened red man broke off the thought, grimacing unhappily.

"Him Apache never go wrong way," he corrected Cavanaugh gently. Then, quickly, and forcing the bright, wall-eyed grin. "Tall Horse make him joke on Junior. Him heap funny sonbitch."

The old scout squinted at him. He was not a funny son of a bitch and he had not meant to make any joke. Yet he did not flare back at the little Lipan in his usual blustery way. He simply looked at him and knew that his red friend of twenty years on the Texas trails was not making a joke either. This was a time that all men dreaded. That made bad dreams for them from the time they were forty. And that suddenly, in some little way just like this, was no longer a dream but a waking, belly-sinking, broad-daylight fact.

"Sure, that's right, Junior," he said softly, putting his

big hand on the little Lipan's thin shoulder. "Only this time the joke's on me. Let's go—"

They went swiftly the rest of the way, coming but minutes later into the tiny boulder-rimmed meadow high on the west haunch of Sierra Blanca, where Junior had said he had more than their horses waiting for them. The Texas Apache was as good as his word. When Jud and Elkanah Cavanaugh broke free of the last of the boulders and saw the horses standing before them, hock-deep in the September hay, their mouths dropped open and their hearts came up in their throats.

Sitting on Junior's slabsided black, holding Jud's iron-gray and her father's rheumatic old white, was Star Cavanaugh.

Cavanaugh himself could not speak. He just stood there, the tears bumping down the channels of his weathered cheeks aglitter in the morning sunlight.

Star, too, began to cry.

Jud couldn't think of anything to say and was feeling pretty well left out of the whole reunion. Junior supplied the spellbreaker.

"Catchum horse from girl," he ordered the two white men. "You ride, me run. No time powwow."

There was, indeed, no time for talk. Jud and Cavanaugh legged it for their horses. Once aboard, they lined them out after Junior who led the way now in a wolf lope; a gait he could hold half a day and which was all the horses could keep up with along the mountainside trail.

The track they were taking plunged steeply downward from the divide of the Tres Cerros Range, aiming straight into a thousand-foot-deep canyon looming directly below them. It appeared the trail would take them and their horses out into the empty air, hurtling them to their deaths on the sawtoothed rocks of the canyon's floor far below. But it hit bottom before long and was good from there south to the open plateau country west of Ruidoso.

When they hit this easier going, Star had her first chance to answer the questions both Jud and Cavanaugh had been gritting at her between leaps down the dangerous trail above.

Sobre had treated her, she said, like an Apache princess. Nothing which could be done for her comfort, within Mescalero limits, was overlooked. Up to the time of Jud's and Cavanaugh's captures, her time among the Three Hills people had been actually exciting. But the mood of the whole camp had changed when they came down off the mountain with Sobre. Grito had convinced most of the band that all of this spying and all of the disaster which was sure to follow it was the direct result of Sobre's having lost his head over the *niña tostada,* the light-brown girl. Overnight, the mood of the people had gone against Star and Sobre had been forced to get her out of the rancheria until the temper of his savage followers might cool. He had moved her over the mountain to an ancient pueblo of the cliff dwellers in the walls of this same canyon they now followed southward. They would see this old ruin around the next turn of the trail, Star now concluded, and it would speak better for itself than she could. Meantime, she added, Junior had somehow discovered Sobre's secret hiding place. He had gotten her out of it only the past midnight, telling her merely that he had stolen into the Apache rancheria earlier that evening, lain up outside the meeting *kinh* and heard the vote go against the captive *nan-tans,* the white scouts. As for the rest, they knew all she did about it. She had done nothing, she insisted, flashing her white-toothed smile, "except hold the horses."

"Well," said her father, when she had finished, "it's clear we all owe Junior one. I don't know, either, how we can ever repay him. What he's did, there ain't six people alive could do, and if I live to be a hundred and sixty-five I'll never understand it."

The old man paused to wave back to the little Lipan who was beckoning for them to quit talking and pick up their gait. Then he shook his head wonderingly.

"Thirty-three days he's lived and kept fat three horses within five miles of one hundred fifty Mescalero Apaches. You realize what that means? God Almighty, there ain't ten white men in the world could do it twenty-four hours. I ain't never heard of a piece of scouting to match it in forty years. It's just plain hard to believe!"

"It *is*," said Jud, unexpectedly quiet about it and scowling at Star when he said it. "And it's not all that's hard to believe about this business."

"Oh?" queried the halfbreed girl, not waiting for her

father to take up the challenge obviously meant for her. "Now what?"

"You," growled the Topaz Creek youth sullenly. "You and that cliff ruin of your friend Sobre's."

"Yes?"

"What kept you there? Why didn't you cut and run when he left you alone? It's only a few miles into Ruidoso—all downhill."

"Sure," said Star Cavanaugh, green eyes flashing, soft voice turned scathingly furious, "and it's only thirty feet from the pueblo to the bottom of the canyon, too—likewise all downhill."

"Huh?" gruffed Jud, blinking like an owl caught in bright sunlight.

"He took the ladder away, you damn fool!" yelled Cavanaugh's daughter, and spurred her horse so suddenly past him she nearly put him into the canyon wall.

The rest of it went so swiftly it was difficult to realize it was happening.

They came to the bend in the canyon beyond which lay the Indian ruins where Sobre had secreted Star Cavanaugh. The heat of the day was mounting and the horses needed a short rest and a little water. Junior took them to the creekside while his three white companions dismounted to ease the saddlecramp of the hard ride down into the canyon. Star was pointing out the site of the ancient pueblo, perhaps a quarter mile ahead, and explaining its features to Cavanaugh. Jud, being thoroughly ignored and resenting it, sat on a water-polished rock eavesdropping sulkily.

He happened to be watching Junior while he was about it and sensed, rather than saw, the shadow of some warning evil above the little Lipan. His eyes leaped upward and cross-canyon. They halted with a jarring flinch on a headland of granite which cropped out from the far wall to spill a tributary creek into the main stream. The bed of the higher canyon lay some three hundred feet above theirs, and there were two throat-constricting things about its present situation with regard to the parent gorge.

First, there was a good switchback pony trail coming down from it to the crossing at which Junior was watering their horses.

Second, the rock outcrop off which the trail led downward was surmounted by the motionless profiles of four dozen Mescalero Apache horsemen.

Jud cried out and leaped to his feet as Grito's rifle snaked shoulderward. Junior tried, belatedly, to get behind the horses. But the white boy's warning cry had come too late. Grito's bullet spun the small Lipan twice around, knocked him back-flat into the shallow stream.

Instantly, a perfect storm of Apache fire drove down at the rearing horses. The wolflike eagerness of the Mescaleros to get down the ponies of their escaped prisoners was all that saved Jud Reeves now.

At the crack of the Apache's rifle, Jud was racing for Junior's fallen body. Before the startled redmen above could guess his intention, he had seized and scooped up the Lipan's slight form and was running, bent beneath its burden, back to the rock from behind which Cavanaugh was covering him with Chavez's carbine. Apache lead bit and snapped at the air around him, smashed at the creek gravel beneath his stumbling feet, whined off the boulders through which he zigzagged toward Star and the old man. But the few seconds of breaking their aims from the squealing horses to put them on the fleeing *Tejano* boy, plus the trickiness of firing downward out of sunlight into shadow, was too great a handicap for the Mescalero marksmen. Jud made it to the big rock without a scratch.

Junior was not so lucky.

He had a hole in his belly you could put your thumb in to the base knuckle and still not plug the pump of the blood. He could live possibly an hour, possibly a day, if they could stop the bleeding.

Decision: take the little Lipan, or leave him, on their dash for the centuries-old pueblo?

Cross-canyon, now, the Mescaleros were cascading down the side-creek trail, baying and howling like so many wolves running a blood trail.

"Pick him up," said Elkanah Cavanaugh, and Jud nodded and reached down to seize the tiny Lipan.

But Junior had reached a different decision.

That hole was in *his* belly and only he could feel the great cold spreading outward from it to creep up his spine and down into his legs.

"Don't touch me!" he pleaded with Jud. "Me *dah-eh-sah,* boy. Tall Horse!" he appealed to Cavanaugh, "you tell boy Junior *dah-eh-sah.*"

The old scout knelt quickly, handing Chavez's Springfield to Jud. He looked into the small man's face and took his tiny red hand in his own great ones and said, "What is it, old friend? Is it that you know?"

"*Anh,* yes!" gasped Junior. "It is *nah-welh-coht kah-el-keh,* I ask of you. It is Indian law. You must do it. Give me my gun and go quickly, *schichobe.* Here is my hand in yours for the last time."

He gave Cavanaugh's huge paw a childlike pat, and the old man handed him his fallen rifle.

"He's right," he said quietly to Jud. "He *is* dead. He asks us, therefore, to let him stay here *nah-welhcoht kah-el-keh.* That's the Apache law that makes the hopelessly wounded ones stay behind to fight off the enemy while the rest of the tribe escapes. We've no choice but to grant it to him. Start running, boy, we're leaving him!" he finished abruptly.

"By God, we can't!" cried Jud. "It's not human!"

"Neither are they," Cavanaugh growled back at him, throwing an arm toward the yelping Mescaleros. "Come on, Star! Run, girl, run—!"

He gave his slim daughter a starting shove, but she twisted back and around him and said determinedly:

"I'm staying with Jud."

"Oh, my God!" groaned the latter, "you can't do that. Come on, run!"

He was pushing her, then, and suddenly they were

235

all three running. Behind them Junior's lever-loading Volcanic rifle began to bark sharply and was immediately ringed about by the heavier baying of the Apaches' Sharps and Springfields and Maynards.

But it was clear from the angry sound of the Mescalero fire that the dying Lipan brave had brought the Three Hills pack to bay. And by the time its savage members had rushed and stormed over the big rock behind which the little red man lay, Junior was grinning his last grin straight up at the blue sky above. He did not feel the slash of the Apache *besh* which took his hair, nor hear the animal snarl with which Askanay, its cursing wielder, ripped loose the pitiful trophy.

The last thing he remembered was Tall Horse Cavanaugh gripping his hand and calling him old friend.

In what better way could a very small man die?

15

IT WAS very quiet in the canyon. So quiet the white fugitives in the cliff ruins could hear the droning of the black deerflies pestering the Apache pony herd. And it was hot. It was so hot that Askanay's spittle fried on the rock where he lanced it in disgust at the situation. Grito, lying with him under the blaze of the noon-high sun, shifted his position to pull a naked red thigh in out of the merciless glare. There was no room for it in the tub-size half round of shade behind their rock, and he had to put the other leg out in the sun in exchange. He growled like a dog-wolf which has just missed an easy kill after a hard chase. Askanay returned the growl, picked up a pebble to suck for want of a cool drink, went back to watching the silent cliff dwelling above.

Chebo squatted in the pleasant shade of an alder clump alongside the creek, tossing little rocks into the water and leaning down to take a long drink whenever he felt the need. Between times he dangled his moccasined feet in the splashing current, whistled back at the mountain jays in the trees above, picked his teeth with the razored point of his *besh,* regarded his burgeoning paunch with the thought that he would need to eat less *socorro* and drink less *pulque* and *tiswin* this coming winter and all the while gave not a look at the cliff above, nor wasted a worry on the foul hunting luck which had allowed the white people to reach it ahead of the Apaches.

Sobre, crouched with Chavez in the rocks upstream and directly across from the old pueblo, shook his head and said to the old man, "I don't know what to do." Nodded Chavez calmly, "Do nothing."

They waited.

On the huge bench of wind- and rain-carved rock hollowed by ten thousand years of weather to hold the mudbrick kivas of the ancient ones, the two white men and the halfbreed girl looked down on the Apache stillness beneath them.

Their own position was impregnable.

There could be no question of a starve-out. They had already been gone nearly six weeks from Mesilla. If Baylor did not already have a force in the field looking for them, he would have within another ten days. And they had food enough from the stores Sobre had brought for Star, plus their own, plus the hordes of rock rats infesting the ruins, to last three times ten days if it came to that. Of water they had a never failing supply from the deep-rock spring in the back of the cavern, and of housekeeping tools and materials they had their choice of the multitude of useful artifacts the ancients had left behind in their mysterious flight those untold hundreds of years gone. Jud and Cavanaugh had discussed these things. Without being overjoyed, they knew their strength. They had better than a fighting chance. They were in the bargainer's seat. Only question: how to prove it to the Apaches.

Said Jud, after they had talked the whole thing out and the silence had ridden along for half an hour, "Cavanaugh, what we going to do?" Answered Cavanaugh, as another old man to another young man before him, "Hold our water."

One o'clock went by. The sun inched west. Out from the far wall of the canyon the shadow of its passing began to envelop the suffering Apaches. The relief was only seeming. The temperature down at streambed level, and in the deepest rockshade, was at least 120°. Two o'clock. The heat stifle, thickened by the sunbake of the east wall, became insufferable. It was like trying to breathe with the head swathed in a sweated horseblanket. Lips began to wither, noses to dry shut, tongues to swell.

Three o'clock.

No movement from above, no sound from below.

Except one.

The plashing gurgle and maddening plink and bubble of the creek foaming, green and glass-clear, down through its moss-grown granite millstones.

"I must have water," gasped Askanay. "I feel the signs. The heat sickness is upon me."

The desert Apache knew dehydration and all its dangers. It was a part of their life. And not infrequently of their death.

Grito looked at his friend and saw that the gray of shock was coming into his face flesh. He reached out and took his hand and it was cold. He felt for the beat of his blood in the wrist, and could not find it.

"Go on," he said, "but be careful. I will give you cover from here."

Askanay groaned a little and vomited before he could get out from behind the rock. Up on the cliff shelf, Elkanah Cavanaugh heard the sound, swung his pale eyes its way.

"Hand me them glasses!" he snapped at Jud.

The tired boy gave him the battered pair of Mexican army fieldglasses borrowed from the jacal of Chavez earlier that same day.

Cavanaugh squinted through them, nodded, handed them back, picked up Chavez's carbine.

"Just wanted to make sure," he said. "My eyes ain't what they used to be."

"Sure of what?"

"That Injun crawling down to the stream yonder."

He raised up to brace his aim across the low wall fronting the cliff shelf. "Looked like he had something on him he wasn't wearing the last time we saw him."

Jud's eyes narrowed as he recognized the Indian below.

"That's Askanay," he said. "Don't miss the son."

"If I do," grunted Cavanaugh, "Junior will never forgive me."

"Junior?"

"As ever was," answered the old man softly. "That's his hair hanging on that bastard's belt."

The carbine boomed and two hundred yards downstream Askanay screamed, leaped to his feet, ran ten yards blindly into a flat-sided boulder, bounced off it and fell on his back, arms outflung on a little beach of white creeksand. Like Junior, he was looking at the sky. But Askanay was not smiling.

"Heart shot," said Cavanaugh, reloading as he leaned forward to confirm his verdict. "Jump. Run. Drop dead. You'll see he won't move a toe."

"Neither will you!" rasped Jud impatiently, "if you don't get back down behind that wall in a hurry."

"I reckon that shines," admitted Cavanaugh, and moved quickly to follow the other's advice. He did not move quickly enough. Like his eyesight and his

Indian smell, his reflexes were not what they were twenty years ago.

Grito's old model Springfield thundered out like artillery in the narrow confines of the canyon's walls. Its big-caliber bullet slammed Cavanaugh six feet backward, into the side of a pottery kiln. He stood upright against it for a moment, then melted at the knees and slid to the cavern floor.

Jud fired three times at Grito with the scooped-up carbine but he was only splashing lead on rock, and knew it.

When the echoes of his third shot had died away down the canyon, there was a return of the former stillness for perhaps fifteen minutes. Then the familiar deep voice of Sobre spoke at last.

"How bad is the old man?" he called up to Jud.

"Not too bad," replied the latter carefully. "Why do you ask?"

"Because everything depends on him. If he can live ten days without help, you will all go free. The Pony Soldiers are coming this way. Can you wait?"

Jud knew that they could not.

Cavanaugh would die if he did not get the care and the primitive nursing which could be provided solely by the Apache women. With their sometimes wonder-working medicinal herbs and their great skill in the cleansing and treatment of gunshot wounds, they were the old man's only chance.

He suspected that Sobre knew as much. There was a certain way that a man spun when he was deeply hit,

241

and the Mescaleros had seen Cavanaugh grab his chest and twist backward.

"We can wait," he said at length to Sobre, but he had waited too long to say it.

"So can we," answered the young chief, and the silence fell again.

That night, after dark, Cavanaugh began to talk off a straight line. It was plain the fever was in him bad.

Star and Jud held a long, subdued discussion of their plight, wincing at the old man's interrupting pleas for them not to let the Apaches bluff them—that all they had to do was wait—that he would be well and fit in no time.

About nine o'clock Jud went to the front wall and asked for Sobre. When the young chief had come up, he inquired of him what his terms might be.

Sobre answered him that they would guarantee to nurse the old man and to let him, Guero, go free. This in exchange for the girl. They would even do more than that. If Guero wanted the girl to go free with him, he could fight for her. The one he would have to fight was Sobre himself. Time of the fight, daylight tomorrow. Its terms, death to the loser.

The one-eyed Mescalero youth set forth the conditions so quickly that the white boy had to call for clarification.

Carefully, Sobre obliged. The principal expansion of the proposal was in regard to the rules of the personal combat. This would be held according to the Apache law which governed such a situation as that between Sobre and Guero, where two men wanted the same woman and physical vanquishment of one of them was the only adequate answer.

Did Guero understand that clearly?

If he fought and won, he could go in peace and take the girl with him. If he fought and lost, everything that was his, including his life, went to Sobre. If Sobre lost, the same held true. All that was his, to the last pony, would belong to Guero to do with as he pleased.

"Le entiende usted?" he queried in Spanish at the end.

"Yes," called down Jud, "I understand. But I will need some time to think."

"Don't be a fool, boy," barked out Chavez, coming into the exchange testily. "We can hear the old man breathing all the way down here. He sounds as though he had been stabbed with a wood rasp. You'd better let us take him tonight. We can throw you up some rope and you can lower him down."

"How do I know you will do as you promise?"

"You don't," said Chavez.

Cavanaugh was now unconscious.

Jud turned to Star and asked, "What will we do?" The halfbreed girl moved past him in the dark and called out, "Chavez—!"

"Anh, nah-lin?" the old Apache's growl inquired.

"Throw up the rope."

Twenty minutes later Cavanaugh was in a pony litter bound up the twisting canyon trail for the rancheria across the Tres Cerros divide.

243

• • •

It was nearing midnight. The air down in the canyon was turning balmy. Far back against the rear wall of the cliff ledge, the drip of the ancient spring ticked like some spirit-wound water clock, telling the time for Jud Reeves and Star Cavanaugh as it had for countless centuries of young Indian couples before them. Earlier, and on Star's suggestion, they had both bathed in the spring, taking their turns at its natural basin of hollowed rock, the one standing guard at the moonlit lip of the ledge while the other went into the icy water. Now, cleansed and rested for the first time in all the weeks since Mesilla, and at ease in his mind that Cavanaugh had been given his chance to live and to stay by his daughter, whichever way tomorrow's fight went, Jud began to remember that he was a man and that his slender co-watcher above the canyon's summer-night stillness was not.

He knew that Star had never forgotten that bitter parting at the pasture spring back at the Atascosa County homeplace. He could tell it in every look and word she had given him during their present brief reunion. She had been right about the ladder to the cliff dwelling, for without it entrance to or escape from the ledge, was impossible. Yet he could not down the dark suspicion that the restless-eyed girl was more than passingly taken with Sobre's savage good looks. And still the latter had told him the girl loved him, Jud. Well, that could be a lie told by Star to keep the Apache Chief away from her.

244

Jud shook his head and didn't know what to do. Instinctively, Star Cavanaugh did.

She eased to his side, sank to her knees in the soundless dust. He knew she was there, but would not, dared not, look at her. Her sultry voice reached out and turned his head like a perfumed hand.

"Jud, look at me."

He brought his eyes around, his lips framing the words with which he would seek to tell her of his continuing indecision, his mind determined that he would say it right this time, and not hurt her again.

But the words never came.

In their place was the sibilant sound of his caught breath being taken in between his clenched teeth.

He had not looked up when Star had joined him from the spring five minutes ago, and further, the girl had taken a place where the wall shadowed her heavily. Now, kneeling before him, her slim body glowed beneath the clear light of the autumn moon.

It was a superb body and it was stark, silken-skinned naked.

Jud waited for the dawn.

He had not slept. He did not feel good inside. His body and his limbs were weak, his mind and heart, troubled.

It was not the fight with Sobre, it was the girl again.

She was a savage.

Her way of love was like the rest of her; wildly exciting, wrong and wicked. She behaved and

245

thought and spoke with the strength and abandon of an animal.

Her pagan way could not be the real love. The genuine article could not be like that. It ought not to disconcert a man as it had Jud. It ought to make him strong and proud and glad, not shaky and sneaky and ashamed.

No, by the Lord, he would still look for his mate among his own color. He didn't hate the girl or anything extreme like that. He wasn't looking down on her and comparing pedigrees, either, when he said he would stick to his lighter kind. It was simply that white boys and breed girls felt and saw things too far apart. A man might never know another experience like this one just past. But the ones he would find with civilized girls would let him rest afterward and look his partners in the face next day, not either of them feeling as though they had done something dirty under a bridge or back of a barn.

He looked over at the girl.

She was sleeping sweet and easy as a child, the last of the moonlight softening the gentle smile on her curving lips.

Jud reached out and pulled the blanket farther over her, covering the brown-nippled breast which had bared itself in her restful turning. His hand accidentally brushed the breast as he did so. He cursed silently and pulled his hand away as though it had touched a sun-hot rock.

Then as suddenly, his scowl deepened and he cursed

again. This time it was Jud Reeves, not the sleeping girl he cursed.

If he couldn't be fair to her, he could at least be honest with himself. She was only a poor little brush-country waif with no rightful idea of how to act. She had not put a pistol in his stomach and *made* him make love to her. She had only *asked* him to do it because they were alone and lonely and because she no doubt believed the sun which was so soon to come would be their last one together. She had been guilty of precisely nothing more than wanting to say goodbye to him in the best and only way she knew how.

What had made him sick and shaky had not been her love-making. It had been his own educated mind building a bad thing out of something completely natural.

To Jud Reeves it had always been the first law of decency to be true to himself. Now he realized he had been unwittingly breaking that Christian rule. He had lied about himself and the halfbreed girl. It was not Star Cavanaugh who needed to feel ashamed, it was Jud Reeves.

When he knew that much of the truth, the crouching Texas boy could guess at the rest of it.

No youth of his birth and upbringing could honestly say what he might eventually do about overcoming that matter of skin color. The actions of his unspoiled heart, however, were another and separate considera-tion. Here and now, as indeed it had from the beginning, Jud's heart skipped wildly at the least thought or slightest touch of Cavanaugh's golden-skinned daughter. If it was not love he felt for her, it was a passing strange affliction which might, God help a man, be even worse.

Unhappily, he broke his worried glance away from the sleeping girl. Damn! why didn't it get light? Why couldn't he get some rest? or at least think about something else?

He must have nodded off, then, for the next thing he knew the slant of the sun's rays off the western canyon top was in his eyes and Star Cavanaugh's slender hand was on his shoulder, her throaty voice stirring him from the depths of half-conscious exhaustion.

He stumbled to his feet, stood staring down over the ancient stone wall of the cliff ruins.

The nerve ends along his spine contracted. The chill raced tinglingly up his back. They were waiting for him down there. The ring was ready. Sobre stood on the far side of it, arms folded, naked to the waist, looking calmly up at him, his handsome face neither angry nor encouraging. Flanking their chief, squatting in a circle to make the fighting ring, fifty Apache warriors crouched chanting a minor-keyed Brave Song of their people.

Jud shivered and slid the ladder over the lip of the wall.

He went down it, hoping they wouldn't see the tremble in his legs.

Star stayed above, sitting on the wall with Chavez's

carbine in clear view of the Indians below. In the dead stillness the slotting of the heavy weapon being loaded and put on cock carried its own message to the waiting Apaches.

They looked up, scowling.

"Watch this," the halfbreed girl instructed them in their own language, and patting the carbine's scarred stock, "for it will be watching you."

"How close, *nah-lin?*" grinned up the irrepressible Chebo, who both liked the girl and was honestly curious as to whether she could shoot the big Pony Soldier gun.

The chubby brave wore a disreputable brown derby hat which he had come by in a Butterfield stage chase and relay station burn-out back in the spring of '59, and of which he was inordinately proud. Star Cavanaugh knew nothing of the hat's history, but recognized in it a relatively certain and suitable target. Chebo's black eyes widened as he saw the carbine barrel point its hollow finger squarely at his round head. In the same instant the fat brave saw the gun come up, the carbine roared. His prized derby bounced off his head, skittered through the air, landed in a heap of fresh horse dung back of Grito's paint gelding, was promptly stepped on and caved-in by the nervous animal.

"That close," said Star Cavanaugh, and put down the gun.

A few of the Apaches actually laughed.

That was pretty good shooting and it was a good

joke that Chebo's round hat went into the horse manure. The mestizo *nah-lin* was all right. She would make a fit mate for Sobre. *Wagh!* Let the fight get on! The sooner Guero was cut up and left to bloat in the September sun, the better. The Pony Soldiers were coming and there was warriors' work to do.

Aha! Anh! Here came the *Tejano* boy, now.

Well, he was walking proud enough, grant him that. But he didn't look good. Pale. Bad around the eyes. Tight in the jaw muscles. There! He almost fell coming across the creek. Very nervous, little doubt of that. But brave enough, brave enough. Give him his *besh* and let there be a quick end to it. *Anh!*

Jud had known it would be with knives.

That was the Indian's weapon.

He grew up with it as a settlement boy grew up with his father's shotgun or his older brother's varmint rifle.

It was natural to him, as it was alien to the white man.

Jud hated knives. He was not good with them. He thought they were vicious weapons, and unfair. He had never used one in a fight or for self-defense in any way, and he knew as he walked up to that slit-eyed Apache circle that should he use one now he was already *dah-eh-sah*.

Accordingly, in the thirty seconds of his walk across the canyon bottom, he had conceived a dangerous idea. And a desperate one. As Chavez, who would administer the fight, stepped toward him with his weapon, now, he tensed himself. When the old Apache came to a stand in front of him and held out the wicked-looking, wooden-handled butcherknife which was the mate to the one held by the motionless Sobre, Jud took it from him and threw it over his shoulder into the water of the creek and said in a loud clear voice, "I will not take *besh* against a brother. Sobre and I have touched hands. We have looked into each other's hearts. I will fight him only as God made me, without weapons."

The rumble which ran the Apache circle was like the growling of a wolf pack in angry surprise.

Honor was involved here. And pride. And something very like treachery.

The white boy had tricked Sobre.

Apache courage had been called and their young chief trapped into fighting on the tall *Tejano's* terms. There was no way out for Sobre, no honorable way, save to accept the contest, *mano a mano,* as Guero had proposed he should and known he must.

Sobre hesitated only long enough to raise his left hand and still the bickering snarls of his people.

Then the flash of his own blade was turning in the air and disappearing into the green water of the creek and he was saying quietly, "Guero is right. It shames my jacal that he had to remind me of my own pledge. Forgive me, Guero. Blame the girl."

"All right then!" barked Chavez, irritated by the delay and stepping back angrily. "*Mano a mano,* if you will. But no more words. Begin now—!"

251

Jud knew the way it must go then.

He stepped into Sobre's gliding rush and smashed the Apache youth into the creek rocks with a right hand that went into his handsome dark face like a fence maker's maul into the brown iron of the splitting wedge. The Indian boy went down and got up without a sound. He came back at Jud the same way. And it went like that, from grim first to brutal last: not a sound save the splintering blows of Jud's big fists, the grunting of the breath being driven out of Sobre's lean body, the roll and rattle of the rocks as he fell among them, or pushed his way back up out of them. In less than five minutes the Three Hills chief was beaten senseless, and Jud Reeves was not even breathing hard.

The Apaches sat in absolute silence.

They had never seen a thing like this done with the bare hands.

It was frightening.

And more. There was something unclean about it. Something indecent and not moral. It was an obscene, wrong thing.

A low sound ran around the silent Apache circle.

Eskim-azan, who had smashed in the head of a little white girl with the butt of his rifle not later than that same summer, got up and went for his pony without a word. Nakay-do-zinny, who had cut the tongue out of the head of the little girl's mother because she had pleaded too loud and too much for her child's life, got up and followed him. Gato, who was called the Cat

252

because he would torture anything alive, and Grito, his full-blood brother, whose crimes of white and Mexican murder were notched into his Springfield's stock from triggerguard to buttplate, arose and stalked off after their fellows.

Still there was no sign nor sound from the others.

Jud, thinking the braves were beginning to depart because they did not want to see him take his prize of their chief's life, stepped forward and cried out to them, "*Dah, dah!* No, no! I do not claim the life of Sobre. See! I give it back to him." He made an eloquent gesture of the handsign for returning something to its rightful owner in justice and good part. "Look! See now! I have made the sign. No one could have fought better than Sobre. I salute him. He is a real Apache."

Two more braves got up and started for their ponies. Three others made move to follow them.

"*Dah,* please!" appealed Jud. *"Enthlay-sit-daou!* Sit down, abide here, be calm, don't move away!"

Here and there about the entire circle, Indians were getting up and leaving now. Not one looked at Jud, nor answered him. Within three minutes forty-six Apaches had walked away from the fight ring by the stream, gotten on their potbellied little horses and ridden off up the canyon. In another sixty seconds the last of them were gone from sight up the rocky defile. In less than ten minutes the whole strange affair was over and Jud stood alone on the banks of the nameless little stream.

Or thought he did.

"Well, boy, come on," said a scratchy voice behind him. "Don't stand there all day!"

"*Anh,* yes!" added another, happier voice. "Come help us clean off your brother."

Jud wheeled about.

It was skinny old Chavez, of course, and faithful fat Chebo. True to their chief beyond any insult to the ethics of Apache murder, or any injury to the notorious poor-loser's ego of the average horseback Indian, the two had stayed behind to see Sobre through whatever Yosen, the Apache Great Spirit, had presently in mind for him. Their stand, taken in the face of the full tribal censor, just delivered, was not only a loyal but a very brave thing to do, and Jud now saluted them for it.

"*De nada,*" shrugged Chavez, slipping into Spanish which he knew the white boy spoke fluently. "When I love a man I do not turn my back on him. Sobre has been like a son to me. I love him like a son."

"I, too, love Sobre," said Chebo earnestly to Jud. "Like a brother, even as you do, Guero."

Old Chavez came quickly to stand in front of the tall Texas youth. He looked up at him, beady-eyed as some wrinkled red ferret. He put a clawlike, dark hand on Jud's broad shoulder. For once, just for a minute, his voice lost its rattler's buzz.

"Listen to me, white boy," he said, "we know why you threw away the knife."

"Hell!" laughed Jud in English, very happy with

254

their loyalty to Sobre yet wanting to cover his own actions for the benefit of Star, who was now approaching across the stream, "I guess we all know that! It was to save my own no-good life!"

"That may be true," said Chavez softly. "But it was also to save Sobre's life. You might have killed him and to prevent that, you threw away the knife."

"My God," said Jud, blushing. "I was scared to death!"

"You gambled with your life. It was a brave thing to do and you did it for Sobre. We honor you," said the old man, putting out his hand, *"schichobe."*

"Schichobe," replied Jud; taking his hand and that of the grinning Chebo after it.

"And now!" snapped Chavez, the rusty file back in his throat, "enough of this nonsense! Pick up the boy and bring him down to the water."

Jud and Chebo took up the unconscious Sobre.

At the creek, Star joined them and took over the washing out of the young chief's lacerations, doing the work with all the authority and natural assumption of a born Three Hills woman. Even as he admired her calmness and quick skill (Sobre's face was a swollen, bloody mask, his body a welter of rock cuts and stone bruises) he was depressed anew with the warning of her dark inheritance which this same hardness and lack of excitement demonstrated so inescapably. A white girl would have fainted at the mere sight of Sobre's bloodied features. This mestizo child, this quarter-bred Sonora Apache daughter of old Elkanah

Cavanaugh, took the multiple ugly abrasions as though they were so many prickly-pear scratches. Jud shook his head and knew he had been right in his last night's decision that she was a savage better off with Sobre's people than with any others. By the time the latter began to sit up and shake the cool creek water from his black mane, he had made a second decision.

As soon as Sobre's mind was completely clear, and the young Apache could understand him without question, he put the burden of this decision to him.

"Sobre, *schichobe*," he said to him, "I am sorry for what has happened here, but I fought like an animal, for my own life. *Dah-eh-sah* makes cowards of us all."

Sobre looked at him curiously. There was no rancor, no bitter race hatred in the look, only the natural embarrassment of having been beaten by another in equal contest. And even that small uneasiness faded as he nodded in receipt of Jud's apology.

"I understand this, Guero, and I am glad to hear you call me *schichobe* again. There is no shame here save Sobre's." He looked at Jud a moment and added low-voiced, "You know, Guero, I could not have killed you either. Not even for the girl."

Jud held up his hand.

"I did not fight for the girl," he told the other youth bluntly. "I fought for myself."

Sobre's surprise was mirrored by Star's shock.

The halfbreed girl looked at Jud as though he had slapped her across the face.

256

"What do you mean?" asked Sobre, genuinely confused.

"I mean she is not my woman. She is a brave girl, very good to look at and very good in her heart. But I do not love her as a man loves his true woman. Do you understand me, my friend?"

Whether or not Sobre did, Cavanaugh's daughter did. Her face went white as wood ash.

"Star," he began lamely, but she cut him off.

"Jud Reeves," she said tonelessly, "you don't need to explain a thing to me. We've come a long trail since Atascosa County and here is where it splits for final keeps. I wouldn't have you if you were the last man alive. I'm staying with Sobre."

It was now the young Apache's turn to furnish the surprised stare. After a moment, he said with simple dignity, "Will you truly wait for me, *nah-lin?*"

Puzzled, Star queried quickly. "*Wait* for you? How is that? Are you going somewhere?"

"Yes, with Guero," he replied, a sadness in his voice which struck into Jud like a knife. "To talk with the Pony Soldier chief at Mesilla. I do not know whether I any longer speak for my people, but if I can arrange a lasting peace for them I will do it."

"*Anh,* yes," nodded Star, continuing in the Apache tongue with deep-syllabled fluency, "I will wait for Sobre—"

She suspended it to stare defiantly at Jud.

Then, addressing it to the young Apache, but slashing it at Jud as though it were a quirt thong, she

257

concluded savagely, *"In your jacal, my chieftain."*

That was the ill-felt, unpleasant end of it.

Within minutes thereafter Star was gone up the rancheria trail with Chebo and Chavez; Sobre and Jud departed down the shallowing canyon toward the Ruidoso plain.

The second meeting of Sobre and Baylor was a travesty on all Indian-White peacetalks.

The Apache chief and the Texas officer reached a complete misunderstanding, settled absolutely nothing, parted with entire friendliness and no idea in the New Mexican world how they were going to get their respective peoples to abide by the handshakes and happy expressions of "good heart" with which they said goodbye to one another that golden September afternoon outside Baylor's headquarters adobe in Mesilla.

Nor was that the greatest irony of it, either.

For his part in bringing the hostile Mescalero chief in, Baylor had breveted Jud Reeves. He was now Second Lieutenant Judah Beaumont Reeves of the 2nd Texas Mounted Rifles and he could thank his Apache brother for the commission.

As for the latter and his final appearance before the Confederate command in New Mexico, Jud could scarcely bring himself to watch and listen.

The difference in this Sobre and the magnificent wild youth who had stalked into the Fort Bliss conference with the "look of eagles" shining in his fierce dark face was a subtle but a devastating thing.

Baylor did not notice it. Hugh Preston, Waller, Herbert—none of his staff, save one—saw anything other than the "same untamable proud devil of a bronco Apache who slaughtered poor May and his company at Fort Davis." The solitary exception to this military myopia was Lieutenant Darrel Royce. As Jud pushed out of the meeting at Sobre's side, he heard the slender dark-haired officer say gratingly to Hugh Preston, "Oh, ignorant savage, my foot, Hugh! The poor bastard's half sick with shame. He's got more sense, yes, by God, and more feelings, too, in his little finger than you and I have in our entire damned bodies. What the hell's come over you, Hugh? Can't you see *anything* anymore?"

Outside, Jud walked with Sobre to his pony.

He stood by in silence as the Mescalero chief stepped up on the little animal. The hearts of both boys were composing things to say, but the tongues of neither were able to say them. Something had happened in that adobe house, just now, which was better left untalked of. Both of them knew this, neither wanted the other to see that he did.

"Goodbye, *schichobe*," smiled Sobre, leaning down to give Jud his hand. "We have each done our best for our people. My heart is good for you."

Jud took his hand, only nodded his return of the feeling, unable, still, to speak.

The Indian turned his pony. The white boy started forward impulsively. "Sobre—!"

The young chief checked the nervous mustang. *"Anh, schichobe?"*

Jud came to his stirrup fender. He put his big, blond-haired hand on the other's smooth bronze knee and looked up at him. Then, in the embarrassing end, he could not say what it was he had wanted to say when he called out to him—that he was sorry, and a thousand times sorry—and so he only took his hand quickly away from the dark knee and stepped back and said, low-voiced, *"Nada, amigo. Vaya con Dios."*

Sunset, September 23, 1861. Very uncomfortable in his new uniform of butternut gray, Second Lieutenant J. B. Reeves sat at Baylor's right in the Officers' Mess at the Confederate command headquarters in Mesilla. The dinner had been a good one. Havana cigars were now being passed around. While the puffings and smackings of lips to produce good lights were running around the long table, Jud took advantage of the rising smokescreen to covertly study his new fellow officers; this before they settled back to look him over.

That they would do so was inevitable.

Any addition to a military staff is welcomed with a certain degree of natural jealousy. Until he can prove himself no threat to any of the incumbents, can, in short, definitely establish to the satisfaction of all, his eminent inferiority, the new man is subjected to an interrogation of hard stares and grapeshot-loaded questions only slightly less hostile than might be tendered a captive foreign agent suspected of being an enemy colonel in disguise.

With a field brevet like Jud Reeves—a backcountry recruit with absolutely no military training or experience—the treatment was certain to be twice as Spartan.

Jud imagined the attack would begin with an innocent, overtly friendly remark. He was not disappointed.

"Well, now, Reeves—" said Hugh Preston, that day made a captain and feeling no more charitable because of it "—tell us how it feels to be an officer and a gentleman—ah, that is, 'officially' of course!"

Preston got his little laugh for the standard trite remark, leaned back with a gracious wave of his cigar.

Jud got awkwardly to his feet.

His bony height, big-knuckled hands and homely sunburned face did nothing for the very bad fit of his Texas-made uniform and he added to the poor impression of his appearance by almost falling over his sword in the process of getting out of his chair. The laugh which covered this bit of confusion was barely polite. The new lieutenant took it with a furious blush and almost bolted the field. But here and there he caught a friendly, sober face among the diners— Colonel Herbert's, young Royce's, Baylor's—and so rallied himself short of a disastrous rout. When the laugh had died away, he took from his inside pocket a small, flat book bound in calfhide and laid it on the table.

At once the staff took interest.

"Gentlemen," said the speaker, "here is a work written by an authority in your field. With your permission I should like to read you something from it. I believe this passage covers the occasion here this evening, and will answer your questions concerning it, and my own reaction to it."

He turned to Baylor, bowing stiffly.

"Colonel, sir, I would like your permission to leave immediately after I have read this," he said, "for I am sure these gentlemen will want to discuss it."

Baylor smiled indulgently. Things were going much better for the self-proclaimed military governor of Arizona Territory these fall days, and he was in no mood to be critical of his own appointments. Furthermore, as a self-made commander, he could understand this fine young fellow Texan's embarrassment at his elevation in rank. He waved his cigar at Jud, agreeing warmly, "Of course, of course. Go on, boy. We all understand your feelings."

"Thank you, sir," Jud said, and picked up the leatherbound book and began to read from it.

. . . Unearned promotions have undermined more military units than disease, desertion, defeat in the field, or even bad food. A soldier of the ranks will put up with brutal sergeants, incompetent lieutenants, faulty equipment, impossible orders, kitchen duty, latrine detail, cancelled leaves, confinement to quarters, no smoking or talking on the march, death, dishonorable discharge and even dysentery.

The officer of the line will do as well or better, as indeed his rank demands.

But the one injustice which no army man, private, corporal or colonel can condone, excuse or otherwise abide, is unearned promotion . . .

Jud closed the book and put it back inside his rough gray uniform coat.

"The title of that book," he said, "is *The Professional Soldier in Command; His Obligations as a Leader of Men.* It was written by my father."

Amid the complete silence which followed, he removed his sword and placed it on the table.

"Colonel Baylor, sir," he said, his homely face mirroring the glad relief he could feel coming up within him at the words, "this thing doesn't fit me, and I don't rightly reckon it ever will. I'd be beholden if you'd hang it on somebody else."

The silence around the Officers' Mess was still holding as the door closed quietly behind the tall blond boy, and his footsteps died away in the dust of the outer courtyard.

"Well, gentlemen—?" said Baylor.

Perhaps ten seconds had passed.

Around the table none of his officers and gentlemen had organized their reactions to Jud Reeves' unorthodox method of resignation. The prevailing sentiment seemed to be surprise rather than resentment, however. The young devil had done it well, you had to grant that. And it was abundantly clear he had not wanted, nor sought the commission Baylor had given him for bringing in that insolent rascal of a Mescalero. Perhaps, after all, the boy was happy as a sergeant and, hence, harmless. Evidently, they had all been overly critical of Baylor's favoritism of him. Reeves or no Reeves, he was just a big backwoods bumpkin, entirely pleased to be a scout with three stripes.

If this new tolerance spreading around the board under Baylor's inquiring gaze was a staff opinion, it was not unanimous. While the Colonel Commanding waited with cocked eyebrows for an answer to his question concerning Jud's blunt action, Captain Hugh Pendleton Preston undertook to supply him with one which did not reflect the apparent popular approval of Jud's honesty.

"Rank insubordination!" snapped Preston. "Intolerable impudence at very least. I would put him under arrest at once!"

Baylor nodded. He had not, after all, missed the implied criticism of himself in the Reeves youngster's awkwardly shrewd move. "Any other opinions?" he now asked quietly.

There was a moment's silence, then Darrel Royce said, "Yes."

"And what would you do, sir?" inquired Baylor.

"It's not what I would do, Colonel, it's what I wouldn't."

"All right, sir," nodded the other, "then what is it you *wouldn't* do?"

"Accept his resignation," said Royce flatly. "He's the best damned man we've got."

"Precisely my own opinion," said Baylor, standing up. "Gentlemen, good evening."

So it was that Jud Reeves did not resign his brevet commission with the 2nd Texas Mounted Rifles.

Baylor needed scarcely more than fifteen minutes with him to convince him that the South's need for leaders was more desperate than ever, and that those of her sons who, like himself, were qualified by birth and breeding to guide her destiny could not ignore their duty.

His commander also had exciting news, and official news, to back up his refusal to consider Jud's request for release.

The war in New Mexico was about to become full scale. Baylor's dream of a Confederate Empire of the Southwest was on the verge of wakening reality. In San Antonio, along the very banks of the Salado which had seen their own start, General Henry Hopkins Sibley was now gathering a great host—two full regiments and an artillery company, plus complete support of the Confederate Government in Richmond, the lack of which had so severely hampered their own efforts to date.

Sibley was a professional soldier and a Texas hero. He had his general's commission and his orders to organize his force and proceed west with all haste, direct from Confederate Secretary of War L. P. Walker, and his field orders from Brigadier General Earl Van Dorn in command of the Confederate Department of Texas at San Antonio.

This was no ragged company of volunteer, buckskin-clad buffalo hunters. This was the regular Confederate Army.

The move up the Rio Grande Valley against Canby at Fort Craig and the subsequent destruction of the Union forces in the Department of New Mexico could now be consummated. The Confederates would celebrate Christmas Day in Albuquerque, New Year's Eve in the Governor's mansion at Santa Fe. The war in the West would be over in sixty days. California and her vast treasures of gold and, through that immense wealth, the final victory in the war in the East would be assured the Confederate cause.

In all this glory and in the emoluments which were certain to follow it, the primary parts of John Robert Baylor and his Rio Salado Buffalo Hunters would not be forgotten by a grateful Southern government. The "Buffalo Brigade" had won the Southwest—and the War—for the Confederacy, by holding Texas, Arizona and New Mexico until superior forces could be brought into the field for final, purely nominal consolidation. But that Baylor and his Iron Men had been the original instruments of this crucial victory, Richmond well knew. And she would never forget the debt.

As for Baylor himself, he would never forget his

debt to those who had served with him and they, in turn, would never regret their loyalty and faith.

Of these latter, young Judah Reeves was an important one to the immediate and future plans of the Fort Craig campaign.

He was in line for a highly specialized and vital assignment and there could be no question whatever of his resignation being considered at this time.

Jud Reeves was neither a clever nor a devious man. Baylor was both.

The Texas boy walked out of his brief closeting with the Mesilla commander convinced that the latter was the greatest patriot since Thomas Jefferson and that all his former cynicism about Baylor's adventuring for personal profit was wrong. Moreover, he still was, and now thought of himself as, Lieutenant J. B. Reeves, 2nd Texas Mounted Rifles.

Even further, he had just been given his first official order under the new rank: ". . . detached service, report immediately to Gen. H. H. Sibley, San Antonio, for reassignment, special duty. . . ."

And, oh yes, there was one other thing. A small matter more or less in the nature of a purely personal favor to his commanding officer. Would he please take charge of an honor guard bearing back to San Antonio the body of Colonel B. F. Horton, who had died two days previous of lung congestion following the black measles? At Fort Bliss the cortege would be joined by the bereaved widow. Since the latter was some in-law or other of Sibley's, and Horton an old Academy classmate of the General's, a properly composed, smartly officered escort was essential to the best impressions all around. It was considerable of a responsibility and he, Baylor, did not confer its honor lightly. He hoped and trusted and knew, indeed, that he had picked the right man in young Jud Reeves.

For his own part, guiding his new bay gelding through the shallows of the Mesilla crossing shortly after nine o'clock, Jud also hoped and trusted that Baylor had made the correct choice.

Directly, after a few minutes of riding through the young night well out ahead of the field ambulance and four troopers bringing Colonel Horton to his last reward at San Antonio, he began to share his C.O.'s optimism. Of course it was no great excitement to be squiring some elderly, red-eyed lady all the way to the Salado with her husband's coffin bumping along behind, but the "special assignment" wording of his orders to report to Sibley could mean almost anything and surely did mean something big. His prospects in the army were rising with his rank.

For a brief moment and for no logical reason he could fathom, the conscience-nudging thought of what Apache fate had befallen old Elkanah Cavanaugh and his angry-hearted daughter obtruded itself. But he shook off that shadow quickly enough. He had done all he could for the old man and it was not his fault that he did not return the girl's unfortunate feeling. Everyone had his own separate troubles.

He had his. Cavanaugh and his halfbreed daughter had theirs. It came out even.

That being righteously that, Lieutenant Jud Reeves straightened his shoulders and rode on.

Taken for all and all, with a good horse once more beneath him and the night wind fresh and strong with the smell of the Rio Grande blowing to him from the fragrant south, a man could not consider himself entirely unhappy with his brevet and his bars.

PART SIX

THE CROSSING

16

M<small>AJOR</small> C<small>ONSIDINE</small>, in command at Fort Bliss, was very glad to see Jud Reeves. The Major was a career man and had known Jud's father. As well, he knew how to treat an obvious favorite of the C.O. at Mesilla. This boy, Considine estimated, would go a long way in a very short while. He was young, not yet twenty years old. He was an intelligent, likable lad, quick and ready to speak or smile, without being in any way obsequious or flippant with either service.

Any small luster which could be imparted to the young man's memory of his treatment at Fort Bliss might very well shine all the way to San Antonio, and at very least would reflect as far as Mesilla.

It was the first time in his life Jud had been wined and dined. He enjoyed that small party in the Officers' Mess at Fort Bliss the night of September 24. As a matter of fact he enjoyed it immensely.

To begin with it was his first party of formal dress. He had never imagined ladies could be so lovely, men so dashing, music so delightful. The glitter of the candlelight and the glow of the French champagne were quite the most exhilarating sensations imaginable. To dance with the perfumed, sparkling-eyed wives of the post's junior officers under these heady circumstances—particularly when it was his party, being given in his honor (although for what reason he was by now having trouble recalling) was the highest point of emotional adventure in the life of Jud Reeves—and then he met Felicia Horton.

She was on the arm of Major Considine, and had asked to meet the young man who was escorting her husband's body to San Antonio. The Widow Horton was being very brave and all the officers and their wives at Fort Bliss admired her spirit in coming to the little party in Jud's honor. She was dressed, of course, in proper black. As well, she bore herself with dignity and restraint and a sort of a sweet, sad, proud courage which touched Jud very deeply. Finally, she was neither elderly nor red-eyed as he had imagined in accepting the onerous chore of squiring her to San Antonio, but rather quite the most smashing looker Jud Reeves had ever laid his sky-blue eyes upon.

Felicia Horton was twenty-six, twenty years her dead mate's junior. She was tall and might have been called too thin, save that where a woman's body should be soft and full, Felicia Horton's figure left nothing to the male viewer's imagination—not even in the severe black lines of her mourning gown. Jud gasped and stared and found himself looking into a pair of bold dark eyes which would not drop. And found himself accepting, too, a slender pink hand which purposely prolonged its lingering in his and, moreover, imparted a deliberate squeeze while doing so which, even to the green lieutenant from Mesilla, did not make sense in a three-day widow.

"So this is the young man about whom we've been hearing so much?" rippled the tall girl, her voice, in its cooler, highly cultured way fully as disturbing as Star Cavanaugh's. "I *am* pleased to meet you, Lieutenant Reeves, and want to thank you for your kindness in this unfortunate hour."

"Well," stammered Jud, retrieving his hand with difficulty, "I don't know what you-all could have been hearing about me, ma'am. I've been with the Indians for the past six weeks."

"Your past six weeks with the Indians is exactly what we've been hearing about, young man. Don't you know you're famous?"

"I surely don't, ma'am." Jud's new collar was suddenly so small he could not believe he had ever gotten it buttoned to begin with. "Now, its been a downright pleasure to meet you, Mrs. Horton. If you'll excuse me, I think I had best—"

"Nonsense, Reeves," interrupted Considine smilingly. "Mrs. Horton wants to talk to you about the trip tomorrow. You know, any little details of what she should take along, things like that. I'd suggest a fresh glass and some slightly less noisy place."

"Perhaps you would walk me home, young man," said Felicia Horton, making it sound as though she were forty and he fourteen. "I really must retire early, Major," she smiled tightly to Considine, "and this *has* been a little trying for me."

"Of course!" bowed the post commander gallantly. "That's an order, Lieutenant Reeves!" he added with a gay, if somewhat misguided wink to the embarrassed youth. "Carry on—!"

"Come along, young man," murmured Felicia Horton, taking his tensed arm and starting for the exit. "You can begin by telling me if we shall encounter any danger from the Indians on our way east."

The walk seemed very long, the talk very small, from there to Mrs. Horton's quarters.

There was a west wind coming in off the river and while the widow chatted, Jud got some of the wine aired out of him and some of the sense exercised back in. He could still hear the fiddles from across the parade ground but they were scraping now, not singing. Also, the messroom adobe did not look so magic from the outside. It looked small and squat and very crowded with the score of perspiring men and women now laughing and dancing in it, and trying to forget they were five hundred miles west of San Antonio and the real thing. Of a sudden, it struck Jud forcibly that there was a dead man lying over there in the post infirmary, that he was walking in the Texas moonlight with the latter's dry-eyed widow, and that he wasn't listening to what she was saying and neither was she. The idea of that did not fit with fiddle music and sweaty dancing and raised voices around the champagne bowl. There was something very wrong with all of this, and a good place to start finding out what it was, was with that slim set of pink fingers still resting unnecessarily on his doubled biceps.

He dropped his bent arm and Felicia Horton took the hint. She moved carefully away from him, very graceful about it, but very prompt and proper too. It was as though she wished to let her young escort know he had misinterpreted her touch, and to do so without hurting his feelings in any way.

Jud breathed easier. By the time they had come to her door she had him feeling completely guilty for his former thoughts, and yet had done it so skillfully and with such ladylike sensitivity and entire social ease that he was in no way uncomfortable when she took his hand again to say goodnight.

The fact that, before saying that goodnight, she used the hand to draw him swiftly into the shadows of the house wall was something else again. As was the fact that, once in those shadows, she leaned up to press her perfumed cheek impulsively against his and to kiss him lightly and teasingly on the left ear.

But even then she left him in confusion and doubt.

"That, young man," she said, stepping back from him and into the doorway of her quarters as though it were ordinary procedure to thus reward any escort detail, "was for being so nice. I know you understand this is a difficult time for me, and that you will realize my emotions are overwrought. A woman needs a strong arm upon which to lean when she has just lost—oh dear, now," she interrupted herself bravely, "I vowed I wasn't going to talk like that! There, now, you *are* a darling. Run along, young man, I shall see you in the morning. I know we'll get on first rate."

"Ma'am," Jud bowed clumsily, "you get yourself a good night's sleep and don't you worry about a thing. And ma'am," he reached out a big hand, put it lightly on her shoulder, "I *do* understand how you feel, just losing your husband and all. Any woman needs a man to be near at a time like that. I remember how my own mother was when my father died. You just go right on and lean on me all you want. That's why I'm here."

Felicia Horton seized his hand, turned it over, buried her soft lips in its rough palm. Jud blushed, but knew it was only the wordless gratitude of a bereaved woman. Even as the thought took him, she proved it was right by dropping the hand and murmuring with heartfelt intensity, "Oh, God bless you, Lieutenant Reeves!" Then, before he could answer or even say goodnight, she had turned and fled sobbingly into her darkened quarters.

Jud waited until he saw the glow of the lamplight spring up inside, then nodded to himself and marched back off across the parade ground. That Mrs. Horton was certainly a fine, brave little woman. It would be a real pleasure and a rare privilege to chaperon her to San Antonio. A man just hoped there wouldn't be any trouble along the way to upset her or to spoil the trip. And, of course, he knew there wouldn't. And equally of course, he meant to see there *wasn't!*

God knew he would never forget his mother when the news came about "her General." So he could surely understand the hell this other little Southern lady was trying so gamely to smile her way through. That took breeding, mister! that kind of courage. That was something you got by blood and birth and no other way, and this poor little bride of Colonel Horton's was certainly showing her pedigree tonight.

Jud straightened his shoulders, smartened his stride, feeling better and better about the whole prospect with every step—especially about the grown man's part he had just played in being there to steady her when she had needed it most.

A man could pleasure himself a little along that line, he reckoned, without he was anyway vain about it.

The trip to San Antonio was an eighteen-day idyll.

It was an impossible dream set to the living reality of a perfect and indescribably delightful companionship with a beautiful, captivatingly talented girl.

Felicia had been to finishing school abroad. She had a nodding acquaintance with the classics, managed to completely enchant Jud with campfire-side discussions of the English poets, the German philosophers, the Italian romanticists and the French political freedomists.

In between low-voiced lecturings on the civilized works of Old World art, the Colonel's lady was furnishing the boy from Topaz Creek with a liberal course in the application of the calculated science of the shyly averted glance, the purposely accidental exposure of the shapely calf, the furious blush, the startled half-parting of the lips upon being caught staring, the innocently lingering touch, the leaning close for just the suggestion of a mad moment's whiff of foreign eau de cologne, the deliberate let-slip of the softly called first name, the stammered apology for the same boldness, and all the other artful mixed bag of tricks of the world's oldest trade, in the exciting practice whereof few wantons and no nice women exceeded the talents of Colonel B. F. Horton's shapely widow, Felicia.

The result of all this weeks-long witchcraft was that Second Lieutenant J. B. Reeves arrived in San Antonio, Texas, October 12, 1861, completely infatuated with a tall black-haired young woman nearly seven years his senior and whose wealthy, elderly husband was not yet a full month dead in his flag-draped coffin. As far as Jud was concerned Felicia was everything right and sweet and wonderful in a woman, and everything he had known he would find some day providing he believed and prayed enough and meanwhile didn't give in to the first girl who put her hands on him, or let him put his on her, the way most poor dumb fellows seemed to do.

The feeling, of course, called up the image of Star Cavanaugh. He had felt something for the wild half-breed girl, there was no denying that. But it hadn't been the right, the clean, the Christian and proper kind of thing Felicia and he had found in those eighteen wonderful days from Fort Bliss. Why, he hadn't laid a hand on the latter, yet he was so entirely in love with her one look would chill him to his bootsoles, or one brush of her little fingertips make him tremble and go weak inside for twenty minutes. In the other direction, he had actually been with Star and all it had done was to shake him up so bad he couldn't stand to look at her next day. It had only made him ashamed and guilty-feeling and half sick later on, no matter that it had nearly killed him with wildness and excitement at the time.

Riding up the Salado now, on his way to report in to General Sibley after delivering his and the Colonel's lady to the General's wife in her San Antonio home, Jud cursed out loud at the way, even now, the tawny breed girl could seize his imagination and drag it down onto the blanket with her.

His meeting with Henry Hopkins Sibley was brief but lastingly impressive. As well, it was highly exciting.

Sibley, a robustly handsome, fiercely bearded, pre-maturely gray man with arrogant face and piercing eye, struck Jud as the very soul and symbolization of the professional soldier.

With him when Jud entered the big command tent, which structure (the Sibley tent) was, by the way, the invention of the dashing Confederate commander and destined to gain him a fame far greater than his military genius, was a Captain Burke O'Roark. This pleasant-faced young Irishman was introduced to Jud as the "leader of my scout company," by Sibley. O'Roark acknowledged the title by grinning contagiously and telling the new arrival that, "outside the General's hearing they call us 'Sibley's Spies,'" and going on to say that the General had privileged him to be the one to tell Jud that the "further assignment" in his orders from Baylor to report to Sibley was O'Roark's personal request to have him for his junior executive in the scout company.

The appointment carried a promotion to first lieutenant and Jud was too numb to argue it. As a result he walked out of the headquarters tent on the Salado but one step away from his family heritage and his beginning ambition and vow that long-ago afternoon when he had set out from the Topaz Creek homeplace to fight for the South. He was second-in-command of a combat unit in the regular Confederate Army! One rifle ball; one saber cut; one charge of grape; a horse's stumble; a simple change in orders, an illness in the field, or an eccentric commanding general's unpredictable whim could make him a leader of men!

This was the excitement that straightened Jud Reeves' back and put the high pride of blood and breeding in his bearing as he now rode the bay gelding back down the river toward town.

What a past three weeks and a last thirty minutes this had been!

He had met and fallen in love with the most wonderful girl in the world. He had been given a commission in the regular army. He was second-ranked scout in the entire Department of Texas. And he was, at the latter's parting insistence that "he would want to do no less for General Reeves' son, officer or private of the line," on his way to report in as house guest at the historic, high-walled hacienda of Brigadier General Henry Hopkins Sibley, in storied old San Antonio de Bexar!

Could any drop be added to that cup of pure delight?

Yes. A dark-eyed, raven-haired one. And especially the fact that fortune had appointed her, as well, a house guest of the Sibleys in San Antonio!

There was little a simple Texas ranch boy could do with such a sinfully lucky situation save to touch up his flashy little bay gelding and get the good news, at a chicken-scattering gallop, to the brave and beautiful girl who had given him every reason to believe she returned his heartfelt devotions.

At the Sibleys', a moment's disappointment—no one was home but the house servants. The women had gone early to dine on the town and would go from their demitasses directly to a Spanish costume *baile* being given that night in the junior officers' ballroom out by the Alamo. It would be possible, of course, the Mexican *mayordomo* told Jud to get him an invitation for the affair. Or he could simply go back out to the Salado and accompany the General, who was going to the dance from the camp.

Jud considered the situation, decided to settle for a note to Felicia, outlining his good luck and asking to have breakfast with her in the morning. The poor dear had earned a good party by her bearing up under the hardships of eight days by canvas-covered buckboard from Fort Bliss, and he certainly did not want to obtrude his mooning presence on her prospects for the evening ahead. He drew the note, gave it over to the *mayordomo* for delivery at the restaurant, retired to his room and to the long-deferred joys of a tub bath and fresh underclothes. An hour later he was resting by the fountain in the patio garden, watching the moon rise over the high wall and listening to the mockers singing sweetly in the coffeebean trees. The smoke of one of the General's fine Havana cheroots was compounding the pleasures of the young evening, and its fragrant luxury had been preceded by a generous peg of the high-proof Kentucky whiskey with which Sibley's sideboard—and the General himself before it, Jud's nose seemed to have told him out on the Salado—was so amply fortified. Thus, he had within him and about him all the elements, save one, for utter contentment. As to that one—

He never got to finish the thought about Felicia.

It was interrupted by the slight sound of the patio's wall gate being eased open, then the rustle of satins and the swish of lace coming along the terra cotta tiles toward the fountain. With that, Jud was on his feet and Felicia Horton was standing there in the moonlight before him.

"What's the matter?" he blurted, assuming something had to be, to account for her surprise arrival.

"Nothing, *now*." She smiled, bowing her dark head demurely. "I did have a fearful headache at the restaurant, and asked to be excused."

"Did you get my note?" he sparred.

"Just as I was leaving." She raised her head, the smile flashing white-toothed in the reflected light of the fountain's spray. "I don't know why I thought I would find you here, but I did. That's why I crept in by the wall gate. I didn't want to bother the servants if you had retired or gone out, and this way I could go right to my room had I missed you. It's just across the patio, there."

"I know," said Jud. "I've been sitting here watching it and praying you'd appear out of it by magic. Then, just like that you're here! That's pretty close to magic, I guess."

"It's not magic, it's music," trilled Felicia. "The wonderful kind that comes when two hearts are in tune."

Jud stood quiet, luxuriating in the thrill of that poetic stroke.

"Felicia—" he started awkwardly, but she put a pink finger to his lips and said, "Wait here like a good boy. I must get out of these stays. I can't breathe. I'm quite sure they gave me my headache. That Mexican girl pulled them so tight—" She was gone without awaiting his reply, and he fell to pacing the patio tiles beside the fountain with a sudden new eagerness and strange unrest that had him breathing tight and hard in half a dozen nervestrung turns. He had no sooner begun to realize he was mightily stirred up about nothing—*or about something*—when the caress of her cool voice was calling softly from the darkness of the cross-patio archways.

She was standing in the open doorway of her room as he came up. The moon, striking in under the arches of the *galería,* framed her with its glowing halo. She had her highnecked ballroom gown down off her shoulders and held protectively gathered at her breast, exposing the lace-edged top bonings of the offending corset, and the frilly trim of the camisole which covered it. She was clearly and obviously embarrassed, yet carrying it off, as she did everything, with a true lady's dignity and graceful propriety. "I'm so sorry," she smiled at the open-mouthed Texas youth, "it's *this* pesky thing." She gestured helplessly to the garment in question. "I didn't want to wake the girl, or bother anyone in the house." She turned her white shoulders shyly to him. "Could you—?" She begged, low-voiced.

Jud knew the whole thing was perfectly innocent. He knew his heart shouldn't pound like that, and the thick blood come up in his throat like it was doing, so fast and heavy it was suffocating him.

He set his teeth and said, "Why, I reckon I can, if you say so—" and took the corsetlace ends in his fingers and began to pull gently upon them.

He had no more than touched them, it seemed, when they ran under his hands like a thread raveling out of a ripped feed sack. The corset came open before him, breaking away down the center and springing apart. He dropped his hands away from it and the force of its spreading, catching its wearer by surprise, pulled the breast-held gown from her startled grasp. Too late,

Felicia Horton moved to retrieve it. In writhing about her clutching fingers missed the folds of the falling dress and the dark-eyed girl stood half turned toward Jud in the autumn moonlight, the only cover for her gleaming body the helpless shielding of her breasts by her crossed arms.

Even then, as Jud stared at her powerless either to drop or to turn away his eyes, Felicia Horton did all any decent woman could do in such an unfortunate circumstance.

Low-voiced, she murmured, "Oh, Judah, I am so sorry," and knelt quickly to bring the dress back up about her and to step, behind its scant protection, toward the darkened sanctuary of her room.

But she stepped slowly and with silken deliberacy, like a retreating cat, and her burning eyes never left Jud's. Nor did the sensuous husk of her apology match the patent innocence of its words. Nor, really, did it need to. Jud never heard the apology. He saw only the flexing of that slender body as it bent to recover the fallen gown, then slid wantonly away from him into the shadows of the arch. And he heard only the feline lure of that voice calling him on into those same shadows after its gliding owner.

He moved forward, came under the archway, went across it into the silent room beyond.

Automatically, he felt behind him, found and swung shut the door.

Its closure plunged the room into yet deeper darkness, accenting the blue-white pool of moonlight which lay around the waiting four-poster bed. Crouched by the bed, caught full in the glare of the moon and still clutching the retrieved gown before her, was Felicia Horton.

As she saw Jud's tall form block the open doorway and his long arm snake out to swing shut the heavy panels behind him, she straightened and dropped the gown away from her.

Across the room she heard him draw in his breath and make a deep sound in his chest, and she began to move her body for him and to answer him with low, throaty sounds of her own. She heard, then, the inarticulate growling of his wordless reply, and the closing in toward her of his heavy breathing from out of the sightless dark beyond the bed.

She started to cry softly, throwing open her arms, arching her back, driving forward her hips and pleading frantically for him to hurry! hurry! hurry!

17

JUD WAS IN San Antonio the better part of five weeks. In the whole time he scarcely had a full night's sleep. History was being rehearsed out along the Salado and he was being brought up in his lines for his part in the coming triumph of the Confederacy in the far West.

Sibley's name was a beacon light which shone over the prairies by dark and by day, calling in the bearded, shaggy-haired horsemen from every corner of the Lone Star state. Men waited in long, dusty queues, standing for hours in the hot October sun to sign the muster rolls. Excitement was epidemic. It ran like some contagious disease throughout the whole of the vast, sprawling bivouac on the riverbank. As with Baylor's buffalo hunters the new recruits each furnished his own mount and armament. Yet there was a significant difference in the two armies past that point.

Those forerunning, first volunteers who had gathered along the Salado four months before had deserted almost as swiftly as they had come in. Baylor had been forced to march long before he was ready to do so, simply to insure himself of having a command with which to march at all.

But Sibley, ah, Sibley!

His problem was not holding his followers together but restraining them from enlisting so fast their swollen ranks would burst the seams of Richmond's authorized two regiments of cavalry and one battery of howitzers.

There were, in fact, so many wrought-up Texans pouring into the original camp on the Salado that a second camp on the Leona River had been set up just prior to Jud's arrival and now, during the term of his stay, a third camp had been needed to handle the throng of Rebel-yelling mustangers galloping into San Antonio to "throw in with Old Henry and his Arizona Brigade."

Compelled thus to go beyond his authorization or turn away hundreds of these wild riding, finest light cavalry troops in the world, Sibley organized a third unit and established a second encampment on the Salado, Camp Manassas, two miles above his own Camp Sibley. Preparations for departure now became intensified.

Within Jud's own few brief weeks of drilling with O'Roark's Scouts on the Salado by day and dallying with the elite of Sibley's officer corps in San Antonio by night (and far into next day) the Arizona Brigade came from a gray, amorphous mass of wild men and half-wild horses into its final lean, professionally ordered marching strength; and with sunset of October 21, 1861, the first unit of this superb frontier cavalry was ready to blow "Boots and Saddles" for the 500-mile advance to Fort Bliss.

Departure time was set at daybreak of the 22nd.

Sibley's men were ready for it.

Promptly as the first streak of red cloud lit up over the distant Trinity, the buglers sounded the call and Colonel Riely's Fourth Regiment mounted up to jingle smartly down out of the hills and into the dusty streets of San Antonio.

It was a wondrous hail and farewell.

Even at this unlikely hour in the morning the ladies of the town were up and cheering on their brave boys.

At the plaza the troops were presented with a hand-made regimental and a makeshift Confederate flag and General Sibley spoke extemporaneously and with inspired eloquence from the unsteady and prancing platform of his spirited stallion's back. Jud Reeves, standing in the latter's honor guard not fifty feet from him, could not hear a word the General uttered. The cheering was so hoarsely incessant that nothing short of a cannon's roar could have broken through it. But Sibley was on fire and so were the aroused men of his command. Failing a military band, the hundreds of raw throats struck up a strident chorus of "The Texas Ranger" and to this great old melody, sweetened by the high-voiced cries of their waving fair ones, the heroes of the Fourth Regiment, Texas Volunteer Cavalry, marched out of town and off west across the llano to disappear into a cloud of horse dust and regional controversy destined to tower into the following century.

The remaining departures were very tightly scheduled owing to a continuing southwest-wide drought and resultant feed and water scarcity along the route.

Colonel Tom Green's Fifth Regiment units began to leave on November 2, those of Colonel Steele's Seventh Regiment to follow on the 20th. Sibley and his brigade staff, including a very impatient Jud Reeves, preceded the latter units by forty-eight hours, departing on the 18th.

The General had become inordinately fond of the Topaz Creek youth, insisting on attaching him to his headquarters company as a special courier to maintain contact with O'Roark in the field, precisely as Baylor had done with him in regard to Elkanah Cavanaugh. It was a bitter blow to Jud, denying him his chance in command as O'Roark's second. But Sibley promised to return him to the scout company at first opportunity "beyond Fort Bliss," and he had been required to accept the situation "as an order" and on that basis.

His young aide's unhappiness at being held back aside, Sibley's start from the ancient city of the Alamo was made under pleasantly auspicious circumstances.

But good beginnings have never guaranteed good endings.

Almost from the hour its last units quit San Antonio, Sibley's Arizona Brigade was in trouble.

And the long journey of Jud Reeves, the tall, quiet-eyed general's son from Topaz Creek, drew swiftly toward its last river and its final crossing.

Henry Hopkins Sibley resigned his commission as a major in the U. S. Army May 31st, 1861. July 6th, 1861 he was appointed brigadier general in the Confederate States Army. Sometime after sunrise November 18th, 1861 and under title of Commander of the Army of the Confederate States of America in the Southwest, he marched from San Antonio for Fort Bliss. Arrived at that post on December 14th, he advanced up the Valley of the Rio Grande toward the Union bastion at Fort Craig, New Mexico during the first week in February, 1862. By early May he was back in Fort Bliss. In June he reached San Antonio once more. There, he furloughed his remaining force, composed his apologia and contemplated his resignation, both thoroughly deserved, neither ever tendered. He had left Texas with 3,700 officers and men of perhaps the deadliest cavalry brigade ever organized. He returned with fewer than 2,000 ragged, hungry and demoralized troops unfit for further immediate service. He was the archetype and the prophetic example of the Southern failure in command. With everything in his favor and easy victory—and empire—within an hour's grasp Sibley, rumored drunk in his wagon, was absent from the field at Glorieta Pass and the South lost Santa Fe, the Southwest, and the War.

The great and fateful dream begun so gloriously the spring before by John Robert Baylor was ended by Henry Hopkins Sibley in something less than six brief months of actual field command. And every single day, every tragic solitary mile of the way, young Jud Reeves rode as close to the Confederate commander as his next heartbeat. There was nothing in all that grand advance, in any of that terrible retreat, which the Texas boy did not see, did not hear, did not smell.

The long march from Sibley's camp on the Rio Salado to the Union salient at Fort Craig on the upper Rio Grande was in itself a major military achievement.

Three days out they reached Sabinal. The country was very dry. Of water there was almost none. What little there was, was scummed and tankish, scarcely fit for the stock, let alone the men. Beyond Sabinal, Indians picked them up and rode their flanks for ten days. They were in large number and the possibility of an attack appeared very real. When the Indians disappeared, disease struck. Measles, heavy chest coughs and virulent bowel looseness devastated the prairie men who had no useful resistance to these urban illnesses. One regiment lost fifteen men to measles alone. Another lost seventeen to bloody dysentery. The unseen hosts continued to march westward with the Texas column; sickness, scarce water, poor grass, furnace heat.

At Fort Quitman on the lower Rio Grande, Sibley held up—waiting for all units to rendezvous for the full dress approach to El Paso and Fort Bliss. Here it was learned that Colonel Steele's regiment had lost one third of its mounts to the trailing Comanches, a grave matter indeed. Colonel Tom Green and Colonel James Riely reported further serious inroads of measles and bronchial pneumonia among their ailing troops. Sibley would not delay. On December 10, the march resumed.

In El Paso, on the 14th, a report was in that a big Union army was moving from California to intercept the Arizona Brigade at Mesilla, before it could get up the Rio Grande to attack the key Union force at Fort Craig.

Here Jud saw Baylor again, and heard him attempt to impress Sibley with the reality of this threat. The latter told Baylor that if he believed the California rumor, well and good. He, Sibley, had a date with Federal commander, Colonel E. R. S. Canby, at Fort Craig. Preparations fot the resumed advance began immediately. In the interim, two Mescalero runners (old friends of Jud's: Chebo and Chavez) came in from Sobre to bring a message from Elkanah Cavanaugh. The old man noted that he felt fine and would report for duty before long. Meanwhile he advised Baylor to "keep your damned soldier boys away from the Apaches, and I will see that the Apaches keep away from your damned soldier boys." He said nothing of his daughter, leaving Jud to assume that this was the way both she and Cavanaugh wanted it. Chebo and Chavez, however, upon questioning, revealed that Star was well and strong and appeared content with her choice of the Apache life.

Sibley had meant what he said about not waiting for the California column to materialize.

On February 1, 1862, he suddenly departed Fort Bliss, breaking camp in the middle of the night and upon four hours' notice. The troops rode hard under orders to bypass Fort Fillmore, as there was smallpox there. They began to see some Mexican dead along the way, badly pocked and discolored, and the men did not like it and grew very restive. Bypassing Mesilla for fear of major contagion, Sibley swung back in upon the river north of that town and drove hard for Doña Ana, which was reached on the 2nd, a tremendous thirty-six-hour march from El Paso.

Here the column was held up half the morning waiting upon scout reports. Jud, riding into the settlement with Sibley and his staff, found the townspeople distinctly unfriendly to the Confederate presence.

They were clearly faithful to the Union and for some reason this loyalty, entirely unexpected by the Southerners, shook Jud unpleasantly. The assumption had been they would be welcomed as liberators. They were treated as Hessians, and the feeling was not good.

Later that day they pushed on, reaching the southern flank of the arid *tornado del Muerto,* the desert "journey of death," the following day about noon. Here couriers caught up with the column with bad news from the South. The California threat had been a Federal ruse. The real Union force was landing at Guaymas on the Gulf of Mexico, would march straight across the Mexican state of Chihuahua to strike at Fort Bliss in the Confederate rear. Also, Governor Terrazas of Chihuahua and Governor Pesquiera of Sonora had rejected the Confederate bids to secure the same rights of passage for their own troops, a major reversal.

Sibley thought little of it. Or of the new Union threat. His objective was Fort Craig. And beyond it Albuquerque, Santa Fe, all New Mexico. The Arizona Brigade was *en avant!* he cried to his officers. Let Baylor look to the rear. His optimism swept Jud along with the tide of other nodding and applauding staff members that early February afternoon. An hour later, immediate excitement was added to future anticipation. The brigade commander called in his young "special scout courier" and calmly directed him to ride up and contact O'Roark in the field, returning at his earliest chance with detailed information bearing on Canby's strength and dispositions at Fort Craig, which information O'Roark should by then possess.

Jud made the ride up into the northern reaches of the *Jornada*, and back in ten hours. He had seen O'Roark and the news he brought back from the dashing Irishman was not cheering. Canby had some 70 officers and 4000 men inside the strongest fortification in the Southwest. It could be guaranteed that Colonel Canby was no Major Lynde and that he would fight.

Sibley smiled at Jud and waved him forward toward the map table over which he had been leaning when the former entered with his dispatches from O'Roark.

"Here," he said, putting his finger on a small dot along the river, as Jud bent interestedly, "is Fort Thorn, our immediate march objective. There," he jumped his finger an inch or so northward, "is Fort Craig, our campaign objective. Remember those two points well, young man. Somewhere between them, within the next seven days, we shall resolve this entire matter."

"Do you mean, sir—" Jud began, but Sibley waved and smiled him gently down.

"I mean, sir," he told him, "that when we have defeated Colonel Canby, New Mexico is ours. There is simply no more to it than that."

To the aroused Jud it seemed there would need to be a little more to it than that, for even as he stood there waiitng to be dismissed, a second courier entered to report that Colonel Kit Carson had just come into Fort

Craig with 1000 New Mexican volunteers, bringing the total Union force to a monolithic 5000. Sibley, counting his mule drivers and ambulance teamsters, might have mustered 2500. Jud winced at the news and watched Sibley. The only visible reaction from the latter was a tolerant nod. "New Mexican volunteers, you say?" he asked of the second courier. "I understand that, sir, to mean they are 'native' troops. Is that correct?" The dusty trooper saluted. "'Yes sir," he said. "They're Mexicans." Sibley nodded again, spread his hands along with his expansive, soft-edged smile. "Well then, sir, there is nothing to keep us from enjoying our lunch. They will not stand up to Texas cavalry."

Jud felt very proud of his commander at that moment.

Saluting him stiffly, he turned to go with the other courier. Sibley checked him quickly.

"One moment, Lieutenant. There was another matter."

Jud wheeled about, saluting again. "Yes sir?"

Sibley eyed him a moment. "It has been difficult staying behind with me, has it not, young man?" he inquired presently.

"Yes sir, I guess it has," admitted Jud carefully.

"There is no guessing to it, I am sure, sir. Not with O'Roark and your own company riding out in the advance all these weeks—out there where all the feel of the enemy is. Ah, no, Lieutenant, you needn't guess with me. We all wait on generals in our times."

He paused, looking up at Jud more closely. "But I

told you I would let you go out when I felt the situation to be right for you, and you to be right for the situation. Did I not, sir?"

"Yes sir, you did," granted Jud, his heart tightening with the prospect of an end to the odious headquarters assignment. "You surely did."

"Well," said Sibley, "here is the situation. A scout patrol will go all the way up tomorrow at daybreak. Call it a reconnaissance in limited force. Say half a troop. I will need an alert young officer in command, as this is a discretionary matter calling for both scouting and military ability. Does the requirement suggest anyone to you, sir?"

"Yes sir!" cried Jud. "It certainly does!"

"Good luck, then," said Sibley, standing up. "Major Jackson will give you the details."

Jud's first command was lean and trim. It consisted of twenty troopers on picked mounts, no pack animals and every man stripped to the essentials of arms and uniform.

The Texas mustangs were as tough as the men who rode them. They went north up the right bank of the Rio Grande at a pounding lope, the new day coming up pink and gray shadowed behind them. In their saddles, Jud's troopers rocked gracefully, long legs jammed straight down into let-out stirrups, backs shipping like spring steel to the tireless gaits of the little horses.

Sibley, now but 80 miles from the Union forces at

Fort Craig, was in waiting need of information on the state of the Union command's nerves, and on the disposition of its officers to either come out of, or stay in their fortifications.

Jud's mission was to go around the fort to the east and attempt to cut its mail line, securing what information he could from the pouches of Canby's couriers relative to the situation *inside* the walls of the Union Colonel's massive redoubt,

He was in beginner's luck.

At 11 A.M. of the second day, February 7, a cold gray morning with a sleety drizzle driving in from the northeast, he and eight hardfaced Texas horsemen jumped and rode down a Federal corporal carrying dispatches to the east. Among the latter was one of a nature to light up the eyes of any young Confederate lieutenant out looking for useful information on the enemy.

Twenty-four hours later the document was in Sibley's hands and Jud, standing proudly by, was listening to him read it aloud to a hastily summoned staff meeting.

"All right, gentlemen," the Southern commander began, clearly as pleased with his youthful favorite as was the latter with himself, "I want you to hear what General Reeves' boy has brought us back from the north."

He paused, waving the captured letter for emphasis.

"This is from the Union Territorial Governor of New Mexico, Henry Connelly. It was posted by regular army mail from Fort Craig to Secretary of State Seward on February Five, this instant. Three days ago, gentlemen. Listen to this."

With the admonition, and as his staff eyed Jud, he read Connelly's letter to Seward.

Canby, of course [the chatty missive led off] had originally proposed to go south and take Fort Bliss. He gave up the idea when Capt. Graydon's spies told him Sibley had already left the latter post and was marching north at great speed. Canby then decided to concentrate his forces here at Fort Craig on the Rio Grande, 176 miles from Santa Fe, 140 miles from Fort Bliss, holding the troops in readiness either to attack or defend, as the moves of the Confederate Commander may dictate.

We now hear from Graydon that the Texas cavalry has come up the Rio Grande like a whirlwind, to die like a spring zephyr at Fort Thorn, some 80 miles south of here.

They appeared beyond a doubt to be marching forward to a decisive battle to determine the fate of the Territory. But something seems suddenly to have cooled their ardor. Could it be Canby's calm determination to await their pleasure?

In all events I have no fears of the result.

We shall conquer the Texan forces. If not in the first battle, it will be in the second or subsequent battles. We will overcome them, rest assured. The spirit of our people is good and I have here and enroute 1,000 and more of the elite of the yeomanry of the country to aid in defending their homes and friends . . .

Sibley put down the letter and stood up.

"I do not need to tell you what this means to our own plans," he said. "The enemy clearly means to stay in his shell and it is as clearly up to us to get him out of it. I propose to do that at once."

He waited out the wash of nods which ran around the circle of his staff officers, then smiled benignly.

"I further submit that we owe a vote of thanks to our young friend here on as fine a piece of scouting as I have seen in the service. Lieutenant," he beamed at Jud, "our heartiest congratulations. Your father would be proud of you, sir!"

The sound of agreement which came from the other officers was more of a noise of throats being cleared than of understandable words. Jud caught the reluctant quality of the response to the commander's praise. He did not resent it because he himself considered Sibley's reward a bit overdone. He was proud of his good luck, yes. But he still had humility and good sense enough to know that it had been luck and not ability or talent.

As quickly as he could he asked to be excused but Sibley shook his head and said that he wanted to see him and that, instead, they would excuse the others so that they might have their little talk then and there.

This merely added to the uncomfortable feeling all around, but the staff left without further comment and he was alone with Sibley.

It developed that the latter had not retained him to talk of old times or the honor of the name.

There was work to do.

"Young man," said Sibley—he had trouble with names and oftener than not, throughout his service with him, he called Jud simply young man or lieutenant—"Young man," he smiled in his fatherly way, "you need not think your capture of this document was quite all I just now let on it was. True, it is a valuable piece of information. It does, indeed, let me know what I must do to crack this Yankee turtle's shell. However, I believe in giving a young officer confidence and know of no better way to do it than to praise him in front of his seniors in command. The action also serves to let those fellows know they must keep at work too. Now if you can remember this little secret, we shall get on famously."

"Yes sir," said Jud. "Thank you sir."

"*Por nada*," waved Sibley in graceful Spanish. "Now you will see that my favors do not come so lightly as you may be imagining. When did you last sleep, sir? On the ground, I mean."

"The night before I left here, General."

"At your age sleeping in the saddle is no great hardship, Lieutenant. At least I hope it is not."

"How is that, sir?"

"I want you to go back up north at once. Get fresh

mounts and take a full troop with you this time. No, better make that twenty men, again. I don't want them to think we are advancing, only patrolling."

"And what, really, will we be doing, sir?"

"Acting, sir, playing a part. I am going to go up there with every man we can put in the saddle, but I want them to think we are uncertain and are poking around with patrols trying to make up our minds. While they are discussing you and your twenty men, Lieutenant, I and my twenty-six hundred men will be easing up on their eastern flank. Do you understand the strategy, sir? And do you agree with it?"

Jud straightened and said, "Yes sir, I do."

Then, after a moment's wait while Sibley only stood there pressing his fingertips together and smiling in that pleased, sunshiny way of his:

"Do you want me to leave at once, General?"

"I am waiting for you to do so as politely as I know how, Lieutenant. If there is something I have forgotten—"

"Oh, no sir!" expostulated Jud, backing out hurriedly through the command tent's drawn flaps. "Not a thing, sir. Thank you sir."

He set at once about getting his men and horses together, borrowing both from a company of the old Baylor 2nd Texas outfit, men and mounts he knew had the bottom to go where he must take them, as fast as he must take them and as furtively. As to his own eight troopers of O'Roark's scout company, he would not ask them to share a fourth sleepless night where they did not have to do so and where it was left with his judgment to make the decision. He told himself he was excusing them on the grounds that their weariness might make them less alert, less militarily effective than they should be. Actually, he simply felt sorry for the poor boys and knew he would appreciate a similar courtesy in their places.

It was a kind of thinking one did not learn in reading Von Clausewitz or Blücher, or for that matter, General Judah Beaumont Reeves. But it was the way Jud Reeves saw it, and it was the way he did it.

To the north, Colonel E. R. S. Canby unwittingly cooperated to make of this second assignment of the young Confederate scout officer as clean and signal a success as his interception of Governor Connelly's letter to Seward.

On the morning of February 8 he sent a strong detachment of regular cavalry to probe south along the Rio Grande and determine if troops reported by Graydon's spies to be camped at the edges of the *Jornada del Muerto,* the desolate stretch of desert below Fort Craig, were the main Confederate army or only chance patrols.

This reconnaissance in force went only as far south as Adobe Walls. There it ran head-on into Lieutenant Jud Reeves' decoy patrol troop feeling its way north.

The Union Commander, Captain Ira C. P. Hickerson, hesitated, then backed off and turned around, convinced these were the troops reported by Graydon's scouts and that, hence, all was yet free of main Confederate troop elements on the Federal southern flank.

Jud, correctly diagnosing the Yankee officer's delay, fostered the illusion that his was an unsupported unit by turning tail and fleeing the instant after Hickerson made his appearance and halted to look over the Texas company.

Hickerson returned directly to Fort Craig, glad enough to have completed his mission without firing a shot or losing a horseshoe nail.

His subsequent assurance to his commander that the "main enemy is not yet in sight down below" raised the already high morale within the walls of the waiting fortress to new and contagious levels of overconfidence.

In the subsequent two days Jud hung off the flanks of the *Jornada,* or circled it to let himself be seen now on one side of the river, now the other, by Graydon's scouts. On the third day, the 11th, he struck on up toward the fort itself, going by dark and swiftly, running out a hunch to have one more look at the Yankee mail route before going back to report in to Sibley on the carrying out of his orders to create diversionary doubts in the minds of Canby and his staff.

Once more his beginner's luck rode with him.

In the cold rose flush of first light on the 12th, he caught a special courier galloping north for Santa Fe carrying orders to "spare no needful means" to get the message he carried out of New Mexico and into the hands of Secretary of State Seward in Washington.

Stated the dispatch tersely:

304

The enemy, exceeding an estimated 3,000 men, is within 20 miles of Fort Craig. He looks fit and seems determined. But fully 4,000 men are under arms here, including 1,200 of regulars. Today our forces march out to meet them. The battle will most likely take place on the 13th about 10 miles below. We still have no fears of the result. Enthusiasm prevails throughout our lines.

The document was dated February 11, the day previous, and signed by Governor Connelly.

It made clear the fact that Graydon's scouts had been looking at more than Jud Reeves' demonstrations and had, in fact, detected Sibley's intention to move up in force behind those demonstrations.

Now the matter was narrowing down.

Jud, sensing this, as well as realizing the importance of the information in this second of Connelly's letters to Seward, turned his weary horsemen at once southward.

Finding Sibley in the field, he delivered his new prize and went promptly to bed where, on the General's orders, he was not aroused until he had slept the clock three quarters around.

When, at last, Corporal Bodie did come for him, he dressed quickly and went up to report at the command tent, where a staff meeting was being held up for him.

He could see at once that the situation had tightened yet further.

Sibley was close to the battle now and his entire attitude had undergone a case-hardening of temper which amazed Jud.

Looking at him in that moment, the young lieutenant felt the thrill go clear down into his bootsoles.

Here, by the Lord, was a professional soldier in command! Every line of his proud figure and patrician face, every syllable of his precise, snapping resume of the tactical picture shaping up to the north, were of pure unadulterated military leanness and hard beauty.

Sibley was determined to play a wily Confederate cat to the Union commander's obviously bold, strong mouse.

They would, said the General, slow their advance on Canby's stronghold, loosening their route march column and straggling the various brigade elements in such a manner as to create among Captain Graydon's Union scouts the distinct impression that there was both disunity of command and lack of determination among the troops in the Confederate army, a disposition, let them say, concluded Sibley, "to hang back at the beginning and stage nothing more than an obvious demonstration at the end."

The theory was that Canby, encouraged by the Texans' clear showing of indecision, indeed even doubt, would come dashing out of his redoubt to his immediate and lasting regret. Sibley would be waiting for him and the Yankee boys would get their first taste of gray Confederate steel in the far West.

Meanwhile Captain Graydon's spy company was hard at work for the Union.

306

Its members reported a growing confusion in the gray camp at the edge of the *Jornada* and shortly, when Sibley began making his dispositions to loosen the Confederate advance as per the agreement taken at that final staff meeting, they convinced Canby that the Southern approach had lost all its former drive and was beginning to break up on the march with all signs of halting altogether before getting clear of the *Jornada*.

The conclusion was that the Confederate command did not now contemplate mounting an attack on the fort and that, moreover, its own condition was such as to invite such a move from the Union defenders. The decision of course was Colonel Canby's, but the opportunity was undeniable.

At once the ebullient Union morale soared to even headier plateaus.

Again, self-congratulations for the victory in a battle not yet joined, let alone decided, swept the Yankee garrison. The climate inside the walls was definitely one of warming confidences and rising expectations.

The atmosphere at the fort cooled off a degree just after daylight of February 19 when the Union scouts dashed in with their tails between their legs to report a Confederate field column moving up from the *Jornada* and dropped another ten degrees when, a few moments later, the Texans marched out of the riverbed within plain view of the Federals on the parapets.

The gray column in question was Captain Burke O'Roark's Salado Scouts.

Aside from its twinkling-eyed Irish leader, this first element of the Confederate army to put in an appearance before Fort Craig consisted of Lieutenant J. B. Reeves, two first sergeants, Alvah C. "Chigger" Denton and Jos. E. "Little Joe" Shelby, and two troops of twenty volunteer cavalry, a total of but forty-two men in all.

Each of these forty-two, however, was a picked veteran, a tracker and sharpshooter of exceptional gifts sifted from the literally hundreds of applicants with such frontier skills who had swarmed into the San Antonio recruitment camps. Jud felt the full pride of being one of their number in that dramatic pause on the east bank of the Rio Grande, but he was given small time to exercise his soaring spirits.

O'Roark at once ordered the column across the river to the west bank. There, they went up to the plain behind the fort and reconnoitered it carefully, sending patrols to the north and south and discussing its points of strength and heavy manning for the better part of an hour. They were in the open at all times, within easy howitzer range of the walls, but Canby did not fire.

O'Roark, at length, had seen enough.

Fort Craig, on final inspection, was still as strong as a bank vault. And as jealously and alertly guarded.

When he got his report to the Confederate commander at noon of the 19th, Sibley was yet some half dozen miles south of Fort Craig. But he had his resting column on the road and ready to move inside the hour. By sunset the last of his baggage train was winding into its new wagon park on the east bank of the Rio Grande, directly opposite and within clear eyesight and earshot of Canby's fortress.

With twenty-five hundred tough, bearded Confederate raiders bivouacked almost within rifleshot of Fort Craig that night, the first doubts began to appear within that stronghold.

The nervous Federal troops crowded the upper parapets in silently increasing numbers as dusk came on. Across the river they could plainly hear the Confederate soldiers laughing and talking. With full dark the enemy campfires began to bloom. In the end their number reached upward of three hundred, and the Union chill deepened.

18

At DAYLIGHT Monday, February 20, 1862, the pickets atop the walls at Fort Craig, New Mexico saw the long line of the Confederate supply train curling sinuously out of its park and straightening to snake due north along the river.

Instantly, the post buglers were blowing the assembly and the advance.

Cooked rations for one day and a single extra box of cartridges were issued each trooper.

The coming action, plainly, could not amount to much. The enemy had obviously funked out and were running off. They had taken their look at Fort Craig and not cared for it in the least. The resulting opportunity was evident. If they could now be, by one swift blow, cut off from their baggage train, Canby would be a brigadier and the war in New Mexico over, all in the same morning's work.

Down the steep embankment in front of the fort, company by eager company, the Federal infantry plunged.

Spurred on by the brass throats of the bugles, they splashed across the winter-low Rio Grande, ignoring the bite of the icy waters in the fever of their desire to take a fall out of cocky Johnny Reb.

If there was a little of the shame of self-consciousness from their previous night's fears adding to their good-natured impatience to come to grips with the "Texians," that could be understood. Those ragged mustang riders with their homemade uniforms, fierce beards, sunburned faces, big slouch hats and outlandish assortment of arms—buffalo guns, squirrel rifles, Union carbines, Mexican muskets, Walker Colt revolvers, Comanche tomahawks, Kiowa buffalo lances, Santa Ana cavalry sabers, Bowie knives and sawed-off shotguns barred across their saddlehorns—well, they were simply enough to startle the everlasting daylights out of any civilized Northern recruit. But after the first look, a man had to laugh at them, for if those wild-eyed cowboys were soldiers he had certainly joined the wrong army.

And so, caught up in the spirit of the thing, the Federal troops shook off the cold water along with last night's doubts. Up the east bank of the Rio Grande they went with a yelling rush. On the double and following the leads of their gallant officers, they struck for the low bluffs fronting the mesa atop which the Rebel supply train was moving north, all the while cheering themselves whoopingly on.

On the mesa it was quiet.

And on the mesa the Confederate sharpshooters lay on their bellies and waited.

Behind them, along the crest of a commanding ridge, Sibley had planted his artillery, as he had his troops, by the dark of the previous night.

The steel jaws of the trap were spread.

Through them crawled the rich bait of the wagon train. And out from his adobe den to seize it rushed the Union wolf.

The gray rifle fire began when the blue advance reached midway of the riverbluff rise. It was wicked but this was still the first blooding for either side, and it was not yet that wicked. The Federals came on, fell back only a few yards to regroup, came on again.

The Confederate cannon opened with grape.

The range was little better than long pistol.

On the slope below, screams replaced shouts. Somewhere in the rear a Union bugler shrilled the recall. Officers were suddenly running. Privates were throwing away their guns. The rally became a rout. Down the bluff to insure the slaughter charged O'Roark's Scouts and three companies of the 7th Texas Cavalry.

The Federal column panicked.

Into the chill waters of the Rio Grande dismounted Union officers plunged shamelessly and in full dress. Enlisted soldiers of the line did not argue the poor example. Only the accurate covering fire from the fort on the far side terminated the gray cavalry charge and saved the blue infantry from decimation.

In the brief action Jud Reeves singled out and rode for sixty yards, stirrup to stirrup, with a young Yankee lieutenant but could not bring himself to shoot the whitefaced Northern boy who would not touch his own gun and kept yelling at him, "Go on! Go on! For God's sake why don't you shoot, Johnny Reb!"

He let the other youth go free, wheeling in mid-gallop to find another foe who would shoot back. He saw three blue troopers running on foot directly ahead of him. He swung his carbine onto them, squeezing the trigger. One of the fleeing soldiers looked around and called hoarsely, "Don't do it, Johnny, please don't do it!" and Jud cursed angrily and pulled his aim up and fired harmlessly over their heads into the muddied waters of the crossing.

By that time the fusillade from across the river was cutting into the Confederate horse and O'Roark was waving the retreat. Jud spun his bay around and loped him away from the Rio Grande and toward the bluffs below the mesa.

For a first action, he assured himself, it had not been too bad. It was only a sort of testing of temper for both sides. Nothing had been proved by it beyond teaching Canby not to send a few companies of boys to do the work of a regiment of men. And beyond demonstrating forcibly to Sibley's Texans that their leader was every inch the grand old heller and remarkable military genius which everyone had said he was back on the Salado.

But even as he told himself the small lie, Jud Reeves did not believe it. Something else had been proved just now.

And Jud Reeves knew, too, what that something else was.

He went back of the bluff, now, very quiet and thoughtful and to a considerable degree disturbed with his conduct in this first chance at field action.

What he had done was certainly not worthy of a Reeves. And if that was the best he could do in a minor skirmish with the enemy already broken and running like rabbits, what was to be expected of his resolution in a major engagement?

The Battle of Val Verde began at noon, February 21, 1862.

The weather was clear, hot, windy.

For the first hours the Federals, sent cautiously back out of Fort Craig by Canby under field command of Colonel Ben S. Roberts and with orders only to "make and maintain contact with the enemy," completely dominated the engagement and at 5 P.M. held every important position on the field.

But by 6 P.M. they were beginning to retreat and by 6:30 P.M. they were in utter panic rout.

The difference was the terrible Texas cavalry which at the crucial sunset hour charged to the muzzles of McRae's murderous Union artillery, galloping into a literal hail of grape and double canister to take the Federal battery intact and unspiked.

Instantly, Colonel Canby, late on the scene and furious with Roberts for having chosen to engage without authorization from him, sent forward a startling order:

"Retreat to the fort! Let every man escape the best he can!"

The instruction completed the forming panic.

Their artillery gone, their officers demoralized by Canby's peculiar order, their ranks galled by the storm of Confederate smallarms fire now creeping toward them out of the smoke clouds of Sibley's cannon, the blue troopers broke to the man.

The field was entirely cleared and silent within thirty minutes.

The Union casualties were 68 killed, 160 wounded, 35 missing. On the Confederate side the toll was 36 dead, 150 wounded, 1 missing.

The first of the dead of both armies were buried that same twilight under flags of truce beside the muddy channel of the Rio Grande.

In the lull and by violating the terms of the burial agreement, Canby got his nerveshot survivors whipped back into Fort Craig. Sibley, graciously, did not choose to deny the enemy this small comfort. A Confederate bugler blew tattoo from the edge of the mesa as the short winter day died into darkness, and the Battle of Val Verde was ended.

That it had been a real battle there could be no question.

The action was full scale, fiercely and very well fought. Casualties on the Southern side were significantly above the ten percent accepted by tactical students as "heavy" in the bloody arithmetic of professional war.

A hundred men had died on the field, other scores would succumb off it to the triple battleground specters of gangrene, tetanus and post-wound pneumonia. This had, then, to be called the real thing. And for every hour of its powder-burned passage, Jud Reeves had ridden and wheeled in the van of the fighting.

He had, too, in the last grim minutes before the Union artillery died, found the answer to his yesterday's doubts.

That answer had come to him when the Salado Scouts had spearheaded the fantastic "shotgun charge" of the Confederate Cavalry which had torn apart every man at the guns of McRae's gallant battery with point-blank blasts of bird and buckshot.

In that charge Jud had killed his first man in field action combat.

He had seen the frightened, smoke-grimed face looking up at him and he had seen its features melt away as the cylinder bore in his hands had bucked twice and the double charge of #4 buckshot in the old

Ethan Allen 12-gauge had hailed into that face. After that he had loaded and fired again and again until there was no foe left standing before him, and no more brass shells left beneath the digging of his fingers into the emptiness of his canvas ammunition pouch.

Then the little bay had quit wheeling and plunging and had stood suddenly very quiet. The stillness and the smell of death had shut down over the silent guns of McRae's Battery. And Jud had known that he could kill a man in battle passion, and that his own resolution under enemy fire was no longer in professional or personal question.

The knowing had not left him proud.

It had left him sick.

Thirty-six hours later, in the small hours of the second night, Jud Reeves sat shivering under an oilskin poncho in the Confederate camp seven miles north of Fort Craig, New Mexico, trying to write a long deferred letter.

But reminiscences of the battle would not down.

He had seen naked war, now, and the pictures of it would not readily withdraw themselves from his weary mind.

The burial details were still out by the river, and would be there for another full day. The camp was quiet but did not lie easy. Jud knew why. Too many fine comrades were gone, too many brave boys were at rest to wake no more, too many bright smiles were faded forever, for there to be any elation in the Confederate ranks. And there were other matters of grave concern to darken the Southern outlook. Yesterday morning, before daybreak, two hundred head of wagon teams had broken loose from the picketlines to seek water at the river. There, the Yankees had captured them to the last head. The loss could be critical, even decisive. It meant that fifty wagons and supplies and munitions would have to be destroyed, reducing the Confederate column's route march rations to five days.

Sibley, of course, would hear none of such pessimism. But Sibley was not the shining light he had been forty-eight hours before. He had not been seen on the forward lines in all of yesterday's fighting. The rumor ran the camp that he had been confined to his ambulance the entire time, too much under the influence to sit a horse. Colonel Tom Green, who commanded in his absence, had issued a gallant denial of the allegation but the private soldiers still whispered over their fires and the spirit was not the same in the Southern camp. Jud had caught the air of change. It depressed him, but he fought against it. He would have to have seen Sibley, himself, to have believed it. He had been too positively magnificent in command the previous day on the mesa. No leader could have been better. Crisp. Sharp. Decisive. No, it was a lie. There were always small men to snap at the heels of great ones. The General was a professional soldier; Jud could not see him otherwise.

His restless mind moved on, coming to the death of

Little Jo Shelby. The cheerful boy had taken a saber cut across the collarbone from a Union artillery sergeant; an unbelievable wound going completely into the lungs and with which he had lived two full hours. But Jud could also see another terrible wound staining a uniform of a different color, and he knew that Little Jo was no more brutally or honorably dead than the Union boy without the face beside the Number Four gun of McRae's battery.

Jud shook his head, forcing his thoughts away from the dead.

That was yesterday and this was today, and would soon be tomorrow. He looked at the blank page of letter paper beneath his hand. On the point of again putting pencil to it, he was interrupted by an order to report to Sibley's tent. He went up, forthwith, curious, despite his great fatigue, to know what it was that would call the General's staff together at 4 A.M.

Another Union dispatch rider had been captured. His intelligences were from Canby at Fort Craig to the area commanders at Santa Fe, Albuquerque and Fort Lyon. In detail, under date of February 21, the principal document stated:

After a severe battle today, the enemy succeeded in effecting a lodgment on the river above this place, and will probably succeed in cutting off your communications with the upper country. You will hold yourself prepared to remove or destroy all public property, and particularly provisions, so that nothing that is useful may fall into the hands of the enemy. All trains and detachments now on the way should be turned back.

Sibley's decision was immediate. The gentlemen of his staff concurred in it with feeling. The thirty miles to Socorro would be made by forced march. There the sick and wounded would be left, the combat force striking at once north for Albuquerque: rendezvous for the field column: Belen, thirty-five miles south of Albuquerque; the time, March 1.

Jud returned to his camp spot feeling better.

The General had been clear-eyed and alert as a child. His diction had been brisk, thoughts keen as steel, hand and eye steady as a rock. Dr. Covey, the brigade surgeon, had put around the word that it was chronic dysentery which had held the commander to his wagon at Val Verde. Major Jackson, Sibley's adjutant, had cemented this claim with the statement that the General had suffered from the complaint since Monterrey in the Mexican War. Jud, with no reason to doubt either affirmation, accepted both. Still, the improvement in spirit was but one part of his problem. There remained the matter of the letter.

Once more, he squared himself away. He frowned with a good deal of determination, made a threateningly serious flourish with the pencil. It was no good. He drew off, then moved in again. He made two or three running starts, each time bringing up abruptly. He scratched out, "My Darling," and "Dearest One" and "My Lovely Sweetheart," finally settled grimly on "Dear Felicia."

Then he sat there.

More would not come.

He tore up four sheets of paper before he got down what he wanted on the fifth. Even then it was a hobbled effort, crow-hopping along as though ankle-clogged. Still it was the best he could do with such a confusing subject in so short a time. Anxiously, now, he scowled his way through what he had written.

> Camp Val Verde,
> Feb. 23, 1862,
> Daybreak—

Dear Felicia,

You are never out of my mind. I worry continuously whether you can truly love a poor country cowboy with no money and little prospects. You are so beautiful and so accustomed to all that is rich and fine, that my own poverty and plainness seem like sins of the worst sort to me. I wish for your sake that I were truly *El Gringo mas opulento*, as I heard myself described by two of the Sibleys' foolish Mexican housegirls outside my room one day.

It is strange. Once a family has had wealth and holdings, it seems people cannot forget it. One remains *un gran patrón,* regardless of all the bank failures and bad investments in the world.

I sensed this very keenly in San Antonio.

I know those good people did not realize my father died penniless and for some reason—I suppose of family pride—I could not bring myself to tell them of their mistake. Just as surely, though, I know you did guess my little masquerade and I shall always thank you for helping me to carry it off.

Conscience truly does make cowards of us all, for here am I confessing my gratitude from the safety of this fair valley in far off New Mexico.

Forgive me all my unworthiness and God bless you until our parting promise (do you remember it?) is fulfilled and I can return to find you waiting for me at Fort Bliss. Meanwhile, you may write me in the field and it will come to me in the Staff mailbag. My best to Maj. Considine and his fine wife, with whom I understand you are staying.

Your obedient servant,

J.B.R.

Jud put down the letter, shook his head, still frowning and lip-pursing his displeasure with it.

It was not right. Not right at all.

Still, it would have to go as it was and with no changes.

Up in front of Sibley's tent the dispatch rider was loading the last of the Fort Bliss mail. Over east the horizon was going from black to dirty gray. To the west, whipping in across the river, the rising wind was beginning to spit a thin rain between its sharp teeth.

Jud Reeves shivered and blew out the wagonlamp. The rain hissed onto its hot glass as he hung it back on the field ambulance from which he had taken it. The sound made him shiver again. He hunched deeper into the oilproofed poncho, set off swiftly up the hill toward the darkly shadowed figures in front of the command tent.

The Belen rendezvous was kept to the hour. By daybreak of the following morning, March 2, 1862, the Confederate column was in sight of Albuquerque. The view of the city from the southern hills was spectacular. In the wine-clear New Mexico air no detail of the distant metropolis of the North could be confused. The truth towered black and greasy against the pale green of the daylight sky. Jud and his weary companions all saw the smoke; they all knew what it meant.

They had lost their forced-march race to beat the Union garrison to the torch.

Jud heard one hungry, hopeful rider of the 4th Texas Cavalry, the advance unit of the halted column in line just behind O'Roark's Scouts at its head, express precisely the military situation and bitter disappointment of himself and all his empty-bellied fellow Confederates when he stood in his stirrups to announce to the surrounding stillness *"Sonofabitch, they've burnt her!"*

Expressed either pointedly or politely, the Confederate failure to outmarch Canby's dispatch riders and seize the huge stores of Union subsistence rations at

Albuquerque was a serious loss to the ill-fed Texas troops. The Southern cavalry was sweeping the field and starving to death on the ashes of each new triumph.

Delay now became intolerable. Pausing only to garrison the gutted town, Sibley drove on for Sante Fe.

The advance, begun March 3, went badly from the first. Its forward elements under Major Pyron, recently promoted for his prominence at Val Verde, were no farther along than Algodones, twenty-two miles north of Albuquerque, on March 5. And here the matter of column supply, particularly of food and clothing, became critical. Sibley would not be halted by any such logistical nonsense, and called upon O'Roark to repair the deficiency at once.

Fortunately, the Irish Captain had a solution.

A spy had just come in to report an unburned dump of Federal supplies of all kinds at the tiny Mexican hamlet of Cubero, sixty-five miles to the west. O'Roark's suggestion to Sibley: Go and get the goods. Sibley's reply to O'Roark: Do so at once, sir! The mutual choice of subordinate officer to lead the raid: Lieutenant Judah Beaumont Reeves, second-in-command of the hard-riding Salado Scouts.

The Scouts made the detour to Cubero in four days. But the twenty-one wagonloads of precious material which they captured there were a full week in reaching the stalled column.

It was March 13 before Jud returned and the "Forward ho!" echoed down the long gray lines to send the momentarily revitalized Arizona Brigade once more toward Santa Fe.

In that city Union Commander Major Donaldson, listening to his fainthearted scout patrols, decided that his post was not defendable and not so by virtue of defamed Major Lynde's earlier rationalization of the Fort Fillmore debacle, "because it was commanded on all sides by hills."

When Jud Reeves heard of the spineless surrender of Santa Fe and its subsequent commendation from the Union high command through captured dispatches while the Confederate column was still many miles south of the abandoned territorial capital, his contempt for the military game as played to the rules of the regular United States Army—begun by his witnessing of the Fillmore shame—was bitterly completed.

Thank a just and generous Providence, he told himself, that the South did not fight that way.

Wars were won by going forward, and Sibley had not backed off an inch since leaving Fort Bliss.

As a matter of fact there was a good deal more than regional loyalty behind Jud Reeves' convictions.

The Union Command believed itself in terminal trouble.

As of sunrise, March 4, Donaldson began moving out of Sante Fe.

By that night most of his troops and a tremendous supply train of one hundred and twenty wagons were under march toward Canby's new point of concentration at Fort Union, some sixty mountainous miles to the northeast. Until daylight faded their ugly redness, the night skies over the deserted city were stained with the smoke and flame of the demolition fires left burning by the fleeing Federals. By high noon of March 5 the smoke had lifted and the last Union soldier was gone. Santa Fe, the ancient capital of the *Conquistadores,* lay prostrate before the Confederate approach, not a solitary pistol shot having been fired in its defense by the retreating U. S. troops.

Again what should have proved a rich banquet, became in fact only another grim belt tightening.

With the uncontested surrender of Sante Fe the soundness of Canby's strategy of scorched retreat became clear to all but the most faithfully obtuse of Sibley's staff. The latter, to the amazement of his juniors when they confronted him with their dark fears, refused utterly to consider any such negative theories. There could be no possible question of taking pause to consolidate and refit the command at this time. Instead, they must drive on for Fort Union without delay. Beyond that powerful redoubt, by far the most important in the Southwest, no place remained for the Union troops to retreat. Seize this last bastion of Federal strength and New Mexico and Arizona would belong to the South. That, sirs! was a positive theory! Could there by any least doubt or reasonable question of its validity?

There was no adequate defense against such heady persuasion.

Jud Reeves and the remainder of the recaptivated staff were picked up and carried along despite their logical doubts.

The Confederates occupied Santa Fe on March 23, 1862.

Forty-eight hours later they marched for Fort Union.

The war in New Mexico at that moment, and by majority opinion on both sides, was considered to be within its final week.

At daybreak of March 26 the situation was this:

The 1st Colorado Volunteers under Colonel John Slough, a Denver lawyer turned soldier, were moving west out of Fort Union for Santa Fe. His second-in-command, Major J. M. Chivington, when not fighting for his country an ordained Elder of the Methodist Church, with about 400 troops of the 1st in his independent force was moving in the same direction from Bernal Springs. The combined strength of the converging commands was over 1300. They were for the most part volunteer militia seasoned with a little stiffening of regulars. The Colorado units had pushed down from Denver through the high mountain country in the dead of winter to occupy Santa Fe. Hearing that Donaldson had given over that city to the enemy, they had marched to Fort Union, refitted, picking up the regular companies, struck out on the present morning not to threaten Santa Fe but to turn off their route at Galisteo, march south for a juncture in the field with the column Canby was reported to have moving north out of Fort Craig, thus to slash the Confederate rear and isolate Sibley at Santa Fe.

Major Pyron, for the Confederates, with five hundred picked cavalry, including O'Roark's Salado Scouts and Lieutenant Judah Beaumont Reeves, was jingling eastward out of the fallen capital under orders to proceed to Glorieta at the western approaches of Apache Canyon for a rendezvous with Scurry and the 4th Texas.

Apache Canyon, through which ran the military road from Santa Fe to Fort Union, was a wild, 1000-foot-deep defile whose precipitous cedar- and pine-topped walls were within cannonshot of one another at their tops, and whose merciless wagon road to summit at Glorieta Pass would have intimidated a Missouri muleskinner with a six-team hitch on an empty field ambulance. What it was to the heavily loaded, under-teamed army freighters of the Southern supply train had scarcely begun to be appreciated that March morning of 1862. There was, in fact, no doubt anywhere in the Confederate column. All of Pyron's battalion were fresh and eager for the assault on the Federal redoubt of last resort at Fort Union, now but a single day's march away.

In the same hour of high optimism, indomitable Colonel Wm. R. Scurry and his fabled "Fighting Fourth" were en route from Albuquerque, via Bernalillo, with orders to effect the joining with Pyron at Glorieta. At the time, the alkali-cured veterans of the 4th Texas were fighting mainly dismounted owing to the great loss of horses at Val Verde. This indignity only spurred their desire to get at the Federal remount at Fort Union and to turn in shanks' mare for a good fat Yankee gelding. With Scurry, however, and to give him some reconnaissance force, was one battalion of the 7th Texas, mounted.

High noon, now; all units, Confederate and Union, continue the cautious march toward the approaches, east and west, of Apache Canyon.

Afternoon; the late winter sunset comes early, catching the forward elements in opposite ends of the narrow defile and forcing a choice of field camps and a holding up in poor positions on the parts of all four Northern and Southern commanders.

Day's end; the long night of last waiting begins.

Pyron and Scurry, Slough and Chivington. Their lines are drawn, their forces at station and committed for tomorrow's fight. The issue will be joined, perhaps finally settled, by following nightfall. This may be the last hour of the last day for either the North or the South in New Mexico.

And Pyron and Scurry, Chivington and Slough, are ready and waiting in the wings of history.

But where are Canby and Henry Hopkins Sibley?

The end question was the one soldiers on both sides were asking themselves in the endless hours before dawn of March 27. Yet there was a grim difference in their answers. And swiftly, a fateful one.

The boys in blue *knew* where Colonel E. R. S. Canby was.

He was 176 hopeless miles south, sitting in Fort Craig counting his shrinking subsistence rations and worrying that he might starve to death before the Confederates did.

The boys in butternut gray *did not* know where Brigadier General H. H. Sibley was.

They could only guess—and listen to the same old ugly undercurrent of rumor.

The General had not been on the field since Santa Fe, and he was not on it now. There was talk of "the wagon" and of his "Mexican complaint." The question of his certain whereabouts passed around the campfires, unanswered then as it had been through the days and hours before, and as it was destined to pass through the months and years to come.

There was only one hollow reply which Pyron's brave lads and Scurry's exhausted foot cavalry could furnish that last night before the monstrous blunder in Glorieta Pass.

He was not with his men.

At 8 A.M., March 27, from his night camp at Kozlowski's Ranch near the eastern end of Apache Canyon, Major J. M. Chivington began his advance upward toward the pass.

A leisurely hour and a half later, Major Pyron broke his Confederate camp in the west end of the canyon and started his forces up the Santa Fe side of the ascent. The gracious Southern start allowed the early-to-rise Yankee troops to top out first on the summit. The advantage was more dangerous than Pyron appreciated.

Scurry was already twelve hours late. Pyron imagined he could not now be another two or three hours in coming up. Chivington knew better. He had captured a Confederate scout patrol the previous evening carrying dispatches from the commander of the 4th Texas to Pyron at Glorieta, apprising the latter of his delay and approximate position. The crafty Coloradoan had succeeded in getting the aggressive Texas boys of the patrol to confirm their dispatches simply by suggesting they were spurious and in reality the highly touted "Fighting Fourth" had turned tail and was "Scurrying" back to Albuquerque.

Loyal Confederate sergeant, Alvah Clinton "Chigger" Denton, and his proud troopers knew better than that.

Unhappily, they did not know better than to say as much.

They had so, by God! just come from Colonel Scurry and the Fourth. They were only prowling around on this long way home hoping to pick up some information for their own outfit, Lieutenant Reeves' company of Captain Burke O'Roark's Salado Scouts!

The result of this exercise in Southern disobedience and misguided spunk—the old Rebel game of every man for himself once beyond sight of camp—was that Chivington, at the same time Pyron assumed Scurry to be virtually within cannonshot, knew for a fact that he was sixteen miles away across a country so rough and rocky a wild burro could not get over it in less than eight hours.

Chivington caught Pyron extended on the road below him and by infiltrating both canyon slopes above him was able to pin him down and begin enveloping his flanks.

The Confederates fought hard, holding the road and their position upon it with nothing but Southern gumption and two small cannon for several hours. But by midafternoon they were softening and by early sundown they were ready to give way. At once Chivington sent in young Captain Cook's crack company of Colorado Cavalry.

Cook's troopers promptly rode through the Confederate Command from front to rear, and the canyon dam was broken.

The Texas troops now drew back in some disorder but no rout. There was not light enough remaining for a pursuit to conclusion and Chivington broke off the engagement, leaving the field to the battered Southerners and retiring to Pigeon's Ranch, a roadhouse on the Fort Union road near Kozlowski's. His casualties were 5 dead, 14 wounded.

The "victorious" Texans licked their far more serious wounds of 35 killed, 43 wounded, 100 missing in action, at the opposite, western end of the ten-mile canyon, and waited there for another day and another chance at the stubborn damned Yankees.

The Rebel camp was exceedingly quiet. There was still no news of the General and no word from Colonel Scurry and the Fourth. The outlook was chancy. Very chancy.

Then, at 3 A.M. the latter came up with his marched-out horseless cavalry and immediately the incurable Confederate optimism was off and running again.

The rebuff of Pyron's unsupported probe up the canyon could not be called anything worse than bad luck. It was in no sense decisive and the Southern troops were not in the least bit doubtful of a recoupment now that they had a little help.

It was true that the damned "Pikes Peakers," as they were calling the Colorado Volunteers, were a sight less fun to mix with than the Mexican militia they had manhandled at Val Verde. As a matter of honest fact, they were tough as hell. With their black hats and red-slashed blouses they made fine targets to shoot at. But the devil of it was that dropping a few of them did no permanent good at all. The rest of them just came on that much more the merrier. But they had the "Fighting Fourth" with them now, by damn, and those Yankee rascals would soon see the difference that made!

The Southern spirit, as usual, was superb. From regimental colonels to squad corporals the little Texas army was still sound. But where was the brigadier commanding? Where was the Commander of the Army of the Confederate States of America in the

Southwest? No one knew. And the Confederate units gathered in Apache Canyon waiting for daybreak of March 28 were deployed without overall command supervision.

In direct sequence to the lack, they committed the fatal oversight: they left their entire supply train of eighty fully loaded wagons parked at Johnson's Ranch only six miles in their rear and guarded by but one light gun and two hundred pickup troops, including a number of walking wounded and other sick-leave convalescents.

Before dawn "Preacher" Chivington was into the hills, swinging wide around the just wakening Confederate camp.

By 8 A.M. he was in position above the precious wagon train, glassing its park with his telescope. He noted the small quantity and indifferent quality of the guard, put his glass away, moved silently and swiftly on down the timbered spine of the north wall.

Well past the wagon park, he dropped off the high ridge into the canyon, came up again behind the Confederate train and between it and escaped to Santa Fe.

He was in final position by 10 A.M.

Still, he waited.

Shortly before eleven, Scurry opened with his artillery on the Union lines around Pigeon's Ranch. At the sound of the Southern guns across the pass, Chivington jumped the Confederate wagon park.

His fateful work was made even quicker by the fact that ten minutes before Scurry opened fire, the entire force of two hundred Rebel supply train guards, except for seventeen men, dashed off up the canyon to get in on the fight. The breach of orders and the rape of discipline was but another incident of the characteristic Southern disregard for any commands save those of "Captain Whim."

Scurry and Slough, who had come up late on the 27th to support Chivington's advance, fought a draw at Pigeon's Ranch that March 28. It was a good hot fight, although scarcely decisive, and neither of the primary commanders knew, or guessed, the import of what had happened behind their backs. They both left the field content with their performances. Slough returned to Fort Union, saying nothing that is remembered. Colonel Scurry retired upon Santa Fe to claim, for the record, that another victory had been added to the long list of Confederate triumphs in the West.

The ugly truth lay in neither of these actions.

It lay in the dispatch which Major J. M. Chivington wrote on the field shortly before nightfall of March 28, 1862, three full days previous to Scurry's March 31st announcement from Sibley's headquarters in Santa Fe of the overwhelming Southern victory in the Battle of Glorieta Pass.

The Preacher said it all in two terse sentences.

... I have captured the Confederate wagon trains, all loaded with ammunition, clothing, subsistence and forage. All of them were burned on the spot, or otherwise rendered useless ...

The South, regardless, continued to believe its own speeches and quote its own dispatches for several days.

But Sibley was beaten.

All the available supplies of food and ammunition in the Territory of New Mexico were either at Fort Craig or Fort Union. The Confederate command had nothing of its own to load, fire, eat, or issue. It was simply fall back south on Fort Bliss and live to fight a new campaign, or stay in the north and die of slow starvation.

The final straw came on the cold wind of a scout report from Socorro: Canby had left Fort Craig and was marching north. Sibley called his staff together and at 5 A.M., April 3, the decision was taken to abandon New Mexico. Santa Fe was cleared on the 5th. A week later the retreating column passed through Albuquerque, continuing southward along both sides of the Rio Grande. On the 15th a skirmish was fought at Peralta with Canby's forward elements. The retreat resumed, the Federal and Confederate armies marching within voice shot of each other on separate sides of the stream. There was no Union pressure. Canby's force was twice the size of Sibley's. He had supplies for six months, his opponent but for a few days. The outcome seemed obvious, and imminent.

Or did it?

The night of the 16th the Confederate campfires burned until dawn. With daylight of the 17th Canby saw why they had been kept going. But hours before that, in the dead of the preceding night, the details of the sight which widened the Union commander's eyes had been seared, firsthand and forever, into the memory of a gaunt young lieutenant of scouts on Sibley's staff.

Jud Reeves sat waiting, hunched and forlorn, on the old down cottonwood which shielded his company's fire. He had just returned from what must certainly be the last staff meeting of the Arizona Brigade as an organized army. General Sibley's look, and sound, of tragic defeat would have broken the heart of any loyal Texan. And yet the General had much to remember. Those of his staff who knew *how* much, could not help but harden a little toward him. But he was still Sibley. None could deny, not even in that last hour there at Goat Crossing above La Joya, that great warm heart, that sad, distant smile, that magnificent grand old soldier's look.

Perhaps God would forgive him where his own men could not.

The meeting had been brief. In getting over the river that afternoon they had lost more than twenty of their remaining sixty wagons. With them had gone nearly half the mules. In result, General Sibley proposed a desperate measure: abandon camp.

The idea was irrational, shocking, and Sibley would not be talked out of it. His final order: abandon all sick and wounded, leave all supplies save five days' rations, take nothing which could not be carried by muleback or rucksack, be ready to depart within the hour.

That had been forty-five minutes ago. The time seemed to Jud more like five minutes. He must have dreamed or dozed there on the cottonwood log. He shook himself and got to his feet. A whitefaced frown twisted his features. Among the other exigencies of the hour, Burke O'Roark lay breathing raggedly in his blankets beyond the fire. It was smallpox going into pneumonia, and Surgeon Covey had said that to move him would be to kill him. Jud Reeves was at last in command of the Salado Scouts—and what a command it was.

There were but seven men left of it, not even a full squad counting himself. They had one mount, his own rough-coated bay. Beyond the fire now he could see his corporal coming, leading the faithful animal. Behind him came the five privates, one of them proudly towing a stolen packmule. Three of the privates had no shoes, none of them had a recognizable uniform. As they drew near, Jud heard a commotion beyond them and, glancing in its direction, saw Sibley himself approaching.

The General passed by without seeing him. He wore a civilian's tweed greatcoat, a Mexican woman's shawl, a ludicrous pair of Union-captured canvas overshoes, or packs. Jud shivered and dropped his eyes. Could this be the fearless old Lion of the Salado? This the proud leader of the fierce Arizona Brigade? It did not matter. Here were the boys with his horse at last.

Jud Reeves looked up. He took out his campaign watch and squinted to see its hands.

The time was 1.20 A.M., April 17, 1862.

"All right, boys," he said. "Let's go."

19

IT WAS a cruel march.

They went west from the river into the northern end of the arid Sierra Madelena Mountains, picked their way down the bleached spine of this desolate range into the even more forbidding Sierra de San Mateo. Here they struck the dry bed of the Palomas River, turning eastward again to follow along this parched watercourse and so to come, once more, into the green valley of the Rio Grande.

They sighted the latter stream ten days after the start from the ill-fated camp below Peralta.

They had traveled a route of over a hundred miles on five days' rations and three days' water. For one eight-mile section across a high mountain shoulder they had hacked their way with camp axe, Bowie knife, trenching shovel and officer's sword through brush too heavy to pass a man on foot, let alone a loaded pack-mule or a wheeled artillery carriage. In another passage of far less than a mile, going almost straight up to cross the last range, they had been forced to dismantle the remaining guns, which they had hauled by hand every yard of the way from the Rio Grande, and pack them up the incline on their backs, piece by piece. So much vitality was wasted in this futile effort that for simple want of human strength to go back down after it, the last of their precious ammunition was abandoned and left lying at the bottom of the declivity. It was here, too (Eagle Pass), that Jud's little bay broke down and the hollow-eyed youth had to lead him off the narrow trail and put a bullet behind his ear. Abandoned, as well, in the ascent, were most of the other livestock and all equipment still carried by the men. Only Sibley's symbolic guns were saved. The few horses and mules which got across the divide played out in the next few miles beyond it. When the starving Texas troops reached the river forty-eight hours later they were afoot to the man, nothing on their lacerated backs but the shreds of cloth not clawed away by the cruel-taloned brush of Eight Mile Mountain, and no boots or shoes upon their tortured feet save what tied-on strips of harness leather and pack canvas the rock fangs of Egle Pass had not ripped and torn away.

There was no command remaining.

Every man was on his own and they moved loosely together only because of human misery's eternal need for companionship.

They came down out of the hills and to the river below Fort Craig on the morning of April 27. There had been no pursuit from Canby at the north except for a company of Graydon's spies trailing them two days into the Madelenas. There was no pursuit now, either, from Carson in the south. Unmolested, the gaunt skeleton of Sibley's brigade rattled on down the river and came, another four days later, past Elephant Butte, Caballo, Arrey, Rincon and Doña Ana, at last to the broad curve of the Rio Grande above Old Mesilla.

Resting on a low hill in sight of town, Jud Reeves sat and watched the thin lines of beaten, empty-eyed troopers limping along the bend of the river below. As he did, another tattered figure, as forlorn and dust bearded as his own, came around the shoulder of the rise behind him. Jud heard the dragging footsteps and looked up. The newcomer clumped to a halt in front of him. It was Darrel Royce, one-time fellow "buffalo hunter" from Baylor's brigade. Both youths managed a wary nod.

"Light down and set a spell, Lieutenant," invited Jud. "It will be a while before supper."

"Many thanks young man," replied the other. "Can you tell me if the Confederate cause is looked kindly upon in these parts?"

He slumped down onto the grass at Jud's side. "Jesus," he said, "this feels good."

Jud gave him a little time. Presently they would talk. Meanwhile there was a good deal to think about.

He had not seen young Royce to speak to since the latter's transfer from Baylor's to Sibley's staff shortly before Val Verde. Royce had subsequently departed Sibley's staff at about the same time his friend Hugh Preston had been promoted from company to battalion command, just after the taking of Santa Fe. Jud had thought of both of them from time to time but never

340

seriously enough to inquire after them. Now that he and Royce had chosen the same moment to sit down and share the same hillside that sunset of May 1 outside Mesilla, the natural camaraderie of dangers shared and long marches made together asserted itself.

"Royce," he asked softly, "what ever happened to Hugh Preston?"

"He's dead. Went to pieces and ran off the field at Glorieta. One of his own men shot him in the back."

Jud shook his head. "Hard to believe of Preston," he said. "It seemed as though the army was his life."

"Seemed as though," agreed the other youth. "I know one thing for sure. It was his death."

Jud studied his companion frowningly. "Royce," he asked, "what does it all add up to now that it's over?"

Royce shrugged wearily. "The whole damned thing," he said, "never was anything but a sagebrush sideshow. I learned that when Sibley put me in the QM Corps."

"How come him to transfer you?" queried Jud interestedly.

"Didn't like the way I bucked an order to go forward under fire at Val Verde," answered Royce unhesitatingly. He shifted his position, deepened his scowl. "I was about to make a point concerning smalltown tent shows and what I learned about our little war in the Quartermaster's Corps."

He took a breath, plunged on.

"Reeves, those sacrosanct sons of bitches back at Richmond never sent our troops five cents' worth of subsistence or ammunition from the first day at San Antonio to the last at Santa Fe. Do you know what we have been doing out here the past five months? Creating a diversion. That's what the textbooks call it. I've got a better name for it. It was a dirty, miserable, two-wagon sideshow, deliberately sent out on the back road to its own destruction."

He sat up, eyes narrowed angrily.

"Sibley was our lion," he charged raspingly. "He was considered a mangy old specimen who could still roar loud enough to stir up a little excitement out here in Texas, but who wasn't worth letting into the main arena back there along the James and the Potomac. So they shipped him out here to raise his own army and fight his own war and they never intended to give him a penny's worth of backing from the first minute. And do you know what he almost did in spite of them? He damn near won them the war west of the Mississippi, that's all! And did it, by God, on nothing but Texas gall and sweat and guts!"

As suddenly as he had launched his diatribe, Royce dropped it. Jud sensed the shameful truth in his outburst, shared its deep anger with him. He nodded and said, low-voiced, "I reckon that's about it, though I never could have said it half so well."

"I'm sorry, Reeves," answered Royce shortly. "I really don't know any more about this than you do. Maybe I'm wrong. Maybe we haven't lost, been defeated, failed. Who can actually say?" He looked at Jud, a thought occurring to him with the question.

"What do you suppose your father would have called it?" he asked.

"He had only one answer, ever," frowned Jud. "To win."

"Then we lost and we're failures. Thank God we settled that."

"Yes," said Jud Reeves, "thank God we did."

The sunset took over again for a lengthening spell. Jud thoughtfully watched the last of the long gray lines winding past below. At length, nodding toward them, he said quietly, "I wonder how many of those other boys down there are thinking the same thing tonight?"

"That," replied Royce, getting stiffly to his feet, "is something they will never admit—they're Southerners."

He said it with the soft, fierce ring of Confederate pride in it, and Jud understood. He got to his feet, saying no more. The two boys set off down the hill, walking side by side, backs straight, shoulders squared. The first knot of stragglers they drew near peered at them curiously, then saluted awkwardly as they passed. When they had gone on, the rough, bearded troopers laughed and made coarse remarks about the foolishness of their own action. Why, for the love of God, those were the first officers they had saluted since Peralta!

The little company of stragglers disappeared into the twilight down the Mesilla road, still ragging themselves, still threatening to desert, still sneering at the idea of saluting anything which had to do with Henry Hopkins Sibley and the Arizona Brigade.

They never realized they were doing it with their own backs straight and their shoulders resquared.

Sibley reached Fort Bliss on May 3, 1862. From there, on the following day, he submitted his final report on the New Mexican Campaign to General S. Cooper, Adjutant and Inspector General of the Confederate Army at Richmond.

It was a discursive document, notable for its unintentional revelation of two extenuating factors in the old soldier's defeat.

> . . . It is due the brave soldiers I have had the honor to command to premise that from its inception the "Sibley Brigade" has encountered difficulties in its organization and opposition and distaste to the service required at its hands which no other troops have met with.
>
> From misunderstanding, accidents, deficiency of arms, and the like, instead of reaching the field of its operations early in September 1861 as was anticipated, I found myself at this point as late as the middle of January 1862, with only two regiments and a half, poorly armed, thinly clad and almost destitute of blankets . . .
>
> We reached Fort Bliss last winter in rags and blankets . . . We have beaten the enemy in every encounter and against large odds . . . The entire

campaign has been persecuted without a dollar in the quartermaster's department . . .

But, sir, I cannot speak encouragingly for the future, my troops having manifested a dogged, irreconcilable detestation of the country and the people. They have endured much, suffered much and cheerfully; but the prevailing discontent, backed up by the distinguished valor displayed on every field, entitles them to marked consideration and indulgence. These considerations, in connection with the scant supply of provisions and the disposition of our own citizens in this section to depreciate our currency, may determine me, without waiting for instructions, to move by slow marches down the country, both for the purpose of remounting and recruiting our thinned ranks . . .

It is proper that I should express, in the end, the conviction, determined by some experience that, except for its political geographical position, the Territory of New Mexico is not worth a quarter of the blood and treasure already expended in its conquest. As a field of military operations it possesses not a single element, except in the multiplicity of its defensible positions . . .

The indispensable element, food, cannot be relied upon . . .

During the last year hundreds of thousands of sheep and other livestock have been driven off by the Indians. Indeed, such have been the complaints of the people in this respect that I have determined to encourage private enterprises against the Navajos and the Apaches, and to legalize the enslaving of them . . .

Jud Reeves did not see this last report of his general's.

The day before its issuance, in the afternoon of the 3rd at about 4 P.M. and while marching along the old Butterfield stageline road near Cottonwood Station south of Fort Fillmore, the world about him began to sway and spin and before he could call out for support, the ground beneath his feet rose up and struck him in the face.

A great roaring in his ears followed briefly. Then nothing but blackness and muffled silence and the strange, far off sensations of being talked over by voices he could not hear, and touched and taken gently up by hands he could not feel.

After that there was a seemingly interminable time of blurred half visions of light, suffocating descents back into the blackness, terrible fights back upward again into the world of life-giving air. Then, still more dimly conscious impressions of friendly, fleeting faces bending over him, of easy, skillful hands working to soothe and comfort and recall him from the reaching void.

When at last the darkness passed and it was day again, it was the 9th of May and Jud had been in the post hospital at Fort Bliss for five days reaching the crisis in a double lobar pneumonia.

The critical fever broken, his tough body mended

itself with animal speed. Yet it was the fourteenth day of that beautiful spring month before he limped, weak and watery-legged, out into the sunshine and blessed plentiful air of the parade ground.

It was at once apparent to him that he had not been released on an ordinary day.

There was some kind of official doings being readied.

On the quadrangle, color guards were trooping smartly by, rifle squads in dress uniform were forming up to march, thirteen-starred battleflags were flying everywhere and a full fife, drum and bugle corps was piping, beating and blowing up the assembly four ways around the square.

Asking the occasion of a passing soldier, the gaunt survivor of Sibley's ninety-day march to nowhere and return was told cynically, "Why Jesus man! ain't you heard? This is the day. Everybody that's anybody is sashaying out to Magoffinsville to hear the General say goodbye. He's going back to San Antonio to bust up the brigade. Every stupid sonofabitching Salado salamander in the outfit goes on unlimited furlough back there, and that's to be the glorious end of the Old Man and the whole goddam idea, including the ever loving Army of New Mexico, or Arizona Brigade, or whatever the hell you want to call it and amen and thank Christ. Where the hell you been, mister? In bed?"

"More or less," said Jud cryptically, and clumped off to flag down a ride in a field ambulance going out with some double amputees to hear what they had lost

347

their legs about. He was lucky, arriving early enough to find a place in the shade close to the veranda of the Magoffin mansion where he could see and hear everything.

He recognized several of his former comrades-in-arm among the crowd of uniformed soldiers and curious townfolk gathered to gawk at Sibley when he came out, but none of them returned his nod or seemed to know him. He felt as though he were in a company of strangers in a land and time far from his own. He was still too weak and shaky to care overly much, however.

Bracing himself, he waited for the General.

Presently Sibley emerged, flanked by Jackson, Ochiltree, Covey, Brownrigg, Robards, Griffin and the rest of the staff. To look at him in that moment, pausing high-headed at the edge of the veranda to survey the ranks of his listeners, was to see a study in ineffable sadness and unbending pride all in the same swift second of hesitation. Outwardly he was still the Commander of the Army of the Confederate States of America in the Southwest. That was the pride in him. Inwardly, Jud knew he had to be feeling the terrible responsibility, to himself as well as to his silently standing troops, for his crucial failures as a leader of men. And that was the poignant, pervading sadness of it.

The bearded commander's silver-maned head turned slowly as he seemed to search the restless gathering for some sign or signal of encouragement in this most difficult moment of his career. His inquiring glance came abreast of Jud's place in the crowd and, somehow, singled him out from among all those other faces upturned and watching him. Their eyes met and the pale young lieutenant felt the same odd sense of communication he had shared with Sobre that long ago day of the peacetalk with Baylor.

Jud drew himself up and saluted his general. He did it with shoulders back and spine ramrodded in a soldier's stiff, proud way.

Sibley saw and returned the lone salute, and sent after it an eye-crinkled nod and wry twist of a smile which spoke a thousand thank-yous. He did not acknowledge any of the others of his recent comrades present in the crowd, nor did they—not a solitary man among them—raise a hand to honor him in his last appearance before them.

It was as though, even as the young Apache chief before him, the courtly commander of the Arizona Brigade had picked Jud Reeves from among the camp of the enemy and called to him across their pitying and disdainful heads, "I see you, friend, and I am no longer alone."

Unlike the result in Sobre's case, however, Jud never had the opportunity to confirm his feeling of having communicated with the gentle, kindly old Lion of the Salado.

The latter's brief valedictory to his demoralized troops, which followed then, was the last he ever saw or heard of General Henry Hopkins Sibley.

It was an eloquent farewell, emotional, generous, uncomplaining. And, to the singular extent that it ignored all mention of his command's or his own disastrous failures in the field, it was entirely pathetic.

Jud stood through it, head bowed.

When the speech was finished, there was an echoing silence from the packed ranks before the mansion. Sibley stood a moment, as though puzzled, then turned and walked slowly back into the house.

The crowd began at once to drift away. Jud hobbled out to the road and got another ride back to the post. In twenty minutes Magoffunsville was deserted by all but a handful of very old men who stayed behind beneath the coffeebean trees to argue the shameful lack of sand shown by today's Texas boys, and to look back with a great deal of rheumy-eyed pride to a happier day when there were real heroes in the land and real fighters along the frontier.

The war in New Mexico was over.

The long afternoon wore away. Night came on, deepened at last. It was a very warm night, humid and with a hint of summer rain in its freshening west wind. Broken cloud drifted high overhead, separated by great open patches of blazing starfield. A fourth quarter moon was breaking over the rim of the hills beyond the river, its loomy orange glow lighting up the prairie, softening everything in that harsh land, giving life and warmth even to the naked rocks and touching all who moved beneath it, hale and halt alike, with the same rich brush of moondust.

Jud was beholdenly grateful for that.

It had been a rough march from his room in the BOQ across the parade ground to Major Considine's house at the head of officers' row. He was breathing heavily, running wet with perspiration. He knew, from the queasy feeling of his stomach being loose inside him, that his face was white as a bedsheet. No man would want his woman to see him that way, looking like death warmed over and set aside to chill again. Not after all this time, he wouldn't. Not by broad day or inside lamplight, anyway. But here in the outer night, under the orangy wash of the rising moon, it was different. Out here he wouldn't look so bad. He'd take on some color from that old moon and maybe even manage to look a little something like the Jud Reeves she had vowed to wait for, and would naturally expect to see again, when, at last, he came for her, as he was coming now.

Oh, the hell. He was only putting off on himself.

It wasn't that simple.

The white-faced youth shook his head. He stopped his dragging progress toward the Considines' covered porch, standing in the middle of the whitewashed stone bordered quarters walk, trying to think.

The hesitation was too much for him, and he stepped off the walk, in under the friendly shadows of a planted mulberry tree in the near corner of the C.O.'s tiny plot of frontyard grass. Damn it, he wished he could take some courage as well as color from that blessed moon up yonder. There was no use lying to himself any longer. Something about this meeting, of which he had dreamed so fiercely all these aching-lonely months, was already spoiled for him, and he was not happy now on his way to it, but sore afraid and deeply troubled. What in God's name could be wrong? Was he still sick? Had the fever hurt his mind?

He sat down on the little garden bench under the mulberry's drooping shelter to think all of it through one more careful time.

He still knew exactly how it was he wanted to begin it—by giving her to understand, in more detail and truth than he had in the letter, his real status as a prospective husband. To make positively sure she was clear on everything the way it actually, honestly was. Such as the fact that his vast ranch was nothing but so many miles of prairie brush and grass. That the Reeves family fortune had been long ago lost in the land speculations which had been pridefully hushed up at the time and the truth successfully hidden for all the years since. Then, the fact that it was this same embarrassment which had driven General Judah Reeves into the Llano County wilderness where he could sequester the family pride until time and some future stroke of better investor's luck could heal its wounds of poverty and want.

Even past that, he had the rest of it memorized just as pat as anything could ever be.

He would tell her of his handing in his commission to Major Jackson that very afternoon, upon returning from the sadness of Sibley's farewell speech. Then, of Jackson's refusal to accept the resignation. And of his own following insistence that he meant it and that he intended to quit and go home if the action got him court-martialed. And lastly he would tell her of his coming to ask her to go along with him to Topaz Creek to share whatever the future might bring them of great or small fortune, not caring which it was, either, because they would have each other and their true love and so would be the wealthiest people in all Texas come duster or downpour, good grass or bad.

Yes, that was the way he wanted to tell it.

Nothing added to the truth.

Nothing taken away from it.

Just exactly as it had been told in the letter, only stronger and with all the little warm things of love and sentiment added in which a man could not bring himself to put down in cold words on blank paper.

He was glad about the letter, then. Glad he had written it, glad he had sent it. It would make the way easier for both of them, preparing her to listen and himself to speak forth with boldness and clarity on the most important subject any young man was required to broach in the course of a normal lifetime.

Yet the thought of the letter no sooner reassured him than it brought the shadow of doubt to his pale face.

What about that letter?

Why had she not answered it? Why had she not written him in the field? Or had she? Was her answer to his clumsy plea carried by one of the mail riders who did not get past the Apaches? And had she taken his subsequent silence in the same hurt way he had her preceding one? Or had his own letter not gotten through to her at Fort Bliss in the first place?

Well, no—wait.

He knew the answer to that last question.

He had asked Sergeant Wade Haymer about it on his return trip from Bliss. Haymer was the regular mail rider and he had not lost any mail on that run. The Lieutenant's letter to Mrs. Horton, if that was the one the Lieutenant had given him that last night in front of the General's tent at Val Verde, had been delivered to the Fort Bliss P.O. If Mrs. Horton had not gotten it from there, it surely was not Sergeant Haymer's fault.

Well, hang Sergeant Haymer! He wasn't infallible.

Letters had been lost before. It happened every day. Maybe Felicia *had not* gotten that lonely note.

Jud groaned and shook his head.

There was only one way to find out for sure.

Ask her.

He got up stiffly. For an unsteady, frightening few seconds he had to shut his eyes tightly end brace himself against the tree trunk. Then he was all right.

At the door there was another bad spell but he shook it off, set his jaw in the old Jud Reeves way, reached out and put his big knuckles firmly to the door panels.

It was his luck that the Considines had already left for the staff ball being put on for Sibley and his remaining aides.

Felicia Horton was at home, and at home alone.

When he heard the familiar stir and rustle of her party-gown petticoats and the light, quick tap of her dancing slippers moving toward the door, the weakness came back on him and all the old doubts multiplied a hundred times.

Then she opened the door and stood framed in the inner lamplight.

He could only catch his breath and stare. He had forgotten how implausibly lovely she was. Just to look at her poured the strength back into a man like no other food or medicine ever could. He suddenly felt strong as a giant.

"Hello, Felicia," he said calmly. "It's me, Jud Reeves."

He had prepared a thousand beautiful greetings for this moment, and this was surely not one of them. But it was the one he felt and he did not even realize he had said it. It just came out of him quietly and confidently and after it had he simply stood there waiting for her glad cry of recognition and the weeping embrace of sweetheart's welcome which was certain to follow it.

He stood and waited in vain.

Felicia Horton only smiled and said, "Why, Judah Reeves! Wherever in the world did *you* come from? We heard you were dead. Or missing or something like that. At any rate, what on earth *did* happen to you? My! It does seem like such a long time, doesn't it?"

Of a sudden it felt to Jud Reeves as though it had

been a longer time than that of all his previous nineteen years put together. It seemed to him as though he had been standing on that front stoop ever since he had brought her home from that fandango Considine had arranged for him when he had brought old Colonel Horton's body through from Mesilla.

He looked at her carefully, peering to catch the set of her face in the lamplight and moonshadows. She would not look back at him, and dropped her eyes.

"I've been in the hospital," he heard himself say, low-voiced.

"They didn't know who I was until five days ago when the fever broke and I could tell them. Then I didn't want you, or anyone, to see me so sick and all. So I asked them to let me mend a bit and make my own announcements later on. Have you been all right, Felicia?"

"Why, I've been just wonderful, Jud. And I am so relieved and happy to hear that you are back safe. You and all those other poor boys who fought so bravely up there. It must have been terrible."

Jud thought of a young Union artilleryman's face blasted away in that shotgun charge at Val Verde. He thought of the saber slash Little Jo Shelby had taken from his collarbone down almost to the middle of his stomach. He thought of a Southern soldier raising his rifle and shooting a fleeing officer of his own battalion command between the shoulder blades. He thought of the countless bodies of good young Texas boys and just as good young Northern boys down on the field with whole parts of them blown off, and of those other bodies left in their blankets at the camps of both sides scarred by smallpox or strangled by pneumonia and he said very quietly to Felicia Horton, "Yes, it was terrible."

She moved nervously under his granite-faced, unblinking stare. She tried for a smile, and faltered badly.

"I do wish I could ask you in, Jud," she said. "But Colonel Allerdice is coming to take me to the General's Ball. Do you know the Colonel? He's such a dear."

Jud knew the Colonel. Next to Judge Crosby and maybe James Magoffin, Colonel Mason Allerdice was the richest man in West Texas. And he was old enough to be Felicia Horton's father.

"I know him," he nodded. "What about him?"

"Well nothing really. Just that he's a bit late and I'm not quite finished dressing."

For the first time Jud noticed her gown was loose about the shoulders. Clearly, it had not been closed in the back yet. His blue eyes hardened.

"Likely he can help you finish," he said. "You do seem to have a lot of trouble with that camisole, Mrs. Horton."

"Really, Judah—!" she reproved him indignantly. "That's hardly fair!"

She stamped her slippered foot, then, as quickly, smiled and added, "You come by and pick me up in the morning. We can pack a picnic lunch and ride out in the hills. Colonel Allerdice doesn't need to know. Now do be a good boy—"

"Did you get my letter?" Jud interrupted flatly.

"Of course! You took the whole thing in San Antonio the wrong way. We never did talk about anything serious."

"No, I reckon we didn't. Just promised to wait for one another forever, or some such a little spell."

"Oh, Jud! that was moonlight talk. Don't you know the difference yet? Now don't be silly. Nothing's happened that can't be mended by some more moonbeams!"

The remembered bell-like laugh was back again now, the old quick-silver smile flashing once more.

"I simply must go in, Jud." She was edging the door closed even while her dark eyes were beguiling him with their lies about tomorrow. "I'll see you in the morning and we *will* have that picnic. I'm so happy you dropped by, Judah, and that you're back safe. But really I must say goodnight now."

"Felicia—" He stepped forward impulsively.

"Yes, Judah?"

He looked at her one last, lifelong moment, getting the true picture of her into his memory for future, final keeping. It was not a good picture and he said, still very softly, "Goodbye, Felicia," and turned and limped away down the neat, stone-bordered walk and out onto the parade ground.

It did not take Jud Reeves long to change into his old scouting clothes and get his few personal things together. The familiar cling of the fringed doeskin shirt, soft Comanche leggins and blunt-toed Apache

358

boots felt good. After the long months in uniform it was like coming home from town and taking off a pair of pinchy storebought shoes. The relief was welcome sure enough, Jud grinned wanly, but the feet still hurt regardless.

Moving more quickly now, he folded the torn and faded remnant of his cadet-gray officer's fatigue blouse—he had never gotten one of the beautiful Confederate officers' skirted frock coats such as Sibley and the regimental colonels wore—and placed it neatly at the foot of his cot in the Bachelor Officers' Quarters.

He paused for a moment, studying the coat, memorizing the look of its two rows of seven gilt buttons each and its standing collar and cuffs stiff with the embroidered gold sleeve braid and double-barred insignia of a first lieutenant in the Confederate States Army. Then he shook his head and got on with it, moving hurriedly and half angrily as a man will when he does not like what he is doing but knows that he must do it all the same.

From under the cot he took the field officer's sword Baylor had given him with his lieutenancy and laid it across the tarnished buttons of the folded coat. With that, and with the stacking of his high cavalry boots at leaning attention on the floor below the blouse and sword, he was ready. Belting on his old cap-and-ball Colt, he closed the drawstring of his lean rucksack, picked up the rusted Ethan Allen shotgun and started down the moonlit center aisle of the deserted barracks.

At the exit he held up, thinking of something else.

Under the kerosene lamp which feebly lit the threshold stood the BOQ's library—a rough plank table which served as a catch-all repository for barrack-room reading matter ranging from a practically depaged copy of Pierre Andre's *The Sinister Truth About Marie Chastain,* through hound-eared, yellow-paper editions of Cooper's *The Red Rover* and *The Pathfinder,* to an untouched morocco-bound set of Edward Gibbon's *The History of the Decline and Fall of the Roman Empire.*

An expression midway between a bittersweet grin and a fleeting, sad smile moved the corners of Jud's wide mouth.

He opened his rucksack and took from it a slender calf-bound book.

Quickly, he dropped it onto the table and went out of the barracks without so much as an eye-corner glance to see how it fell. The book lit front cover up, atop the pile, the handsome goldleaf of its title glittering in the shift and play of the lamplight.

It was *The Professional Soldier in Command; His Obligations as a Leader of Men.*

Outside, the moon was shoulder-high. Risen clear of the rim of the prairie, it was no longer dusky orange but white and pale and tired looking, like Jud Reeves himself.

He did not know where its waning light might lead him, nor did he greatly care. He only knew that he was going to follow that lonely old moon away from Fort Bliss, far, far away from it, and keep following it until the tiredness and the hurt and the confusion were gone out of him and he was a whole man once more and so could decide which was the right way, and which the wrong, for Jud Reeves.

One way, that of the professional soldier and leader of men, he had already left behind him on the book-littered table by the barrack-room door.

In all the long hard road from San Antonio to Glorieta Pass and the last brave charge of the Salado Scouts, he had seen the price of leadership paid over and over and over again, and always in the same bankrupt moral tender of human misery and suffering. Whether it was a small company of Confederate spies caught by a Union rifle trap in the narrow, dark streets of Mesilla, or a full regiment of gray cavalry shredded by blue cannonfire on the broad, open plains of Val Verde, the terms of the final settlement were no different. To the leader of men, be he squad corporal, regimental colonel, or army corps brigadier the price of victory was the same as the cost of defeat—the lives of the men who followed him.

Jud could not, he would not, any longer attempt to pay that price.

His failure might put the family honor in default, bring to a sorry end Southern history's proud accounting of his father's and his grandfather's names. If so, the blame could not be disowned.

There remained to him, however, the choice of ways in which he might proceed past that shameful first decision.

As he stood there in the growing moonlight attempting to see this choice and to make it, a gaunt shadow detached itself from the dark side of the barracks building and glided soundlessly toward him. The next moment a remembered tart voice was advising him testily that, "If I was an Apache, boy, you'd be a certain goner," and Jud was wheeling about to cry out, *"Cavanaugh! Cavanaugh!"* with a relief and gratitude which rushed up in him so happily his throat closed and he could say no more.

There was nothing more, actually, that he needed to say. He simply took the old man's hand in his and stood there. Both of them understood the moment, neither was embarrassed by it. After a bit, Cavanaugh shifted his hand to Jud's shoulder and said simply, "We been waiting a long time for you to come back, boy."

"We?" said Jud, puzzled.

"Yes," answered the old man. "Me and some other friends of yours."

"What friends?"

"Sobre and what's left of the Tres Cerros. We're going away, boy, and we want you to go with us."

"Cavanaugh," pleaded Jud, "whatever are you talking about? You don't make sense."

"I reckon I do," said the old man slowly. "Boy, a lot has happened while you been away. There's going to be a real Injun war. Sibley and Baylor and Canby have all issued due notice they're going to start killing Apaches on sight. Naturally that don't shine with the Apaches. Grito has gone north to join up with Mangas Coloradas

362

and the Mimbreños. For Sobre it was either fight along-side his own people or get out. He decided to get out."

"I can't believe it," protested Jud. "You mean to tell me the whole tribe is leaving the country?"

"Don't mean to tell you no such thing. The main bunch went with Grito. There ain't many left with Sobre. Only a handful, boy. They're the ones waiting for us down to the crossing."

"The Chihuahua Crossing?" asked Jud hesitantly. "The old Apache trail that goes down into the Mexican Sierra Madres?"

"That's the one, boy. You coming?"

The thought of it took hold of Jud. Of a sudden he straightened. He felt better than he had in many weeks. The old homely grin was back in place, the arid Llano County drawl returned. "Old friend," he said quickly, "I will surely do it. I am that happy to see you, I would follow you off a blind drop. Lead on, 'Tall Horse,' but don't forget you've got your rope on a lame pony."

"Gimme your sack and gun," ordered Cavanaugh. "Lean into my shoulder for a brace. Holler if I go too fast for you."

Jud willingly surrendered the things. He put his left arm around the offered shoulder, nodded wincingly.

"Old Paint, I am ready to go."

Cavanaugh returned the nod, slipped his powerful arm about Jud's shrunken waist, started guiding him carefully off across the Fort Bliss parade ground toward the river.

So it was that the two friends came presently to the old ford below El Paso where the Indian road of the centuries went over the Rio Grande to wind down into the secret Sierra Madre heartland of the Apache people. And so it was, too, that Jud Reeves came at last and haltingly to the hour of his own final crossing.

In the trees nearby the ford, three saddled ponies were waiting. One of them was Cavanaugh's old white plug. The second was Lieutenant May's trim gray gelding, the mount Jud had ridden into the Tres Cerros country in his search for Star Cavanaugh. The third was Sobre's nervous little stallion.

Sobre, waiting with the horses, led them forward into the open moonlight as Cavanaugh and Jud came up. He touched his brow and Jud returned the formal gesture. "*Schichobe*," said Sobre, "I am glad to see you. My heart is full." Jud nodded and put out his hand. Sobre took it and Jud said, "Thank you, *schichobe*, I am glad to be here."

On the south shore, across the shallow channel, a small band of Indian horsemen sat watching them intently. They made no sound, showed no movement. For some reason strangely aroused, Jud limped forward to get a better sight of them. It was then he saw they were not all Indians. One of them who was not— a slender, small and golden-haired one—he would have known a mile away without the moonlight. He stood transfixed, a hundred deeply mixed and remorseful feelings rushing up in him at once.

Behind him, Sobre spoke softly.

"It is true, Guero," he said. "It is your woman who waits for you over there."

"I reckon you can make out the others, too, boy," added Cavanaugh quietly. "I went back to Atascosa County and fetched the whole family out here while you was away. It's why I wasn't able to come see you sooner in the hospital."

"That is also true, Guero," nodded Sobre. "Tall Horse went to his home below the Rio Medina and returned to the Tres Cerros with his wife Maria and the little ones. He did that when he learned I was going down into the Mother Mountains. We agreed to wait for you to come back. We heard that the white man's war in the North was going badly for the new Pony Soldiers from the South. We prayed you would return in time. Now you have come and we are ready to go."

He swept the far bank with a flourish of his lean arm.

"See, *schichobe,* there are faithful fat Chebo and wise gray Chavez waiting for us. And with them there, are some few others; those older, truehearted ones who remembered my father and who would not listen to the ugly sound of Grito crying out against the white man. They are all waiting for us over there now. There is no more time. You must give us your answer. How do you say, old friend?"

"I don't know!" muttered Jud desperately. "Let me think, let me think—"

He did not move to take the gray pony which Sobre had led up for him, but remained peering across the water at the blanketed figures on the far side. There was good reason for the belated delay. If he took the bridle reins from the Mescalero chief and turned with him toward Apacheland, he would have made an irrevocable choice. It would be a decision which would take more real courage than his father or his grandfather had ever known. It would require the moral will to abandon a lawfully governed society of his own blood and color knowing that the act of abandonment, in itself, would make of him a frontier pariah for his whole life. Nor was this the entire depth of the question. There was, as well, the matter of his military and patriotic loyalties. To see the truth about a cause, as he had seen the hopelessness of the Confederacy's struggle against the Union, and to renounce that cause in mid-resolution before the fact of its failure was apparent to all, took three times the grit that it did to cling passionately to it. Yet the onus, of such a renunciation was inescapable. There were many names for men who did what Jud Reeves had already done, let alone what he contemplated doing, and the least of these was deserter.

Jud knew, as he stood there, what he would be reduced to if he took that gray pony from Sobre. He would be a disgrace not only to his family but to every Southerner who might in the future hear the story of his defection and disappearance into the Mexican desert that early May night of 1862. But he also knew, at last, where his true heart lay. Or, at least, where it must lead him. He turned to Sobre.

"Well, Guero," asked the Indian youth, before he could speak, "what shall I do with this gray pony?"

Jud stepped forward. The gelding got his scent and whickered in pleased remembrance. Jud reached out his hand to stroke the animal's soft muzzle and said to Sobre with a glad quick laugh, "Give him to me, old friend!"

He swung up on the gray with a lift of the heart which brought him into the saddle light as an eagle feather.

"Come along," he said happily to Sobre. "Let us ride over this crossing together."

"Yes," agreed the Apache, turning his own restive stallion. "Let us do that as you say, Guero, side by side, like true brothers."

They put their ponies into the shallows of the ancient Chihuahua crossing. Behind them, old Elkanah Cavanaugh grinned acridly, spat to windward, spoke a pleased word to his bony white. All three horses were fresh and wanting to go. They made small bright showers of silver drops rise in the moonlight with the quick chop of their hooves into the quartering current of the Rio Grande.

Across the stream, Chebo nodded to Chavez and said, "See how lovely the water looks falling every which way in the moonlight. Is that not nice, Chavez?"

"To the empty head," rasped the grizzled sub-chief, "all things seem agreeable. But yes, it does look nice. I grant you that."

"This will be a good trip," said Chebo, eying the

patchy sky. "There is going to be some rain. That's a fine thing. It makes me feel good. Everything smells so pretty when it rains. Altogether, I am glad to be here. It is a very fine night."

"Aye," growled Chavez. "It *is* a fine night."

The old Apache was not watching the sky or the night at all. He was studying the light of the fourth-quarter moon reflected in the excited eyes of Star Cavanaugh. Presently he bobbed his head again.

"A very fine night indeed," he repeated with guarded softness to himself. Then, with still more care that no one else should hear the admission, "Even I am glad to be here."

Center Point Publishing
600 Brooks Road ● PO Box 1
Thorndike ME 04986-0001 USA

(207) 568-3717

US & Canada:
1 800 929-9108
www.centerpointlargeprint.com

DATE DUE

SEP 0 1 2009	MAY 3 1 2014	DEC - 4 2014
OCT 1 0 2009	JUN 2 6 2014	
NOV 9 2009	OCT 3 1 2014	
9-6-10	DEC 2 6 2014	
10-12-10		
7/9/11		
8-24-11		
5-12-12		
6-2-12		
7-14-12		
8-18-12		
NOV 07 2012		

LP

F
Henry, Will
The Crossing